THE BLESSED VESSEL

VENUS COX

The Blessed Vessel

Character & scenery illustrations by Aga

Page edges & internal formatting by Painted Wings Publishing Services

ISBNs:

Ebook 979-8-9883470-1-9

Paperback 979-8-9883470-4-0

Paperback (alternate version) 979-8-9883470-0-2

First Edition: July 2023

10 9 8 7 6 5 4 3 2 1

Content Warning

This book is intended for an adult audience.
It has explicit sex and foul language. Lots of it.

Kinks & Tropes

Arranged Marriage
Blood Play
Breeding/Pregnancy (mild symptoms)
Dubious Consent
Fire Play
Group Activities
Hate Sex
Praise/Degradation
Primal Play
Voyeurism & Exhibitionism
"It'll fit."
"Good girl."
"Mine."
"Who hurt you?"

Possible Triggers

Brief mention of harm to a woman and unborn child
General racism/stereotyping between the different fantasy races
LGBTQ+ characters outed (accidental/nonmalicious, not a major focus)
Near drowning
Violence (mild)

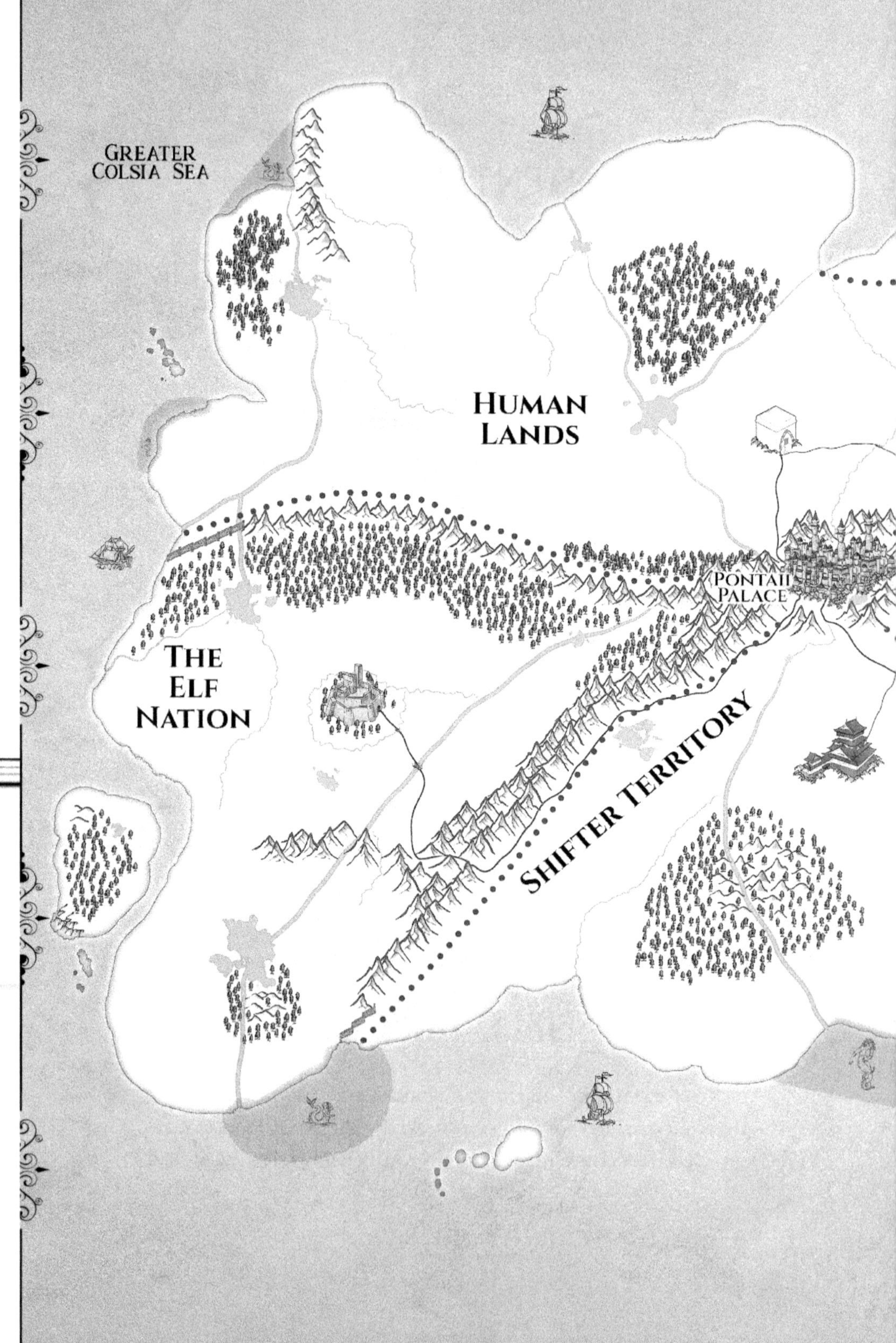

GREATER COLSIA SEA
HUMAN LANDS
THE ELF NATION
SHIFTER TERRITORY
PONTAII PALACE

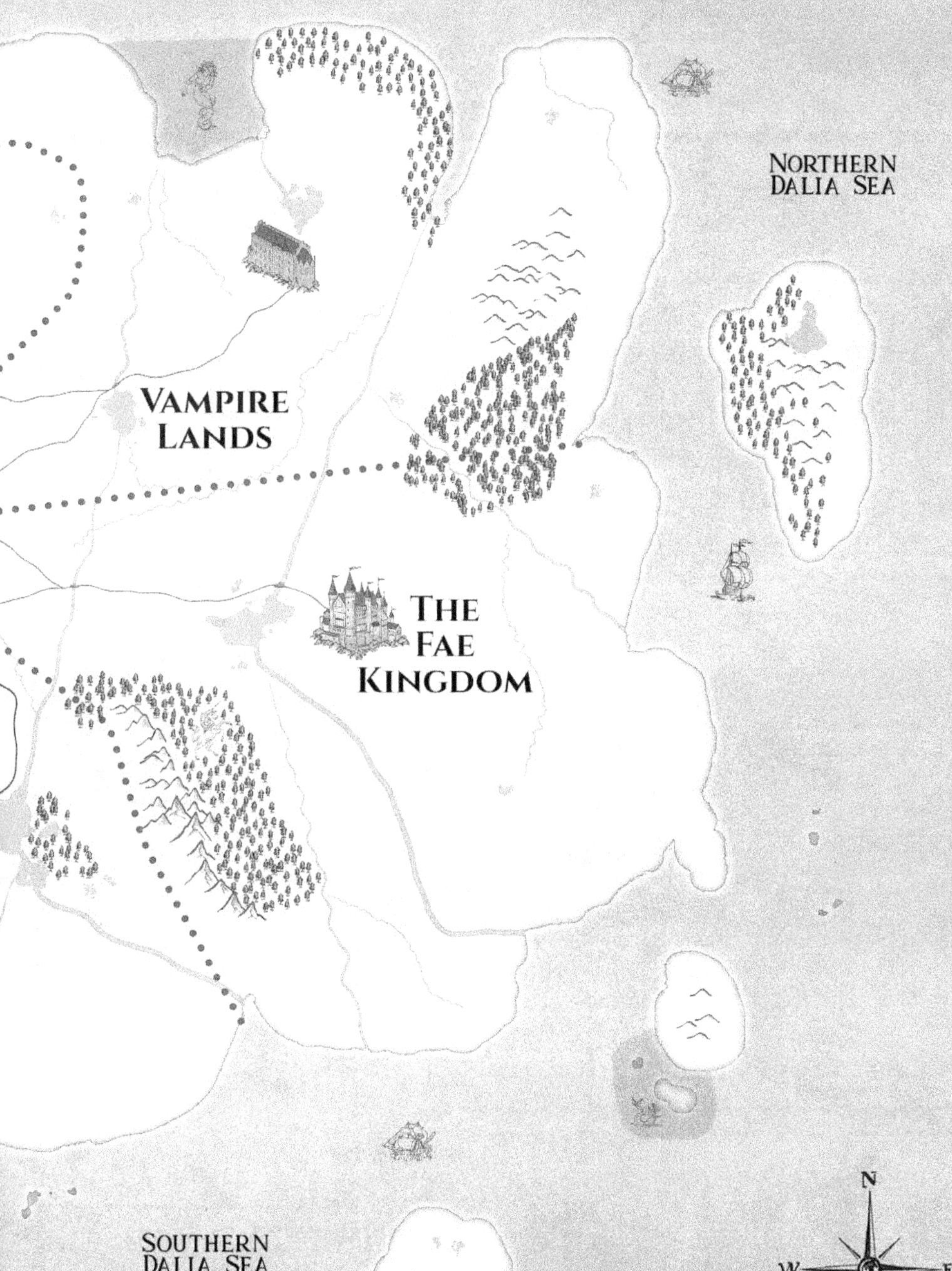

THE REALM OF COLSIA
NORTHERN DALIA SEA
VAMPIRE LANDS
THE FAE KINGDOM
SOUTHERN DALIA SEA
N
W
E
S

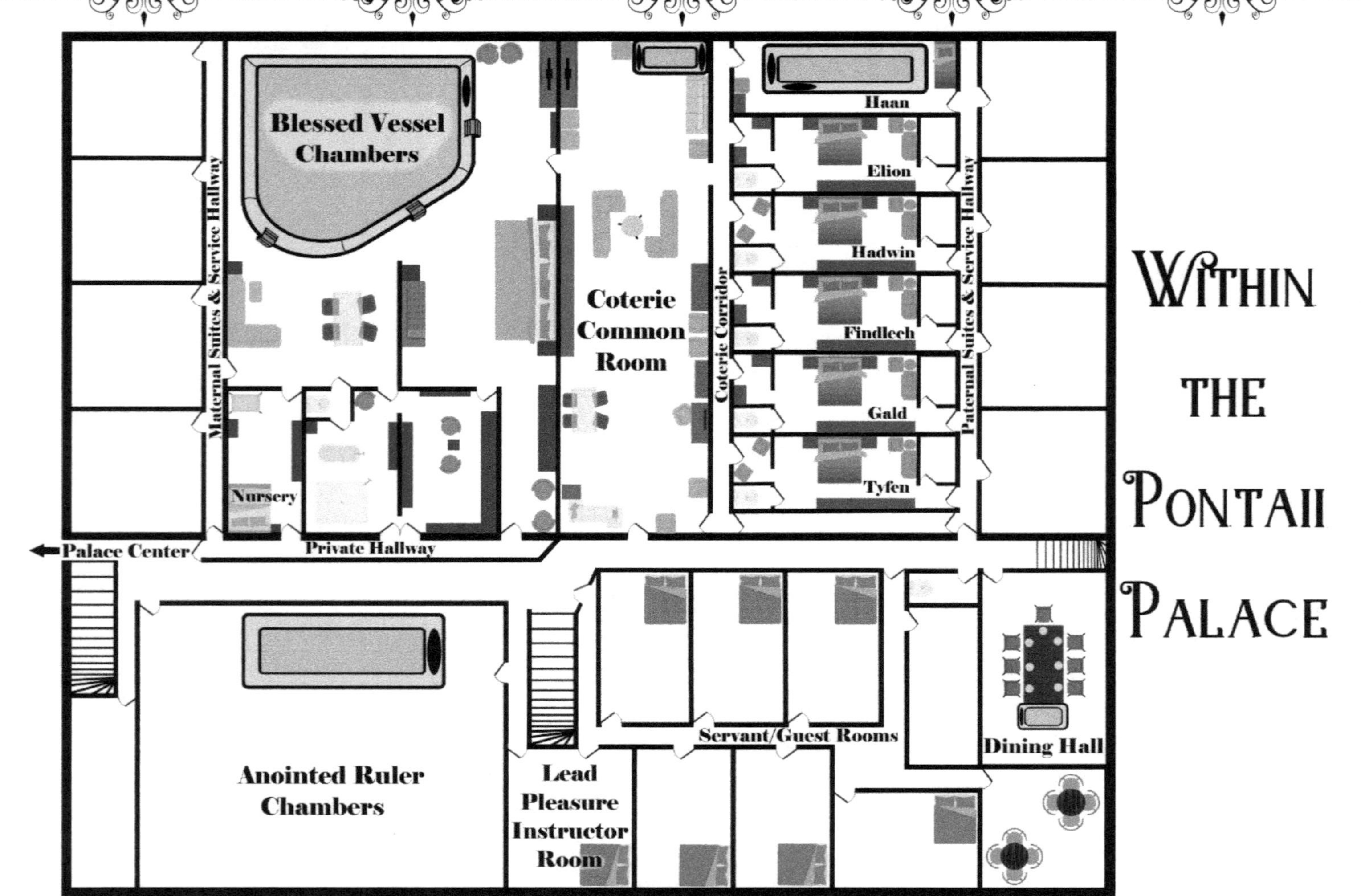
Within the Pontaii Palace
Blessed Vessel Chambers
Maternal Suites & Service Hallway
Coterie Common Room
Coterie Corridor
Haan
Elion
Hadwin
Findlech
Gald
Tyfen
Paternal Suites & Service Hallway
Nursery
Palace Center
Private Hallway
Anointed Ruler Chambers
Lead Pleasure Instructor Room
Servant/Guest Rooms
Dining Hall

Pronunciation Guide

Schamoi: s-chuh-MOY

Sonta Gwynriel: SAWN-tuh gwin-REE-el

Pontaii: PAWN-tie

Coterie: KO-teh-ree

Hoku: HO-koo

Lilah: LIE-luh

Gaffey: GAF-ee

Mammi: mam-EE

Kernov: CARE-naw-v

Cataray: CAT-uh-ray

Leonte: lee-ON-tee

Elout: ee-LOWT

Marsone: mar-SEWN

Findlech/Findie: fin-DLECK/fin-DEE

Bretton: bret-un

Lourel: LOUW-rel

Tyfen: TIE-fen

Hadwin: had-WIN

Elion: EL-ee-on

Danah: duh-NAW

Gald: GAWLD

Haan: HAWN

Vesta: VEST-uh

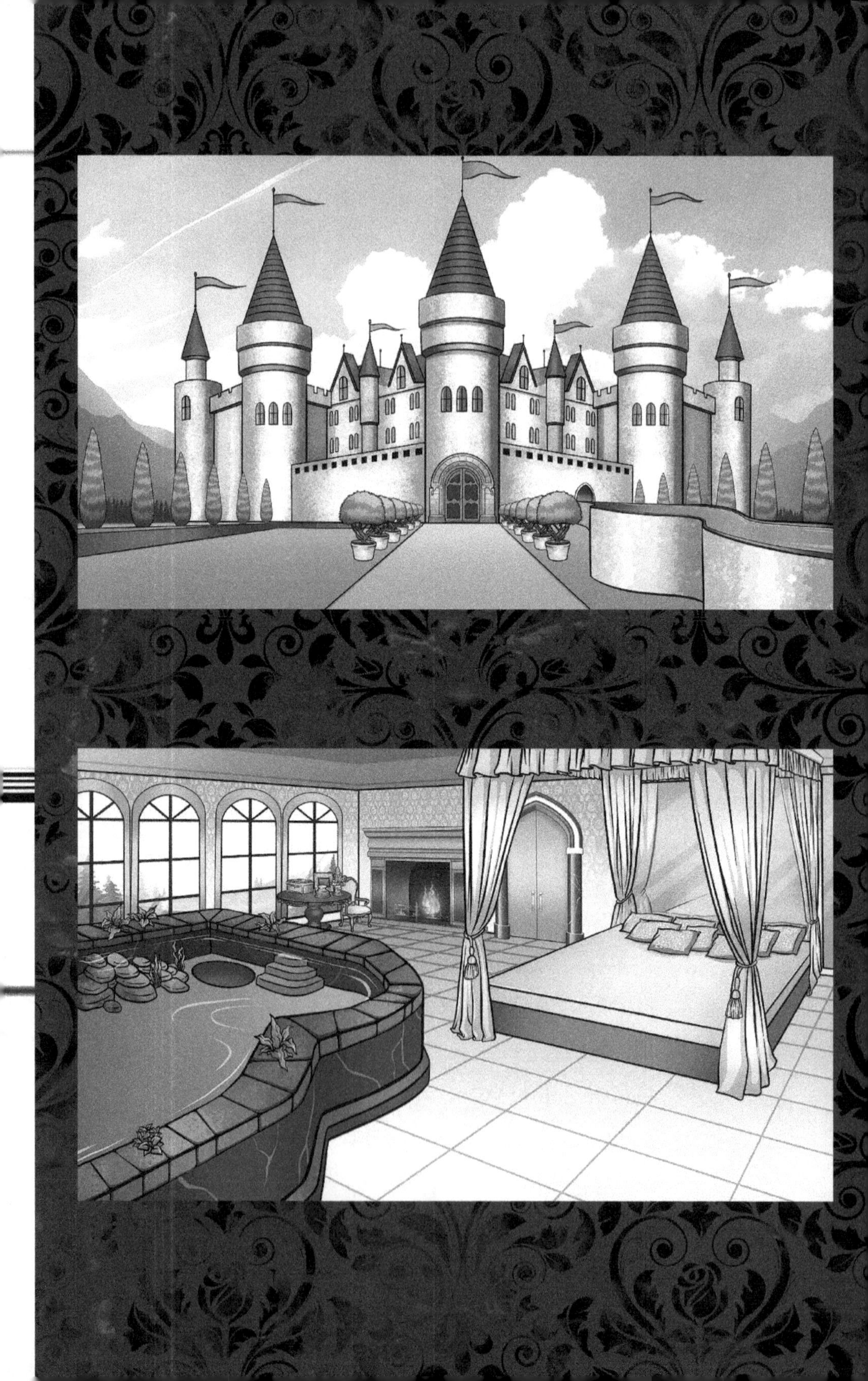

THE PLEASURE INSTRUCTOR

I arched my back, so close to completion, as Schamoi licked my clit once more. He dipped his tongue inside me again, and I couldn't help but tug harder on his hair, my breathing ragged.

He groaned—deep and satisfied. I would miss that groan, his tongue, his everything in the bedroom.

Sliding his hands up, he palmed my breasts, then rubbed my nipples just right.

I was so tight, on the edge of bursting as his tongue stroked me. I barely managed to whisper his name.

Schamoi gave no verbal response, his mouth too busy delivering his gift, but he knew what I needed, what I craved. All it took was a gentle pinch of my nipples to send me over the edge, shaking and gasping.

He didn't stop his work until the waves of pleasure rippled away.

I lay there a moment, spread open upon the end of this giant bed. The breeze from the open windows blew the golden lace curtains hanging from the bedposts. My room's pond trickled softly as it always did when it sang me to sleep, and when it greeted me each morning here in the Pontaii Palace.

Schamoi rubbed my thighs sweetly, then draped his arms over my legs as I cooled. "I'll miss your taste, Sonta."

I gazed down at him with a smile. "Come here."

I admired his form as he crawled back onto the bed. We cuddled facing each other.

"I'll miss your constant companionship," I confessed, caressing his freshly shaven face, taking in his icy blue eyes.

He snickered. "You'll be plenty busy. Stop pretending you'll miss a dull human like me."

I scowled, and he kissed me on the forehead.

The truth was I *would* miss him and our relationship. He'd been my lead pleasure instructor from my first day in the Pontaii Palace. He'd been my primary teacher on even broader topics for five years now.

But he wasn't wrong. I *would* be busy. The Great Ritual was finally here— starting tonight. I would meet my Coterie—my partners and mates—in a few hours, then over the next few weeks, we would fuck until I conceived the next ruler of this realm.

"Not dull." I ran my fingers through his bronze hair. "I'll always be grateful for you, Schamoi. You'll always have a special place in my heart. And you'll always be welcome in my bed after the birth."

His smile was soft. "Time will tell how our paths will tangle."

My offer was genuine. I wasn't allowed to take someone outside my Coterie during the Great Ritual and the months of my pregnancy, but I could choose who I shared my bed with after that. I had dismissed the rest of the pleasure instructors yesterday, opting to spend the night and morning with Schamoi alone. He had been the first of them assigned to me, the first to show me what a real orgasm was, to show me every position my body was capable of.

He'd taught me about myself—what I liked. How to manage my constant craving for more pleasure.

He'd prepared me for the mates and partners I would take tonight and tomorrow night—the many preferences of the many races in fucking and lovemaking.

And just as important, he had warmed my bed and heart when I'd been brought here as a twenty-year-old still sorting out what it meant to be who I am, and understanding what was asked of me.

We had a special love. We were a sexual pair. We were friends.

"No matter what, I'll always be honored to have served the Blessed Daughter." He kissed my lips. "I'll get breakfast."

"Okay."

He rolled out of bed, his perfectly muscled form on display as he dressed. After the door clicked closed, I let out a cleansing breath.

While I wouldn't miss the rigorous political courses and meetings that had prepared me for tonight, it wasn't much of a relief. If anything, my schedule would be nonstop. It was both terrifying *and* exhilarating. And I would finally have to step up and put into practice everything that had been drilled into me for the last five years.

"Come on, Sonta. Get up," I whispered to myself. If I lay in bed all morning, I would waste what little time I had left as the Blessed Daughter—the mortal daughter of Goddess Hoku herself. Soon enough, I would be known as the Blessed Vessel.

I stood and surveyed myself in the wall mirrors. No bruises remained—good. I'd told the three instructors I'd taken to bed yesterday afternoon to be careful, as I didn't want any blemishes for the big ceremony, though I usually healed quickly. It always got rough when I shared, but it had been a fantastic send-off.

The day was bright and sunny, the breeze still blowing in through the open upper windows of my room.

I took the stairs into my raised pond, and enjoyed soaking and swimming. Some of my mates and partners had already arrived at the palace, having traveled far from their native territories. I hoped I liked them.

Unable to stop my reflections on such a nostalgic day, I fondly considered my childhood—that of a fairly standard human girl with a kind mother. I'd never known my father. And we hadn't understood I was the Blessed Daughter—a gift from Hoku, the Goddess of Unity—until my seventeenth year.

We hadn't exactly been destitute when I was a child, but my childhood was a far cry from life in this place. Our house could have fit within the walls of my chambers and dressing room. Then again, there were no other buildings so grand in all the realm.

The door opened, and Schamoi strode in, carrying breakfast on a tray. "Fresh. All your favorite things."

"Get started without me."

He settled at the private dining table in the corner, and I swam a couple of laps in the short marble-lined pond, then toweled off and wrapped myself in a silky robe.

The breakfast spread was mouthwatering. A large bowl full of chopped fruit in every color. Soft whipped eggs from a golden speckled fowl. Sweet buns that melted in your mouth like clouds.

"I love it." I sat and examined the rest of the tray, peeking under a couple of cloches. The first surprise item had me cocking my head. "A raw prawn?"

Schamoi grinned mischievously. "Preparation for when your tastes change. In case the merman's seed wins."

I rolled my eyes. "For the time being, I prefer human food. And my fishes *cooked.*"

Uncovering the remaining cloche, I let out a sigh. It was a small ornamental bowl of blood. "You are horrible."

Schamoi laughed. "But *Sonta…*" His tone was a playful taunt.

"Vampires…" I muttered. I tried to keep my opinions to myself, but a vampire mate was possibly the most terrifying member of the Coterie, honestly. They were death itself, and one would be trying to make life within me. If it took, I would crave blood for much of the pregnancy. But at the moment, the sight of it made me queasy.

I replaced the cloche. "I thought I was supposed to be treated exceptionally well for the Great Ritual."

He gave me a sultry look. "Did I not worship you well enough on my knees an hour ago? Have I lost my touch?"

As he licked his lips, a shiver ran up my spine. He had done well, and he'd insisted upon it being all pleasure on my part—no lessons, no experiments.

"For that, you're mostly forgiven."

He broke off a piece of sweet roll. "Does that mean I need to do more work before your final fitting? A bit more penitence?" He enunciated that last word, drawing it out.

I shrank in embarrassment. I didn't want to seem too attached, too needy on our last day together. "If you don't mind. Once more?"

He lifted a glass of pomegranate juice. "Without hesitation, little dove."

2

Farewells & Fittings

"How would you like it?" Schamoi asked, undoing the tie of my robe.

I didn't hesitate. "Tender. Slow." This would be our last time together for months, and while I would not lack for partners, I wasn't delusional. None of my Coterie would be tender tonight. They would not be gentle or romantic.

Yes, they would focus on that after the initial claimings so they would have more opportunities to win me over. They'd need to gain my favor for more chances at impregnating me. They'd want my approval for future political connections.

But romance was not the point of the first two nights of the Great Ritual. These men were here to perform, to dominate, to ensure at minimum an equal share in securing their seed with the Blessed Vessel.

Schamoi slipped my robe off. "I can take my time."

I took his shirt off, savoring the foreplay with my lips on his chiseled chest in a dozen places.

Slowly, painfully slowly, I started to slide his pants down.

"Take your time, little dove. I don't have anywhere to be today if you don't."

I giggled. His cock was already large, ready for me. Placing his hands on my ass, he pulled me in, letting me feel him at his hip.

Leaning in for a kiss, I stroked his cock as it pressed against me. We didn't always kiss when we fucked—sometimes it was about learning or practicing, or satiating a need quickly. But when we made love—when it was about friendship and togetherness and sweetness—we usually kissed in abundance.

His lips were soft, large, always well moisturized. He still tasted of pomegranate juice from breakfast. I pressed my lips to his time and time again, and when his lips parted for my tongue, I didn't take the opening. Not yet.

Grinding my hips against his, I nibbled his bottom lip. He replied with a groan as he ground back.

He wouldn't let me do all the teasing or work. He guided me toward the bed and up against the mirror wall. I wasn't mad—it always provided a great view of his perfect ass in the mirror on the opposite wall. It was a pity my room was so large, really, that the other mirror was so far away.

Schamoi leaned down, kissing my neck while grabbing his cock to slide it between my legs. He was already wet, and so was I. He thrust softly—between but not in.

It was an appetizer as his lips covered my neck. I wanted hickeys over all of it, but reminded myself—not this time.

My heart and breath quickened with the constant rubbing, the sweet nibbles, and his hands cupping my breasts. Were it another day, I'd be begging him to throw me on the bed already, or to slip inside and take me against the wall. But he did as I had asked—tender and slow.

Only when he was drenched in me and we were both so wet the friction lessened, did he back me up onto the bed.

My core tightened at seeing him fully erect while he mounted me. Every inch of him slid into me slowly. I closed my eyes, focusing on the memory we were creating, on how well I knew his body and he mine. Once he was completely inside me, I flexed around him.

He shivered with satisfaction.

I gazed into his eyes again; they were sweet and sinful. He bent to kiss me while he gave his first thrust. Without hesitation, we were tongue and lips, thrust after thrust. Slow and steady, building our mutual pleasure.

I was tightening, warming.

He slowed to prolong things, suckling my breasts and circling my nipples with his tongue.

I moaned, breathless, bucking my hips to encourage him to go faster again.

He chuckled against my skin, but did not relent.

His lips took mine again, and he slammed into me. I gasped, our lips still locked.

"My little dove," he whispered as he thrust again. Each thrust became harder and faster.

I met him in rhythm until our breath mingled, thick and short. Until his eyelids fluttered and my core was ablaze, my peak so tight, so explosive that all we could do was give in to pure bliss.

I gasped for air as he shook and filled me. He found the strength to keep thrusting as I surrendered to pleasure.

This. This was why he had been chosen as one of my pleasure instructors. He knew how to do it perfectly every time, in every way.

His energy spent, he lay on me, still inside me.

In another lifetime or realm—I would have picked him for a life partner. He may have been enough on his own.

I drew circles on his back, his forehead pressed against mine, both of us sweating. And we lay there, stealing kisses as he shrank inside me, as his cum leaked out.

I felt a little guilty in that moment. Only five years my senior, he had his whole life ahead of him, but he had not made any new plans yet. Released from my service, he could do anything. He could be a farmer, a painter, a husband to some lovely woman or man. But he could not produce his own children. None of my instructors could. They'd all sacrificed that to be in my service.

The Blessed Daughter must not bear a child of a human. As ancient lore went, Hoku had promised the realm a daughter born of humans every generation, one capable of bearing a child to any of the other races. It was a gift given to only one to breed a ruler capable of bringing the realm together despite the differences of the races.

No, Schamoi could not produce a child with those same handsome icy eyes, but he could be anything else he wished to be.

"Thank you," I whispered. "For this. For being with me in the bedding chamber tonight."

He had no obligation to stay. At this very moment, he could get up, leave my chambers, and walk away, never to see me again. His work was done. But he was my friend, and he'd agreed to see things through.

He slid off me, holding me. I almost cried right then and there. I would have been scared to face the claimings without him near.

Stroking my face, he smiled. "How else am I supposed to see if my hard work paid off?"

I stuck out my tongue in defiance, and he nipped at me, demanding to see what that tongue could do.

As he pulled away again, he gave me another soft smile. "Thank you for letting me be your first and last in this position, little dove."

We bathed together in my large tub before parting ways, reminiscing about the countless hours we'd shared here at the palace.

After dressing myself, I headed to the seamstress's room. The hallways of the palace were ornate and elegant, colorful yet not overwhelming. No sooner had I walked into the seamstress's room than my best friend jumped up and greeted me. "Sonta!"

Lilah hugged me, giving me a kiss. "How are you doing?"

I tidied a strand of her curly hair. "Good. Ready for the fun to begin…" Only a hint of sarcasm laced my words. Each minute that passed felt faster, the tasks ahead of me greater.

"Are you ready, Your Holiness?" Madam Gaffey, the seamstress, asked. Her room was more colorful than any of the other rooms I'd ever entered in the palace, with floor-to-ceiling shelves filled with tidy bolts of fabric, and clothing options on racks. Madam Gaffey stuck out in the sea of color, always wearing white, grey, or black.

"That I am," I replied. I would wear many outfits over the next couple of days—one for each of the men in my Coterie for our individual claimings, and a few more.

Madam Gaffey set to work, grabbing garments from a rack as I undressed.

Lilah sat and watched. "I think the fae dress is my favorite."

I smiled. "It's hard to pick a favorite. Because I can't just judge them on beauty. There's practicality to them."

She smiled back, her eyes trailing along my barely clothed body. "They're lucky." She winked.

We'd been best friends since childhood. We'd experimented and become casual lovers before I moved into the palace, but that wasn't the main reason she'd moved here with me. I'd invited her here because we always had fun, and she always supported me and reminded me of where I came from. She was a beacon who drew me back to reality when a pampered life threatened to change me too much, when my duties threatened to make me dull.

"Arms up, please."

I followed directions, and the seamstress slid the dress over my head. This one was for my vampire mate.

"So… We're only doing final details on the three men she'll be with tonight?" Lilah asked, one eyebrow raised.

Madam Gaffey cleared her throat in warning. Very few people were privy to how the selection had landed, and as Lilah was only a guest, she shouldn't have that knowledge.

"It's okay," I said. "Lilah won't tell a *soul* what she's seen." I winked my answer, and Lilah smiled again. I'd only found out the night before which three partners I'd be taking the first night.

We chatted while Madam Gaffey put on the final touches for each of the three dresses, and the magistrate's messenger came to update me on details of the day.

My grand entrance dress was next—one of my favorites. It hugged my curves, flaring out at the bottom, the single strap highlighting my shoulders. Minuscule jewels covered it in every color of the rainbow.

"I don't envy your pussy with that lineup," Lilah commented.

I laughed. "No, *you* wouldn't, would you?" Lilah preferred women by far. Generally, men were my preference.

"At least you don't have the vampire, shifter, and merman all in one night."

My eyes widened. Thank the stars the secret drawing had broken them up a little. They were the three most likely to be aggressive. The merman pairing had its own intricacies—merfolk usually drowned land-walkers they mated with, often unintentionally.

Soon enough, I tried on the last dress of the evening, admiring the royal blue silk. It draped perfectly.

A messenger peeked in right after I'd changed back into my day dress, and announced my mother had arrived. I nearly squealed with excitement. "I'll be right there!"

Lilah hooked her arm through mine, and we bid Madam Gaffey and her assistants goodbye for the time being.

Our footsteps clicked through the hallways as we went to meet my mother.

"I'll admit I'm a little jealous," Lilah murmured.

I paused. "You can't be serious. We both know—"

"I'm not talking about your Coterie. They're not for me. I'll miss time with you."

I frowned. We only enjoyed each other in bed once a month or so, and we'd indulged last week. I'd vowed to follow the strictest interpretation of the divine edicts about my calling, though, and that included not even taking a woman for the duration of my pregnancy.

I faced her, interlacing our fingers. "I'll make time for you today if you want, before the ceremony."

She grinned, stealing a couple of kisses, pulling me back until she stood against the wall. Her lips were the softest, the gentlest. Her skin was smooth, a bit darker than my own.

After a moment, she pressed her forehead to mine. "If you want me before the Great Ritual, I'm happy to oblige. If you're offering for my sake alone, it's not necessary." She quickly added, "Not that I'll turn it down, because I *will* miss you."

I held her waist. "I… I could go either way."

She stole another kiss. "We'll see how the rest of this afternoon plays out. Right now, your mother is waiting for you."

"Okay."

"Plus…" She drew lazy circles on my lower back. "I know you're a rather sexual creature, but please tell me you haven't forgotten I like to spend time doing many other things with you."

I fully blushed. "Obviously. I only offered because, you know … it could be a long time." Gestation varied depending on the race of the man whose seed had done the job.

Her dark brown eyes gazed into my own. She had beautiful lashes. "I'll miss you in every way, because you'll be so busy." Her tone turned playful, almost mocking. "And I know you're all 'goddess blessed' and everything, and those men are going to fight to rail you every two seconds, but you really should learn that everything's not all about you. My bed is warm when I want it to be, whether or not it's with you."

I grinned. "Everything *is* all about me. At least it is today."

We busted out laughing in unison, and she pushed me away. "Hurry up! Let's go see your mother."

She took my hand, and we strode down the hallway again.

"Honestly, Sonta. You've become so spoiled," she whispered in fun.

I reached up and brushed a finger across the dangling crystal earrings she wore. "Says the woman who only lives in the palace because of her spoiled friend."

Lilah snickered. "Fair point." She drew a deep breath as we approached the door. "You're sure you won't forget me? What if your Coterie votes to kick me out?"

I scoffed. "You were here first. And they have little say." I nudged her as we halted at the door. "Plus, my child will need a proper auntie when it's born, and I can't think of anyone better."

Her smile was sweet and satisfied.

3

Lilah's Bedchamber

My mother's arms were around me so tight I could barely breathe.

"Sonta, my girl." Her hair smelled of primroses.

"Mammi," I said, squeezing her in return. She would always be my mother. She had conceived me, brought me into this world, cared for me, and taught me the best she knew how to. My discovery as Hoku's mortal daughter had been a tough one for her. It had been rough navigating the transition. I felt guilty for leaving her. She preferred her privacy, which she had gotten precious little of after I was confirmed to be the Blessed Daughter. With my new wealth, I'd purchased her a cottage far from the town we'd lived in. She cherished the calm.

Today would be anything but calm, but she'd come here for me on one of the most important days of my life.

We sat for tea in her guest room parlor, Lilah joining us. We talked timelines and technicalities, anxieties and anticipation. My mother had offered to arrive a full week early to help with preparations, but I had insisted she didn't need to. She would have been so stressed with the hustle and bustle of the palace leading up to tonight, and she still struggled to understand me in some ways. She, like most humans, didn't have quite the sex drive I had. She didn't have the calling I did. And this place could be downright dull with politics at times.

"I really do appreciate your support, Mammi." I took a sip of my tea. "It means the world to me."

11

She pursed her lips. "I'll always be here for you, even if I don't understand everything."

That truly warmed my heart. I'd never told her Lilah and I had become intimate, and my mother had never shown romantic interest in a woman, but she'd picked up on our affections over the last few years. She had a calming smile that conveyed her desire to understand and appreciate others for their differences.

"That doesn't mean I won't worry," she added.

"I'll be fine." I understood her fear of the Great Ritual, especially when it came to the merman. Oddly, I wasn't as nervous about that claiming as I probably should be.

Lilah slid her hand onto my thigh under the table. "I'll make sure she's well cared for in the bedding chamber."

Her hand on my thigh, the sweetness of her reassurance had me mentally planning time for us alone.

My mother was nervous for me, but she could not stomach watching her only daughter from the closeness of the bedding chamber. She would instead listen from far below in the general audience. I preferred it that way, anyway. It had been enough of a strain on our relationship with the drama I'd stirred up by taking so many young men to bed in our town growing up—before we'd recognized the signs of my calling as Hoku's daughter—and I didn't need her getting a close and personal view of my Coterie claiming me.

There would be *plenty* of spectators without her.

I did my best to dispel any fears my mother held for my well-being, and fears Lilah had, too. As servants delivered lunch, the three of us discussed the political ramifications of my Coterie. I'd assessed them a million times already, but it wouldn't hurt to go over them once more. Then again, I was becoming more tense with each minute.

It didn't help when Kernov appeared to deliver a message from the magistrate himself. This morning and afternoon were *supposed* to be spent the way I'd like—calmly with friends and family.

Lilah's fingers trailed up and down my thigh, distracting me. I couldn't focus on the last of the food on my plate, but I did catch the slight tint in my mother's cheeks as she and Kernov exchanged pleasantries.

I liked Kernov. He was a highly respected and honorable man ten years my mother's senior. His dark hair was peppered with silver, and he was always kind enough to offer to accompany my mother on a stroll—a rather long stroll—around the palace gardens. They liked each other, though neither would admit it openly.

While I wasn't normally a matchmaker, I paused in that moment to truly consider the pair. I slid my hand onto Lilah's, giving it a squeeze. My mother was lonely. Kernov worked himself to death as the magistrate's top advisor.

I had to admit just a smidgen that my motives were also selfish in wanting the pair to come together. Kernov lived at the palace. If he won Mother over, she might move here.

And as much as I had on my plate, I would find immense satisfaction in my mother's happiness. And in having her closer once I became pregnant and bore a child of my own.

"Kernov?" I interrupted rather rudely, snapping back from my musings.

"Yes, Your Holiness?"

"The Coterie meeting is at five thirty?"

He gave me a nod. "Sharp."

Rubbing Lilah's hand, I settled on my plan. "Then I should probably go. Lilah and I were going to see to one last thing before I have to get all dressed up."

"Oh… You don't want to stay for dessert?" Mother asked.

"I'm really not that fond of it right now. With my nerves and stomach…" I faced Kernov, folding the napkin on my lap. "Would you be so kind as to take our place? Keep my mother company for now?"

His assessment was quick and subtle, his lip twitching slightly. Kernov knew *exactly* what I was doing. He was good at reading people, at anticipating their moves and motivations. That was his job, after all.

"I'd be delighted. Always happy to help the Blessed Daughter in whatever way she deems necessary."

Lilah had stayed perfectly still, and I hadn't dared to look at her, but she followed my lead as we stood and said our goodbyes.

"You're sure you don't want to take anything with you for dessert?" my mother asked. "In case your stomach settles?"

Just then, a servant entered with a tray of cakes.

"I'm fine, thanks."

The servant looked a bit confused with two-thirds of the table leaving.

"It'll just be these two." I considered a moment, wanting to be discreet. "Once you've served them, would you please see me in the hallway?"

"Um… Sure, Your Holiness." She set the first plate in front of my mother.

While Mother was also visibly confused, she was easily taken with Kernov. "Please, take a seat, Kernov." She gestured to the chair I had sat in.

"Gladly," he replied with a fondness to his voice I never heard him use for anyone else.

Lilah and I left the room, holding hands. Only when the door closed did she address me. "We need to see to one last thing?" She wore a subtle grin.

My smile matched hers, and I couldn't resist stealing a kiss. Less than a minute later, the servant joined us in the hallway.

"You wanted to speak to me, Your Holiness?"

"Yes. Could you have the kitchen deliver a plate of small desserts to Lilah's room? Bite-size things. And … some honey."

"Right away." She still held her serving tray in front of her. "About the honey… You want honey baked into a dessert, or something to dip into the honey?"

I swallowed, my mouth dry. *Discreet.* 'Enough to lick off Lilah' would not be the appropriate answer.

"Just a small jar of it on the side, thank you. Surprise us with the rest."

The servant curtsied. "I'll have it delivered right away."

Lilah and I lay on her bed, still dressed, cuddling and sharing kisses. She had been acting a little off lately despite her brave face. I couldn't tell what was bothering her, but I could offer some relief.

Her room was much smaller than mine, but still elegant. She'd decorated it herself with fabrics and art in various hues of purple and pink.

A servant knocked on the door, and Lilah jumped up to get it. She thanked him, taking the tray and setting it on her dresser.

"Mmm… Nice selection."

I wrapped my arms around her, peering over her shoulder. "Not bad. Any requests?"

She plucked a chocolate-filled raspberry from the tray, popping it into her mouth. "Oh, that's so good. Want to try one?"

"Sure." I opened my mouth as she picked up another.

Then she placed it on *her* tongue and leaned in for a kiss. As our lips met, her tongue glided against mine, depositing the raspberry.

I let out a soft moan as she pulled back, and I savored the treat. Grasping my hips, she leaned in for another kiss. We stood there for a moment, lost in a tangle of tongues and lips. She may not have had pleasure instructors, but she was good at this—at foreplay and tenderness.

After another minute, she weaved her hands through my ebony hair. "So, *divinely appointed* Blessed Daughter. What do you want?"

I glared at her smug grin. It annoyed me when she addressed me formally, and she knew it.

"Well…" I worked at the knot in her wraparound dress. "What do I want?" After I loosened the knot, I gently disrobed her. My insides were already heating for her with the thin slip she wore. "I want you to call my name in a few minutes. Gasp, moan, or scream—it's your choice."

Lilah giggled. "So confident."

I slid the slip off her, one strap at a time, until it fell on the floor. Stunned by her undergarments, I stared.

Her breasts were astonishing, larger than my own. They weren't the main focus of my attention, though; not exactly…

Unable to help myself, I lifted my hands and traced her areolas with my thumbs. Her bra and underwear were lacy—barely there. Her nipples hardened beneath the peach-colored lace.

"You told me you hadn't planned on us being together today," I said. This set of lingerie had been a gift—from me—that she only wore on special occasions.

She bit her lip. "Well… You had Schamoi this morning, and you'll have the three later tonight…"

"And?" I applied light pressure.

"I knew you'd make time for me if you wanted to. But I truly don't expect it. Things are changing, and I can see that. But even if we didn't end up enjoying time together today, I wanted to support you. In all ways. In my own little way." She looked down, embarrassed.

"I love you, Lilah. In all ways." I claimed her mouth with my own as I reached behind her and undid the bra. She worked at the ties of my dress, though they were too tricky to undo that way.

Slowly, I glided my hands down, tucking my thumbs under the band on her underwear. I took my time lowering it to the floor, appreciating every curve on her body as I went.

"All right, let's get this thing off you." She turned me around as soon as I stood, more hurriedly undoing the lacing of my dress.

"Really?" Her voice was perky as she grasped my naked ass after the dress fell. "So, bare all morning?"

I chuckled. "It's refreshing. You ought to try it."

She didn't reply as she set to work on my corset, planting the occasional kiss on my neck. "Seriously, Sonta. Make half of you easily accessible, but the other half a fortress?"

I laughed even harder.

Despite her playful complaints, she worked quickly, freeing me completely from my clothing. As soon as she tossed my corset to the side, she held me from behind, her hands cupping my breasts, my ass nestled against her.

"I love you, too, Sonta," she whispered into my ear.

I leaned into her, safe in her arms. Sex or no sex—we had always been a pair. If you had trouble with one of us, you had trouble with both of us. When we got into mischief growing up, we had either dove into that mischief together, or we'd been there to cover for the other.

We just stood there a moment, skin to skin, drinking up the last of this type of intimacy we'd have for some time. No words needed to be said.

Eventually, Lilah's cupped hands shifted, and she worked circles around my nipples, repaying the favor. "So… We don't have all day today, do we?"

Part of me wished we did.

"I suppose it's either us or that dessert… Or are we meant to be the dessert for each other?"

Smirking, I removed her hands and kissed each on the palm. "Get on the bed." I faced her.

She pouted. "So bossy… So high and mighty, O Blessed—"

I covered her mouth with my hand. "Don't you even…"

Her eyes twinkled. After prying my hand from her mouth, she leaned in, grazing her lips so delicately against mine. "But you said I would call your name in the form of… What was it? A gasp or moan?"

Our lips touching, I repeated myself. "Get on the bed, or I'll put you there, Lilah."

She chuckled. "It *is* your special day. I can be obedient this once."

4

Love & Lust

Lilah lay on her bed, watching me, her dark brown curls cascading over the hand she propped her head up on. It was hard to not get distracted. As much as I absolutely loved a man's cock inside me, men just didn't bring the same satisfaction when it came to curves.

Food play was also at a whole nother level when it came to the female body. Body hair on men was handsome in its own right, but not ideal for licking and consuming things.

I surveyed the tray of desserts, mentally designing a map for Lilah's body. After moving a few things around, I set the tray on her bed to the side.

She gave it a curious glance.

"One more thing," I said. We had few secrets between us, and since we didn't have all day, I rounded the bed and straightaway opened her bedside table's top drawer. Inside lay a few tools of the trade. I studied them, assessing their usefulness. This was another thing Lilah had educated me on. Some were knobbed glass of different shapes, others made of softer material. Two in particular were specially charmed by mages.

Grinning, I picked the shorter of the two and closed the drawer.

"Interesting choice," Lilah commented.

We sometimes used the longer of the two contraptions—it fit inside us both simultaneously. It was a divine finish when we wanted something quick.

"My treat," I replied, setting it next to the food tray. It was all right if I didn't come. I wanted *her* to enjoy this—I wanted to see the way her long eyelashes fluttered as she finished, the way her perfect lips parted as she fought for breath.

Without further delay, I climbed in her bed and straddled her.

"First, do *you* have any requests of desserts you want to eat? Because, in all fairness, I plan to do most of the eating here…"

Her hands grasping my hips, she glanced at the tray. "Surprise me."

I picked another chocolate-filled raspberry, popping it into my mouth as she smiled back. Then she lifted her hands above her head, surrendering to me. How was she so graceful in every move?

Leaning down, I transferred the raspberry to her mouth. She savored the bite with a soft moan while I selected another couple of treats to feed her. Nothing quite compared to the feeling of our naked breasts pressed tightly to each other, our more intimate lips kissing with no barrier.

After I fed her a few more treats, it was time to move on. I tried to not rush, to not get distracted by the clock. This time was ours and ours alone.

I started at her neck, plucking up the small jar of honey. I twirled the honey stick, picking up plenty, then carefully let it drip. She'd moved her hair to the side once she saw it coming.

No sooner had I replaced the honey on the tray than I glanced back at her, noting I'd drizzled a tad too much. Honey dripped down the side of her neck, and I swiftly halted it with a finger, wiping it up.

"Let me see that," she said, opening her mouth for a taste.

I obliged, and she sucked my finger, taking it deeper into her mouth than needed. I was already wet.

After reclaiming my hand, I snuck a quick kiss, then continued on my path downward. I slathered a whipped fruit mousse on her nipples, already yearning to suck it off.

With a swipe of a finger through a dish of caramel sauce, I drew a squiggly line from her breasts to her navel. She giggled and squirmed a bit, the more ticklish of the two of us.

The raspberries were so fresh that I chose another and placed it on her navel.

Lastly, I took a piece of chocolate, sliding it between her labia. I sat back and prepared myself to feast. She only gazed back at me, wearing a full smile with brilliant white teeth.

I scooted back, giving myself better access. My tongue glided through her center, the chocolate just small enough for me to scoop up with the tip. She shivered under my touch.

The chocolate melting in my mouth, I went back for a couple more swipes of my tongue, focusing on her clit. The bitter creaminess of the chocolate mingled with her scent and salt.

"Sonta," she breathed.

I stopped after another lick. "You called my name. Does that mean we're done here?"

Lilah threw me a withering glare. I wouldn't dare leave her unsatisfied, or covered in food.

Drawing my tongue through her center one more time, I reached the raspberry at her navel. She liked my tongue in there as well—she always kept it immaculately clean.

Inch by inch, I made my way up her body, savoring the caramel sauce mingled with the taste of her. I paid special attention to the curve of her underbreasts.

I halted for a moment, contemplative. "Do you remember our first time?"

She grinned. "You were so awkward." She chuckled at my expense.

It was true, though. "Well, that's what you get for sharing your bed with a girl who'd only ever screwed a half dozen young men."

Even so, I'd learned most of lesbian pleasure from Lilah. My pleasure instructors had taught me a fair bit about self-pleasure, but most of their education had been about preparing me for the variety of races that would join my Coterie—all men, mostly focused on conception.

Lilah was sweetness, sin, and pleasure—no strings attached. It had started with hand-holding, with lingering gazes and trailing fingers on lower backs. Then a stolen kiss. It had taken us months to admit we wanted to share a bed. And most of the time, with Lilah, it was lovemaking, not just fucking.

"Hopefully I've improved," I said, lowering my lips to her nipples, suckling the mousse from them, taking in as much of her as I could manage.

She softly threaded her fingers through my hair. "Goddess damned, you've improved," she muttered.

A smile graced my face as I tackled the next breast. She ground her hips, begging for penetration. I was *almost* ready to give it to her.

I gave her another lingering kiss, ensuring my hair didn't dip into the honey. She grabbed my ass like her life depended on it, hungry, desperate, her breathing ragged.

Then, only then, did I grab the tool. It was a curious thing. With a tap of a rune on the bottom, it vibrated. Five taps gave it five levels of strength. Not wanting her to go off immediately, I kept it on the lowest setting.

Her eyes followed me as I scooted back. She was drenched, making it easy to insert. Easing her open, I slid it in.

Lilah lost all speech as she enjoyed the pleasure, and I was tempted to take it out and finish her myself, but I stuck to my plan. I crawled back up, voraciously cleaning her neck and nibbling her ears as she ground against me. Though it was solely inside her, the residual vibration brought me pleasure too.

She fondled my breasts as I propped myself up, and I wholeheartedly claimed her mouth, wrestling through each panting breath.

She was tight. I was tight. I greedily regretted my pick of tools, that I had not chosen the one for us both.

In no time, her whispered praise became gasps of ecstasy, her grinding turned into shaking. I rested myself atop her pussy, enjoying the tightness myself while watching her. Her profile was beautiful as she arched her back, as her chin tilted up, as her knuckles whitened around the bars of her headboard.

Careful to monitor her, I allowed the warmth to build in my core. Short of me reaching my peak, her shakes and expression settled into that point of overstimulation when pleasure turned to pain.

My hand darted in, and I tapped a rune on the opposite side, quieting the magic.

Spent, Lilah calmed, smiling up at me.

After a moment, I pulled the tool out and set it on the food tray.

I savored a couple of sweet kisses as she thanked me, then I got up to put the dessert tray back on the dresser so it would be out of the way.

"Come back here," she said softly, rolling onto her side.

I obeyed, cuddling with her, our legs intertwined. Brushing the hair out of her face, I took in her beauty once more.

"You should change your mind about tonight and run away with me," Lilah said.

I let out a breathy chuckle. She didn't mean it—it was a running joke between us. My life and womb were not mine to direct; they hadn't been since my discovery as Hoku's daughter. Oddly enough, I had never resented this position. These men would fulfill my every need. I had power and status. I could take care of the ones I loved most. And part of me was genuinely excited to bear a child.

Still, I caressed Lilah's face. "Don't play with me. I know I'm not your favorite lover."

She grunted, throwing yet another scowl at me. "Favorite is a profane word in my love life."

Unable to stop myself, I chuckled again. It was true. We both shared that mentality. It wasn't about a better or worse lover, but about appreciating the differences each offered. That was something I looked forward to with the men of my Coterie—they would each bring something different to the bedroom, and to our realm's leadership.

Her hand massaged my hip as we gazed into each other's eyes.

"I…" She hesitated. "I wanted to ask you something."

I smiled. "Anything."

"You know Cataray?"

"Yes. I don't keep track of all your girlfriends, but give me a *little* credit…" Lilah brought Cataray around the most of any of her lovers. She'd dined with us several times here at the palace.

"Well… Of course… I just…"

"You can tell me anything. You know that. That will never change."

Lilah closed her eyes, sucking in a breath. "She wants to be exclusive."

My heart hurt. I shouldn't be jealous. And I usually wasn't. Lilah deserved to live her life in whatever way she deemed fit, whatever made her happiest. I just … hadn't realized things would change so quickly.

"If that's what would make you happy, then I support you."

She opened her eyes, a frown playing across her lips. "But I don't think it would. I don't want that. I honestly don't know if I'll ever be ready for that."

I rubbed her shoulder, adjusting my leg hooked around hers. "Do you think that's a deal breaker for you? Either way, she could move here if that would help things… I just want you to be happy."

She smiled sweetly. "I think she'll understand. I love her, but … I'm not there yet."

I nodded. "Okay." I searched her eyes, a little confused about the topic at hand. We spoke openly about lovers, but usually not while in bed with each other. "Is this … about … being at the palace?" I arched an eyebrow.

Her mouth hung open a moment. "Not exactly… I was wondering if, after the child is born and you're free to take other lovers again, if you'd like to try something with the two of us."

Imagine how much more fun that could be—a full day with three of us taking turns. Goddess damned, that sounded divine right now.

"If she likes the idea, then I'm all for it."

Lilah swooped in, stealing my breath with a fervent kiss. "Thank you."

One kiss became ten as we lay there. My desire built again, and I couldn't resist grinding against her.

Lilah's fingers trailed down my hip, making their way to my entrance. She inserted one finger, then two, gently pumping as I ground in rhythm.

It was paradise itself in her arms. The tension was so tight, my core on fire, her every touch exquisite.

A loud knock at the door brought us to a screeching halt. My breathing heavy, the devastation set in. We both stared at the door. We couldn't ignore it, couldn't pretend we hadn't heard—not today of all days.

Another knock changed the rhythm of my heartbeat, squashing the mood entirely. "I'll get it."

I stood and grabbed a blanket from a chair in Lilah's sitting area. After wrapping myself, I opened the door.

"Yes?" I tried to keep my annoyance out of my tone.

"His Eminence wishes to speak with you."

I groaned, glancing over my shoulder at the clock. Lilah and I had spent longer together than I'd planned, but I still had plenty of time to get ready for the meeting before the big feast.

The servant surveyed my blanket-wrapped form. "He wishes to have a few words before the Coterie meeting, and he'd like you fully dressed and prepared." Worry tinted her words.

Five minutes. Just five more minutes and I would have been in pure ecstasy. "Fine. Where?"

"His private study, Your Holiness."

"I'll be there shortly."

I closed the door and pressed my forehead against it. The reality of the tasks ahead of me was suddenly such a massive weight on my shoulders.

"I'm sorry," Lilah said behind me. "Here, let me help."

Her footsteps padded across the stone floor and into her washroom. A rush of water splashed, then quieted. In no time, Lilah stood beside me, placing a kiss on my shoulder. "Here."

I faced her, trying not to let the moment be completely ruined.

Her smile was strained but encouraging as she handed me a warm, wet washcloth. "I could be quick if you want to finish, if you think His Eminence would be patient enough…"

Fighting a frown, I used the washcloth to wipe myself—despite my best efforts to lick Lilah clean, I always got a little sticky. "It's okay. I wanted to see *you* finish." A genuine smile tugged at my lips. "I'm sure my fae partner will be glad to have me already prepared for him. Or at least *I'll* be grateful for it."

Lilah wiped herself with a washcloth as well. "You're welcome, then. Glad I could help." She giggled, wiping her center. "An appetizer for your main course."

I lifted her chin. "Never something lesser."

She smiled softly. "I know, Sonta. I was kidding." She held out a hand for my washcloth, and I surrendered it.

While she returned the cloths to the washroom, I picked up our clothes from the floor and placed them on the bed.

"Before we get you back into that half fortress…" She pulled me into her arms. Her presence was so calming.

"Do you want to join me in my chambers tonight?" I whispered. "Just cuddling?"

Tonight would be an odd juxtaposition, a lonely bedtime after the first evening of the Great Ritual.

Lilah held me tighter. "I'd love to."

We remained embracing for as long as I could manage before my anxiety forced me to get back to task. Lilah held up my corset. "Let's get you ready."

5

PREPARATIONS

It took me a little longer to primp myself than I'd planned before leaving Lilah's room to see the magistrate. My hair had gotten rather messy with our toss in the sheets, but Lilah made sure I looked presentable before I left. I wouldn't see her again until the big feast.

I knocked on the door to the magistrate's private study, and it opened immediately.

"Oh…" I paused, surprised to find the room so full.

"Join us, Sonta," Magistrate Leonte offered. He was a midsized man, an elected official who ruled in tandem with the emperor.

"Certainly, Your Eminence." I gave him a courtesy bow and entered the room.

The emperor himself was also in attendance. I bowed lower. "Your Magnificence."

The elderly half-elf gave me a slight nod, nothing more. He was a man of few words, and when he spoke, he did not falter with his meaning. He'd intimidated me since the day I first met him. A lot of that had to do with his nature, and the rest had to do with the nuance of our relationship. With his elf nature and upbringing, he carried physical and personality traits from his father's side. Elves liked to keep to themselves; they were a quiet, proud, and stubborn bunch. They were calculating and cunning. They were strict but generally fair.

The emperor had not inherited immortality from his father, though; none of the mixling rulers did. While his freckled face did show signs of aging, it didn't betray his true age. His years were counted.

My child would be his replacement.

"Would you like a seat?" Magistrate Leonte offered, gesturing to an empty chair by his desk.

"Thank you." I readily took it.

"Nothing troubling. We simply wanted to discuss final appointments for protocol."

I swallowed, my face warming.

Leonte named the other six people in the room I didn't recognize. Part of me didn't even want to know their names. They had been selected as attestants, impartial witnesses who would track my every move, from the start of the Great Ritual to the end of the claimings tomorrow night.

While I'd taken all five of my pleasure instructors to my bed at once, I had never practiced any sort of open exhibitionism, no mass voyeurism. The claimings were public, just as the birth would be. And these strangers would have front-row tickets. They would be peering into some of my most vulnerable and private moments for the sake of properly fulfilling divine prophecy and keeping the peace in our realm.

I felt completely naked already. My gaze kept shooting to the bookshelves and pictures in the room rather than the eyes of the attestants.

"And, of course, the security teams will guarantee your safety and that nothing goes awry," Leonte reassured me.

The realm always had its scuffles and differences amongst the territories and races, but things had been relatively calm for some time. That didn't mean it was safe. The Great Ritual was supposed to be something beautiful, but it was also an opportune time to stage a coup, to attempt to overthrow the empire. To take my life and stunt Hoku's blessings for an entire generation until another Blessed Daughter was born and discovered.

I gulped. "Of course." *Generally*, I was at peace with my placement here, but at moments like this I was beyond uneasy.

Luckily, the meeting was short, and I was happy to leave. Wasting no time, I made a beeline for Madam Gaffey's room.

"About time," she scolded as I walked in.

"Sorry. His Magnificence and Eminence wanted to see me."

"No excuses. We don't have time to waste, Your Holiness."

Her assistants quickly stripped me down and got me into my gorgeous jewel-covered gown. I could barely breathe, mostly out of nerves, not from it being too tight.

They fussed with my hair and makeup, ensuring every part of me glowed. Talk was minimal as they did me up, and I couldn't help but ponder my calling as Hoku's daughter.

People worshiped me for something I had never earned. I hadn't even understood my true nature until my seventeenth year. I wasn't a deity—I had only been touched by one in my mother's womb.

I did recognize Hoku's presence sometimes, mostly in visions but also in moments of meditation and decision. But I didn't have any notable mortal pedigree, nor decades—never mind an immortal's centuries—of experience in leadership. I mostly followed the moral compass my mother had ingrained in me, and the law my palace tutors had drilled me on.

I had not even entered most of the territories or met some of the races I would now be linked to for the rest of my life.

But the realm trusted me, simply because a goddess had given me a gift.

I prayed in that moment, as the stylists set my curls. I said a silent prayer to my divine mother. *Bless me with your wisdom, and the strength to keep the peace. Bless me to know how to nurture my child.*

Minutes later, I was all primped and set, not a hair out of place. I looked stunning. My ebony hair was done up in intricate braids and curls. My lips glistened, tinted radish red. My eye makeup was slightly smoky. I took a second to admire the rainbow sea of miniscule jewels adorning my gown.

I thanked the workers for their job well done. They dismissed me, reminding me they'd see me a few more times tonight.

No sooner had I opened the door than Lilah tackled me with a hug.

"Careful," Schamoi chastised softly. "Our dove needs to look impeccable."

I smiled, returning Lilah's embrace. A pace behind her, Schamoi grinned at me, handsomely dressed.

Releasing Lilah, I held out my arms for Schamoi. He scooped me up into a hug.

"We couldn't resist seeing you one more time," Lilah said, giddy. She still glowed from our earlier encounter.

Schamoi stepped back, tucking his hands into his pockets. "We're proud of you."

I swallowed hard. "Thank you." I really ought to get going, but my heart thudded in my chest. Glancing between the two, I opened my mouth. "Schamoi, where are you sleeping tonight?"

It wasn't like he was being booted out of the palace immediately. "My room."

Lilah would be okay with him joining us tonight; that much I knew. And I wanted both of them there with me for my lonely, crazy night. "Would you join Lilah and me in my chamber? Obviously…"

Obviously no sex.

He took my hand, kissing it. "It would be my honor."

Beaming, I wanted to steal a kiss, but I wouldn't dare mess up the look I'd just had done.

"Your Holiness," a servant called from the end of the corridor. "I'm here to escort you. We need to make haste."

I drew a deep breath. "Right. Yes."

Lilah took my hand. "We'll walk you to the last corridor?"

Schamoi offered his hand as well, and I quickly took it.

"I appreciate that."

We strode toward the servant, and he turned. For a minute, we followed in silence. My heart beat harder with each footstep in the quiet, panic nearly setting in as I imagined the eyes of the men soon to claim me, some more inhuman than others.

I gripped Lilah and Schamoi's hands tighter, hanging on to them like tethers to the past I suddenly didn't want to break.

"You really do look ravishing, Sonta," Lilah said. "That dress does your breasts justice."

I grinned. Did she like them better in this dress? Or how they'd been pressed against her own little over an hour ago?

Schamoi hummed. "I will admit, she is rather enjoyable to ravish."

I busted out laughing, and they followed suit. The servant remained quiet, no doubt used to this crass humor from my side of the palace.

While I appreciated the levity to help distract me, it didn't last long. We reached the corridor where we had to part ways. I paused, my hands clammy. I could do this. Right?

Schamoi pressed a kiss to my hair. "It's time to fly, little dove."

Lilah's smile was encouraging. I summoned the strength to release their hands. "I'll see you soon."

"We'll see you soon. You'll do great."

Sucking in another breath, I stepped forward, following the servant down the last hallway. A few heartbeats later, we stood outside a small ballroom. I would be entering solo.

"Ready, Your Holiness?"

Ignoring the thumping in my chest, I nodded.

He grasped the door handle. "May Hoku multiply her blessings on you."

6

THE FEAST

"Wait," I spat out before the servant opened the ballroom door. Concern covered his face. "Your Holiness, can I—"

"I just need a moment." I stepped back, forcing myself to breathe. A butterfly—why couldn't I be a butterfly? Or rather a caterpillar? A beautiful and free creature whose transition took place in private, in the warmth of a cocoon? Or perhaps a bird in a tall tree, far from all eyes?

The fact remained—I was not a flying creature. I was the mortal daughter of a goddess. And I had a job to do.

Mostly, I feared a loveless life. All duty. I wanted a child, but not for every single aspect of my identity to be tied to the emperor or empress I would bring into this world.

I wanted to be loved for me, too. I had that with Lilah and Schamoi. There were no guarantees I would share any such connection with the members of my Coterie.

"Your Holiness, should I tell them—"

I straightened. "I'm fine." Standing tall, I fixed my expression as I'd been taught to. I was not a frail young human walking into a room of predators. They were not powerful ancient leaders towering over me.

I am Hoku's daughter. The treaties and peace rely upon me. They need me.

As for love and connection with the men in my Coterie, I would soon find out.

"Thank you for your escort. I'm ready."

With only a brief pause, he turned the knob and opened the door.

Loud chatter filling the room quickly died as I entered. I kept my head high.

"Her Holiness, Sonta Gwynriel, the Blessed Daughter," an official announcer boomed.

Every head bowed, dozens of them—the magistrate's and emperor's as well, though they didn't usually.

I nodded back, taking in the room. "Thank you."

Magistrate Leonte came to my side, escorting me fully into the room.

Despite the dozens of attendees, this was a 'small and private' gathering. It gave me a chance to chat for a few minutes with each of the men I'd be bound to before they fucked me in front of a crowd of a thousand.

It also gave me the opportunity to meet some of the most important rulers within the realm.

Each race huddled pretty closely in their own groups, only lightly mingling with some of the others.

"Let's see His Magnificence first, shall we?" Leonte suggested.

I followed along, walking toward the emperor and offering a curtsy. He stood by the elves.

"Sonta," he replied, his voice shaky with age. "High Lord Elout, his High Lady Marsone." He gestured to a tall graceful couple. They extended their hands and clasped mine in turn. Each race had their own way of greeting, but in the capital, all handshakes were doublehanded.

The emperor continued. "And Lord Findlech."

Lord Findlech assessed me, his face unreadable. He was centuries old, but with the grace and beauty of an elf, he looked no older than forty. He extended his hands, and I took them to shake.

"An honor," he said. His skin, long hair, and eyes were all dark, his lips handsome. He wore a delicate circlet befitting his station.

"I…" I wasn't normally one to stutter. Maybe it was all the eyes on me. Or perhaps it was the fact this man stood before me, one of my partners, and I had actually seen him before. I had been given details about each of them to prepare, but I hadn't thought I'd ever seen any of them.

But Lord Findlech had been at the palace before, visiting the emperor, presumably on business.

Gathering myself, I managed to recover. "I am honored. I look forward to knowing you, to learning more of your people."

"May Hoku multiply her blessings," Lord Findlech uttered.

No sooner had we taken our hands back than another group approached.

"Elout, good to see you," the fae king declared, though his tone didn't convey any true warmth. And he *had* to be the king with how adorned he was.

High Lord Elout gave him a wry smile. "Indeed, it is."

The fae and elves were the most closely related of the races, actually able to interbreed, though it was almost never done. The cousin races had succumbed to treacherous rulers centuries ago, enslaving and slaughtering many across the realm. Most of the inhabitants of the realm, however, held blame for that dark past, especially before Hoku put an end to it and established her line in mortality.

Magistrate Leonte introduced the fae rulers. "King Bretton and Queen Lourel."

We exchanged greetings.

"And I'm Tyfen," a breathtakingly gorgeous man said, extending his hands. "Prince Tyfen."

Another member of my Coterie. He kissed my hand. His grip was tight and warm. The cousin races were so similar, yet so different. Their arrogance and pride were of a different brand. And elves usually stood taller, and had pointier ears. But the ethereal beauty of them both was hard to ignore.

Tyfen had an air of confidence, his attire immaculate, a simple silver crown adorning his head, tattoos covering his brown arms and neck. My insides tightened as I wondered what they all looked like, where all they covered. I'd get a good view in just over two hours' time because he would be the first to formally claim me.

"Sonta," I breathed. "Nice … to meet you."

A small smile tugged at his lips. "Indeed."

Not quite rushing me, Magistrate Leonte guided me from group to group. We didn't have long, but I took in first impressions of each of the rulers, and of the men in my Coterie—them especially.

I was met with a mix of sweetness—no doubt starting their attempts to buy my affection and loyalty—and curiosity. I had been raked over by all hues of eyes by the end of the short meeting.

The vampires' hands were colder than I'd imagined, but my mate's eyes softer. The shifter had a pure sort of kindness to his mannerisms and adorable lycan eyes, a dull grey capable of shimmering metallic silver. The mage—the second youngest of the lot—had a mop of curly red hair that took me by surprise, three visible piercings, and a crooked smile that made me question him.

Sadly, my merman partner had not arrived yet. A solo messenger occupied the tank in the room, informing us he would be here shortly. There had been trouble along the way and record-breaking riptides delaying his arrival from the far south sea.

At the end of the short meeting, one of the magistrate's advisors led me out of the room.

My heart burst with joy at the sight of another surprise supporter. "Mammi, what are you doing here?"

She smiled, all dolled up. "I had to sneak away. How was it?"

Meeting the men, albeit briefly, had calmed me. By the end, I'd undressed them all mentally, their personalities and their physiques. "It'll be great. They all seem like good men, I swear." I tucked in a hairpin of hers that had wiggled loose. "I'll be safe."

She gave me a quick hug but had to return to her seat in the banquet hall. As a commoner, my mother wouldn't have a special entrance. Being who she was, she wouldn't want one anyway. The next hour would be a feast loaded with formal introductions and ceremony. It would be dull, full of pomp and circumstance. I truly wasn't sure if I'd rather we skipped it and went straight to the claimings… Get it over with.

After arriving at my designated entry point, I listened to each announcement of dignitaries and royalty as they were ushered into the banquet hall. While the small ballroom had been full of dozens of dignitaries and staff waiting on them, this banquet room held hundreds.

After every single race and their representatives had been called in to join, it was my turn.

They did their usual formal introduction—Hoku's daughter, Blessed Daughter, all that.

"May Hoku multiply her blessings," the emperor said. Hundreds of voices shook the hall in echoed reply. "May Hoku multiply her blessings."

My mouth went positively dry as I stepped through the curtain I'd waited behind.

The sight of so many gathered to celebrate me was astounding, and also familiar. Thousands had gathered at my local temple and at the palace to glimpse me upon my discovery as the Blessed Daughter in the first place. I had grown so much since then.

I stepped to my appointed place on the high stage; the dignitaries were on different levels for the best views.

The sunset bathing the dining hall mingled with soft fae lights, and my dress glittered. This was that moment—one I would never forget.

"I'm honored to serve our people." I bowed, sweating already. "I'm privileged to bear the light of Hoku within me, to bring unity to this realm. I pledge my life to this beautiful empire, to honor the culture and traditions of each race."

I had practiced this speech so many times—with the right pauses and emphasis—that I could not falter. My eyes scanned the room as I recited it, catching on a friendly sight that warmed my heart. Kernov had escorted my mother to the dinner, and was even holding her hand for support. Schamoi and Lilah sat next to them. I kept my expression neutral despite the smile in my heart.

I carried on with my speech. "I welcome a worthy representative of each territory to join me tonight and tomorrow night to share in the Great Ritual, to form a new life Hoku will be proud of."

Just then, Lilah made a vulgar gesture to Schamoi, one that indicated 'welcoming them to join me' actually meant 'fuck me senseless.' And Schamoi, that bastard, had the gall to silently chuckle.

It took all I had to keep a straight face.

I made sure to recognize and honor my human mother, then finished my speech. "I give myself to the people tonight, to the will of our goddess. May she multiply her blessings upon us all."

They thundered their reply about Hoku's blessings, and I took a seat.

Magistrate Leonte stood again, welcoming the people to eat from the richly stacked plates before them.

I ate slowly, mildly less comfortable in this dress when sitting. I tried not to stare at the different groups and their meals. I became queasy at the goblets the vampires lifted, given what they were filled with.

Midmeal, the merfolk group finally arrived, taking their place in a side tank. They were announced, and people went about their business. I tried not to stare at the one who would be mine. He was a beautiful brute of a man, the most foreign of them all to me.

Nibbling on some sauteed herbed mushrooms, I couldn't help but note the lack of garlic. I adored garlic, but it wouldn't do for now. Silly rumors had been passed around ages ago about it being dangerous for vampires, but that was a ridiculous claim. In truth, no one liked garlic breath during intimacy, and vampires just didn't like the bitterness it imparted to a human's blood.

Tearing a roll in half, I glanced again at my special group of people. Lilah, ever irreverent, met my eyes, dipped her finger in gravy, and sucked it off.

I could almost taste that honey on her neck again, that mousse on her hard nipples.

Goddess damn me.

She had left me wet and wanting, and Schamoi next to her… It had been an eventful day already. And honestly, that small playful gesture had reignited my ever-present desire.

I finished a bite of venison and gulped down some wine, then gestured for an attendant.

"Yes, Your Holiness?"

"I'm ready to take my leave, to go prepare."

"Of course. The staff is waiting for you."

I stood, trying to not cause too big of a disruption to everyone else's meals. It didn't really work since I was the center of attention tonight. Straightening my dress, I glanced at the man I would claim in less than an hour's time. Tyfen, the beautiful fae prince, eyed me, munching on something. His expression was subtle, but the longer our eyes remained locked, the more a sinister grin grew on his face. Like I was the next course, and he had left plenty of room to devour me. Whether sexually or politically, I didn't know.

7

PRINCE TYFEN

Back in the dressing room, the seamstress and her assistants set to work, peeling me out of my entrance gown and into the one meant to honor the fae people, to please Prince Tyfen for our claiming. A few of my curls got twisted into more braids, but little changed with that. My eye makeup became smokier, my lips now tinted dusty rose.

I smiled as they tugged the leather onto me—this was Lilah's favorite of the dresses. The dress was fashioned of skintight black leather. I wore no undergarments. The bodice did a fair job keeping my breasts up without a corset. And both the top and midthigh-length skirt were held together with latches and ties.

"Hmm." Madam Gaffey stepped back, admiring her work. "Tight enough to show off your secrets. Hopefully he doesn't thrash it off you. That took a lot of work for how simple a design it is."

I grinned. He didn't even know me, but we had time to sort that out. Tonight and tomorrow were about giving each of the races a fair chance at a mixling who could rule the empire. He need only follow the divine instructions and surrender his seed.

And what did I know of the man? He had dark brown hair, bright green eyes, and those damned tattoos that made me want to know more. A firm handshake, large hands, and a few extra tidbits I'd been informed of. Tyfen—like many fae— enjoyed hunting, and was well trained with a blade. He was a commander in his

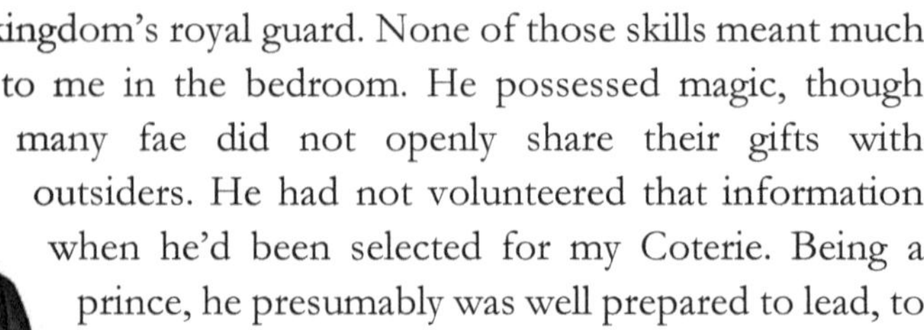

kingdom's royal guard. None of those skills meant much to me in the bedroom. He possessed magic, though many fae did not openly share their gifts with outsiders. He had not volunteered that information when he'd been selected for my Coterie. Being a prince, he presumably was well prepared to lead, to raise a child with me.

How much of that mattered right now? None of it. We were about to copulate under public and official scrutiny. There was no romance to it.

Still, I looked sexy. This leather couldn't hide a thing. My ass looked phenomenal.

"And here's a little something more to honor and entice," an assistant added, patting a bit of wild rose oil on my neck and down my chest.

They wished me luck, pride gleaming in their eyes, and of course spouted off the whole 'may Hoku multiply your blessings' bit. I really did respect my divine mother; we had a special connection no one else had, but the rote wishes got old fast in my position.

A pair of guards escorted me to the grand ballroom—the largest of them in all the palace, in all the realm. It had taken staff a month of hard labor to prepare it just right for the Great Ritual.

More than a thousand attendees stood on the dance floor, while dignitaries sat in designated alcoves. The bedding chamber alcove sat highest in the room to allow some semblance of privacy. A platform stage extension had been erected high in the room to reach it, stairs connecting the bedding chamber platform to a couple of other important alcoves for the ceremony.

Even with limited access to the bedding chamber, and the general privacy the alcove allowed, there would be many witnesses to the ritual claimings up here.

Voices thundered from the ballroom, the chatter of hundreds who had been at the feast joined by many more.

The guards positioned me behind a curtain and notified the magistrate I was ready. Luckily, he would not be in the bedding chamber. I wouldn't have been able to look him in the eye if he had wanted to be. He and the emperor had a place on a lower platform.

After a couple of minutes, the roar of the crowd died down, and Magistrate Leonte's voice boomed. His speech carried authority and respect as he recited the divine instructions, the old lore, the meaning behind this all. As he nearly gushed—a sickeningly sweet politician's touch, really—about the *noble* fae people and their contributions to this realm.

I had nothing against them, but I also could not turn a blind eye to their faults.

Leonte more properly presented Prince Tyfen as the second eldest prince of the fae kingdom.

Tyfen responded, formally accepting this calling as a member of my Coterie, pledging his life to my safety, that of the current emperor, and of the future emperor or empress I would bear—regardless of the paternity outcome.

My stomach tightened at his acceptance. While these men were gaining a lot out of this—power and pleasure—they were also sacrificing things.

I was not Prince Tyfen's mate. I couldn't be. It had been centuries since fate herself had chosen a human mate for a fae partner. We had become too different in our biological making, many said.

As a human, I didn't crave a mate the way he did. And he may grow to like me, even love me, but I could never stand in that place for him, not even as the Blessed Daughter, the Blessed Vessel. He clearly hadn't found a mate in his two hundred and nineteen years, and his pledge of loyalty to me may mean he never would.

"This is you, Your Holiness," the guard to my right whispered.

"With Hoku's blessing," Leonte finished, "the first claiming shall take place."

My heart slammed so hard in my chest, it might have been visible for others to see.

"Her Holiness, the Blessed Daughter—Sonta."

The guards parted the curtain, and I entered. Other dignitaries had received cheers and applause, but that was nothing compared to this. I stepped to the edge of the bedding chamber platform, passing the bed decorated fae-style. Tyfen joined me, and Leonte climbed the stairs to appear with us momentarily.

He nodded to us both, and we followed tradition, taking each other by the arm, just under the elbows.

"Sonta, do you accept this man into your Coterie? For unity, cooperation, and fertility?"

I swallowed, but did not allow my voice to expose any hesitation or fear. "I accept."

Tyfen's face was unreadable, save for the moment his gaze lingered on my breasts. He revealed an inkling of pleasure there.

At Leonte's prompting, Tyfen formally accepted his place at my side, now in my presence. He barely even made eye contact with me, almost as if disinterested. I couldn't blame him—inevitably, for some of these men, it was merely a political chore to impart his seed. And if that was his only hope here, so be it.

Leonte pronounced the union blessed and took the stairs back to his lower platform. Tyfen and I remained in place as a beautifully adorned fae woman approached.

She rubbed a fragrant oil on our foreheads with her thumb, smiling. "Blessings."

Each race was allowed a certain level of magic or tincture for general fertility as desired.

After the woman retreated, there were no other instructions. All that had to be done was … he had to bed me, with a thousand people below listening, dozens watching from the bedding chamber.

"Your Holiness," Tyfen said, gesturing to the bed.

I sucked in a breath, retreating to relative privacy where those below would not see. Part of me felt so small in the moment, waiting for him to tell me what he wanted. I knew two things about fae sex in general—they liked it rough, and the men were hung well. Besides that, I knew nothing of this one's preferences.

Shy as a doe staring at a hunter, as a virgin who'd never been with a man, I stood at the end of the bed, wringing my hands.

Tyfen's gaze raked over me, and he reached for a button on his leather jacket. "Lie down."

I didn't need to be told twice. I lay on the bed as he unbuttoned his shirt. Maybe he wanted more range of motion? He certainly didn't need his shirt off for his cock to be freed.

After he removed his jacket and shirt, I visually traced his arms and chest, which were full of tattoos—swirls and symbols I didn't understand. They definitely extended below the belt he reached for after removing his crown.

A rustle to my left caught my attention, and my brain stuttered. How had I not even noticed *all* the witnesses? I'd sped right past them to greet Tyfen. In addition to the six official attestants, each race had three witnesses in the bedding chamber with us—humans included. The other five men in my Coterie watched on as well from the opposite side of the room.

Lilah and Schamoi—my special guests—stood in the middle of the group on my left, offering me encouraging smiles. Whether Lilah was excited or nervous, I couldn't tell, but she grabbed Schamoi's hand, giving it a white-knuckle squeeze.

Tyfen's pants came off while I was distracted.

Damn, that bulge under his shorts.

I was already wet, my desire growing. It had been hours since I'd gotten so close with Lilah…

Tyfen turned, exposing his back to me. The tattoos accentuated his muscles. He stripped his shorts off, tossing them onto the edge of the bed, but still not looking at me. Why did I have such a thing for asses? I couldn't imagine not liking a man with that kind of ass.

Clearing his throat, he stepped forward *toward the edge of the platform*, away from me.

What the hell?

I didn't have to guess when he came into full view of the spectators below. The whispers told it all.

My gaze shot to Lilah, who was fully amused. Schamoi gave me a confused shrug.

Queen Lourel, however, Prince Tyfen's own mother, was livid. She didn't hide her exasperation well at all.

Tyfen's display didn't last long, though. He turned and strode back to me.

I should have focused on his face, but that was not what drew my eye. As he reached the end of the bed, I did look up. He wore a self-satisfied grin.

Kneeling on the bed, he hovered over me. "I want to see you."

He set to work undoing the ties and latches on my top. The leather easily released me, putting my whole torso on display.

Part of me felt shame, so unused to strangers watching. He didn't need me to be bare, but if it helped him prepare, if this was his preference, I could swallow that embarrassment.

I would have felt better, though, had he shown more appreciation. Instead, he stared at my breasts for a long moment, expressionless save the knob in his throat bobbing.

"Right." He blinked. "And the rest of you." Reaching for the ties and latches on my skirt, he said nothing else.

"What was your display about?" I asked.

His lips twitched. "They came for a show, didn't they? I gave them a nice start."

My ears burned. I wanted to lay into him about the blasphemy and disrespect he dripped, and I almost did. But this wasn't the time or place.

With my skirt undone, he finally touched me, sliding his hands onto my stomach, over my womb. I furrowed my brow. He was an arrogant prick one second, seemingly kind another.

Tyfen stared at his hands on me. It got awkward for a moment as he did nothing else. Was he using magic? I didn't feel any different.

A breath later, he pulled his hands back, clearing his throat again.

"All right. All of you," he ordered.

I paused, completely bare. What more did he need to see? Maybe he wanted to take me from behind? I turned, exposing my back to him.

"Sufficient," he said, his tone cold and casual. "You can turn back over."

Uncharacteristically, I kept my legs closed after turning over. *Never* had a man or woman I'd shared a bed with assessed me so blandly, like chattel. The sheer arrogance of this ass!

Tyfen nodded to two of the official attestants I'd met just earlier today. They approached, standing a mere two feet away on either side of us.

Despite his generous size, Tyfen was not yet erect. I tried to console myself that I wasn't everyone's taste… Some of these claimings would be purely business, and that was what this was.

Tyfen began pumping himself, and I would have offered to help had he been a little more gentlemanly, but I let him arouse himself.

The wicked part of me, the part not satiated earlier, wondered what it would be like to taste him, though, to fit him inside my mouth, to wrap my hands around him. The more I stared, the more my eyes widened.

I was properly scared by the time he became fully erect, my breath hitching. He was *massive*. And while I'd been warned about fae and elf sizes, and my pleasure instructors had helped me prepare with tools, somehow none of that had prepared me enough.

"You can close your mouth," Tyfen said with the smallest hint of amusement. "It's not going in *there*."

I clamped my mouth closed.

"Don't worry." He rested his hands on my knees. "It'll fit." He spread my legs.

The official attestants inched closer, and I wasn't sure whether I should be further humiliated or grateful for the distraction at the moment. They were there to ensure the strictest demands of the divine edict were met. They needed a close view to ensure he was indeed penetrating me properly.

I closed my eyes, trying to relax my opening for him to slide in, though the rest of me was tensed in case he drove right into me.

His tip entered, and he surprised me by easing in. I despaired as each inch of him stretched me, rubbed me so well without any added friction. I clenched my teeth to keep in a moan. He didn't deserve a moan from me, but damn that cock…

Once he was fully inside me, the attestants retreated a pace.

Tyfen muttered something under his breath, pulling back, and plunged into me.

I shuddered.

"I'll make this quick," he whispered.

I didn't want him to make it quick, not when it felt *this* good.

Tyfen withdrew, nearly to the tip, then slammed into me. Again and again and again.

I gripped the bedding to my sides, clenching my teeth to keep in the absolutely treacherous moans that tried to make their way out.

Schamoi's joke about how boring human men could be was … not just self-deprecating humor…

Unrelenting, Tyfen continued in perfect rhythm, his ferocity scooting me further and further up the bed. His panting mingled with mine.

I was so damn tight, ready to beg for release when his final thrust sent us both over the edge.

I unashamedly gasped. He remained quiet, but his shivers of pleasure shook me, his release inside me complete.

He did not lie on me, rather choosing to hover as he filled me, as we both rippled with divine satisfaction.

We quieted, catching our breath. He stayed inside me as required. The attestants were off on the sidelines timing us. Each of my men needed to stay inside for a while to ensure the best chance of his seed finding its way and not just spilling out.

The silence was deafening. I opened my eyes, barely catching a glimpse of Tyfen's bright green eyes before he looked away. And we lay there, as required, with him buried inside me.

I didn't know what to say. Probably nothing, given the audience. I could whisper, but what? What's your favorite color?

In due time, an attestant with a timer nodded. The required period to stay inside me was over.

"We lift our prayers to Hoku, seeking prosperity for this realm, for the fae kingdom, and for the Blessed Vessel," someone announced. The people echoed the sentiment as the giant curtains around the bedding chamber closed to allow us privacy. Tyfen pulled himself out and reached for a set of washcloths near the head of the bed.

"Here." He handed me one.

Maybe I was too spoiled with my instructors and Lilah, but I usually didn't just get tossed something to clean myself.

Most of the witnesses in the bedding chamber filed out—the merfolk through a tunnel connected to their tank, the land-walkers through a side exit—though the attestants remained. I wouldn't have a minute to myself over the next day.

I glanced at Queen Lourel as she exited the room, her face still full of displeasure. Had she not been pleased with the way her son had performed? There hadn't seemed any frustration between them in our previous meeting. No matter the cause for her sour expression, I was grateful my own mother was far below, unable to see me on display, that she had not volunteered nor been required to witness our copulation.

Before Tyfen could wipe himself clean, the attestants approached to confirm that he had indeed spilled himself, that he could produce a child for his people. Tyfen's expression darkened as they inspected him.

Part of me—a very petty part of me—found satisfaction in his apparent anger, his humiliation at having his own dick scrutinized. How humbling was that for a prince of more than two centuries?

Good.

The attestants gave him another nod that they approved, and he wiped himself clean, still not sparing me any notice. After I cleaned myself, I stood from the bed. A servant rushed to bring me a silk robe, and I let them put it on me. I wouldn't be wearing that dress again. It had been a costume meant to please Tyfen.

My pride was wounded that he said nothing, that he *felt* nothing, even now. That other than a moment's release, he had not truly felt pleasure inside me.

And what they'd just announced, what they'd called me moments ago—the Blessed Vessel. That was my new title. I was to be the vessel for Hoku's Anointed Ruler. Instead of cherishing that transition, I stood here, staring at him as he refused a robe and mumbled about putting on his clothes himself.

His clothes had not been a costume as mine had been. This was who he was. Cold and heartless.

Part of my heart cracked. I wanted him to love me. To cherish me. Hell, even just to like me. I very much wanted to at least be on good terms with the members of my Coterie.

"Tyfen?" I dared to speak, though I was not sure what would follow. Tears pricked at the corners of my eyes.

"It was a pleasure, Blessed Vessel," he replied, wholly disinterested as he finished fastening his pants.

"So…" *Is this how it's going to be?* Why had I bought his smiles in the meeting earlier? It had all been a façade. And he had no duty to care for me. I'd known that.

He tugged on his shirt and jacket. "I expect to have you at least once a day." He finally met my gaze. "Until it's confirmed you've conceived." He placed his crown on his head, taming his hair.

I gritted my teeth, nodding. Fair share for the child. "That sounds like a demand, Your Highness." If he wanted to use titles, so would I.

He shrugged. "Call it what you like. It's not an unreasonable request."

Unable to stop myself, I marched up to him. He towered over me, but I would not be intimidated. It didn't hurt we still had attestants and guards.

I grabbed his shirt. "You don't get to tell me what to do. The only requirement of the Great Ritual is that you get *one chance* to fuck me, and you just got that. Any other opportunities with my body are at *my* discretion. If you want more chances for your cock to do its job, to bring pride and power to yourself and your people, to have *any* part in the future ruler's life, then you would do well to be kind to me. To *earn* those opportunities." I released his shirt, pushing him. I was irrationally angry but couldn't stop myself. Not that he budged. He was all muscle.

He said nothing, sizing me up.

"I have plenty of other men in my Coterie who will happily take your place as lovers and fathers, so I don't need you. And I'm frankly shocked you were the choice. I thought the fae would favor brains and charm over idiotic nepotism that doesn't even know how to decently bed a woman."

His lips pursed, all he did was look away.

My fists clenched, and if I didn't leave that very moment, I would do something I fully regretted.

I turned and stomped out of the room, back through the private corridor I had arrived through, an attestant and guard hot on my trail to escort me.

8

PRINCE PRICK

"Are you all right, Your Holiness?" the guard asked as I stormed through the corridor toward my dressing room.

"Yes," I gritted out. Physically, I was fine. Tyfen's massive cock had hurt me a bit, but it was the nice kind of pain. My pride, on the other hand, was severely wounded.

"A whore," I muttered. That was what he'd made me feel like. I was ashamed I'd lusted after him at all, ashamed I'd enjoyed him inside me so much. But the fact he wouldn't even make eye contact, that he'd called me 'sufficient.'

"Excuse me?" the attestant trailing behind me asked for clarification.

"Nothing." Most people didn't know my mother's history. She hid it well. Just before her sixteenth birthday, her parents had kicked her out of the house for disobedience. Homeless and without any support, she'd had a choice—either sell her blood to local vampires or sell herself to local human men in the form of prostitution.

I had been conceived through prostitution, and I wasn't ashamed of that. My mother had done her best; she'd done what she'd needed to do. But the men my mother would spend her time with … they were often dirty, often made *her* feel dirty and cheap.

That was how I felt right now.

"Sufficient," I mumbled.

Finally reaching my bathing room, I slammed the door open. The attendants startled.

"Your Holiness?"

I still had *so* much pent-up aggression. I needed to get it out. It didn't matter that all the servants stared at me.

"That." I pointed to a vase. "Is it expensive? Precious? Rare?"

"Well… Uh…" one servant stuttered. "I imagine so, Your Holiness…"

I needed to break something, but I also held on to the tiniest thread of rationality and did not want to do something I'd regret. I glanced around.

Next to the bath drawn for me sat a stack of towels. I snatched one up, covered my face, and *screamed.*

Loud and long, my hands gripping and twisting the fabric like my life depended on it.

Once I'd gotten it all out, the room fell silent despite the half dozen witnesses. I was not prone to a short temper, to tantrums, and certainly not in front of others.

While the urge tugged at my heart to fall to the floor and cry, I restrained myself. I lowered the towel from my face. "Sorry," I whispered.

"Are you hurt, Your Holiness?"

"No." I gently set the towel back down. "I'm fine. Let's bathe me."

They exchanged looks amongst themselves at my irregular behavior while I undid my robe and got into the clawfoot tub.

"I'm required to remind you—" the attestant started.

"I'm well aware of the edicts," I said, perhaps too sharply. The water was warm and fragrant, soothing to my body but not yet to my uneasy soul. An attendant behind me pulled my hair up to ensure it didn't get wet.

"I'll follow the letter of the law," I assured the attestant.

She was there to certify I was properly cleansed between copulations, and also to guarantee I did not douche.

And I did want to douche. I wanted to get Tyfen's seed out of me, out of pure spite. But the law—my divine mother's rules—dictated I could not. It would be an unfair disadvantage for me to give any of the races in the Great Ritual.

It was also important I be cleansed between the men during the claimings, though that was more about the men's preferences to not have another man's scent or fluids all over me when they took me.

"Here," the attendant behind me said, draping a soft towel over the edge of the tub. "Lay your head back and relax. Just mind your hair."

I obeyed. Relaxing was just what I needed. I needed to calm down and focus on the task at hand.

For a moment, I allowed the hot water to heal me, to soothe and hug me. Only the rustle of the servants quietly working around me filled my ears, and the trickle of water as I gently swished my hands back and forth.

The door creaked open. "Miss Lilah is here, if you'd like her to join you."

I smiled, opening my eyes. "Of course!"

Lilah ran in, a huge grin on her face as she knelt at the end of the tub. "I told you you were ravishing in that dress! And damn, that cock." Her eyes were wide. "If you need help down the road, *I* might even consider riding him!"

I rolled my eyes. "You can have him."

She frowned, leaning her chin on the tub. "What's wrong? It was a little odd in there, and I'm sure it was awkward having barely met him, but … you did seem to enjoy him as he did his job…"

"He's a prick." I bunched my toes. "Remind me: are fae susceptible to poison?"

Her jaw dropped. "You can't joke about something like that!"

The servants all eyed me, shocked.

"She *is* joking," Lilah added.

I glanced at the guard, witness, and attendants. "I *am* joking. Sorry, that was inappropriate."

Lilah reached into the water and rubbed my ankle, frowning. "What happened?"

"He wouldn't even look at me," I said, folding my arms.

"Maybe he was shy, nervous to perform?"

Cocking my head, I gave her a dead stare. "Yes, his exhibitionism to the audience below was definitely him being shy."

She wrinkled her nose. "Yes, that was a bit unexpected."

I glanced at my chest. A flower petal floated across the water. "He didn't even like my tits. I thought he did when we first made our vows, but once he fully saw them… He said nothing, did nothing."

Lilah chuckled. "You joke about assassination of a prince because he didn't appreciate your breasts? Come now, Sonta."

"It's not just that." I narrowed my eyes. I wasn't *that* vain, was I? No, it had been so much more.

"Plus, he's not *the* fae prince," I retorted. "He's *a* fae prince. He's the second born. Not the heir. The second-in-line, the spare."

Angling her head and wrapping both hands around my ankles, she reasoned with me. "I don't know what all happened between you just now, how he unraveled you so … but the Sonta *I* know wouldn't consider herself so much above any kind of prince…"

I frowned. She was right. Neither of us had been raised in high society. Even with her connections to me, Lilah would be extremely lucky for a prince or princess of any kind to pay her attention.

Looking down in shame, I chased a flower petal with my finger. "I know. I'll get over it. I guess I just started with high hopes, and to have my first of the Coterie treat me that way…"

"That's right," Lilah said. "He was only the first. While not as muscled or tanned, I think your next suitor looks dashing in his own way."

Letting out a puff of air, I allowed myself to focus on the next claiming. It would take place in less than two hours. "Vampire…"

Lilah grinned wickedly. "You shouldn't be so afraid. And you would appreciate them more if you'd ever joined me at the Suck and Fuck."

I rolled my eyes again. Vampire society mingled quite a bit with human society. They preferred our blood, and many poor humans turned to the blood business to make ends meet. But there were erotic establishments as well—which many of us crudely referred to as the Suck and Fucks—where skilled vampires knew how to pleasure with blood play. The right bite, the right sucking and rubbing was incredibly pleasing. Making the blood flow through precise points in a body could make you instantly wet. The vampires themselves also got great pleasure from feedings—the fresh blood in their system helped things circulate, come alive, become large and erect.

Lilah had gone there twice before we'd moved to the palace, and had absolutely raved about the two female vampires who had pleasured her, but she hadn't been back in years.

"And why don't you still go?" I asked, taking a washcloth from the edge of the tub, starting to scrub myself.

Pursing her lips, Lilah gave no reply.

Vampires could be some of the friendliest sorts, not that they could usually have children, so I had none as peers growing up, but they could also be dangerous, even deadly.

High-class folk could enjoy erotic vampire escorts in the privacy of their homes, but most common folk had to go to the Suck and Fuck, and they were often in seedy parts of towns. Before Lilah had saved money to go a third time, a vicious killer vampire had been caught near the establishment she'd previously been to. I forbade her from going alone again, though I hadn't needed to. She'd been properly frightened on her own.

"Well…" Lilah said. "It's about time I give it another try." She grinned again. "I've been scoping out the Coterie's parties and their servants. There are a couple of lovely vampire ladies. I'll have to see if they're skilled in the art."

"Lilah!" I scolded.

She shrugged. "They may want fresh blood. I don't think they brought that many human servants along for feeding. I'd be doing them a favor, really…"

I giggled. "You're wicked."

"The divine law demands rules around *your* pussy right now, not mine." She stuck out her tongue.

I shrugged, looking away playfully. "Try if you want. I'll be here to sop up your tears when they all turn you down."

She splashed me. "You brat!"

"Mind her hair!" an attendant snapped.

"Sorry." Lilah bit her lip, glancing at me while containing a laugh.

I gave her a mock reprimanding expression.

"Miss Lilah, we do need to prepare her. If you're going to distract her so, you'll need to leave."

Lilah frowned, and I more seriously washed myself down with the cloth. "You probably should go. Keep Schamoi and my mother company."

She nodded. "He says hi." With a contemplative look, she added, "I'm sorry your first one didn't turn out like you'd hoped. But I'm sure you two can work something out, even if it's only for the sake of the child and the realm, you know? And you have others who I'm sure will adore you, especially the next two who require mating marks…"

I smirked. "How refreshing. They'll want to rail me and protect me for the sake of their biological urges alone. I do feel I'm living in a dream world now."

Narrowing her eyes, she stood, straightening her dress. "Mating bond or not, they'll love you because of your spirit. Not just for your womb, either." Her deep brown eyes were kind, her tone genuine. "They'll get to know your heart like I do, Sonta. Give it time."

I offered her an appreciative frown. "Thank you."

"And … if they're all stupid enough to not appreciate your breasts, know that I always will." She winked. "Excited to see you bright and brilliant for round two. Don't let those old pricks intimidate you."

She strode toward the door, having calmed me, having restored my hope. "Lilah," I called as she twisted the door handle. "I love you in that dress." She'd had a special one tailored for each night of the claimings, and I'd been too distracted to compliment her earlier.

Her beautiful, lush lips formed a smile. "I love you, too, in or out of any dress."

She left the room, and the servants bustled a little more.

"Come now, Your Holiness, let's get you ready for your second."

9

FACING THE VAMPIRE

I stood in place again as Madam Gaffey and her assistants dressed me. While stunning, this particular dress was a little cliché for a vampire to bed me. Black? Really? And two black dresses back to back?

"He won't be able to resist you," Madam Gaffey replied, fiddling with the lace.

It was true that black was a staple color for many vampires' wardrobes from what I'd witnessed in my own hometown. In darker days, it had been a tool to help them remain unseen in the night as they waged war. Nowadays, many wore black purely as a fashion choice—it contrasted well with the pallor of their skin. When I was young, I'd thought perhaps they liked it to draw in warmth from the sun since their skin was so cold, but that was a silly notion. They disliked the sun very much as a race because they were highly sensitive to it, and it caused great discomfort.

"Either way, it is beautiful," I said. Hopefully he didn't want to assess all of me like Tyfen had, because this dress would be harder to remove.

Half-inch-wide straps held up the top half of my dress. It was snug with support built in, the fabric barely covering the bottom of my breasts. Only a white lace sewn into the top covered my nipples. The bodice clung to me until my hips, then flowed freely. Floor length, the silky fabric split on either thigh for easy access. I wouldn't be wearing undergarments for any of the claimings—it was a waste, given the purpose of these outfits. I wasn't even wearing shoes, though that was a personal choice.

"Just a couple more touches," an assistant said, adding another pin to my hair.

I now wore a high bun, the base of it circled with braids, a couple of strands of ringlets hanging forward. My previous makeup had been scrubbed off, and I now wore a simpler nude eye and a bright cherry lipstick.

As the servants completed their work, I couldn't stop thinking about what Lilah had said about me, and about the men of my Coterie.

"Madam Gaffey?" I asked the seamstress as she fussed to make sure the thigh splits hit the right spot.

"Yes, dear?"

"Would you tell me if I were out of touch?"

"Oh, you're fine, child."

I frowned nonetheless. Lilah had implied I was snobbish for insulting Tyfen for being a second-born prince. Perhaps she was right? Did I think too highly of myself since my discovery as Hoku's daughter? I didn't leave the palace much at all. I was too busy with lessons in politics, and in fantastic sex. I had Lilah here, too, and a great support system. Maybe too great. Maybe they all lied to me to make me feel better.

Pouting, I stared into the mirror. "You're sure I don't walk around with an air of superiority? I don't want to become a horrible person." I didn't want to lose myself.

She stood straight, cradling my face in her hands. "Is our Blessed Vessel afraid she has a goddess complex? Because I'll remind you—you *are* the chosen daughter of a goddess. You're allowed to have a complex. Allowed to accept a certain place of superiority."

Madam Gaffey could be all business at times, but she also had her sweet maternal side.

"And the truth is, Sonta dear, most horrible people don't go around worrying they're horrible. They don't see it, so they don't take the time to fear it. You're fine, child."

I smiled. "Thank you."

She glanced at the clock. "You're all ready. We'll see you for your third tonight. Make sure to let us know if his jaw drops." Her smile was as warm as mine.

"I will."

Two guards and an attestant escorted me through my private corridor. The steady flow of water from the built-in waterway on the other side of the wall made for a nice background noise.

I held my head high. Madam Gaffey was right—I was Hoku's daughter. And Lilah was right—I wasn't going to let these old men intimidate me.

And they *were* all older than me. Some, like Tyfen, were centuries older—born and raised rulers. I was nothing to them, but at the same time, I was *everything* to them and their people, and they needed to look past my age and limited experience and respect me as an equal.

Nothing about me was just *sufficient*. Not my heart or mind, and certainly not my ass or tits. I worked hard for them all.

The guards beside me listened carefully, as did I, to the same sort of speech from Magistrate Leonte about my vampire mate as he'd given for Prince Tyfen.

Duke Hadwin was the name of my vampire mate. Despite often being rather intertwined with human society, many vampires kept their privacy well guarded. He hadn't given us much to profile in the way of personal interests.

But he had kind hazel eyes, blond hair and a short beard. He wasn't much taller than me, and, of course, he was extremely pale. He was currently eighty-four, which was surprisingly young for an immortal such as himself. His body had to have been envenomated when he was in his thirties by the look of him.

"All right, Your Holiness," the guard to my right said.

Leonte had ended his speech.

Minding my posture, I passed through the curtain and glided to the edge of the stage to greet Leonte and Duke Hadwin.

Hadwin smiled gently. He really did look well put together like Lilah had said. His hair was parted, reaching midway to his shoulders. He wore a collared burgundy dress shirt with elegant black trousers.

We swore our loyalty, both accepting his place in my Coterie, and accepting the blessings of Hoku for fertility.

It twisted my heart a little that the rote wishes were not as loud for Hadwin. As far as I or any of the palace advisors knew, he was a good man. But if there was a black sheep of the races in this realm, vampires would take that slot every time.

There was still great prejudice against them after previous brutalities. People considered them a plague, an unnatural thing. And I hated the part of myself that feared them so, because I did not want to judge them that way.

Hoku herself had chosen the races worthy of ruling this realm. She had given me the divine ability to conceive a half-vampire child, and that in itself was a miracle. Vampires were half-dead beings. They had exchanged their humanity for immortality and other gifts, part of their curse being sterility.

As Madam Gaffey had so recently reminded me— I was different, a human capable of giving them a fair chance at rulership and peace. Were it up to most of the nonhuman races, they would have been eradicated long ago. I couldn't fault them their reasoning, though. In old war days, vampires had committed some of the most ghastly sins.

To envenomate a human meant to create a new vampire. To envenomate one of the other races meant to create an oni—a ferocious monster they could control. Direct descendants of humans, vampires did not distort our humanity so much with their venom, but a fae, shifter, or elf… They became barely sentient beastly killing machines. Most of the creatures had long since been hunted down, but many forests and mountains were still not traveled for fear of them after wicked masters had unleashed them.

Hadwin and his kind had both my fear and compassion.

"Your Holiness," he whispered, "are you ready?"

I blinked, still holding his arm and he mine.

The room of a thousand people was silent. Leonte had already descended the stairs to his alcove. And I stood here like a statue.

My cheeks warm, I dropped my hand. "Yes."

I hastened to the foot of the bed, avoiding eye contact with anyone in the bedding chamber. How was I already mortified? It was hard to keep confident when I made an oaf of myself so publicly by zoning out.

Hadwin followed close behind me.

"Sorry," I whispered, facing him. "I… I forgot you have no fertility blessings."

That was a lie, but better than admitting the truth about where my mind had wandered during such an important moment. Better to pretend I had been waiting for someone to walk up and smear lucky oil on my forehead again. Unlike some of the other races, vampires didn't have any sort of fertility magic or blessings. Why would they when they normally could not conceive?

His smile was warm again. "That's quite all right."

"Great." Were my palms sweaty? They were sweaty. Attestants weren't here to ensure we *chatted* properly. I should have taken a survey in our meeting earlier and just asked how they liked it, because I didn't know right now what Hadwin liked. Some vampires enjoyed blood play with human partners, but not all, and not all were skilled in it. And this wasn't really about pleasure, anyway.

I could ask. I could wait for him to tell me. Or I could just do what I was compelled to do, and if he wanted something different, he'd have to tell me. I was flexible.

I eased myself onto the bed, keeping my eyes on him. He would mark me as his mate before claiming me with his cock, and while he wouldn't draw too much blood with his bite, I would probably simply faint out of fear. Better to do this lying down.

My guts twisted at the fact the new sheets were red to hide any unsightly blood drops that might escape.

I scooted back on the bed to give Hadwin more space, and laid myself down. Focusing on the chandelier above, I waited. Still fully clothed, Hadwin straddled me.

His warm hazel eyes searched my face. "You consent to be my mate, Your Holiness?"

Already, I didn't hate being under his weight. "Yes, Your Grace." I slid my hands to his thighs for support. "And you can call me Sonta." It seemed silly to use titles for my Coterie, especially the ones I'd be biologically imprinted by.

His smile warmed further. "And you can call me Hadwin."

I turned my head to the side to give him a good angle at my neck, closing my eyes so I didn't have to see any of the witnesses.

The bed shifted as he leaned forward. He wore a cologne I would have associated with a human, but it mingled nicely with the herbaceous perfume I wore for him.

When the mattress shifted next to my shoulders, I had to calm my breathing. I was really doing this. I was letting a vampire bite me. He was going to drink my blood. The rational part of my brain kept trying to tell me I was safe. There were guards in the bedding chamber—more than with some of the other claimings, actually. The other men of my Coterie had all had to surrender their weapons; Hadwin's weapons were built in.

But the guards would stop him if he drew too much, if he became frenzied. Hell, Lilah and Schamoi would rip him off me and shove him off the platform for me, not to mention the others of my Coterie. I was safe. It usually took more than one vampire to drain a human anyway.

I was *safe*.

My heart and lungs, however, were not connecting with my brain. His cold lips caressed my neck, and I flinched, gripping his thighs tighter.

"Are you okay?" he whispered in my ear.

"Yes," I lied. I was not prone to panic attacks, and I couldn't bear to insult him and his people. I needed to be strong. Even if his closeness terrified me senseless. Even if all I could think about in the moment was that his saliva and fangs could do both beautiful and horrific things. He could either numb me and bring me pleasure, or he could inject a venom that stole my life from me, that tore down this empire.

And he *could* tear down this empire, because his venom would seal my womb, would deprive an entire generation of a Hoku-blessed ruler. It would bring instant war. It would be a terribly stupid decision, given he'd be tortured in unimaginable ways for hurting the Blessed Vessel, but it would also be a spectacular declaration should his intentions not be pure.

Not in all my life had I been this terrified.

"I would never hurt you, Sonta," he reassured me.

"I know." *Please just get it done with.*

He pressed his lips to my neck again, opening them. Two dagger-sharp fangs rested on my skin.

I curled my toes, preparing for the pain. My heart tried to beat right out of my chest.

He didn't puncture me, and it started to feel cruel, like he was taking his time to torture me. Perhaps he enjoyed that dominance.

"Your heart thunders," he said softly.

"Sorry. I'm fine." It almost came out in a whimper.

"Would you like a distraction?"

"Yes," I whispered, my voice shaky.

Shifting himself, he freed a hand and moved the center flap of my dress, sliding a chilled finger straight to my clit.

The Vampire Mate

adwin was skilled with his finger, gently rubbing, applying just enough pressure to my clit.

The coldness of his hand easily faded with the warmth building inside me as he stroked. I even found myself grinding, my greed growing, my heart calming.

And then he bit me.

I took a sharp breath at the momentary pain, but it soon dissipated as he sucked from my neck. He didn't stop rubbing me, either.

His saliva numbed the injury, but it didn't stop the sensation of my blood rushing to him. It tickled and burned in all the right ways. It was not venomous or gluttonous, but a lover's bite.

Goddess damn me, Lilah knows what she's talking about.

Granted, Lilah had not been claimed as a mate by a lover's bite, but this was divine all the same.

I was wet and wanting. From his sucking, from his rubbing. His deep breathing carried satisfaction as he sucked harder.

My desire mingled with curiosity, and I glided a hand up his thigh to his crotch. The bulge was telling. He shuddered with a single stroke of my hand across the strained fabric.

Hadwin slowly removed his finger as he stopped sucking, readjusting himself. My body calmed and cooled as he kissed my neck and put a cloth to my bite.

He lingered there a minute. "The bleeding should stop soon."

I dared to finally turn my head and look up at him. His eyes had darkened marvelously. They were dilated, the honey color now overtaken by deep bloodred.

Normally, I would have been terrified to be straddled by a vampire looking at me this way, but the desire in that gaze mirrored my own at the moment.

He craned his neck, studying mine after removing the cloth. He wore a small satisfied smile, setting the cloth to the side. "That will heal nicely."

Scooting back, Hadwin gave me space to sit up. He still straddled me closely, though, because the mating bites were not quite finished. At least not symbolically.

I sat and reached for a spiked ring on the bedside table. A single spike had been set into the gold ring. I swallowed hard. I'd just overcome my fear of the worst happening, but I didn't want to hurt him, and I definitely didn't want to drink blood myself. I didn't even like my venison bloody.

Careful to hide any disgust, I slipped the large ring onto my thumb. Until we'd ordered this one recently, I had only ever seen one of these ceremonial rings before. My mother and I had sometimes perused jeweler's shops when I was a girl to enjoy the beautiful colors and designs, though we usually couldn't afford anything.

I had commented how inefficient this type of ring was for a self-defense tool since the spike was so short. The jeweler had chuckled and explained. Vampires normally took vampire mates. Immortals generally paired best to avoid continual heartbreak from the loss of loves who expired so quickly, but the heart didn't always choose wisely. Since a human, such as myself, didn't have sharp fangs, should they wish to form a mating bond with a vampire, they often did a symbolic bite with this type of ring, then took a taste of their blood to seal the bond.

Despite our bond as mates, I would never fully reciprocate the strong tug Hadwin (or the shifter, for that matter) had toward me. In her gift, Hoku had designed me that way so my loyalty could not be unrighteously swayed by such a bond. I was human, but not a normal one.

This part of the ceremony changed practically nothing. Hadwin had already given me a love bite, had tasted me with consent and intent. I was his mate. He was bound to me for as long as I lived, not just by word but also by urge. But, however much I disliked blood, it would be a massive slight to his people to reject their tradition.

Hadwin stretched his neck, presenting it to me, and I wrapped my hand around the back of it, holding out my thumb to find the right placement.

My nerves jumbled again as I hesitated.

"You won't hurt me," he whispered with a hint of amusement, softly placing his hands on my hips.

Vampires didn't easily feel pain, but it still felt wrong. Schamoi had to be mentally screaming at me for my hesitation. How many thousands of times had we gone over where exactly I ought to punch the hole? How many poor melons had I massacred to practice?

I didn't want to offend anyone, disappoint anyone, or appear a coward. Straightening, I found the right position, and punctured.

The resistance made me want to vomit on the spot. Hadwin, however, didn't even flinch.

I withdrew the spike. It was coated with thick blood, but none escaped his neck. Holding my breath, I leaned in and covered the hole with my lips, taking the tiniest suck. He may have been happy to feast, but I only needed a drop.

Cool metallic blood coated my mouth, and I choked it down, pulling away. I swiped my tongue across my teeth and swallowed a couple of times to make sure it was all gone. What I wouldn't have done to guzzle a glass of water. But with a well-practiced smile, I gave him a nod, removed the ring, and replaced it on the table.

My desire had cooled from having to do my part, but at least I was still wet for him to take me, and I was grateful to have the most nerve-racking parts of this done.

"Did you want to lie back down?" he asked.

I nodded and did so. He didn't move to strip me, and I was grateful. I could only handle so much per claiming with an audience. Instead, he reached to where his trousers laced up and undid them. He was still large. With a tug, he freed himself through an opening in his shorts.

The prying attestants moved forward, and Hadwin further opened the slits in my dress for proof he was doing it properly. He halted, though.

"I … am cold," he warned.

Every part of him was cold, and I actually looked forward to that sensation the next time he bedded me, but I feared the shock this time might clamp me up further. "Could I help warm you?"

"If you desire."

I reached down and grasped his cock. He was an average size compared to any I'd ever had inside me; he'd been born a human, after all.

But he did grow a little as I held him, as I warmed him. I couldn't look him in the eyes for some reason, but I felt his stare. I also couldn't hide a small smile as he pulsed and twitched in my hand.

He was ready to take me. I gently squeezed, moving my hands to a new position, and he let out another deep desire-filled breath.

Why did I want to tease him so badly? Despite all these people, I wanted to take my time and play. But I shouldn't.

I finally met those fresh vampire eyes. "Thank you."

Hadwin furrowed his brow. "I haven't exactly finished the job. I'm not sure why you're thanking me already."

I answered honestly. "For being kind." Despite the lack of privacy in these claimings, despite this one being far more terrifying and disgusting than the first, his kindness had made all the difference. So much so that I genuinely wanted to give myself to him, not just out of duty.

He offered me a half smile, but said nothing.

After a minute more, he was warm enough, but I gave him one good long stroke as I removed my hands. His tip was wet; we were both ready.

I lay back down, spreading myself more, and he leaned in, inserting his tip. The attestants approved and backed up to give us a smidge more privacy.

He was still cold, just not shockingly so for my entrance. It actually felt marvelous after the ache Tyfen had left me with.

Not rushing, Hadwin pushed in. He slid in easily, and I caressed his cock with a couple of pelvic squeezes. His breath shuddered, and I grinned. I loved doing that to men—I practiced often.

He adjusted his position, more fully over me as he thrust the first time. With a clear view of my breasts, the way they bounced, my nipples peeking out from the lace, he smiled.

Then he looked up, and I could see the predator in him. He was going to claim me, and I was going to love it. I squeezed him once more to tell him to not hold back. Without a word exchanged between us, he seemed to understand.

Hadwin only pulled out halfway before he thrust into me again. He didn't pause before repeating himself, plunging harder, deeper, faster. Stronger each time, and I loved every damned second of it. My instructors and I had practiced with chilled tools and menthol to try to mimic vampire dick, but this—this was something else.

The cold of Hadwin's cock prolonged the buildup, and I worked in tandem with him. He would not remove his eyes from mine, and I was not ashamed to share ragged breath as I grew painfully tense, as every nerve screamed for relief from the friction, each time we met in the middle.

The veins on his neck bulged, and he let out a low grunt.

With one more slam into me, he careened first into ecstasy. I joined him soon after, both of us still making an attempt at a good rhythm.

Had we been alone, I would have called his name as he filled me. It was so cold it almost felt warm to have him cum.

After he stopped shaking, he leaned forward, pressing his forehead to my chest. "You're marvelous, darling."

I couldn't stop smiling. "So…" I ran a hand through his hair. "Can I thank you *now*?"

His breath tickled as he chuckled against my skin, and the movement sent another wave of pleasure through me.

I liked this. Him on me while he remained inside. Me stroking his hair as a lover would.

After a minute, he lifted his head, glancing at me. "Could I…" He didn't finish.

"Could you what?"

Studying my face, he pursed his lips. "Never mind."

Before I could urge him to ask what he wanted, an attestant spoke up.

The time required for him to keep his seed in elapsed. Voices were lifted in blessing and prayers for our fertility, and the curtains closed.

Most of the observers filed out of the bedding chamber as they had before. Blowing out a breath, Hadwin withdrew himself and presented his cock for inspection. The fluid that covered him was essentially clear, which didn't really serve as proof of release, but the attestants seemed satisfied enough.

I reached for the washcloths this time.

"Would you like me to clean you?" he offered, and I appreciated the offer.

"Not this time, but thank you." I handed him one. Since he'd not taken off his pants, he had to clean himself up first to avoid making a mess.

We wiped up in silence. I did get a little distracted watching him. Hoku's miracle to allow a half vampire conception was so puzzling. Common wisdom stated a male vampire's seed expired with his humanity. Scholars in Hoku's temples, however, postulated the seed must be dormant, and only the divinity within me could wake it.

Hadwin finished cleaning himself and set his cloth to the side. What ought I to say? It felt silly in the moment to say I'd enjoyed it. Was I holding back, expecting him to drop his pleasant façade like Tyfen had, to demand more opportunities to fill my womb?

I set aside my own cloth, pulling my dress down again, eyeing him as he tucked himself back in and did his trousers up.

He finally looked at me, and spoke. "Sonta, I know I'm not your first choice, but I'm yours whenever you want me."

Why did that make me sad all of a sudden? He'd just offered himself, not demanded a quota. It was in the tone, and the dismissal of how wonderful he'd just been. 'I'm not your first choice.'

How could he possibly know that? I hadn't even been with half my Coterie yet. But a sinking feeling told me why he'd said that—my hesitation.

"Have I offended you?" I swallowed the lump in my throat. It would crush me if he'd been hurt, and I worried about offending his witnesses.

"Not at all," he stated simply, though the words didn't ring genuine.

"But…"

Hadwin rose from the bed, extending a hand to help me. I let him.

He slid his hands onto my waist as a lover would. "You were nervous, darling. No one can fault you for hesitating to perform under these circumstances."

I nodded, but the lie offended my own conscience. I wished it had been that.

"Just… Just because I'm not a normal mate—vampire or human…" I couldn't promise I'd love him the same. I truly couldn't, but I already held a great fondness for him. "I don't pick favorites that way, so you shouldn't sell yourself short."

The warmth of his smile defied the coldness of his touch. He leaned in, placing a gentle kiss on my forehead. "I know how this realm works, and my people will never be the first pick, but I appreciate your attempts to create equality. You truly are Hoku's daughter."

Despite the praise, I frowned. To contradict the assessment of his people's place in the realm would be to lie.

He slid a hand to my ass, gazing down at my breasts. "Either way, I very much look forward to sharing a bed. Next time … without all the prying eyes."

Damn if that look in his eyes didn't drip honesty, and damn if I wasn't absolutely blushing.

I wanted to know what his lips could do, but before I found out, he let me go.

"I have to go meet with my people," he said. "And you certainly have somewhere to be. I'll see you in a couple of hours."

11

MY SHIFTER MATE

I sat in my fresh bath, chasing the flower petals, smiling. Absolutely grinning like a giddy girl. I had a crush. I liked Duke Hadwin.

The attestant watched on, and the guard at the door let Lilah in to see me.

She smirked as she sat next to the tub. "I was right, wasn't I?"

"Yeah." I bit my lip.

"Though, the ladies at the Suck and Fuck didn't actually go for my neck, but was it good?" She focused on my love bite.

"Oh… Yeah, it *was* pretty nice." I hadn't initially remarked on the bite.

Lilah narrowed her eyes. "What were *you* referring to?"

I swiped the wet cloth over my arm. "Just that it would get better after Prince Asshole's turn."

She nodded. "Don't get me wrong, I'm eating it up watching you, but it's also really fun to observe the other witnesses. Especially your Coterie…"

"I avoid looking so it's not so awkward…"

"Does that mean you don't want to know what I think?" She clicked her tongue.

I switched which arm I was washing. "I didn't say that…"

Obviously, witnesses on my behalf were closely monitoring everything, but Lilah usually judged people fairly.

She went on, talking about how each of the men had reacted during the first two claimings. It was mostly a mix of curiosity and indifference, though that was to be expected. More than desiring an opportunity to screw me, these men were playing a political game. They often wore a mask to assess without giving anything away.

"Well, I'm utterly offended they aren't burning with jealousy," I kidded. They didn't know me yet, nor had they been mated with me yet. There were no personal feelings that would induce jealousy.

Lilah adjusted a clip in her hair. "Honestly, I'm not so sure on Prince Tyfen…"

I laughed. "Tyfen? Jealous? Of Hadwin?"

Lilah shrugged. "Okay, well, he did do a lot of looking away. And I really couldn't tell how much was annoyance and how much was jealousy. But I swear there was something there…"

Rolling my eyes, I scoffed. "He was probably upset he had to stand around for so long." Hadwin's claiming had admittedly taken a decent amount longer, with the bite marks added, and my hesitation. "Do you think I offended the vampires?"

Biting her lip, Lilah took a deep breath.

Not a great sign…

"I'm sure they'll be fine. It was a little odd when you zoned out at the edge of the platform."

I frowned.

"And … you were as pale as your duke during the love bites."

Looking down in shame, I swallowed hard. Despite my uplifted spirits upon returning to my dressing room, the first thing I'd done was down a vat of water and gargle with a strong mint brew.

"What did Schamoi say?"

She shrugged. "Nothing, really. He was proud. And so was I. We both knew how hard that would be for you, and the others probably didn't understand your hesitation as much. The other vampires weren't visibly upset…"

I scrubbed down my torso, trying to bounce back to my giddiness. I couldn't undo my performance. I would have a chance to sort things out with Hadwin down the road. First impressions mattered, but so did all the others after…

"What was he like? What did he say? You two whispered so much, but I couldn't catch anything."

My smile returned.

"You're obviously a fan of his cock."

I giggled. "He's really sweet."

"Even his blood?"

I almost gagged, and Lilah laughed at my expense.

"I mean … I suppose I would expect a commoner vampire to be kind, but not a duke, you know?"

We chatted a while about him and the profile we had on him. His kindness was probably a result of his youth. Eighty-four was young for a duke, and so he was perhaps not as stuck in his ways, and did not harbor so much hatred for other races given his lack of life experience.

After a while, Lilah left me, and the attendants finished stripping my makeup and bathing me to prepare for the final claiming of the night. My thoughts ebbed and flowed mostly between the vision of Hadwin's blood eyes and my anticipation of the next claiming.

My dress for the shifter would be one of the simpler gowns for the Great Ritual, but I still loved it. In honor of the shifters' close connection with nature, gold embroidered stars scattered on a bed of royal blue silk. It was strapless and draped perfectly.

We had washed my hair this time, and I wore it in a slicked-back ponytail.

"Hopefully he doesn't pull anything out," Madam Gaffey muttered as she fastened a necklace.

I smirked because I *wanted* the shifter to pull my hair. Wolf shifter instincts ran deep and wild, and while the idea of his impending ferocity unnerved me a bit, everything he'd want to do to me sounded like a hell of a good time. I'd practiced plenty for this pairing with my instructors.

"And let's not forget the cedarwood," an assistant said, dabbing the earthy perfume on me.

My makeup was minimal, only darkening and lengthening my lashes and adding a subtle blush to my cheeks.

Once I was ready, they wished me luck and blessings, as well as a good night. I wouldn't see them again until tomorrow.

On my walk to the bedding chamber, I recited everything I knew and all my plans. I wasn't going to commit any offenses or be awkward this time. By now, I'd gotten the layout and process sorted.

I reflected on the shifters I'd met in the meeting just hours ago. My mate—Elion—had no formal title, but his father was the high alpha. It was odd to have such a young untitled non-alpha be chosen to claim me. I'd expected a more influential and experienced representative. Elion was only two years my senior, shockingly young. But I wasn't complaining. I'd take friendly youth over crusty old crabs any day. And he *had* seemed genuinely friendly in our meeting.

A twinge of annoyance had me curling my lip. Prince Tyfen had seemed nice, too. Then again, Tyfen had been more charming, really, than friendly, and the two were not always synonymous.

As usual, I arrived with enough time to listen to the magistrate's speech from behind a curtain. He made sure to honor all the shifters, for they were not all wolves. The wolves were just the governing species of shifters, the caretakers of their lands and of many smaller shifters.

Once it was my time to appear, I stepped through the curtain. This time, Hadwin caught my gaze as I strode by. I properly blushed at his subtle smile. Tyfen dared to look my way, too, though he flicked his gaze away, disinterested.

Fae were tough, but could they survive falling from this high of a platform? The fantasy of me *accidentally* shoving him off danced in my mind.

The thought was fleeting as I passed the men and returned my focus to the spotlight of this claiming.

Elion was handsome in a boyish way compared to the others. He had soft features with narrow grey eyes. He looked at me eagerly, but his expression wasn't lust-filled.

Magistrate Leonte did his whole spiel about us pledging loyalty to each other and the realm. We both answered accordingly, holding each other by the arm.

Once we were wished well, we stayed in place as Leonte retreated. Elion's mother approached, smiling wide. She had been chosen for our additional fertility blessing.

She first pressed her forehead to mine, and we breathed the same air. "May Danah multiply your fruitfulness," she uttered.

Danah was another of the goddesses, a goddess of nature, most worshiped by the shifters. Nature, when unhampered, always brought forth fruit, so her blessing in their eyes, when paired with Hoku's for unity, was an extra measure.

Elion's mother then repeated the motion with her son, drawing a deep breath with him and reciting the blessing.

As she descended the stairs from the platform, Elion released my arm and took my hand, giving me a smile. His hand was soft and strong as he guided me to the bedding chamber alcove without a word.

Despite the audience far below us to hear, despite all the witnesses on either side of the bedding chamber, I was excited for this one.

Elion led me to the foot of the bed. "Sit." While his mannerisms were gentlemanly, his tone was half invitation, half command.

I paused, just long enough to notice the flicker in his eyes. Shifter rules of engagement and foreplay were nuanced yet simple, widely known, yet often misread.

After a short moment, I sat, having conveyed enough to him and the witnesses. A hint of defiance while still obeying. I would let him imprint on me, claim me as his life mate, but we were equal. I would not simply submit in this arrangement. It was understood. Personally and sexually, I submitted only when I wanted to. Politically and theologically, I submitted to the will of Hoku and the law.

Elion didn't hesitate to proceed. He dropped to his knees and lifted my skirt. The fluid action made me wonder if any of these men even appreciated the dresses I wore for them, or if they were too set on their goals to notice.

Somewhat gently spreading my legs, he put his face straight to my pussy. In my usual fashion, I looked forward, avoiding eye contact with any witnesses. Trying to distract myself, I admired the tall windows across from me in the enormous ballroom. This part was admittedly a bit awkward. Even shifters usually did imprinting in private, but here we were.

Elion sniffed me, and I stiffened. Lilah had to be stifling a giggle as she watched. Schamoi would be proud, though, that I was following protocol so well.

Picking up my scent, Elion then tasted me, licking through my center. It sent a shiver up my spine.

He licked again.

Then he poked his head back out, his eyes hungry. He reached into his pocket and pulled out a white handkerchief. This was usually not necessary in shifter imprinting practices, but it was solely for my consideration since we were in public.

Holding the handkerchief out to me, Elion said, "My mate." This time, it was said mostly in command, in dominance, but soft enough to not offend.

I took the handkerchief and bit down because the wolf's bite would hurt like hell. His saliva held no numbing properties like the vampires' did.

My toes curled and fingers firmly gripping the bedding beside me, I prepared for the pain.

Elion dipped back under my skirt, angled his head, and picked a spot on the inside of my upper thigh. First he licked, then his teeth scraped against my skin.

He clamped down. All things considered, I did a decent job of containing a scream as I dug my teeth into the handkerchief, trying to act unfazed while my chest heaved. It was a brief pain before he released, but sharp as he pinched and punctured.

It stung in the way all fresh injuries did, and I was still tense, trying not to cry, trying not to show how much pain I was in.

Elion's tongue stroked over the wound a few times, and it helped soothe the pain. His hands gripped my legs tighter, and he resumed licking my center.

There—there was that balance of pain and pleasure I often enjoyed. The pain dulled as the pleasure increased, and the pleasure was warmer from the residual pain.

Elion didn't stay distracted with his mouth for long. And I didn't need him to. While the imprint didn't affect me nearly as much as it did him, it did offer me quick arousal, quick wetness.

He stopped, then brought his head back up. His eyes were twice as bright, his expression fierce. The mating fever had set in. For him, the world would have blurred away, and I was the only one he cared about, the only object of his desire.

His breathing was ragged, his nostrils flared, as he fought to restrain himself. "I want..." was all he could get out as his hands tightened on my legs.

Had I also been a shifter, there would be no hesitation, no words, no consent even necessary. We'd both be in animal form and fucking each other senseless already.

But we were not both shifters, and a very strong and disciplined part of him clung to decorum in this room of witnesses.

I took the handkerchief from my mouth and set it on the bed beside me. The bite's pain was now just a steady thrum in the background of desire and anticipation.

"You can do what you want," I said, a smile lacing the words.

A guttural breath escaped him as he pushed me back onto the bed. He reached for his pants, making swift work of unbuckling his belt and dropping trou. I was genuinely surprised he was going to take me lying down.

But he didn't mount me right away, and I barely even got a glance in at his engorged cock before he grabbed me. Flipping me, he slammed me down on my stomach.

That's more like it.

A couple of witnesses in the bedding chamber let out small gasps. They would have been made aware of the kinds of things that might happen in here, but most of them knew how to show better restraint, or were not so beastly in their fucking to begin with. In the end, if they truly believed I was being harmed, the guards would intervene.

My smile grew. While my pleasure instructors lacked the strength or stamina of a shifter, they had taken *plenty* of opportunities to throw me around to prepare me for Elion. I *always* loved it.

I barely took a breath when Elion plunged himself into me, and he did not hold back. There was fast fucking, and then there was fevered mating.

He thrust like a drowning man thrashing in a riptide to reach the surface, like he would die if he didn't do it harder, faster.

"Sir," one of the attestants said from a few feet away.

Elion growled, stopping, firmly clutching my hips. He remained in human form, but the sensible part of his brain was suppressed right now by the fevered beast that lurked under his skin.

A footstep advanced toward the bed, and Elion growled louder, his fingers gripping me like claws. He felt threatened, possessive, protective of his new mate.

"We just need to see," the voice calmly reasoned.

Elion's growl was low, and he did not move.

I stayed right where I was, waiting for Elion to sort it out, to push through the fevered haze. He was already knotted inside me, so I couldn't do a whole lot to move anyway, and I wasn't sure if I ought to say something.

A commanding snarl came from one side of the room. I dared to glance. His father—the high alpha—stood as one of the witnesses. The snarl had come from him.

Keeping himself pressed to me, fully inside me, Elion panted. Slowly, he pulled up the bottom of my dress, sliding himself out just enough for the attestants to confirm he was in the right place, that his seed would not be wasted.

"Thank you," one said.

I reached up, grasping the edge of the bed, and decided to entice Elion more, help him recover from the distraction.

Shifters generally enjoyed a good chase. Even if he hadn't already knotted inside me, I wouldn't have let him chase and tackle me in the bedding chamber. The room was too small, and a chase would have been inappropriate given the witnesses and divine purpose of the Great Ritual.

That didn't mean I couldn't give him a little playful resistance for enticement. Before he reamed me again, I tugged myself forward on the bed.

I was met with a swift reward—he growled, shoved himself in deep, and pulled my hair to keep me in place. The soft growl of warning was prolonged.

I eased back the smallest amount and flexed my pelvic muscles to hug him.

Oh my goddess. I almost moaned instantly. I hadn't understood how exquisite the tightness against his cock knot could be.

He liked it too as I did it a couple more times. Convinced I wouldn't try to flee and sufficiently enticed to start again, he released my hair, gripped my shoulders, and drove himself into me.

In ecstasy for every second of it, I let him ravage me at a speed I'd never experienced, every moment gasping as his cock rubbed me in a way a standard human's couldn't.

I lost myself on that bed, tumbling through the eternities while I held on for dear life. Nothing else mattered other than what he was doing to me, and the incomparable tightness that gripped him. It built with each thrust, and he did not slow down.

If it were possible to die from the release, I would have died happy and with no regrets. My release was explosive, and I had zero control over the noises that escaped my lips as I shook and stiffened.

Elion came soon after me, fevered bliss filling his grunts and gasps.

As we both gulped air, our tightness ever so slowly easing, he rested on me.

I lay there, stunned. Shifters were believed to have the strongest biological mating bond. The other men in my Coterie may choose to leave my side someday, but Elion would never, regardless of the outcome. He was my personal guard and lover. I would have felt guilty about the one-sided loyalty if it weren't for how much I'd enjoyed this claiming. I would never want for an orgasm with him by my side. And if his heart truly matched the warmth I'd already seen from him, I would never wish him away.

Cooling, I regretted we weren't naked so I could feel his chest on my back as we lay there. I craved that intimacy in the moment. Then again, my sense of the moment was returning, and I was well aware we had dozens of witnesses staring at us. Staring at Elion's ass in the air, covering me.

I gave him another squeeze to let him know I'd enjoyed it. A deep rumble in his throat let me know he'd enjoyed me as well, that he was well pleased with his new mate.

Soon enough, the minimum required postejaculation time had been met. The blessings of Hoku and fertility were wished yet again. In addition, as the bedding chamber curtains closed, it was announced I would be retiring for the night to meditate to Hoku. Attendees were invited to remain for libations and celebration, as we'd hit the halfway mark of the Great Ritual claimings.

Up in the bedding chamber, the witnesses filed away as usual. Elion remained inside me another minute. Shifter knotting often took longer to dissipate than the timing requirements for the Great Ritual.

As footsteps tapped past us, our breathing returned to normal. Elion sweetly stroked my shoulder. "My mate," he whispered.

I smiled. "Yes."

We were both spent, and I was beyond grateful he'd taken me as the last of the day and not the first, because I may not be able to stand for long over the next few hours.

He placed a couple of lazy kisses on my shoulder, still stroking.

The attestants and guards wouldn't allow us to stay like this forever, though I'd happily remain in this bed with him inside me all night. Still, Elion's cock had returned to normal.

"We need to get up," I whispered.

His lips pressed to my skin again. "I know." After drawing a long breath, he pushed himself up and back, removing himself from me.

I turned on the bed, every muscle properly aching as I faced up.

Holding his cock, he stared at me like I was the most precious thing in the world.

I smiled.

"We need to confirm," an attestant said, approaching to inspect Elion. It was laughable. How could anyone have seen what had just happened and wonder if he'd done his job?

I'd felt the gush after he'd pulled out. I was sticky with him, and I loved it.

The attestant confirmed the divine requirements had been met, and allowed us more privacy.

I reached for the washcloths.

"Can I clean you?" Elion asked.

Nodding, I handed them to him. Rough in the bed, soft when standing—I liked that combination.

First, he quickly wiped himself down, and pulled his pants back up. I had no shame in watching and appreciating what had brought me so much pleasure.

I scooted to the edge of the bed, and Elion knelt. He didn't use the cloth to wipe me clean. Instead, he lifted my dress again, smiling at the bite mark. He licked that first. It still stung, but his saliva had healing properties that would help.

Satisfied with that, he looked up. His eyes were still bright, but the mating fever had cleared enough for the moment for him to be rational, to be mostly himself, like before he'd bitten me.

"Is there anything you dislike that I should know about?" he asked.

Unable to resist, I took his face between my hands, admiring his youthful beauty. "I… I would prefer not to mate with you fully shifted. I would prefer to make love, or whatever you call it, with a man, not an animal." I hesitated. "And that doesn't mean I don't accept you or that you have to change who you are…"

He smiled, rubbing the tops of my thighs. "I only shift during sex when my partner does. Since you cannot, that's not a problem."

It gave me great relief that he took no offense.

"Other than that," I added, "I'm up to trying anything once."

He nodded. "Great. Let me clean you?"

I spread my legs a little more, and he dove in, licking my center clean. It was like he'd run a feather down a deep bruise—it tickled and tensed in all the right ways, while simultaneously brushing an ache from the intense action the area had just received.

He was thorough, and damn if I didn't love every second of it. I didn't say a word, still exhausted, still in otherworldly ecstasy.

After he finished cleaning me, he stood and extended his hands. I took them and stood. My legs were a bit shaky, but he supported me, holding on to my sides.

"You're beautiful," he said.

"Thank you. And you're handsome."

"And … I never knew how good it could be until I was inside you."

My cheeks warmed. Some of that was definitely the mating fever talking. His thirst for me would be unquenchable for some time. While I'd become confident in sexual pleasure, I still had things to learn hands-on with a shifter.

He pulled me closer, wrapping his arms around me and kissing the top of my head. "I don't know how I'm going to get through the next day."

I frowned. "I'm sorry the lot didn't fall in your favor to have you last tomorrow."

He wasn't allowed to bed me again until the final three men had claimed me. It wasn't fair for his seed to be given a greater chance. Elion would suffer tonight and tomorrow until he could have me again. Shifters often didn't leave their homes for up to a month after the imprinting, screwing each other nonstop to satiate their urges.

Elion held me tight. "It's not fair. You're sure there's not an exception?" His voice was almost pleading.

"No, there's no exception." I hugged him back to comfort him.

His pants already bulged again, pressing against me. My heart broke for him. "Please?" he begged softly.

I hadn't realized how horrible this would feel. "I'm sorry."

He held me tighter, gripping my dress, clinging to me. His breathing was labored. "Can I walk you to your chambers?"

Carefully, I tried to pull back, hoping it would help. He hung on for dear life, like he had when the attestant had approached after insertion.

I might have been a little scared if the two attestants and the guards weren't still watching. If Elion tried to take me again before the last three got a chance, they would use whatever force was necessary to keep him away.

I didn't want him hurt—his pride or any other part of him.

"No, Elion. I know it will be hard, but you *can* be without me for a full day. I promise."

He shook his head.

I tried to gently pull back again, but his grip was impossibly tight.

"Please," he begged again.

I relaxed, leaning into him without a word, giving him one more minute. I couldn't imagine his suffering. It truly was unjust they couldn't have made him last.

Violins in the ballroom below played their tune, joined by the chatter of a thousand happy souls celebrating three unions that could potentially produce the next ruler of the realm.

I wouldn't be partaking in the merriment tonight, nor would Elion. The others in my Coterie were probably down there with their people, but Elion would have to be monitored and controlled, out of the public eye. It was rotten.

Drawing a deep breath, I calculated how to get him off me so I could leave, without involving any of the guards. How I treated him when he was most vulnerable mattered. For our relationship, and for political relationships.

He was a statue, not moving an inch.

I didn't know what to say. I hadn't expected it to be quite this hard, despite what I'd been told.

"Son," a gruff voice behind me called.

The voice was his father's. Relief washed over me for the intervention.

"Come," he called.

The tiniest whimper escaped Elion as he finally loosened his grip on me.

A familiar snarl from his father made him let me go at last.

He gave me the saddest possible look for a grown man, like a child whose favorite toy had been ripped from their hands and burned in front of them.

His head low, Elion walked to his father. The alpha put an arm around his son, guiding him to an exit.

"You'll be okay," I said, no confidence to my words.

His father looked at me with a gentle smile and nod that told me he knew his son, and the fever, and that he knew how to take care of him. The small gesture brought immense relief. From the minimal interaction I'd had with the shifter alpha and his mate, I really liked them. They seemed so approachable for leaders of a nation. They *would* take care of their son.

I straightened my dress and tightened my ponytail, still glancing at the exit he'd left through. I knew one thing for certain—his hands would probably be cramping tomorrow from all the work he was going to have to do to try to keep a semblance of sanity while away from me. As a member of my Coterie, he couldn't even be with anyone else to help him relieve his urges.

I finally glanced toward my private corridor. It was a little unsettling having the attestants and guards still all staring at the exit Elion had left through, cautious as though he might break free from his father and come back to bed me again by force.

"So…" I wrung my hands.

"We should get you back to your chambers," a guard said.

"I think that's a great idea."

12

THE AFTERMATH OF DAY ONE

I took my time walking back to my chambers. Every muscle in my body was sore, and for all the right reasons.

Poor Elion…

It was going to be a rough night for him.

Lilah was already in my bathing room when I arrived. She jumped up from a chair and drew me into a hug. "What took you so long? Did you let him take you a second time?"

I rolled my eyes and pulled back. "Yes, the attestants and guards decided 'Divine instructions? What are those?' And 'It's not that important if people find out and it starts a war…'"

She took her seat again, crossing her legs, still in her lavish ball gown. I allowed the attendants to peel my dress off me, and I crawled into the fresh tub. Steam rose from the water, and I was grateful for the relief it gave me.

"So…" Lilah prodded.

I frowned.

"Not what I was expecting after the sounds that escaped your lips." She grinned, stealing a glance at my chest.

My cheeks warmed. "How bad was it, really?"

She didn't even have the decency to lie to me. "Honestly, other than Princeboy's exhibition at the beginning, I think the audience below has been bored. But Wolfboy… They didn't need to see what was going on to get the picture."

The vision of my own mother listening the whole time flashed through my mind, and I was fully ready to die. The only other time I'd ever been so mortified was shortly before the temple had confirmed I was the Blessed Daughter. My mother had come home from a long day of work to find not one but two young men inside me. And while she now understood and accepted my regular cravings, it was still not something I discussed much with her.

As for the moans and gasps… I was often a vocal creature in bed, but could usually control myself if needed. But Elion had undone me, *thoroughly* undone me.

I blew out a breath. "Well, that's it. I'm going to sink into the bathtub, and I'm issuing official orders that no one is allowed to retrieve me until I'm fully drowned."

My attestant spoke up. "Unfortunately, your death would destroy the seed and its potential within you. Divine law demands I override your orders and save you."

I flopped my head to the side, glaring at her. Sure, she was an official palace-appointed attestant, but did she have no sense of humor?

Then she grinned.

I rolled my eyes again. "You're horrible."

Lilah chuckled. "People will be glad you enjoyed yourself. Don't fret so much." She bobbed her head in thought. "Then again, I'm not sure how much your Coterie enjoyed him taking you that way."

Cringing, I grabbed the washcloth from the side of the tub. "Go on."

"Most of them looked away for quite a bit of it. I think either embarrassed or offended. A couple watched on, though, with their usual cold, disinterested masks."

I shrugged. "Not my problem if they're embarrassed or offended." I wanted to strike a balance that would be reasonable for different sensibilities, but at the same time, the whole principle of Hoku's gift was to help us appreciate each other where we were so different. There would have to be some give and take from all sides.

Standing, Lilah grabbed a candy from a tray on a counter. "So, why did you frown first thing when I asked you about Elion taking you?"

"Oh… I took so long getting back because he … didn't want to let me go." I wiped my groin, which was properly sore from the day's work. A half dozen daily orgasms was easy for me, but I hadn't been with such voracious partners before. It would be a task to keep up.

She nodded, popping the candy into her mouth. "Clingy, that one. I'll take a woman, or even the right man, if they can make me feel the way you sounded with him, but I'd rather not go through all that."

"Yeah." I frowned again. He'd calm down eventually. It would just complicate the dynamic of the Coterie until he did.

"What do you suppose he's doing right now?" she asked. "Punching his dick to try to make it go down?"

I swallowed my lip to keep a laugh in.

"Surely they would have made his chambers safe… Imagine he found a thin vase and cut himself trying to peg anything he could get his hands on…"

My eyes went wide.

She let out a little giggle and sat. "I'm sure he's fine."

Continuing to scrub myself, I worked on my feet. "They told me they'd provide him with plenty of chilled hand cloths to … cool … himself. And a strong calming tea to help him sleep away a good deal of the fever."

"Hopefully that's enough."

I considered what else my tutors had mentioned. "They told me something with my scent may be comforting to him. I didn't originally have anything delivered to his room because it felt a little odd sending that to a man I hadn't met, but now I'm reconsidering."

"The dress? That has both of you all over it."

The attendants had already whisked it away for laundering, and I didn't want to defile Madam Gaffey's hard work in that way. "Think smaller." I smiled.

Lilah lifted an eyebrow, her perfect lips pursed. "Underwear?"

"Exactly."

She raked her eyes over me as a lover would. "Sonta, how fresh does it need to be? I, for one, know you didn't wear a stitch of it all day…"

I grinned, focusing on her beautiful eyes. "No, I didn't. Did I?"

Ever so casually, she tilted her head. "And how much fabric is needed? The kind you wear rarely has much to it. Is it enough to even carry a scent?"

I bit my lip, mentally back in her room, undressing her in the barely there lace undergarments I'd gifted her. We had similar tastes.

She sat back in her chair, folding her arms, wearing a self-satisfied smirk. I suddenly regretted not having taken a few more minutes in her arms to let her finish me off earlier.

"I wore something a couple of days ago and set it aside so the servants wouldn't wash it, just in case, thank you very much."

She still smirked.

"Don't look at me that way, Lilah. I'm either going to invite you into this tub with me or kick you out if you keep it up."

Chuckling, she stood again. Rounding the tub, she sat behind me and freed my hair, running her nails over my scalp. My head went limp into her hands as she worked magic.

"I should get back to the ballroom. Schamoi and I are going to party it up while you meditate and all that. He confessed he doesn't have anyone to rail when he returns to his hometown, and that's a travesty considering how much you've given him over the years."

I silently laughed, my shoulders shaking. "Yes, please help poor Schamoi find someone to please him as he transitions. I'm sure he won't be able to find a soul to appreciate his perfect ass, cock, technique, or work history…"

"Well…" She stopped scratching and leaned forward, gliding her hands into the water to hold my breasts. "If not Schamoi, then I have to think of myself, don't I? Cataray is gone for a while on holiday, and I won't have you. But if that duke has a vampire friend who wants to play…"

Her lips brushed against my ear. "Or maybe one of those badger shifters can make me gasp like you did." She stroked my areolas.

Sometimes, easy arousal was not a gift, because I wanted her to slip those fingers inside me despite my current aches. It wouldn't happen, though. Not with the attestant eyeing us both right now. We hadn't quite crossed the line of propriety yet, but…

"So, *just* cuddles in my chamber tonight, right?" I asked.

She slid her hands to my shoulders. "Yes. *Always* friends first, love." After kissing the top of my head, she stood. "You enjoy your relaxation and meditation. Schamoi and I will be up late with the celebration. If you want our company early, don't hesitate to send a servant."

She smiled as I nodded. About to be thoroughly pampered, I wouldn't regret missing the celebration.

After Lilah left, I soaked and scrubbed until the bathwater chilled. I was immensely grateful to have a masseuse as well. He worked on me for an hour, slathering lavender oil and rubbing out the knots and aches.

I was supposed to meditate, and since I wasn't that familiar with the masseuse, I didn't feel all that chatty. Deciding to fulfill that requirement in my own way, I meditated while on the table.

Most people assumed I was extremely devout in the worship of my divine mother, but I wasn't really, not in the way some were. My own mortal mother hadn't been all that devout in the worship of any of the goddesses when I was young, so I simply hadn't been raised that way.

Despite that, I did feel a connection to the divine—in thoughts, feelings, impressions. In visions of places and things I had no right to know. But Hoku had never asked me to worship her. She'd asked for my respect, my trust, and my loyalty. I'd never hesitated to accept this role for her and this realm.

"Is there anything else I can help you with, Your Holiness?" the masseuse asked after finishing.

My body was a puddle on the table, so relaxed, so happy. "Carry me to my bed?"

"Okay."

I chuckled. "That was a joke. I'm fine, thank you for your assistance."

He gave me a smile, a nod, and a blessing for the rest of the Great Ritual before leaving.

After forcing myself to get up, I dressed and asked the only remaining attendant to let my mother know I was headed to my room for the night. I had told my mother to wait to come see me until I was all finished for the day because it would have been more stressful for her otherwise.

I slipped on the most comfortable sleeping gown I had, a silky plum number that reached my knees. Before crawling into the comfort of my bed, I prepared a box and had it delivered to Elion's room. I sent a pair of my worn underwear, and a simple letter encouraging him—letting him know I looked forward to being with him again as his mate. Though we didn't know each other well, he had a special place in my heart already.

While waiting for my mother, I picked over a delectable tray of desserts that had been brought to me, and savored the quiet ambiance of the pond's trickle.

I even offered some of the desserts to my attestant, who would be watching me all night to ensure there was no foul play in the Great Ritual.

Not much later, my mother arrived, all smiles.

I jumped out of bed and hugged her. "You really do look stunning in your dress."

She didn't let me go. "You looked beautiful in all yours." She squeezed tighter. "How are you doing?" Her whisper was full of maternal concern.

Stepping back, I gestured to the bed. I sat on the edge and pulled the covers over my legs, and she sat in an armchair next to me.

"I'm fine. It was … fine."

She eyed me. "Fine?"

I shrugged. "Better in some ways, worse in others."

Reaching a hand up, she felt the love bite on my neck. I winced at the residual pain.

"Does it hurt?"

"Only when people poke it." I gave her a silly smile.

"And your … other one?"

This was going to be awkward no matter what. She hadn't watched the events, but she'd heard some of it… And she knew how much activity happened in this room. Luckily, she was clueless to the fact that Schamoi had ground into me less than a day ago just a foot away from where she now sat. The mirror had been washed and was streak-free.

"The shifter bite is fine, too. I promise—I'm okay. If anything, the worst part was the rudeness of the one who *didn't* bite me."

She asked for details, but I didn't get too much into it. Politics were not her concern, and she needn't worry, but she still vowed to dislike Tyfen for offending me.

We chatted for another good half hour about the feast and other events surrounding the Great Ritual. My eyelids grew heavy as we talked about the celebration I was absent from.

She rested a hand on mine. "You're sleepy. Rest up. We'll catch up more in the morning."

I nodded, slipping under the covers to my neck. "Go have fun. Tell Kernov hi."

"I will." She kissed my forehead, brushing some of my hair to the side.

"Will we be sharing brunch in your room, or Kernov's?"

My mother blinked. "In mine, of course…"

"Okay. If that changes, have a servant notify me. I wouldn't want you to have to sneak halfway across the palace to get back to your rooms just for brunch." I grinned wickedly.

She narrowed her eyes. "Sonta," she whispered. "He's a nice man, but he's busy and important."

She'd always struggled with confidence around men. And I could understand why others might hesitate to pair them. They were night and day in many aspects. His skin was much darker than hers, his upbringing more elite. Her past as a lowly prostitute wasn't exactly the glowing résumé a man of such political position liked to parade around. Despite their differences, they were good for each other, and that should be enough.

"He *is* a nice man. And he likes you, and always makes time for you when you visit. He's not too busy for a relationship; he would make time."

"You don't need to fret about me. You have enough on your plate."

I wrinkled my nose. "I'm Hoku's daughter, as well as yours. I'm sure she would enjoy your being happy. She does support unity, too, does she not?"

Resting her hands on her hips, my mother cocked her head. "You did not just try to issue me a divine order about being with a man, did you?"

I let out a silly, sleepy giggle. "You deserve to be happy, Mammi. Give Kernov a chance."

She kissed me again, this time on the cheek. "Good night, tired girl. I love you."

"Love you too." I rolled onto my side, succumbing to sleep before the door even opened for her to exit.

Sometime late into the night, Lilah and Schamoi woke me when they found their way back to my chambers.

Groggy, I moved over a bit. "Have fun?"

Lilah giggled.

"We did," Schamoi said.

Clothes hit the floor, and they both slid into bed with me, each taking a side. I treasured their warmth as they cuddled up.

Lilah kissed me on the lips, her breath laced with wine. "All sorts of fun, love."

I acknowledged her kiss with a soft moan. "How did I do on my first day, Schamoi?"

"Mmm." He rested a hand on my hip. "Great, little dove. Let's talk in the morning."

13

Party of Three

I slept like a rock. Harder than a rock, if that was even possible. I was usually a heavy sleeper, but this was exquisite rest.

A bird chirped at the window. My eyes still closed, I savored Lilah and Schamoi's warmth, their soft breath. I also assessed where all our skin touched.

Schamoi had stripped down to his shorts, which was more than he normally wore to bed with me. Then again, he was usually free to fuck me. For now, he held my breast, pressed to my back.

Lilah didn't seem to have a stitch of clothing on her, and I was pressed to her back, my hand on her breast as I held her.

I couldn't resist fondling her softly. "Good morning," I whispered.

She shifted, slowly grinding her ass against my groin.

Goddess save me. This wasn't fair. My craving was already back.

And her grinding against me made Schamoi hard behind me.

"You two are wicked," I whispered.

Schamoi let out a sleepy moan, his cock large against me. "Do you want me to go?"

No. I didn't. I wanted a release.

I glanced at the end of the giant bed to find the attestant fully awake, already scrutinizing us. Neither Schamoi nor Lilah were allowed to get me off, nor I them, until I'd birthed a child of my Coterie.

And damned if I didn't want them *both* inside me right now.

I pressed myself to Lilah, craving more pressure, though she'd stopped grinding. Where was Elion when I needed him? Or Hadwin? He'd do the job well. Hell, I even craved Tyfen's massive cock right now if I didn't have to look at his stupid face…

I shuddered a breath. It was going to be a long day. I wasn't going to be able to find full relief until my next claiming, and that wasn't until this evening. The gap was meant to allow me a break from the night before, but I didn't need it.

Lilah rolled over to face me. "I'd love to help… You could use a tool… We could leave so you're not tempted."

Her nipples were hard; Schamoi was hard. They wanted it as much as I did.

"Whatever you want," Schamoi said, caressing my hip while pulling his cock away from my back.

Lilah gazed into my eyes, and I wanted to steal a kiss.

I pushed past my yearning. "I'll be fine. I can take care of myself."

"Do you want us to stay or leave?" she asked.

I'd had enough of being on display in the last day, and while I normally wouldn't shoo them from my bed, it also wouldn't be fair to leave them unsatisfied while I fulfilled myself.

Lilah and Schamoi held two very different places in my life. They were my friends and lovers, but in such different ways. Schamoi had always been with me in an official capacity. Lilah just happened to live here as my friend. They'd spent more time together in the last twenty-four hours to support me than they probably had in the previous five years I'd spent here.

That didn't mean they might not enjoy a toss in the sheets.

"If…" I wasn't trying to start anything with them, but I also wasn't suggesting anything I didn't already know they'd be open to. "If the two of you want to take each other, I could watch while I manage myself."

Her eyes wide, Lilah blushed. Schamoi said nothing.

While he'd been bound to me up until a day ago, he had eyes. I'd seen him take her in more than once as their paths had crossed, and I couldn't fault his appreciation for her body when I myself admired it.

His silence wasn't unexpected. He may hesitate to seem eager so quickly after being with me, or because of my friendship with Lilah, though it probably was his lack of knowledge about her sexuality. Lilah only ever had women visit her here at the palace. The few men she had hooked up with over the years were usually back in our hometown or elsewhere, picked up from a tavern while visiting family.

Lilah bit her lip, her smile growing. She'd confessed to me a list of men she would let bed her without hesitation. Schamoi was on that list, after all the praise I'd given him.

Still, her eyes questioned. And I winked my answer. He was now free to do what he wished with other women, and he was moving away. This was her chance to fulfill that dream.

"I'll have Schamoi if he'll have me," she said.

He gave the briefest pause, then propped himself up behind me, a skeptical smile on his lips. "Really?"

"Surely, if you can handle Sonta, you can handle me." Her taunt was well aimed. "Or are you afraid you don't know how to please someone other than her after all this time?"

His lips twitched as he narrowed his eyes. "I accept."

Lilah beamed, giving me a peck on the cheek. Getting up on her knees, she stretched, likely for a good show.

Schamoi's throat bobbed, his cock still pressing against his shorts. First, though, he turned to me. "Do you need us to get anything for you?"

"No. Enjoy yourselves." I slid back on the bed, up against the headboard. Unable to wait any longer, I slipped a finger up my nightgown and gave my center a stroke. The perfect tingle of anticipation tightened me.

Schamoi freed himself of his shorts, and they both scooted a bit away from me on the enormous bed. I happily took them both in—sensual curves, familiar bodies, beautiful hearts.

"I thought … you liked women," he said. "Have you ever…"

Wrapping her arms around his neck, she pressed her breasts to his bare chest. Her lips brushing his, she said, "I've had more than one cock inside me. Don't think you're so special."

He chuckled, stealing a kiss while gliding his hands onto her ass.

Goddess damn me, it was hot to watch, and I was wet and desperate.

"How do you like it, Lilah?" he asked.

She raked her fingers through his hair. "I trust Sonta's judgment. She said you can do no wrong."

I blushed when Schamoi shot me a satisfied glance.

Not wasting another moment, he turned to Lilah, placing another kiss on her lips. He sucked on her bottom lip, and I was beyond jealous of them both.

I stroked myself as he focused on her neck—slowly, preciously trailing down every inch. Her posture loosening, Lilah surrendered to him.

Shifting on the bed, Schamoi held Lilah's breasts. "You're beautiful, Lilah."

She licked her lips. "You're not so bad yourself."

He bent down and sucked her nipples. I panted out a breath. I knew how great her tits felt in my mouth, and how skilled he was at doing things with that mouth of his.

They could take their time, but I was suffering. I slipped two fingers inside myself; they glided in effortlessly.

I pumped as slowly as I could, building the pressure, as Schamoi prepared Lilah.

Luckily, he didn't take long. Soon enough, he'd laid her down, spread her legs, and leaned in. I imagined it was me he inserted himself into as I stroked myself, hot with desire.

He went slow, and it reminded me of how gentle he'd been our first time together, and also our last.

Lilah shuddered, bucking her hips once he was fully in. "You won't break me."

Schamoi took the invitation.

It was beautiful, really. I'd never seen Lilah from this angle, nor Schamoi. Lilah and I had never had another person in the room with us when we made love. And while I'd done group activities with my pleasure instructors, Schamoi hadn't been interested in exploring with the other men.

But this gave me a great view of all their best parts. I took care of myself to their rhythm for a while, and as my tension grew, as my core ached, memories of being with them washed over me. As well as the recollection of the three men of my Coterie from the night before.

I came before Lilah and Schamoi. It was softer than I was used to, but still took the edge off as I'd so dearly needed. After collecting myself, I smiled and watched them complete. He took good care of her like I'd known he would.

He straddled her, still inside her, as they calmed. "Thank you," he said, gazing down at her.

Her smile was bright, her arms stretched out over her head. "I think we're officially friends now."

His laughter was always so sweet and bewitching. "So, this is how one becomes friends with the Blessed Vessel's mysterious best friend?"

Acknowledging me again, Lilah glanced in my direction. "I'm mysterious? So exciting!"

I laughed and reached for washcloths for us all, chucking a couple at them.

I watched them fondly as we all cleaned up. There was an ebb and flow in my life at the moment. I was still clinging to the past while embracing the future. I wished I had a clearer foresight—that that had been a divine gift from Hoku—

to know how things would settle in a year's time. But I did not have that gift, and I needed to enjoy making the memories as they came.

I painted a portrait of this moment for my memories to keep.

After a minute, Lilah glanced at the attestant, nervous. She asked if this would go in any official records, and the attestant stated it would not. They had not touched me too much, and the divine edict did not forbid me from satisfying myself.

The two of them took positions next to me again under the sheets, our backs to the headboard.

"Did you enjoy the show?" Lilah asked.

I gave her a toothy smile. "Without a doubt. Plus, now I feel things are a little more balanced. You two are getting six shows with me in that bedding chamber, and now I've at least enjoyed one show myself." I winked again.

She leaned her head on my shoulder.

Schamoi rested a hand on my knee. "Speaking of the bedding chamber, did you want to get caught up on all that?"

I bit my lip, anxious, but nodded. He was here for support, and his assessment and approval meant the world to me.

He felt my performance so far had gone fairly well, that my nerves had been understandable. I resolved to not let myself get frazzled with tonight's claimings.

While he wasn't privy to information exchanged in official meetings, he shared his assessment of yesterday. Lilah piped up occasionally too. Everything had seemed calm, the people happy. Officials were always a little tense when all the races were packed together for the Great Ritual, but nothing this time felt out of the ordinary.

Apparently, *both* the fae king and queen appeared rather discontent with their son's behavior, and possibly not just because of his exhibitionism. That might be in my favor if they humbled him to respect me more.

Schamoi shared my personal opinion of the shifters—he optimistically approved of Elion and his parents. I pitied Elion for how hard my absence from him was, considering I myself was yearning for full satisfaction.

And luckily the vampire leaders didn't seem too bothered by my hesitation when Duke Hadwin had taken me.

Lilah and Schamoi shared fun stories about the celebration I'd missed. Lilah had not yet found a new lover, but she was going to keep her eyes peeled.

I discussed my nerves for tonight's claimings. Really, the biggest concern was the last—the merman. But I would not let that anticipation spoil the day for me. I'd be fine.

After a while, we all got up and ready for the day. I took a quick swim in my pond to loosen up while they shared a bath.

I invited them both to breakfast with my mother, though Schamoi declined. He said he preferred to pack his own belongings instead of having servants do it, and he still had some left to do.

It was a calming stroll to my mother's chambers, Lilah's arm hooked through mine. My mother gave us each a strong hug and a kiss on the cheek when we arrived.

"No stocking on the doorknob," I commented, sitting down at her breakfast table.

Her eyes went wide. "Sonta!"

Lilah giggled. She and I may have conspiratorially chatted about my mother and Kernov from time to time, and she'd informed me they'd danced and held hands a good deal at the celebration last night.

"Come now, Mammi Gwynriel," Lilah said, choosing her chair. "We're old enough to chat with you about lovers, aren't we?"

My mother had always been a second mother to her. "Do you discuss such things with your parents?"

Lilah cringed.

My mother gave a self-satisfied hum as she sat with us.

I flourished my hands in the air. "But ... blossoming love…"

Mother couldn't resist a smile. "Either way, he'll be joining us, and I don't want him walking in on any gossip, thank you very much." She sat up straight, regal.

I nodded in mock solemnity. "As the Blessed Vessel, I give you my word."

Lilah snickered, and my mother rolled her eyes at the sanctimonious pronouncement.

Servants brought breakfast, and Kernov arrived late, full of apologies.

As I buttered my toast, I had to choke back a comment wondering how he could possibly be late since he must be familiar with the route to my mother's chambers by now. I chose politeness this time…

It was a nice breakfast, a good distraction from all the noise and business. In the end, though, Kernov and I had to leave earlier than I liked for official meetings.

We walked the corridors, side by side, on our way to the emperor's council room.

"Are you all right, Sonta?" he asked.

I smiled. While his concern for my well-being no doubt stemmed from his position as the magistrate's advisor, his voice had been laced with friendship, perhaps even with a fatherly concern.

"I'm fine. I'm not that shy, and I understand my purpose in this." I adjusted my earring. "Plus, I'm already quite fond of the two I'm mated to."

"Good," he said. "Ready for a riveting meeting?"

Chuckling, I took his arm as we approached the room. "Ready as ever."

Mysteries & Magic

My purpose as the Blessed Vessel extended beyond fertility. The Coterie wasn't simply about fucking and bearing new life to rule the realm.

As the child's mother, I would help mold them into who they would become. As would their father, and any of the Coterie who remained by my side, who the two of us allowed to be a part of her or his life. I would only allow good influences in the child's life, and help balance their understanding of the world.

Gaining my favor in bed to impregnate me only got the men of my Coterie so far. They could not guarantee their seed would prevail, but they would try to remain an influence and a voice for their people, through me, and eventually through my child.

I entered the council room first, Kernov after me. Greetings were exchanged between myself and the emperor and magistrate, and also the other attending advisors. None of the individual representatives of the six territories were in attendance for this meeting.

At first, the meeting was rather dull. Security staffing was discussed, as well as changes that needed to take place for high-ranking-guest accommodations.

I was used to these meetings by now. Technically, I held no authority here beyond that of my divine appointment to birth a child of my Coterie. That didn't mean I was inept.

The emperor was the anointed high ruler. The magistrate was an elected official serving in tandem with the ruling emperor, but his or her rule was shorter, and the final say rested with the emperor.

Should the emperor die before my child was of ruling age, the magistrate would step up as the high ruler in the interim, and I would become a secondary voice in my child's stead. It had all been a sharp learning curve for me once my identity had been discovered.

"And you're well, Your Holiness?" one of the advisors asked me as the conversation turned.

Giving her a polite nod, I sat up straighter. "Yes, thank you."

Most of the people in this room had been in a different alcove than the bedding chamber, but every single one of them had to have heard me when Elion had taken me. I refused to be embarrassed. And I wasn't insulted by the casual question, either. We wouldn't delve into my feelings for each man or how well they'd railed me. These people respected and even revered me as Hoku's daughter, and they would not make a mockery of me. And this was not a meeting to discuss silly crushes or how good it had felt to have those men inside me. They simply wanted to know I was uninjured, and to exchange political information.

"Do you have more information on Prince Tyfen?" the magistrate asked.

I blinked. "What sort of information?" I tried to think of anything that mattered. He'd insulted me, and his cock had been huge, and he'd made a bit of a display of himself, but none of that was secret or important for this meeting.

"There's been a bit of unrest with himself and the king and queen since their arrival, so I'm hoping something he said last night may give us some insights."

I took a moment to replay it all. "I know nothing about that. His mother was obviously displeased by his ... performance."

The emperor grumbled. "Performance indeed. Rather distasteful."

Many would find Tyfen's exhibitionism distasteful, though some had likely enjoyed the show. It was a shame his personality didn't complement his features.

"Keep an eye out," Magistrate Leonte said. "And while you're at it, keep your ears open about Lord Findlech in regards to the fae."

I raised an eyebrow, confused. "You're afraid the fae and elves are colluding?" That notion genuinely made me uneasy, given their domination in ages past.

"No," Leonte assured me. "But something is off. King Bretton assures me there is nothing foul afoot, and that any tension we've witnessed is of a personal nature, but it would be better to know."

He was right about tension. There had been a little something there between the fae king and queen and the elf high lord and lady when we'd briefly met yesterday, but I'd assumed that had just been their general prideful attitudes.

The emperor abstained from commenting.

"I'll be watchful," I said.

Leonte nodded. "And the king and queen wanted to extend personal apologies to you for the prince's behavior."

Pursing my lips, I simply nodded in return. It was doubtful anyone other than the guards or attestants left behind in that bedding chamber knew how rude he'd been by demanding time with me. They probably were only apologizing for his nudity display.

Leonte continued. "They plead for you to still give their people a fair chance, that you will not hold Tyfen's actions against them."

The request gave me pause. Perhaps the king and queen knew more. Then again, the queen *had* been a witness at the claiming, and it had to have been obvious how humiliating it was to have him strip me, to call me just 'sufficient.' Why would they send a son—a representative—for their kingdom who would play so poorly in the game of love and politics? They certainly weren't teaming up with the elves for a takeover if they couldn't even control their own son.

I shook the curiosity from my head. "I'll of course consider their people. I wouldn't punish millions for the sake of one." *Even if that one is an ass.*

With those in the room satisfied with my response, the conversation shifted again, and we discussed the others in my Coterie. Each race had a nuance to their traditions and mode of operation. And as much research as the palace had put into learning about the men of my Coterie once the territories had submitted the names, much was still shrouded in mystery.

Duke Hadwin was still mostly unknown to us. He was not that established as a vampire, at a mere eighty-four years old, and did not have a public pedigree. I fought a smile at the mention of him.

Elion was also a surprise representative because of his youth. My feelings were mixed with him. I asked how he was doing, and I was assured he would cope with my absence a little longer.

"Odd they'd pick such a young pup," an advisor said. "Had he a few more years behind him, he'd be able to control his mating fever better."

Another advisor shrugged. "Is the high alpha sending his son so different from King Bretton sending his?"

We discussed tonight's claimings. The merman, unsurprisingly, came from a visitor-friendly region. The reminder calmed my nerves about him taking me. Something about his smile from across the room at the banquet hall had been disarming. He was also the most colorful of the bunch with purple eyes and turquoise scales, and the most unique with his deep-sea jewelry. I looked forward to getting to know him on a personal level and learning more of his culture.

Lord Findlech of the elves was a mystery in his own right. Elves were arguably the most closed-off society, at least for land-walkers. He was also the oldest man in my Coterie. We knew almost nothing about him. It wasn't uncommon for territories to send the same immortal men to try to sire multiple generations of rulers at the palace, but this was Findlech's first time in a Blessed Vessel's Coterie. By his title alone, we knew he had wealth and his people's respect.

And that was all, other than random tidbits like food preferences his people had supplied the palace. The territories had no obligation to share information they didn't want to, and I had no right to refuse their pick as a member of my Coterie, at least not for the one claiming of the Great Ritual.

I took comfort in my place of power despite my lack of choices. The territories sent great lovers, handsome men, and charming personalities—doing so was in their best interest.

The mage, who was to be my first claiming of the evening, was one we all kept an eye on. Some feared he had a radical agenda, and that as a result, he'd won the confidence of his community to take this place so young. As much as I'd be getting intimate with his body, I needed to get intimate with his intentions for his people's place in this realm.

Overall, the meeting did a fair job of putting me on guard but also giving me more confidence. I could tackle these men's political agendas amidst them tackling me in the bedroom.

After the meeting, I spent more time with Lilah and my mother. The grounds around the palace were filled with people who would be elated to meet me in person, but that was a security risk, and frankly too much for me to handle at the moment.

Instead, we soaked in my pond and got massages. It helped loosen my muscles and prepare me.

Eventually, the time arrived for my first visit to Madam Gaffey's room. After trying on the final three claiming dresses for tonight, I climbed into my first dress of the evening. It was a stunning long dusty rose number for dinner—it crossed over my chest, made of light fabric that flowed like a cloud.

I entered the banquet hall with my head held high. These hundreds of people had seen me the night before, and I them. I was less nervous this time around.

Doing my best to maintain an appearance of neutrality, I acknowledged each of the men in my Coterie with a nod as we ate from our separate tables. It was hard to keep a scowl hidden when Tyfen acknowledged me with the most hideously fake smile.

It was also hard to hide a blush at the way Hadwin winked at me while sipping from his goblet of blood. I tried to not think of the blood, but rather his eyes, which had cooled to their natural hazel. He didn't hesitate to lock eyes with me, to flirt. Butterflies danced in my stomach. I had to force myself to focus on my salad.

Part of me had wondered if Elion would opt to not attend the banquet. While skipping would usually be frowned upon, people would understand with his mating fever so fresh.

He did attend, and he looked pitifully desperate, his eyes glued to me for every second, as though he'd happily break away from his table and take me in front of everyone.

Not wanting to spur him on or torture him, I offered him a small smile of encouragement. My mind turned to my underwear… What had he been doing with it? Did he have it tucked in a pocket on his person right now?

Unfortunately, it all ended up being too much for him. Halfway through dinner, I caught him rubbing himself under the table. His father again led him out of the room. He did it tastefully, but it destroyed me a little inside. I didn't want Elion to be publicly humiliated, and his departure doubled the glances of people. People who had all heard me gasp and moan the night before from the bedding chamber.

Elion's mother gave me a sweet smile from the shifters' table, and it helped calm me.

As for the three men who would claim me tonight, our visual exchanges were brief. We'd sort out our deeper intentions with each other soon enough.

After I'd had my fill, I tried to slip out of the banquet early again. The mage caught my eye one more time, raking his gaze over me. His plate was nearly empty, but the confident look on his face told me he was still plenty hungry. For me.

I hadn't forgotten the warnings to be especially wary of him and his political agenda. How much of that hunger was lust? How much was mischief?

I swallowed as my eyes stayed on him a moment longer. Part of me didn't even care what his motives were at the moment—the part of me that begged for relief because I had restrained myself since this morning.

He leaned back in his chair, armed with those boyish curls and a smug grin. A septum piercing and lip ring adorned his face, drawing my eye to his lips. To my credit, I held my composure, only giving him a simple nod as I left the room, all the while wondering what kind of magic he was capable of—in and out of the bedroom.

15

The Magical Bond

"What do you think?" Madam Gaffey asked.

I spun in front of the long mirror, taking in the dress. My hair was down in ringlets. I wore a headband that matched the dress; it was a beautiful accessory, though I did worry it might mess up my hair more in the bedding chamber.

The dress itself was a stunning shade of violet with delicate golden embroidery of the twin moons around the hem. While the straps were extra thin and the front and back low, the skirt hung to the ground.

"It really is beautiful." I smiled.

They dabbed perfume behind my ears and on my wrists—amethyst and black currant.

After taking a deep breath to bolster my courage, I left the seamstress's room with escorts to my place behind the bedding chamber's curtains.

I was definitely calmer than the night before. We were halfway there.

Magistrate Leonte went through his usual introductions and explanation of the divine role the Great Ritual played, and honored humans and the mages. I waited patiently as he did it all. Many people feared or disliked mages, though that could be said of any of the races in our realm. Some of it had to do with their powers and the way they often handled them, and some of it had to do with the fact they were technically human.

All mages were humans who had been born with magic. Many argued they should not be allowed a place in the Great Ritual at all because a resulting child wasn't really a mixling. The child was wholly human with added magic, or simply a watered-down mage. While they had a point, it was a moot point. Just like the controversial participation of vampires and merfolk in the Ritual, mages had been included by Hoku. The goddess had decreed they be involved, that they have a say. Legend held their magic was a gift from the stars themselves, and if my divine mother decreed they should have a place here, I would fight for that right.

Hoku herself had been a mage during her mortal years. While some may say she showed favoritism by including mages in the Great Ritual, others would argue mages automatically deserved a seat at the table *because* of her service and sacrifice for all of us long ago. I couldn't imagine living in the dark times she had.

Leonte eventually called for me, and I played my part, walking onto the platform. Lilah and Schamoi smiled reassuringly as I strode past. My heart broke for Elion. He looked pained, as though his hand were in an animal trap, and he was about to have to watch three other men take me before he was allowed access to me again. While the members of my Coterie usually stood on the right side of the bedding chamber with the other witnesses on the left, his father and another shifter witness now stood behind him, subtly restraining him by the wrists.

I hoped the next three took me quickly and without any hang-ups, just for his sake.

Once I reached my designated place on the platform, the mage—Gald—and I took each other by the arm, making our vows of unity. Leonte called for the blessings of Hoku for us and departed.

Gald's smile was still a crooked one, and I couldn't make out if it was swagger or mischief, but it didn't throw me off. He had changed clothes since the feast, wearing a ceremonial robe over a rather fetching outfit. His white button-up shirt was half unbuttoned, exposing his chest, and his trousers were dark grey.

This time, a Demali mage priestess approached us, bowing low and offering a vial. Gald picked it up.

"Blessings," she whispered as she stood and retreated.

The vial shimmered with gold liquid. Gald removed the cork and handed the vial to me. "A potion for the Blessed Vessel's womb."

I would not hesitate despite my nerves. Drinking a potion made me as uncomfortable as giving myself to Hadwin had—risking death by poison or venom. As I thanked Gald and drained the fertility potion, I took solace in the knowledge the potion had been strictly monitored from its creation to the moment it met my lips.

The potion tasted of fresh cherries and raspberries with a hint of medicinal herbs.

After draining the vial, I gave it back to Gald. He tucked it in a pocket of his robe and took my hand. "Shall we?"

I nodded, and we retreated from the public eye, back into the somewhat private bedding chamber. Despite Elion's heavy breathing, I refused to look at him; it would only cause him more pain as he watched. Despite the soft trickle of water in the merman's tank, I wouldn't look at anyone.

Gald led me to the bed. "Would you like to sit first?"

"Sure." I did so, easing down on the edge.

He knelt before me, his smile replaced with a solemn look. "Will you make a bond with me, Your Holiness?"

I had anticipated this happening, though my heart fought it. My fear was irrational. Part of me considered this so unnecessary. It was unfair of me to think this way, though. The shifters always wanted the mating bond, as did the vampires. They wanted that way to link themselves to me. And why wouldn't the mages want to stake their claim?

"I will share a bond with you," I replied. To deny it would be to give offense, to send a message to the realm the mages could not be trusted.

He smiled. "Then it shall be done." Standing, he nodded to his witnesses. One pulled a short wand from their robe and approached us, along with two guards and two attestants. The magical bond could not be reversed, and they were here to ensure it did not go awry.

I rested my arm on my leg, exposing my wrist. Gald knelt before me again and pulled up the sleeve of his robe to expose his own wrist. He touched the wand to his wrist, indicating where his matching mark would be inked, then put the wand to my skin.

"My life to your life," he said.

I swallowed. "My life to your life."

He drew a circle with the wand tip, depositing a black mark. By magic, an identical mark appeared on his own wrist.

"No harm shall come between us," he uttered.

"No harm shall come between us."

He drew a wavy line down the middle.

"With the mark of friendship."

Smiling, I repeated. He drew a small symbol to match.

"With the mark of allyship."

I repeated, and he drew another symbol. Each inking carried a small tickle, but nothing more.

"With the mark of lovers." His smile grew to a grin.

My cheeks warmed, and I didn't care if I looked silly. These three marks didn't do much more than declare our intentions toward one another. There didn't need to be any marks at all—that wasn't the binding part.

"With the mark of lovers," I accepted, and he swished the last mark onto my skin.

He sealed the bond with the wand in the center, invoking the blessings of Hoku, Danah, and another goddess often worshiped by mages.

He returned his wand to his witness, and the group resumed their places, satisfied he had not harmed me or broken protocol.

Mages were not allowed to use magic during the claimings. Dampening stones had been installed on this platform, anyway, to dull his powers in case he tried anything. And as the others withdrew, I became more at ease. The bond was a weak one—there were much more serious and dark ones out there. This one was simple. The only real danger this posed me was harm if I directly harmed him. Were I to stab him, I would receive the same wound. This technically protected both of us, though not much. I could still have him assassinated without receiving a wound myself.

Despite the weak and purely symbolic nature of the bond, it was permanent. And I didn't dislike the intent he'd included with it—friends, allies, lovers.

Gald focused on me, a smile dancing in his eyes. "Well, that's official. Now… Do you have any preferences?"

"Not really."

He nodded. "I'm a bit limited without magic, but I'm not completely unskilled. Would you like some attention to prepare you?"

I rubbed my knee. As much as it would be helpful in the moment, I didn't want to prolong this, and I was tense from lack of release. "I'm fine without anything as long as you start slow."

"Lovely." He paused. "Can I kiss you?"

That surprised me. "Yes."

Leaning, I met him in the middle. His lips were soft, the ring in the center of his lower lip as warm as his body, and I wanted more, but he only gave me the one kiss.

"There," he said. "I generally do like kissing people before I fuck them." His tone and expression were all play.

I let out a breathy chuckle. "Not a horrible thing."

He beamed. "All right."

He undid his pants, revealing himself to me with a bit of privacy thanks to his robe. Gald wasn't that particularly muscular or intimidating compared to his rivals in my Coterie, but it wasn't like my pleasure instructors—mere humans— hadn't done an exceptional job simply because they were also humans.

"Do you want help?" I offered.

"I appreciate it."

He was already partially hard, but I wrapped my hands around his cock and gently pumped. He shuddered. Placing his hands over mine, he helped until he was ready.

"That's good. Would you like to lie back?"

Wordlessly, I pulled myself further up the bed. He followed, kneeling over me. He was gentle as he lifted my dress.

The sensation of him touching his tip to my entrance already had me wet. I'd been so damned starved for intimate touch today.

He slowly pressed in, and I almost begged for him to go faster, closing my eyes, enjoying each inch gained.

Gald paused for a moment, and someone cleared their throat.

I opened my eyes, having not even realized the attestants had approached to witness the penetration.

Gald threw one of them a dirty look. "I do trust the divine mother desires her daughter to be comfortable and not rushed." His tone held an edge, and I appreciated him standing up for me.

The attestant looked properly ashamed.

Returning his focus to me, Gald smiled, pushing in the rest of the way. I loved the way he filled me, how my body caressed him. He momentarily exposed us to the attestants before covering back up with his cloak.

His rhythm started slow and steady. *Too* slow. I gave him some encouragement, thrusting my hips. It became a dance as he matched me, as we pushed and pulled, as the pressure built.

I'd been worried about not being able to fully finish with him—a human stripped of his magic—but that fear was unfounded. He clearly knew what he was doing with each thrust, as though he'd had a thousand lovers in his short lifetime to hone his skills.

As was usually the case with me—thank the stars—I released as he did, tumbling together into that beautiful thing of friction and fantasy, of climax and cum.

"Sonta," he panted as he tried to recover. It was endearing the way my name was on his lips so casually. Like a friend, an ally, and a lover.

Once he calmed, he steadied himself for the required rest time.

I smiled. "Gald."

He returned the smile.

The announcement was made that the claiming had been successful, and the usual blessings were uttered as the curtain closed. Witnesses filed out, and I swore Elion squeaked out, "Mate." I didn't look at him for fear of making him wild with more envy.

In due time, Gald pulled himself out and unashamedly presented himself to the attestants to inspect. He held me down with a hand and insisted on cleaning us both up.

"You know," he said, "next time, I'll happily use my magic and have you gasping the way you did with your hound."

My eyes widened at his casual tone.

He simply shrugged as I sat up. "We're bound, but not mates. I'm not a jealous creature, Sonta. I've enjoyed watching you each time."

That was oddly refreshing. While loyalty like Elion's was endearing, the attached jealousy was also exhausting. Still, I didn't want him reduced to urges he could not control at the moment. "Please don't call him a hound. That's not kind."

Folding the cleaning cloths, Gald sighed. "Some may call him rabid with the mating fever, but you're right—I do know better. I've traveled enough to understand his plight. Sorry for the dismissal."

He helped me to stand. "I may not burn for you the way the others do, but I'm confident you and I will enjoy our time together." He held my hands. "Bond or no, oath or no, I intend to always be loyal to you, to always aid you." Glancing down toward my stomach, he added, "No matter the outcome of the Great Ritual."

I appreciated the assurance, and he was so sweet. I didn't quite fawn over him, though, not fully. Not with the apprehensions I had about him and his almost too smooth delivery.

"And you can promise all that while representing your people?" I asked.

He smiled with understanding. "I'm not trying to hide my intentions. I came, first and foremost, to sire the next ruler. Becoming lovers with a breathtaking woman touched by a divine hand is a secondary benefit. You don't get to be in my position without hard work and big goals, and I trust you don't fault me for that."

His eyes were a brilliant blue, and I searched them for truth and integrity. "I would not fault you for any of that."

"Good." He leaned in, his lips close to mine once more. "Because I'm more than happy to mingle lovemaking and law." He kissed me, each pass more intense, stringing me along with the tiniest hint of his pierced tongue before he pulled back. "I look forward to seeing you in a few more stunning dresses tonight, Your Holiness, just as much as I look forward to finally seeing you with nothing on at all while under me."

Turning, he simply walked away. I blinked for a moment. How had the man just bound me to him, fucked me, teased me, and pleased me, and yet I felt like I knew nothing of him? He could still be a threat, or he could be a friend and lover for the rest of my life. Shouldn't I know which it was by now?

16

ALMOST A BRIDE

As she'd done the night before, Lilah came to visit me while I bathed. She was stunning in her silver dress with a plunging neckline. She tortured me with an update on how much Elion had struggled through the claiming.

"Just two more, then I can help him out." I frowned, warm in the tub.

"He'll get over it." She smiled. "But this one—the mage—he kissed you…"

"Mmmm." I closed my eyes, and we chatted more. It was a little hard not to rank them from first impressions. How much had they pleased me in bed? How much had their personality made an impression thus far?

An hour later, I stood in Madam Gaffey's fitting room, staring at myself in the mirror. I looked a bit like a bride, or at least what many would consider a human bride. But this dress was specifically intended to please Lord Findlech— the elf in my Coterie.

While human society was rich with culture from its neighboring societies, elven traditions were often the most favored. Or at least what people *thought* were elven traditions. They were the most reclusive society. Many elves never left their hidden communities beyond their border mountains.

This tradition had to at least be a true elven one, though, to mimic it in the Great Ritual. The white lace gown hugged my curves and touched the floor. It even had long sleeves. While gorgeous, it was a bit blinding. I even had to wear a veil.

"I look like a mountaintop in winter," I said.

"A lovely mountaintop," an assistant said, dabbing a honey rose perfume on my neck and ankles.

"You can't get much use out of something so long and white, though. Think of the stains." I smoothed out the fabric over my stomach, though it didn't need it.

Madam Gaffey smiled, adjusting a pin in my hair. "Not to be crude, Your Holiness, but white is probably the best color for you to be wearing during the Great Ritual, isn't it? You won't even notice if his seed spills on it."

I pressed my lips together, both stifling a laugh and trying not to think too much about it. The Great Ritual was definitely a messy thing… "Well, there's that."

She stood back, assessing me. "And you look like a proper bride." She hesitated. "Do you wish, with all this, that you'd been born normal? That you could have chosen to be a regular bride with only one spouse?"

Without hesitation, I shook my head. "Not really. I always knew I'd take a different path." Just not this one.

My mother had never set the example or expectation of matrimony for me. And in my own unique way, I was bound to each of the men in my Coterie as a bride might be, in a much more open arrangement.

"Life has twists and turns we don't anticipate," I said. "And I'm confident I'll be able to navigate this. I'm already fond of most of the men."

A half hour later, I stood behind that bedding chamber curtain for the fifth time. Lord Findlech had tried the least to charm me in our initial meeting yesterday, so I was curious how this would go. He may have just been cold due to his elven nature, or due to the fact we'd been interrupted by the fae king and queen in our initial meeting. It could also be his age that made him standoffish— he was the oldest of my Coterie at 834 years old.

After a moment lost in thought, I returned my focus to the ceremony. Lord Findlech accepted his calling as a member of my Coterie, pledging his life.

I quickly lowered my veil as elven tradition required and took my cue, strolling in and across the bedding chamber to the platform edge.

Magistrate Leonte gave me a bright smile, and Lord Findlech gave me a small one as well.

While elven tradition dictated their brides generally be veiled for the entirety of their vow ceremonies, I wouldn't be. To Findlech, I may be some sort of bride, but to all the people of the realm, I was the daughter of a goddess, and I would not—could not—be hidden.

Findlech did the honor of lifting my veil before taking me by the arm for our exchange. Hopefully he appreciated the gesture of the lace accessory despite us breaking his people's tradition.

It was hard to tell, honestly. His emotions were as veiled as my face had been.

Despite our initial lack of emotional connection, I did find him handsome. His smooth and deceptively youthful skin was the darkest of my Coterie, his pointed ears the tallest. His locks of black hair the longest.

After we took our vows to each other, Leonte left the platform. As planned, Findlech and I remained. A sweet-looking elf approached us for fertility blessings, carrying an ivy vine.

Findlech took my hand, giving me another mild and reassuring smile. The woman wrapped the vine around our wrists, binding us, then bowed. Holding our hands, she pressed her forehead to them, uttering something in Elvish. The language was so ancient and complex I hadn't ever dared to try to learn it, but it was beautifully ethereal.

She ended her part with the anticipated 'May Hoku multiply her blessings,' and stood. She gingerly removed the vine, giving us one more bow, then retreated from the platform.

"Your Holiness." Findlech's voice was deep. He gestured to the bed, and I followed without a word.

I stood at the end, unsure. I'd always struggled to read the few elves I'd met, the emperor included.

"Please get comfortable," Findlech said.

I sat on the bed and scooted myself up. As much as I'd be happy to follow the order, it was actually harder to maneuver in this dress. It was the most difficult to move in, and get in and out of. And, frankly, the most awkward to access my pussy in.

First, Findlech used a clip to restrain his long locks. Still unreadable, he nodded to his witnesses, and one brought a small vial of clear gel. He thanked them, and they returned to their place.

"This should make things more comfortable," he said, kneeling over me. After I rolled up my dress so I could spread my legs for him, he opened the vial and tipped out a decent amount onto two fingers, then aimed straight for my center.

He rubbed the gel around, inserting his fingers into me just a little. While not rough, he did so in a utilitarian way, not at all sensually. I braced myself for the reality that he would not even be trying to prepare me by arousal. I had understood some of the Great Ritual may go this way, but I'd still prefer to crave a man before he took me.

Luckily, the gel not only provided lubrication, but a bit of numbing and tingling. At least I enjoyed the tingling.

As he freed his cock from his pants, I was also glad for the numbing. He wasn't Prince Tyfen, but Findlech was still plenty well endowed.

Findlech rubbed some of the gel on his cock and pumped himself to harden. I didn't have the same urge as I'd had with the others to offer to help. This all felt oddly transactional. At least he wasn't rude or cruel like Tyfen had been.

Soon enough, Findlech gently slid inside me. Despite my lack of arousal, it was nice. After the attestants were content he'd entered properly, Findlech did the job.

It was … decent. It wasn't making love, and I wouldn't even classify it as fucking. It was simply sex—him moving inside me, building up for a release. The tingling gel was lovely, and the friction was always welcome to satisfy my cravings.

Findlech didn't look me in the eye as he focused on his duty. I closed my eyes, gently assisting him to try to finish quicker.

With each thrust, I imagined myself in a glen full of wildflowers, with a warm breeze blowing over me. The quiet chatter of the people far below in the ballroom pierced that imagery, reminding me where I was, as did Elion's fevered breathing from the side and the trickle of the nearby merfolk tanks.

While Findlech's work was almost clinical, it *was* pleasurable. I still tightened, hoping he would get me there. I mused about my dress as he plunged into me, harder and faster with each go. It supported my breasts well. They were still so perky and barely even bounced as he worked me.

Realizing he grew close to completion, I stopped my daydreaming, forcing myself to more actively participate so we could both enjoy the ending.

With a pant and a shudder, he braced himself over me, filling me. Despite it not being mind-blowing sex, I did enjoy a small orgasm to relieve some of my tension.

As he cooled, he finally made eye contact, giving me a polite smile. I gave him one back. There had been mutual pleasure, no matter how mild, and we had fulfilled the Great Ritual requirements for him to cum inside me.

The waiting period passed for him to stay inside, and the curtains closed. Like Tyfen, Findlech didn't seem keen to have his cock inspected, but he submitted to the requirement. As the room full of witnesses emptied, Findlech reached for the wiping cloths.

"Would you like…"

I blinked. "Um… I can take care of myself." I held out a hand for one.

We wiped up in silence for a moment.

After putting himself back in his pants, he stood and bowed. "An honor, Your Holiness."

"You too," I said, somewhat perplexed. I couldn't wrap my head around the way I felt. Until it hit me. I had probably been so distracted because this reminded me of the very way I'd been conceived—as part of a task.

My mother had spent years under strange men to afford a roof over our heads, and it wasn't that different from me accepting my role in this palace and government by agreeing to share my body and bed with multiple men. Then again, mine came by divine appointment, with loads of honor and choice. My mother's had been out of personal need and carried shame in much of society.

My heart hurt for her, and I understood in that moment why she hesitated so much to embrace my place as the Blessed Vessel. She hadn't only had a realm placed between her and her daughter, but she also feared—despite my honesty about accepting this role—that I was coerced or hesitant. I vowed in my heart to spend more time with her, to make sure she got to know those I connected with most in my Coterie. Because, despite Tyfen's rudeness, and despite the blandness of Findlech's bedding, I was happy and full of hope. And I wanted her to play a large role in my child's life without hesitation.

Drawing me back to the present, Findlech held out a hand and helped me up from the bed.

I really should say something…

Opening my mouth, I paused. He was an absolute mystery—an elf lord. Not the high lord, nor closely related to the high lord from what I understood. Where to start to build something between us?

He gave me a nod. "We ought to go so the workers can start preparing the room for your final … bedding."

"Right…" Extra workers had to be waiting outside the door to complete the next task in a hurry. And it was kind of silly to call it a proper bedding. The merman would take me in a tank.

"I'll see you later, then." He walked away.

I couldn't really say much to that. "Bye." I shrugged and simply strode for my personal corridor.

17

DANGEROUS WATERS

Lord Findlech and I had chatted so little after our claiming that I returned to the bathing room in record time, beating Lilah there. After getting help from the attendants to strip me from the white dress, I soaked and scrubbed as I had after each bedding, an attestant watching me.

The door creaked open, and Lilah popped in, her face already screwed up. "Well, that was…"

I chuckled. "He got the job done."

She immediately snagged a candy from the counter before sitting down at my feet. "You'd think a man who's lived over eight hundred years would know how to … I don't know … do better?"

"Maybe he's so old he's gotten tired of the act."

We laughed together, though I did feel a hint of guilt at the jab.

Dipping her hand in the bathwater, Lilah swished gently. "What a contrast for your last two, right? Dry and dull to wet and wild." She winked.

I gulped, my nerves building already. "Yeah. I'm…"

She frowned with understanding. "You'll be fine. Lots of security. Just hold on tight…"

I drew a deep breath. "Right. And if they fail me, you'll personally rescue me?"

Lilah leaned back in her chair as if it were a throne she ruled from. "Of course."

That was a fat lie, and we both knew it. Duke Hadwin's claiming had been dangerous because of his venom, but it was ultimately safe because of his intentions.

Merfolk, however, often drowned land-walkers, and sex was a prime time for that. If there was one race that part of me wished Hoku had left out of the Great Ritual, it would be the merfolk. I was terrified despite all my practice and preparations.

"He's a chancellor, Sonta," Lilah reassured me. "He's cultured and prepared to be careful. They wouldn't send someone from the bogs, you know."

My stomach churned. "I know."

The merfolk most certainly wouldn't send one of the dark creatures from dangerous swamps or bogs as a representative. Most merfolk denounced the dastardly creatures, claiming they were remnant monstrosities from old wars, a type of oni created by vampire bites. Vampires, of course, vehemently denied any involvement, calling those rumors propaganda, since the creatures readily procreated, not requiring a vampire's bite to create more. They had probably been proper beauties at some point in history, and fully self-aware, but got caught up in a stream and became landlocked, disconnected from their warm salty waters. They often fed on unsuspecting animals and small children whose parents foolishly let them get close to murky waters.

"Though it's a pity he's not from a coastal resort," Lilah added. "I hear they're a great deal of fun."

I almost snorted at that. No, he would not be from a coastal resort, either. While most of mer-culture was a mystery—owing to the fact we land-walkers literally could not swim to the depths most merfolk lived at—those of us with legs could at least observe the interesting spectrum of their society.

At one end: sunken eyes, murderous, living in murky places. These were the monsters the majority of their people considered past hope.

As for the coastal resort type? They had chosen not only to mend things with land-walkers after the old wars, but embraced coexistence. Merfolk had taken sides in our wars, too, though to a much smaller degree, but they'd blocked water travel for any land-walkers they hadn't sided with. Their coasts and ports were ripped from them in many places as retribution. And while they spent almost all their time in the deep seas, they did often enjoy basking on the beaches for contrast.

Hoku herself had put a stop to all the fighting, and merfolk had received their coastal land back. But many land-walkers had already settled there, and in several places, they'd decided to cohabitate.

The locations were beautiful, the skilled entertainment breathtaking. I'd never seen one of the places with my own eyes, but I'd seen it in a vision once, and I'd been present for each yearly exhibit of entertainers here at the palace since I'd moved in.

That said, just as the merfolk of the bogs were shunned, many traditionalist merfolk considered the coastal resort type to be sellouts, and disowned them.

Most merfolk landed somewhere in the middle of the spectrum, and that was where their primary leadership hailed from—the majority, deep underwater.

I gave no response to Lilah's commentary, lost in thought and worries, bunching and unbunching my toes against the tub.

"You're sad he won't appreciate your tits, aren't you?" Lilah asked lightheartedly, almost mocking. "They haven't gotten any love all day. Do you need help with that?" She stared right at them.

That brought a grin to my face. "It's a shame, really, that merfolk don't understand the joy of tits or foreplay."

She wiggled in her chair, cupping her own breasts. "You'll have to teach him."

A shiver ran down my spine. I wanted to taste her again, damn it.

But I doubted I'd be teaching him anything, honestly. Merfolk—especially those from the deep seas—were both predictable and unpredictable all at once. They were strictly heterosexual, though rarely monogamous. Tits and lips were utilitarian things for consuming nutrients, not for pleasure. And consent was a foreign word altogether. In the wild of the seas, they took what they wanted from whom they wanted when the urge arose. If you didn't want to fuck and were strong enough to swim away, then you were fine. If not...

Swallowing hard, I focused on the salty aroma of this bath.

They weren't unruly creatures, truly. They were beautiful, and just happened to live under a different code than most of us land-walkers, and were therefore vilified. And it wasn't just their code of conduct; some of it was in their nature.

Their instincts, not their culture, were what I feared.

They'd gained a negative reputation not from the bog creatures, but from numerous incidents over the centuries involving run-of-the-mill merfolk. Specifically older adolescents who had less control over their urges.

When merfolk were stimulated and seeking sexual pleasure, they would bob their head. Some idiots considered it a fun challenge to fuck a merman or mermaid, and would seek them out. Some poor souls unintentionally swam in merfolk-heavy waters and hadn't read the signs of one on the hunt. When a young merperson wanted a release, they followed their instincts.

Unfortunately for those of us who require a constant flow of air in our lungs, we weren't compatible.

For a merperson, to claim a partner meant to thrash that partner until the merperson was satisfied. It was mildly inconvenient for merfolk if the act hadn't been mutually desired, but not as devastating as it was for us. They entered a full-on frenzy, often knocking out the person they were having sex with or dragging them under the water too long.

And it was almost never a sinister act. But like a shark to blood, their logic and senses often took a backseat to their instinct and desire for pleasure.

In less than two hours, I would be in a tank with one, letting him take me.

"Sonta." Lilah spoke softly. "I promise you'll be fine. He understands the risks if he hurts you."

I nodded, trying not to drown in my fears. A well-aimed swish of a merperson's tail could knock you out or break your neck. They were *strong*. But I was the Blessed Vessel, and the realm would hunt the merfolk to extinction should this one kill me. All Hoku's mortal daughters had survived the Great Rituals, but that hadn't meant there weren't some close calls over the years.

Soldiers—not just guards—would be in the bedding chamber, armed with spears. They would do their best to preserve my life if things went too far.

"Yay…" I said with weak sarcasm. "If I don't drown, I might get speared in an attempt to save me."

Lilah refused to allow me to wallow. "I thought you preferred men spearing you. And he *will* have the longest cock of your whole Coterie." She wiggled her eyebrows, earning a chuckle. "And it's going to take them a while to prepare for this claiming. If you need help with more practice, I'll hold your head under the water in this very tub until the guards pull me off you."

I laughed, though the attestant was not at all pleased, throwing Lilah a scowl for joking about attempting to murder a goddess's daughter.

"I appreciate the offer, but I'll pass this time."

With the mood lightened, I was more at ease to chat about other things and distract myself. Lilah gave the usual rundown about everything I'd missed out on, and also details about her plans to collect as many lovers as possible for herself and Schamoi during the celebration tonight. I was expected to attend this one, and I told her I'd keep an eye out.

Before the water grew cold, I finished washing myself. I had an extra hour before the merman's claiming so the setup could be completed.

Lilah wrapped me in the tightest hug as I left the dressing room to go to Madam Gaffey's.

Fucking in a tank required practical clothing. I wouldn't want to be weighed down or have something catch, making it harder for me to resurface or fix my positioning. Frankly, it would be safer and easier to enter nude, but I did have *some* sense of modesty with dozens of witnesses, guards, and soldiers watching.

Due to mobility restrictions, my claiming with Chancellor Haan would be different, anyway, held in two parts.

My dress also had two parts to it. Over the simple outfit I'd wear in the tank, I wore a flowy wrap dress made in two shades of coral. It was light and bright.

Owing to the thrashing I would go through, my hair had nothing ornamental in it, and I wore no jewelry. I didn't wear anything perfumed, either, since merfolk were sensitive to foreign scents in their water; we'd been careful to avoid any during my bath, as well.

My anxiety started to return as Madam Gaffey gave me one last look.

"Take care, dear." She pressed her lips into a thin line. "I want to see you happy and well for the last dress change, you understand?"

I choked down the lump in my throat. "Yes. I'll be fine."

My walk to the designated ballroom was slow and contemplative, and on a slightly different route than the others.

The palace was massive, easily spotted from great distances because of its three main towers. The towers belonged to the three primary residents and rulers here—the emperor, the magistrate, and the Blessed Daughter/Blessed Vessel, and their loved ones. The public and official rooms such as the ballrooms rested in the middle of the structure.

It had taken me ages to find my way around the palace when I'd moved in. There were so many pathways and corridors, staircases and gardens. Part of the size of the building was due to the accessibility requirements of the merfolk when they came to visit or live here. Great care had been taken to work in waterways throughout so they would not have to suffer the indignity of being carried to reach most destinations, and they wouldn't be excluded from activities at the seat of the empire.

I personally enjoyed the quiet trickle from the pond in my chambers and the steady flow of water heard from different parts of the palace.

"This way, Your Holiness." One of my guards gestured to me as a reminder to divert from my regular path.

The bedding chamber was adequate for the actual 'bedding,' even for the merman's turn, but not ideal for the initial portion when we took loyalty vows. That part always took place at a lower level so the people could watch.

We arrived with more than enough time for the assembly beyond my curtain to settle. Leonte had just barely begun his speech honoring the merfolk. I tried not to pick at my fingernails as I listened, but allowed my mind to drift. What would my child look like if they were a merfolk mixling? Statistically, merfolk were usually underrepresented in the outcome of the historical Great Ritual.

But the child would be beautiful. They would have patches matching their father's scales, though legs like mine. They'd still have gills, which would enable them to travel to the deep waters of their ancestors, but they would need help due to them missing a tail.

Leonte directly addressed Chancellor Haan, and Haan accepted his place in my Coterie, just as the others had done. That made me smile a little. Soon, we would be a complete group, and we could sort things out beyond the public eye.

After Haan's acceptance, I strode in on cue, holding my head high. I would not show any fear to the people, especially at this closer location.

Haan smiled at me as I strode to his tank. He held himself upright by leaning on the edge of the clear tank, his magnificently muscled tail shimmering a lovely shade of turquoise. My gaze caught on his bare chest, a sheen of brass to his brown skin. His hair was brown, and his eyes were as lovely and mesmerizing as his scales. They were the most inhuman eyes of the lot of my Coterie, with rich purple irises and slits for pupils ideal for deep and dark waters. I admired his earrings with a glance—they were fashioned from shells and urchin spines, a bar, rings, and studs.

They were all rather becoming on him.

I gave him a polite nod, which he returned as we grasped each other's arms. We made the required vow of the Great Ritual. His voice, like all merfolk, was airy yet husky at the same time. It was a beautiful sound that tickled the ears and put me at ease.

Once our vows were made, we released each other. His merfolk witnesses, who had been in a corner of a secondary tank, dove to take the waterways up to the bedding chamber.

"I'll meet you there soon," Haan said.

The kind warmth I had gleaned from him lost a bit of its glow as I accepted what would happen next. "See you soon."

Saltwater & Spears

After leaving the general assembly, I followed my escorts to the bedding chamber. I had to constantly repeat to myself reassurances that this would be fine.

I was strong and well toned—my daily regimen had ensured that.

I was prepared—my pleasure instructors and I had practiced countless times for this encounter.

Multiple security measures had been taken for this—guards with spears, and the setup of the tank itself.

To further soothe my nerves with each step, I recalled visions and journal entries.

Hoku sometimes blessed me with pictures of this world and the people in it. Despite my lack of travel, I had an understanding of others and their ways, and it was no different with merfolk. In my mind, I'd swum in the deepest of seas to breathtaking cities no land-walker had ever truly set eyes on.

Previous Blessed Vessels had also kept records in private journals to share with the next in line. I'd read them all, and all my older divine sisters agreed they had been afraid of the merfolk claiming, but once they'd found that sweet spot between respect for the water and the danger it posed and an inner calm to relax despite it, the sex could be mind-blowing.

I rounded my shoulders as I approached the upper platform's curtain.

The first step is survival. Then we'll see about pleasure.

No announcement halted my approach, though I took a moment to strip free of the outer layer of my dress. Also coral, the bodice of the short dress clung to me as tightly as I'd be hoarding the air in my lungs in a few minutes' time. The dress flared out at my waist, short enough to provide a *little* cover, though barely enough to conceal my ass when dry and upright.

I walked through the curtain, this time taking in all the witnesses and the bonus soldiers with spears in hand. I gulped at that sight in particular.

Poor Elion was again subtly restrained by his alpha father and another witness. He looked terrified, though I couldn't tell if that was genuine concern for my well-being or the mating fever and his need for me.

Hadwin pursed his handsome lips, giving me a solemn nod. Gald, my sweet but mischievous mage, sent me an encouraging smile. Neither my fae nor elf partners seemed all that interested. In the grand scheme of things, who was I to them? Clearly not a lover. Just a twenty-five-year-old girl.

Chancellor Haan already waited for me in the claiming tank, his witnesses in their usual tank to the side.

The claiming tank was not as ornate as the others, due to the safety concerns and ritual requirements. It had been fashioned of thick glass to take a beating, charmed by powerful mages in the emperor's employ to be soft enough to not crack my skull with the force I would be thrashed with. A dozen ropes hung over the edges of the tank, touching the bottom, for me to grasp if I needed more stability, or if I needed to fight my way to the surface for air.

Elion had been a challenge for the attestants with his mating fever, but Haan would be impossible to tear from me without serious force in intervention.

For the most part, I would be on my own in there.

My mouth and pussy were both bone dry as I approached the tank, ready to face my fate. On the side nearest the platform edge where I'd previously vowed myself to my Coterie five times, a set of stairs held three soldiers prepared with spears.

My heart thundered as I reached the steps meant for me on the other side of the tank.

Attestants already surrounded the tank to verify the penetration was valid when he took me.

Haan, in his kind merfolk voice, caught my attention before I climbed the stairs. "Your Holiness?"

I met his eyes. "Yes?"

Propping himself up on the glass with his elbows, he reached both hands for me. I took them in a handshake, grateful for the gesture.

"I regret having missed the original meeting, that we have not had time to get to know each other," he said.

Perhaps that was why I was so nervous. I'd met all the others in the brief meeting before the Great Ritual had even started, but he had been absent.

"I regret that too," I confessed. "But I look forward to getting to know you and learning more about your people." I offered him a weak smile as he still held my hand.

"I look forward to it as well. And I will be as gentle as possible."

While my heart kept its rapid pace, my worries eased a bit. Despite the sheer unadulterated beast that lurked beneath his skin and scales, he was rather considerate. A lot of that probably had to do with his age. Relative to each race's life span, he was the oldest member of my Coterie at the age of forty-eight. While forty-eight was a drop in the bucket for immortals like Tyfen, Hadwin, and Findlech, it was a mature age for a human like me, and the other mortals like Elion and Gald.

"Thank you," I told Haan.

With a nod, he released my hands.

I forced myself to climb the stairs, but froze at the top.

"It's warm," he crooned.

I touched a toe to the water, and he was right. Like all the palace waterways and even the pond in my room, it was a lovely temperature, and slightly salty. I anticipated the salt stinging my eyes as I drew a deep breath. Hopefully the salt would soothe any bruises I got, and wouldn't sting any extra injuries I sustained.

I took the plunge, so to say, lowering myself in. The skirt of my dress floated up, exposing my lower half for all to see. I quickly tamped it down.

Wanting to get it over with, I glanced at his lips, but that would not induce him to take me. Granted, I'd want to be in the right position for it all to happen before he worked himself into a frenzy anyway…

Haan swam up to me at the edge of the tank, bracing himself. "Are you ready?" Had he been a couple of decades younger, he likely would not have asked.

I didn't answer, too afraid the tone of my lie would speak louder than the words. Instead, I did what I needed to.

Wrapping my arms around his neck, I lifted myself, throwing my legs around his body. I positioned myself where I needed to be—skin to scale where his cock would emerge.

"Well done," he whispered, his voice husky and airy.

I gazed into his eyes, begging for my life without saying a word as I gently coaxed him by grinding against him.

The moment he let out a soft guttural moan and gave me a frenzied head bob, there was no going back.

My eyes wide, I tightened my grip on him, chest to chest.

Merman cock was different than that of the land-walkers, and no matter how much I'd prepared myself for this encounter, I couldn't have truly understood the sensation.

Like an eel, his cock was the longest and thinnest of those of my Coterie. It emerged from behind a large central scale, snaking its way to my well-positioned opening. I allowed myself to focus on his insertion, though it happened in the blink of an eye.

Well lubricated, it found its target, entering me, hardening and coiling once his full length was inside me. A slight sharp pain jolted me—the barbed end, like the shifter's knot, had moored inside me.

Long, thin, and flexible were not usually traits associated with a good bedding, but when he filled me—that friction could be exquisite.

Achieving that friction could be deadly.

Still grasping the edge of the tank, he thrust me against the glass with immense force, pulled himself back and thrust again.

The world became a blur as I focused on all my training. I took cautious breaths while my head was above water, so as not to hyperventilate. I gripped him tightly and engaged my muscles to prevent injury.

Haan delivered several thrusts, more hungry and greedy with each one. I allowed myself to relax my pelvic muscles to enjoy his hard work. And damned if it didn't actually feel great, the way he glided in and out, the way he bunched and loosened inside me, stroking and rubbing me differently each time. It was better than any of the tools Lilah or I had for pleasure.

With a particularly rough slam into the tank's glass, my legs became unlatched from his waist.

Shit.

In a split second, I gulped in as much air as I could. His hands pushed off the tank, and that meant only one thing.

Haan grabbed my ass, ramming himself into me, and plunged under the water.

It took me a second to regain my footing, wrapping myself securely around him.

He was merciless in his frenzy, beating me into the tank with each swish of his tail.

My mind raced, what with the pleasure between my legs, the need to hold him tight, and pure gratitude for the mages' work on this tank to keep me safe.

Even merfolk were often scarred from sexual encounters, having their backs and heads pounded into coral and rock with their partner's fervor to plunge deeper and faster.

This tank was large, but still more restrictive than the open sea or a bay. Haan thrashed me, swimming in circles.

I often enjoyed the right kind of pain—the barb pinching inside me as he dug in, my back hitting the wall. As my hair tangled around us and flowed behind me, I even enjoyed the burn building in my lungs.

I did fear, though, that with a wrong move, he would push the wind right out of me.

As the pressure in my chest matched the tightness of his work, I freed a hand, searching for a rope to resurface.

My hand bumped into a rope, but he pulled me along too swiftly for me to get a good grip. I did my best not to panic as my lungs burned.

With no other choice, I let go with both hands, still clutching him with my legs.

The saltwater burning my eyes, I opened them, searching for a rope, and lunged for one, barely snatching it, and holding on for dear life.

He yanked me so hard I nearly screamed from the way it wrenched my shoulders, but to do so would be to let the last of my air go. He released my ass to pull the rest of me closer to him.

Five years. *Five years* I had lived at the Pontaii Palace, and it had not all been tutors and pleasure. I had trained for this, and I could prove I was strong enough to do this, strong enough to bear and raise the next ruler.

With a death grip, I clung to that rope, using all my strength to pull my head to the surface. Haan was all animal instinct, fighting me. In one swift motion, I unhooked my legs and pushed away.

He was still inside me and would be swift to grab me again, but a mere moment of disorientation was all I needed. My window would be short, so I blew out my lungs and yanked myself up with everything I had.

The second my face surfaced, I sucked in a huge breath, barely closing my mouth before he pulled me back under.

He drove deep—into me and to the bottom of the tank, now taking me against the floor. I clutched him and let it happen, praying to Hoku he would come before I ran out of air again.

In another life, I would have enjoyed being a mermaid. Something about the water was so pure and serene, even with him railing me. The bubbles created by his frenzy tickled as they brushed against my skin. The slap of the water against the tank beat to his furious rhythm. His scales scratched me in an oddly satisfying way.

And damn, that dick was something else, the way it slid around, caressing me.

He didn't need to care about tits, lips, or even clits with the way his strokes landed. With each plunge, I grew tenser, warmer, craving him inside me.

It was torture, really. I could not moan, gasp, or call his name, because to do so would be to drown. Had I been above water, I would have done all those things.

Soon enough, my lungs burned again, just as much as my core, and my aching muscles, and my damn pussy begging for a few more well-placed thrusts. The pains all mingled, and I could have cried with how exquisitely it all came to a head.

Lost in pleasure and pain, I almost gave in to the sensation, forgetting the danger. Perhaps it was the haze of near climax, or my brain starved for oxygen, but I started thrusting back between each of his. He reacted in kind and changed his direction, slamming me against the side.

I craved every inch of him inside every inch of me, and the passion nearly drove me senseless. The smallest part of me that clung on to humanity remembered my mother and Lilah, and that I still needed to breathe. This would be the perfect way to die, but I was not ready to do so, and Hoku had blessed me to bring life, not waste it.

Snapping out of my spiral, I opened my eyes again, my lungs pushing past the pleasurable-ache threshold. I grabbed another rope and tried to encourage Haan up with me this time, thrusting while slowly pulling us up.

His speed did not change, but something about his strokes did. He grew thicker with shorter movements—he was as wound up as I was, so close to going over the edge.

I didn't gain much ground with my pulling on the rope, but I held fast.

Haan found his release, slamming my ass against the glass.

Goddess help me.

My own rush of release soon found me as his explosive seed filled me like I'd never experienced before.

I moaned, expelling all my air.

In a panic, I yanked the rope for dear life, and Haan came with me, not resisting, merely keeping me against the glass with each pulse of his cock.

My face crested the water, and I gasped—for air and for pleasure, unable to control myself.

I didn't even open my eyes as I panted out, "I'm fine!"

Haan's strokes dwindled in power as he milked himself inside me; that sweet ache and friction ran chills down my spine.

After a moment, he more firmly pressed himself into me against the glass, and reached for the edges to keep his cock inside me.

I fought for air still, my lungs calming, my orgasm so fresh.

It was done. I'd survived.

I opened my eyes, instantly startled by the soldiers above me. They stood, anxious, spears aimed in front of me.

"I'm fine," I quickly reassured them.

They stepped back, more at ease.

Haan still pulsed inside me, now resting his head against my chest. Each pulse brought a moan to my lips.

He soon resurfaced, holding himself to me.

I always enjoyed those sweet moments with lovers, right after we'd both found satisfaction.

With Haan more aware of his surroundings and what had happened, concern shaded those slitted eyes. "Are you hurt?" he asked.

I clung to him and pecked him on the lips. "I'm great."

He gave me a warm smile. His cock twitched within me as he shrank, the attestants intensely watching our connection through the tank.

His barb released me, and his cock uncoiled and receded despite his efforts to stay inside me, which was to be expected. He'd all but tucked himself behind his opening scale when the required time was met, the announcement made, and the curtains of the bedding chamber closed.

Not a whisper rose from the thousand listeners below, nor from the dozens of witnesses in the bedding chamber. I dared to glance around the room, only to find dropped jaws and blinking wide eyes. That gave me an odd sense of pride, actually.

It was unlikely any in this assembly had seen a merperson take a land-walker, and the walker had walked away.

An attestant cleared their throat. "Privacy." A reminder for those in the room to vacate, save a few guards and officials.

I stayed there, fully aware my ass was on display against the glass, not really caring because of my triumph. It was a special kind of high to thwart death, to freely breathe again.

Haan stayed pressed against me, as if shielding or protecting me as everyone left. "You did well."

I couldn't refrain from smiling at the praise. "And you showed great restraint." It truly could have been much worse.

He surprised me by leaning in, touching his lips to mine. He didn't properly pucker them or really do anything, but it was a sweet gesture.

"What was that for?"

He searched my eyes. "A kiss."

I ran a hand through his wet hair. "But merfolk don't kiss for pleasure."

His grin was sweet. "And humans don't usually risk their lives to spin in the water with us."

My smile brightened. I was grateful he was making an effort, no matter how poor the delivery or unbalanced the gesture. "I really do look forward to getting to know you more, Haan. I mean, Chancellor."

"Haan," he murmured. "As do I, Sonta."

Somehow, despite the ache of every muscle in my body, I wanted more of him, more time in this water. But the time wasn't right.

"I should let you go." He backed away.

I made my way to my stairs. Luckily, the water in the tank was filtered quickly, so the murkiness our activity had created had all disappeared. "I'll see you at the celebration?"

He nodded. "Of course."

19

Titles & Tiaras

very muscle throbbed as I made my way back to my chambers. My legs even shook. I dripped a path behind me, but I smiled all the way.

I'd done it. I'd managed each of my Coterie partners.

I was taken aback when I entered my dressing room. My mother paced the floor.

"Mammi?"

Her attention shot to me at once. "Are you all right?" She rushed to me and hugged me.

I hugged her back. "I'm perfectly fine. You didn't need to leave the celebration." She must have rushed out of the ballroom to beat me to my room.

"Are you injured?" She pulled back and assessed me.

"I'm…" I hesitated to lie. "You don't need to worry. I'm well taken care of."

The door to my dressing room burst open, and Lilah strode in, not a word escaping her lips. She didn't need to utter anything—her reaction was painted on her face. Her eyes were wide, her jaw agape.

"How bad was it?" my mother asked her.

"That was…" Lilah glanced between us, assessing whether she should be honest. "It was interesting, but Sonta had it all under control."

"You're a horrible liar, Lilah. You always have been," my mother scolded like we were little girls getting into mischief again.

I took my mother by the shoulders. "It's a waste to fret over something that has already happened. I made it out and completed the claimings—that's all that matters."

She hugged me again. "Promise me you won't go into the waters with him again."

I glanced at Lilah over my mother's shoulder. She lifted an eyebrow in question. Truthfully, I couldn't make that promise. "You don't have to worry about me."

"That's not a promise, Sonta," Mother whispered.

I rested my head against hers. "You're getting your dress all wet."

"I don't care. If I ever meet Hoku in person, I'll…"

"Don't blaspheme her, Mammi. She has good intentions."

I stood there a moment, growing colder from my sopping clothes and hair, allowing her to hold me.

A knock sounded at the door, and an attendant cracked it open.

A man cleared his throat in the hallway. "I am so sorry to invade your privacy like this, Sonta, but did Vesta come here?" It was Kernov, concern in his voice.

I fought a full smile. He'd not only called my mother by her given name, but he'd left his place by the magistrate to come find her after she'd left in a panic. "You can come in."

He hesitated. "You're … dressed?"

I released my mother. "Yes." A servant had offered me a robe as I'd left the bedding chamber.

Kernov really was dashing. He surveyed us as he entered. All the attendants stood around, waiting to do their jobs while we held our conversation.

He inclined his head to my mother. "I told you she would be safe." His gaze turned to me. "You *are* well, aren't you?"

Every single muscle screamed, but I kept my composure. "Yes. Unless I stand here too long like a damp rat and catch a sickness, instead of climbing into the hot bath these lovely people have drawn for me." I faced my mother. "Go with Kernov. Go dance. Have fun. No harm will come to me while I ready myself for the celebration."

She considered, and Kernov held out a hand. "Come, Vesta." His beckon was soft and sweet.

Nodding, she cast one more glance in my direction. "I'll see you soon?"

"Of course."

Lilah and I silently watched as they left, Kernov giving me a half smile as he rested a hand on my mother's back.

The moment the door closed, Lilah returned her attention to me, her eyes wide. "That was madness."

I let out a breathy chuckle, peeling myself out of the robe and soaked dress. Two attendants rushed to help me, and I soon sighed in relief, stepping into the piping hot tub sprinkled with aromatic flower petals in my bathing room.

"Truthfully," Lilah demanded, sitting at the foot of the tub again. "You're all right?"

I rubbed my arms. My hands were raw from the rope, but it was soothing to start my massage. "Yes. I'm just sore."

Without hesitation, she reached in and rubbed one of my calves. I moaned.

"I don't know whether to be angry with your divine mother for putting you in that position, or in awe that you handled that so well."

I simply smiled wide.

The next little while was a rush of attendants helping me. They gave me a tincture to help ease the salty sting in my eyes, as well as a soothing tea for my aches and pains, my head included.

We found a few bruises developing, but I always healed rather quickly.

Lilah didn't stay too long, returning to the celebration at my urging to check on my mother and keep Schamoi company.

I wanted peace and quiet, anyway. The tub did wonders as I soaked, and my masseuse arrived when I was ready. I would label him a god by the way he worked me and tended to each ache.

I did my required meditation while he helped me, and half my supplication was gratitude for making it through the two big nights of the Great Ritual. I could breathe more easily now.

Instead of heading to bed, I plodded along to Madam Gaffey's room for one last dress change.

She gave me the brightest smile as I entered. "We all knew you would be successful."

Liar. "Thank you."

"Come now, they're all waiting for your arrival. Let's make haste."

An assistant swiftly handed me a mug of tea. "Spiced to help invigorate you."

I guzzled it, happy for the gift. Tonight's celebration would last all night, and I wished for my bed to rest, but duty called.

It didn't take long for the herbs to kick in, bringing me renewed strength and alertness. Madam Gaffey and her assistants rushed about, braiding my hair and setting some curls. They weaved fine strands of gold into my locks.

After stripping my robe off, they fitted me into my last gown of the night. It was possibly the most regal thing I'd ever worn—a deep royal purple that flowed to the floor. The sleeves were loose, somewhat transparent, and cuffed at the wrists. I would have liked something off the shoulder, but this was better to hide bruising.

It was backless, though, with a flattering neckline, and they used cosmetic cream to help conceal any injuries.

I smiled at how much the dress glittered in the lights. A thousand crystals had been sewn into it—enough to dazzle, but not so many as to weigh it down.

They went heavier with the cosmetics this time, darkening my eyeline with black to a sharp point, giving me a blush on my cheeks, and tinting my lips a glowing deep red.

All that remained was the jewelry. A necklace draped around my neck—gold, custom made for this event. The casting was intricate, encompassing official symbols for each territory of our empire, as well as the empire's symbol itself. Hoku's likeness and ancient script for 'Blessed Vessel' rested on the other side. I faced that side out as I made my formal debut as the Blessed Vessel, keeping the other side close to my heart.

My earrings were light but dangly, matching the sparkle of my dress, and the crowning touch was, well, a tiara.

I rarely wore one, as it wasn't often required or even appropriate. My place as the Blessed Daughter had not been as high as it was now as the Blessed Vessel, and once my child ascended the throne as emperor or empress, I would again take a backseat.

But this was *my* time, and my cheeks hurt from smiling at how elegant I looked.

Madam Gaffey held a hand over her heart, admiring me as well. "You're lovely."

I couldn't dawdle, though. My escort and attestant strode alongside me through the palace corridors. The clack of my shoes punctuated the silence. I grew giddy with each footstep.

I couldn't wait to see my mother and Kernov, Lilah and Schamoi. And my Coterie. And the rulers. And the people.

There would be food—and I was starving again—as well as dance and merriment. It was a celebration of life and unity.

When I arrived at the grand ballroom, I had to wait a bit. Guards notified the emperor and magistrate that I'd arrived, and the music faded away. The people hushed, and the announcement was made that I was to enter.

I wrung my hands, my heart beating without mercy.

"Her Holiness, the daughter of divinity herself, may she bring forth renewed peace to our realm—Sonta Gwynriel, the Blessed Vessel."

I drew a deep breath as the doors opened for me. Collectively, hundreds of people bowed as I walked in. Even the emperor and magistrate bowed.

Swallowing, I remained confident. I strode to the platform the emperor and magistrate sat on, my footfalls echoing in the massive room.

Once I reached them, I held out my hands, first to Magistrate Leonte.

He stood, raising his hands to hold mine. "May your health and happiness endure for your service."

I gave him a nod of thanks, and he released my hands, then I approached the emperor.

He took my hands as well, a soft smile on the elegant lines of his half-elven face. "May your wisdom be beyond your years in your service."

I thanked him with another nod.

I had practiced every step, every word so many times. It didn't seem real that we were finally here.

A third and central throne sat at the top of the platform, especially for me. It was a temporary spot, an honorary place, but I had been born for this, and I would not shrink from the honor or responsibility.

I turned and stood before my place, surveying the hundreds of people in the room, all still bowed.

"I am honored to serve you as the daughter of Hoku." I wanted to mention my mortal mother as well because she had done everything for me, but to do so would stray too far from protocol, too far from what she would even be comfortable with.

I continued. "I happily accept this seat before you in the hopes of further unity and prolonged peace. May my divine mother multiply her blessings for us all."

In unison, they echoed the sentiments for Hoku's blessings, rising to meet my gaze.

I smiled in awe. Every eye was on me, and I was so humbled to not only have the weight of the realm on me, but also the support of it.

Taking my seat on the throne, I minded my posture, nodding to the people.

The emperor was swift to speak next. "We are honored on this occasion of the Great Ritual, to celebrate Her Holiness and her Coterie, and all the noble leaders of this realm. Please, enjoy yourselves."

The orchestra struck up a new tune, and attendees began to rustle, though many eyes remained glued to me. I wouldn't stay on the throne all night, but I remained for the time being.

Lilah and Schamoi smiled. So did Mother and Kernov. My heart melted at his arm around her. I avoided direct eye contact with my Coterie, a little nervous about moving forward.

Most people still wore a look of awe. I couldn't decipher if it was respect for the title or shock that I'd just survived a spin in the water with a merman. To be fair, the merfolk seemed less shocked as they mingled from their tank on the west side of the room.

Next to me, the emperor leaned toward me. "Well done, Sonta."

The simple praise brought me so much joy. "Thank you, Your Magnificence."

After a few minutes, I made eye contact with Kernov. He stood from the table he shared with my mother, Lilah and the others. With the poise of the magistrate's top advisor, he strode to me, taking the stairs to the platform.

"Your Holiness." He grinned, then pressed my hand to his forehead. "It would be my honor to escort you this evening."

It was merely a formality to release me from the throne for the celebration, but I was glad for it.

"Thank you. I accept." I stood, taking his arm. We descended together, into the heart of the lively room.

20

Little Dove

The room grew louder with chatter and the clinking of dishes. While Kernov wouldn't be at my side all night, he did escort me for a while as we made our rounds, greeting the rulers again—most of whom I'd briefly met right before all the claimings.

The fae king and queen were first. They were elegantly dressed, and the queen had lovely earrings accenting the soft point of her ears.

We offered each other a small bow.

"Congratulations," the king uttered.

"We wish you happiness and fruitfulness," she said.

"Thank you."

A servant swooped in, placing goblets in my and Kernov's hands.

Prince Tyfen stood next to his parents, wearing his usual disinterested expression. I waited for him to say something, but he didn't.

"Tyfen is … shy…" his mother excused. "But I assure you he's *humbled* to be a member of your Coterie. It truly is a *great honor* for him."

His bright green eyes met mine. "An honor."

He'd said it so blandly, so insincerely, that the statement stung with the same insult as the assessment he'd given me right before bedding me, right after stripping me down unnecessarily before the witnesses.

I gave him a curt smile. It was a shame he had the largest cock, yet the foulest personality.

Kernov—often my savior—picked up on the mutual distaste. "Please do reach out if you have any concerns. We'll take our leave so as to allow Her Holiness to make her rounds before tiring."

The royal family accepted the excuse.

Kernov only hummed his curiosity after we were out of earshot. I forced a smile. "I'm not everyone's cup of tea."

He nodded his understanding, but I feared his disappointment. Tyfen and I hadn't really had enough interaction to be so properly cross with each other, and it was kind of my responsibility to not only choose wisely, but also to keep people's love and respect for me, especially my own Coterie.

"Things will settle," Kernov assured me as we visited the next set of rulers.

It was refreshing to have his support as I faced each of these noble people, and each of my Coterie, after having been fucked repeatedly so publicly.

The elves were their usual selves—tall, proper, of few words.

The vampires were accepting, Duke Hadwin wearing a fond smile while glancing at my neck for his mark.

Gald and his fellow mages were charming yet aloof.

Chancellor Haan and his party of merfolk were eager to chat. I hadn't formally met most of them, and they were kind. My cheeks warmed a bit at the proximity to Haan so soon after our claiming.

One table we didn't dawdle at was the shifter head table. Poor Elion was beyond pale, even sickly. So as not to slight the shifters, we cautiously approached just to share a word.

His parents carefully greeted us.

"We're so happy you're well," his mother said.

"Thank you for your service," Elion's father said.

They stood as a barrier between us.

"I need you," Elion blurted in a shaky whisper, cracking my heart in two.

I swallowed, making eye contact. His mating fever made it tremendously hard to control himself. It also had an effect on me—I was already wet for him.

"Your Holiness, we should—" Kernov started.

"Please," Elion begged.

His parents frowned, making it clear it would be a kindness for me to back away. None of us wanted him to be shamed, to make an embarrassment of himself.

And I wouldn't dare reach a hand out to shake or soothe. If I let him so much as touch me, he'd take me, right then and there in front of hundreds.

"Soon," I promised, letting Kernov steer me away.

"It's his youth," Kernov quietly assured me. "It will pass."

A part of my heart remained with Elion as Kernov and I walked toward other empire officials, chatting.

I was beyond grateful when the formalities ended. Most commoners wouldn't dare to approach the Blessed Vessel on this eve. The few times I'd gone out in public since my formal debut, children had happily swooped in to greet me, but the Great Ritual wasn't exactly a place for small eyes and ears. Few commoners had even been invited.

My stomach protested over how long it had been since the feast, and Kernov led me to his table. I sat with him and my closest loved ones while servants left to fetch me food.

Luckily, my mother had calmed. "You look lovely."

"Thank you. And I'm feeling much better."

"You do look *stunning*, Sonta," Lilah praised. Her tone carried the softness of my lifelong best friend.

"Thanks."

Schamoi simply shrugged. "Not bad."

I glared.

He chuckled. "Don't tell me you've been starved for compliments lately."

I couldn't resist laughing. The servants were quick to bring me food, and I dug in—as much as I could in a civilized fashion. We chatted and reminisced for quite some time.

Nostalgia sank in again. I would miss Schamoi's laughter and smile. "You're sure you want to move out tomorrow?" I took a bite of pastry.

A small frown on his lips, he nodded. "My time here is done. I'll only be in the way."

My emotions hit me so hard, tears pricking at my eyes. "I'll miss you."

"Don't you dare," he said.

I subtly wiped away a tear and took another bite, averting my gaze. Had we been in private, he would have held me, would have taken my hand to reassure me, would have kissed me.

But we were in public, and the Great Ritual had begun. It wasn't appropriate for any romantic or sexual partners outside my Coterie to claim my affections or time, least of all a former pleasure instructor.

He did comfort me under the table, though, his foot gently stroking my calf. "Even little doves have to learn to fly."

I bit my lip, nodding. "I would ask you to dance if I could." Sharing a table with him was already pushing the bounds of propriety, given our former relationship.

His eyes were soft. "And I would have loved it."

Lilah sipped her wine. "He's not forbidden from visiting, or even dancing on another night. He's not *dying*, Sonta."

"I know…"

"Another night," he said.

"Plus…" Lilah leaned into him, slipping her hand under the table. "He might have more than one reason to visit now and then."

He glanced at her, a question in his gaze.

A wicked smile grew on her lips, and I didn't have to guess what magic she worked with her hand under the table. How had it only been this morning they'd shared my bed, and I'd watched them as I pleasured myself?

Apparently, Lilah had enjoyed it enough to make another offer. I hoped Schamoi wouldn't get too wrapped up in her seduction, though. He *was* the exception rather than the rule when it came to her preferences, after all. I enjoyed the idea of them happy in bed, but neither would truly make each other happy in any sort of long-term romantic relationship.

My mother claimed my attention, asking another question. Conversation ebbed and flowed, and the food was exquisite.

Lilah eventually returned her focus to me. "So, are you going to introduce me to these important people so I can find new … friends?"

I held back a laugh. She wouldn't waste an opportunity to find new partners, especially not exotic ones like shifters or vampires.

"I would be glad to."

"No merfolk," she quickly added. "Well, not that I wouldn't be happy to meet them, but…"

But she wasn't all that interested in being thrashed by a merman with the risk of injury or worse, even if the ladies all had their breasts on full display for her to ogle.

"Noted." I sipped my drink again, and stood.

Lilah followed suit, downing the rest of her goblet of wine. "Did you want to join us, Schamoi?" She grinned.

It wouldn't be proper for me to go around introducing him as my former lover, and she knew that. And only the two of them knew how long and how well she'd stroked him under the table.

Blinking, Schamoi gave her a tight-lipped smile. "I think I'll stay here, thank you."

It was cruel of her, but also funny to see him so out of sorts when he was normally so confident.

"Come on, Lilah."

She joined me, and we had fun making more rounds. As the wine took hold of people's courage, the celebration eased from its formality, and we chatted with several commoners, along with several dignitaries. I tried not to approach the actual rulers, but general groups.

Having spent plenty of time with me here at the palace, Lilah now acted the part of a proper lady—charming everyone she spoke to. She quickly gained friends in a way I never had. When we were young, I didn't have all that many friends, and that was likely due to poverty as well as unrecognized signs of my divine calling.

After I became a teenager, much of my attention turned to my enormous sex drive. While she experimented with other girls, I'd found more than enough company with young men. At least the girls seemed to enjoy her personality. The young men, well, they enjoyed the ample opportunities I gave them when we were out of the view of adults.

As an adult now, as the Blessed Daughter and now Blessed Vessel, everyone loved me. But few knew my heart.

"There's no greater gift than having been raised with Sonta as my closest friend," Lilah told a group of vampires. She rested a hand on my bare back, and I had to stop myself from leaning into her.

I smiled at her. "And Lilah's amazing."

Lilah wouldn't be so bold or foolish as to openly ask anyone here to accompany her back to her room, at least not without another goblet or two of wine, but she dropped her subtle hints.

Duke Hadwin approached, joining the conversation. His deep bloodred eyes had softened to hazel again, and his smile made him immensely approachable. "I'm glad you're well."

He made my heart flutter in a way none of the others had, and my cheeks were suddenly on fire. "Thank you." I looked forward to bedding him again, and craved his cool touch.

"Sonta," a familiar voice called behind me.

Gald joined us, nodding to Hadwin. "Hope you don't mind me interrupting." He took my hand, lifting it and placing a kiss on my wrist where our magical bond had been inked. "Would you dance with me?"

My brain stuttered. People had danced the whole night in the center of the room, but I had not intended to. "It's … not really traditional…" The Blessed Vessel didn't usually dance at the celebration, mostly because people assumed she was tired. They weren't wrong.

He still held my hand, stroking it with his thumb. "I like breaking tradition. You look remarkably well, and it would be great evidence of your strength to be seen making the effort, would it not?"

I couldn't put a finger on it, but Gald had a way of making me question every motive while simultaneously tearing down any barrier.

"Or are you afraid of what people will think?" He leaned in, whispering into my ear. "Because they already know what we've done, right?"

I bit back a laugh. "You're not wrong."

"Dance with me."

I let my hesitation go. It wasn't against divine protocol for me to dance, after all. "One dance."

"Lovely." He led me to the dance floor and rested his hands on my hips. "Thank you for accepting."

His brilliant blue eyes and curly red hair gave him a boyish look that contrasted with his sexy piercings and sharp clothing—he'd shed his ceremonial robe before approaching me.

"You like dancing?" I asked.

"I do. And you?"

"I only started lessons when I moved here, so I'm not that great, but I'm learning."

"I think you're doing quite well. In all aspects." He pulled me closer.

"Are you being honest? Or flirting with me? Or flattering me?"

He smirked. "It can't be all of them?"

I narrowed my eyes. He liked playing, and while I enjoyed a good game, I wouldn't risk my heart on someone who put on appearances solely to get more time in my bed for politics.

Gald laughed. "I do like what I know of you. I've followed your journey since you were formally presented at the palace as our new Blessed Daughter. You come from humble beginnings, like me."

I'd learned as much about his childhood as he likely had about mine, but I hadn't realized he had followed my journey from its inception.

"And despite any political motive, I *do* like you. I think we'll get along great." He glided his fingers across the small of my back as he turned me. "And I'm attracted to you. I do believe I got rather hard watching your ass pressed against that tank glass."

My mouth went dry. He had teased about looking forward to having me under him again. "You're horrible to say something like that in such a public place."

He had no shame whatsoever. "Are you telling me you're not attracted to me as well?"

I cocked my head, assessing him, nearly missing a step in the dance.

"You wound me with your delay."

I rolled my eyes. He wasn't the type I'd naturally gravitate toward. It was probably the hair. But I still liked him, and he'd done a good job in the bedding chamber. I was particularly grateful for him covering me and standing up for me when the attestants got too pushy. I returned his sentiments. "I like what I know of you so far. I think we'll get along well. As for ass to glass, I can't say, but I look forward to learning what you can do with your magic."

A greedy glint lit his gaze as the song ended. "I'll do my best."

21

DARING DANCES

No sooner had Gald and I stopped dancing than Lord Findlech approached. "Are you up for another dance, Your Holiness?"

Findlech? The man who bedded me like it was a chore? What excuse did I really have to turn him down?

"Of course. I'm honored." I thanked Gald for the dance, and Findlech took my hand.

The orchestra struck a new tune, this time a traditional elvish one. Only then did I realize how many eyes were still glued to me, that they had paid attention to my dancing, and to my partner.

"Interesting choice," Findlech observed.

"What choice?"

He lifted an eyebrow, gliding me across the floor with impeccable grace. He'd had over eight hundred years to practice dancing, so he'd better be good at it.

"Breaking tradition to dance," he said.

I shrugged. "It's just a dance."

"Is it? *Just* a dance?"

Perhaps it was the tone of his voice, or his intimidating height and pointed ears, or the sheer difference in our ages, but his questions were loaded with judgment.

"I'd have thought the Blessed Vessel understood her position in this capital and this realm. *All* you do, especially now, will be scrutinized."

I stood taller. "I understand that. I'm following all protocol, and dancing does not taint me."

"But it speaks to your favoritism." He smiled. "Hundreds watched as you danced with a mage first. It makes a statement."

"You don't like mages?"

He didn't miss a step as the dance sped up. "I have no quarrels at all. I'm simply analyzing the situation as anyone would when they understand the politics of your partners."

Elves could be so cold and calculating, and I hated to stereotype them, but he was getting on my nerves rather quickly.

"I appreciate your feedback, Lord Findlech. I'll take that into consideration." I gave him a sickeningly sweet smile—since he was so keen on making sure the people watching had a good show. He hadn't come to dance with me as a partner, or even to offer advice. He'd swooped in after Gald to make a public statement. He wasn't the first to dance with me, but he refused to be the last.

Neither of us could openly disrespect each other at the moment, not with him in my Coterie, but I wasn't always the best at keeping my mouth closed.

"I think we should come to an agreement," I said.

"And what is that?"

I kept my voice low as I leaned in. "I gather you prefer silence when you fuck me. I can be fine with that. But I think I'd prefer silence when dancing with you, thank you very much."

He spun me, unfazed. "As you wish, Your Holiness. The information was kindly shared."

"No, it wasn't."

He gazed into my eyes. "Paying special attention to only two-thirds of your Coterie on such a monumental night is an interesting choice. Or have you worked out how you'll dance with the chancellor, or your new shifter mate?"

My heart dropped into my stomach. He was right. I wouldn't be crawling into the water again in this dress, and I wouldn't risk it with Elion in this room full of people. I averted my eyes, throwing my full attention into the dance for the remainder of it.

"A pleasure," he said, releasing me with a bow as the song ended.

"Likewise," I lied.

He stepped away, revealing Hadwin. Hadwin gave me the kindest smile. My gut twisted at the confirmation of my idiocy—they would all want attention. But Hadwin's warm presence was also comforting.

"Rumor has it the Blessed Vessel is dancing with her Coterie tonight," he said, offering his hand.

I accepted. "Rumors are often unreliable and shouldn't always be trusted."

He smirked, pulling me in. "Wise words."

Only then did the orchestra start a traditional vampire song.

Hadwin slid his hand to my back. His cold touch sent a shiver down my spine.

"Sorry." He took his hand back.

"No. I like it."

Narrowing his eyes a bit, he returned his hand, caressing my bare back.

"How are you enjoying the celebration?" I asked.

"It's lively, though I'll confess… The merfolk renditions of all the songs are not my favorite."

I agreed. "Compromise." Merfolk were sensitive to certain pitches and sounds, so the orchestra played music that would not offend their ears at the event. It was always a bit more somber and off-tune in my opinion.

"Are you all right?" Hadwin asked, his voice soft, his expression mildly concerned.

"Yes?" Was he asking about the music still? No, surely he was referring to the tank adventure. "I'm fine. I wasn't seriously hurt. I've practiced a lot for the claimings, though I'm glad they're over."

He nodded, then pulled me to him. It wasn't sensual the way Gald had done it, but more like a hug.

"I was also talking about your last dance partner," he whispered. "You seemed … unhappy."

"Oh…" *Great…* I'd done a horrible job at disguising my frustration.

Something told me I could be honest with Hadwin. "Findlech and I just don't see eye to eye. Not my favorite."

"Hmm. Picking favorites already?" His lips brushed my ear. "A mate might wonder what the lineup looks like."

"I… Well, no. Just…"

He chuckled. "You don't have to explain yourself, darling."

Darling… He instantly put me at ease.

"I look forward to getting to know you more, Hadwin." I was sincere. He was sweet and thoughtful, playful and charming, and I knew practically nothing about him.

Most older generations of vampires shared their genealogy with pride, but Hadwin's was not public knowledge.

"And I look forward to knowing you better."

We chatted more as he led me. In all honesty, his dance steps were not the smoothest, but he still did a great job. He commented on how delightful Lilah was, how it was obvious she and I had grown up around vampires. I didn't dare ask on her behalf if any in his company were into human women—we weren't there yet.

I could have spent all night in Hadwin's arms, chatting and swaying, but the song came to an end.

Panicking, I debated if I should ask what I wanted. "Would you … like a spot next to me tonight?" My giant bed would finally fulfill its purpose—fitting my entire Coterie on it. While we wouldn't share every night, it was tradition for them to all join the Blessed Vessel on the first night together.

I instantly regretted asking as Hadwin searched my eyes. I was being too forward, too vulnerable.

"I would love nothing more." He lifted my hand, kissing it. "I look forward to it."

Butterflies flitted in my stomach. "Thank you."

He bid me farewell, returning to his fellow vampires.

And I stood there, like a fool, expecting a fourth member of my Coterie to be lined up to dance with me. Part of me wanted to cry from how mortifying it was to have all eyes on me. Even the orchestra waited for a cue. Elion wouldn't be allowed to approach me, and Haan certainly wouldn't drag himself from the tank to make an attempt.

Tyfen.

I didn't even care to dance with him, but the expectation had been set, and he wasn't there.

Panicking, I made eye contact with Lilah. Her eyes were wide, and she dropped her conversation, striding toward me.

"Your Holiness." Tyfen addressed me from behind. "A dance?"

I turned, snatching his hand so the orchestra would start up. They saved my pride by doing so to the tune of a popular fae song.

Tyfen held me, his face casual. "I hate this song. Out of all the options, it has to be this one?"

I pursed my lips, angry he had made me wait. Had it just been theatrics to throw me off again, like his exhibitionism? His criticism of the song only dug deeper.

"I think it's a great song," I snipped. "They chose it because it's one I've memorized the steps to."

He hummed. "Right… Inexperienced, so they picked an easy one."

Prick. He was an *absolute* prick. "I'm sorry if my mortality isn't *sufficient* for you. I haven't had two centuries to master all your dances, but somehow, Hoku considers me worthy."

He bunched his eyebrows. "You certainly are a feisty one, aren't you?"

I glared, visions of daggers to his throat dancing in my mind. The barely sane part of me forced restraint, softening. People were watching.

Smiling, I straightened. "You're here to impregnate me, Your Highness. That's all. It takes more than a nice ass and cock to earn my favor in bed. You should remember that."

His asinine smile was smug. "I appreciate the compliment."

I gaped. "Which one of us had their head bashed into glass tonight? I tell you I find your personality detestable, and that's a compliment?"

He slid his hand to cup my ass, right there in front of everyone, pressing into me. "You said you like my ass and cock."

I blinked. How had that slipped out? "I…"

"It's okay. I've been known to leave women speechless."

My ears burned as I stood tall to whisper into his. "Take your hand off my ass, or you'll lose your cock."

He took his time sliding it up to my back. The picture of regality, he smiled. "You think you're rather important, don't you? To threaten a member of your own Coterie? To threaten a prince of the fae kingdom—arguably the greatest influence in this empire?"

My temper had gotten away with me again, but he'd earned every bit of it. "I think *I'm* important? You're the *second-born* prince. And we *both* came by our positions by birth. How many people in this realm can say they have a goddess for a mother?"

Only one at the moment.

Right when I thought I'd gotten him, he humbled me further. "You aren't the first Blessed Vessel in my lifetime, and you won't be the last." He pursed his lips, looking away. "Beyond my responsibility to my people, you mean nothing to me."

My anger turned to pain. Why did his barbs dig so deep? Why did I even care?

We finished the dance in silence; it took all I had to put on a brave face for the crowd. Lilah certainly didn't buy it.

At the end of the dance, he pulled back. I glanced up at him. "You know, tonight…" I stopped before I said something I couldn't take back. I almost told him he could join the others in my room, but he should sleep in the pond with Haan, and that he should keep his head under the water indefinitely.

"Never mind." I walked away.

Lilah headed toward me again, but I brushed her off with a slight shake of the head.

I didn't want to be rescued. I didn't want to be seen as weak and unwanted. Instead, I continued on my path, straight for the merfolk tank.

The orchestra began playing a human tune—merfolk instruments didn't work above the water, and the orchestra was only composed of land-walkers.

"Haan," I said, a giant smile on my face.

He greeted me with a return smile. "Sonta."

"Are you enjoying yourself?"

"I am. I hope you'll forgive me for not joining you on the dance floor. What do land-walkers sometimes say? I have two left feet?"

I chuckled. "Yes." Maybe it was rude of me to overdo the flirting to compensate, but I took advantage of the situation, resting my hands on his flexed biceps as he held the edge of the tank. "I appreciate spending time with you nonetheless."

We chatted for several minutes, and I enjoyed getting to know his people more. When it came to a natural pause in the conversation, I leaned in to ask him about his sleeping preferences.

"You're welcome in the bed with the others if you'd like tonight. But I'm assuming you'd prefer the pond in my chambers."

"Yes, I would."

I grasped his hand. "All right. I just wanted to be sure."

As the evening waxed late, I considered how I would honor Elion with my time for the sake of public scrutiny. I couldn't give him a dance, and I couldn't hold his hands or biceps and just chat.

But … I could give him *something*.

22

Secret Hookups

After a brief request to a guard, I cautiously approached Elion's group. His father held his arm while his mother stopped me several feet from the table.

He whimpered for me, and the mating bond even strained on me, my body craving him.

"We understand you're not able to dance with him," his mother said softly. "Please." She frowned.

I wasn't there to torture him, or really even to give him extra attention for the public eye. Everyone could see how much he struggled, and the simple gesture of me acknowledging him would have to be enough. That wasn't the full reason I had come to talk.

"I can help him," I whispered.

She angled her head. "Are you retiring for the night?"

Not yet. It would still be at least another hour or two before it would be acceptable to head to my chambers, pulling my entire Coterie from the celebration.

"No, but there's another way." I leaned in and gave her instructions, directions. Many Blessed Vessels before me had found a way to see to their desperate mate's needs during the long celebration, and so could I.

I stepped back from my conspiratorial whisper. "As long as you can ensure he's discreet. And that he waits the allotted time."

She nodded. "We can make that happen."

I gave her a smile and a handshake. "I'm glad to help."

"We like you," she added before releasing my hands.

That warmed my heart. "I like you, too. You should meet my mother."

She said she would, and I left her, finally returning to Lilah.

"Is it always going to be this way?" Lilah asked.

I blew out a breath. "I hope things calm down. But right now, I need your help."

"Anything."

Cupping my hand to her ear, I shared my secret.

"*Sonta*," she chastised in feigned shock. "How naughty. You need help with a distraction? I can down another goblet of wine and break my ankle or something."

I laughed. "Not something so self-sacrificing or worrisome. Just leave the room with me. Give me an alibi, that way if he and I are missing at the same time, people may not put two and two together."

Lilah gave me a seductive look, biting her lip. "Do I get to watch?"

"It's a small room…"

She shrugged. "How utterly selfish."

I jabbed a finger into her arm, and she giggled.

"Come on, Sonta." She hooked her arm through mine. "Let's find that washroom." She spoke entirely too loud for our formal surroundings, but I didn't bother to look ashamed.

We made eye contact and waved at Schamoi as we strode for a private door. He would be a witness to two best friends leaving, not me and a member of my Coterie.

A guard nodded as we approached, allowing us access. Very few people were allowed this exit, and I was luckily one of them.

"Isn't it nice not having an attestant follow you everywhere now?" Lilah asked.

"Yes!" It was beyond refreshing. The moment I'd entered the ballroom for the celebration, the restriction had been lifted. "No more shadows."

We turned down a dark corridor, and she took my hand. "If he doesn't show, *we* could…"

I halted. "Lilah, don't." Her even mentioning intimacy with me tugged at my heartstrings.

"Kidding." Her tone was less than convincing. "I only meant kissing. Kissing is still allowed, just not the full thing, right?"

It was iffy. My loyalty *should* be strictly to my Coterie until I birthed, but it wasn't like the attestants had protested what they'd seen of us already.

"Are you really going to be okay?" I asked, resting my hands on her hips. "Because it's not like you and I are…"

"I know. We're not exclusive. Our friendship comes first." She pressed her forehead to mine. "I'm being selfish. I just don't like being told I can't have something." She held my waist. "Sorry. I didn't mean to make you feel guilty. I was only trying to have some fun."

It would be bad if Elion walked in on us embracing—his fever and jealousy would go wild. But he *was* supposed to wait several minutes…

I leaned in, pressing my lips to hers. She took the opening, holding me tight, gliding her tongue against mine, sliding her hand inside my plunging dress to caress my breasts.

It was a stolen moment between lovers, and every ounce of me again regretted not letting her finish me yesterday in her room. Fully aware of the time crunch, we groped and grinded, panting and stealing kisses.

Part of me knew it was my craving for Elion, and that this wasn't fair to either of them. She and I had already had our goodbye.

I pulled myself away. "I really shouldn't… I'm sorry."

"It's okay," she assured me. "It was more than I'd hoped for. You have somewhere to be."

I hesitated. "You're sure?"

She caressed my cheek. "I love you, and that won't ever change. We were just warming each other up." Her playful, adventurous tone had returned. "You for the man you *gasped* for yesterday, and me for whomever I lead to my bed tonight. Maybe Schamoi."

"Okay. I, uh, I'll be halfway down the hall. You should probably go hide near the entrance we came in so he doesn't notice you when he comes in the other entrance."

She stole one last kiss, then giggled. "If you gasp too loud, I'll have a coughing fit or something to cover it up."

"You're wicked."

She shoved me down the hall, and I picked up my skirt to make a dash for the private washroom in case Elion came early.

It really was small in here, and while everything in the palace was luxurious, fucking in a toilet room was not my ideal. I tried not to let my guilt set in about kissing Lilah as I waited. I'd gone most of my life without being her lover; we could last a few months apart.

After a couple of minutes, the door opened. Elion stood, feverishly staring at me as though he may eat me whole. "My mate. I need you." He undid the buckle on his belt.

I held up my hands, taking a tiny step back. "I know. We shouldn't let the others know, though."

"Okay," he panted, advancing a step. He was ready to pounce, and his restraint was impressive.

I gave him one more caution as I gathered my skirt. "Don't mess up my dress, hair, or makeup."

He unzipped his bulging pants, and pulled himself out. My mouth watered at the sight.

I hiked my dress up and faced the washing counter. The gilded mirror in front of me gave me a perfect view of his face as he bent me over and took me from behind like he had in the bedding chamber.

He fit perfectly inside me, and his lycan eyes brightened with hunger.

His hands gripped me so tightly, and I in turn gripped the counter.

Each thrust was desperate, needy, and powerful. His stamina and speed were impressive as we panted and moaned together, as we gave in to pure desire.

It didn't take long for him to bring us both satisfaction, given the ferocity with which he took me. My arms burned from my earlier exertion in the tank, but it echoed the sheer fire inside me as Elion filled me.

"My mate," he groaned over and over again, still thrusting, still tenderly knotted inside.

I was simply trying to catch my breath. Mate or not, I wished I'd known earlier how beautifully feral shifters were at lovemaking.

Elion kept gently thrusting, slipping his hands inside my dress to caress my chest. "Thank you."

Each and every stroke within me made me shudder. I couldn't even speak. The prolonged ecstasy was exquisite.

He kissed my back and neck. "And thank you for sending something… I thought I was going to die without you…"

He had to mean my underwear. "You're welcome. And you'll be okay." His mating fever would tame over time, and there was nothing to keep us apart now.

His knot rubbed me just right. He was still engorged, and I would have stayed there for an hour with him, groping and grinding, but we couldn't. We needed to get back to the celebration before people noticed we'd both slipped out, and every muscle in my body quivered from the day's exertions.

"We need to go," I whispered.

He slowed, frowning. "When can I have you next?"

"Soon." I didn't want to make any promises. The others would get jealous if he had more chances with me than they did.

His fever having calmed, he placed one more sweet kiss on my back, and stopped thrusting. "Thank you."

We waited a moment for him to shrink, grabbing drying towels from a rack within reach to preserve our clothing. He gently cleaned us up after pulling himself out. I made sure no evidence had dripped onto my dress, and that everything else looked fine.

He fastened his belt as I turned around and admired him.

"I love what you do to me," I said. Selfishly, I didn't feel guilty for his biological mating bond tying us together. Not with how good of a lover he was.

Grinning, his face was closer to the clear-minded man I'd first met before the claimings. "I love what you do to me, too."

I smiled softly. He was kindhearted, fierce at fucking, and I couldn't imagine finding fault with him. Granted, I hadn't learned much of his hobbies, interests, or political stances, and those were important too. But we had time to sort that all out—a lifetime.

I wanted to kiss him, to embrace him for a moment before sending him away, but it wasn't wise, given how hard it had been to peel him off me after our claiming. I didn't want to have to scream for the guard at the end of the hallway...

"You go first," I prompted.

He held my gaze. "Will I be able to hold you tonight?"

I nodded. Hadwin had already claimed a spot next to me, and I'd assumed Elion wouldn't take no for an answer on the matter of being on the other side.

Elion reached for my hand, but I pulled away. "Please, Elion. We'll be together soon. You need to go."

He closed his eyes, visibly fighting his fever for a minute. "Okay."

Without another word, he opened the door and left.

I waited a while, collecting myself and spacing out our returns.

After a couple more minutes, I stepped into the hallway. Lilah leaned against the wall near the entrance.

"How good was it?"

My cheeks warmed. "Not bad."

She grinned. "Mhmm..."

I hooked my arm through hers. "Let's go enjoy the rest of the evening."

We reentered the ballroom without a fuss, then gabbed and enjoyed food and drink. Elion sat at his table with his parents, the color in his face and his lucidity much improved.

I allowed myself to properly celebrate with the people. I had faced death itself in that tank earlier. I had accepted my full Coterie. And I was fulfilling Hoku's divine mission to unite this realm.

Peace and joy, despite any of the roughness with some of my Coterie, dominated my spirits. I spent plenty of time with my mother and Kernov, laughing and watching him slide his arm around her. Lilah and Schamoi didn't hesitate to partake of more wine and socialize throughout the room.

The night grew late, and my energy waned.

"You look tired," Kernov remarked.

I gave him a lazy smile. "I could use some more invigorating tea… Or I could call it a night."

"If you're ready, I'll notify them myself," he said.

Rousing my strength, I sat straighter in my chair. "Let's do that."

He stood and took a turn about the room to inform my Coterie it was time to leave, that they needed to wrap up their business and pleasantries.

Before the room understood it was time for our departure and all eyes returned to me, I shook Schamoi's hands. He promised he'd be in touch and would visit soon.

I briefly hugged Lilah, and she made me promise I'd catch her up on everything.

Then I turned to my mother for a nice long squeeze.

"You will get some sleep, right?" Mother asked.

I rested my hands on her shoulders. "I'm exhausted. Yes. Lots of sleep."

She kissed my forehead as Kernov returned.

"They're waiting on you, Your Holiness."

I nodded, wearing a confident smile despite fresh nerves. Solo, I strode to the throne platform, where the emperor and magistrate sat. I took my place next to them and swept my gaze over the crowd, searching for my Coterie.

Haan swam to the closest position to the throne, and the other five members of my Coterie walked to their places at the base of the stairs.

The orchestra ended their song, and the ballroom fell silent.

Without a word, I stood again, acknowledging the room with an intentional glance. Then I descended the stairs, aiming for the large doors at the end of the ballroom where people had cleared space. Each member of my Coterie fell into place behind me with the exception of Haan, who swam away to the side.

It was a bit theatrical, but we were the focus of the event, and it was always done this way.

Guards opened the large doors as I approached, and we filed through. We didn't stop until we passed a foyer full of additional attendees.

I tried to avoid eye contact, but a variety of onlookers caught my attention for a moment. People were excited, and many of them probably had to think we were all about to share in a great orgy the moment we arrived at my room. It had gone that way for previous Blessed Vessels, though I was far too tired to consider it right now.

No, this was simply the beginning of a new arrangement, and all the ups and downs that came with it.

THE GIANT BED

We didn't head straight to my chambers. I first led them to a Coterie common room that connected their rooms to mine. None of these rooms had been used in decades, not since the last Blessed Vessel and her Coterie had chosen to retire from the palace. *Most* of this floor hadn't been used in ages.

Floor-to-ceiling drapes covered a giant window on one side of the long, thin room. A generous fireplace in the corner mirrored one in my chambers, and a tank for Haan sat opposite. Several chairs and sofas, tables and bookshelves provided activities and a place for the men to chat and share time.

They all took in the room, some with more interest than the others. "Thank you for a lovely celebration," I said. "And the dances." I gave Haan and Elion a smile. "And the extra time chatting."

Elion's lips twitched with satisfaction.

"Please go see your rooms and make sure they're to your liking, just through that door." I pointed to a door opposite the one leading to my chambers. "Your things should have all been moved and set up to your specifications, and the doors have been labeled."

Quietly, the men nodded, leaving the common room. All save Elion. He took the opportunity to slide his arms around my waist and kiss my head. "I'm fine looking later."

His desire was still strong, and it made me yearn for him, but one of us had to use the logical part of our bodies. "Please go look at your room."

"I…" He pressed himself against my hip, erect.

Damn it.

"Elion," I said more firmly. "Later. Please, do as I ask."

He left me with another kiss on the head. "Okay." He only mildly sulked as he rubbed himself and walked through the door.

I sat on a chair, waiting, taking in the common room more fully. I'd had no reason to enter during my five years here, so I'd only seen it during my initial tour and when the servants dusted it to prepare for my Coterie.

My gaze rested on the ornate ceiling, and I imagined the men all on my bed. Hopefully this wouldn't be awkward, given my tension with Findlech and Tyfen.

"Tired?" Hadwin asked.

I startled, sitting upright. "You're so quiet. I didn't hear you come back."

He took a seat near me.

"Your room is to your liking?"

"It's perfect. Thank you."

Just moments later, Haan returned, and then the others.

Standing, I wrung my hands. "Don't hesitate to let the servants know if you need anything…" I swallowed, growing more awkward. "Your room is your own sanctuary, and I may claim my own chambers to myself at times, but it's customary on the first night to share. So, I'd like to welcome you all to stay with me." I avoided looking at Findlech and Tyfen. "If you'd like to. It's not compulsory."

"Will there be any more contributions tonight?" Findlech asked.

Contributions… I could think of more creative or savory ways of phrasing 'sex.'

"No. I'm quite tired. Tomorrow."

He nodded.

Elion, his hands concealing his bulge, looked devastated by my answer.

I averted my gaze. "Well, I want to take some time to freshen up, and you may all do the same. I'll meet you in here again when I'm ready."

After muttered agreements, I turned and opened the door to my chambers.

I blew out a breath, surveying the room under candlelight.

Glancing at the bed, I tried to decide how we would share it. I could lie in the center, and the five land-walkers would just have to surround me, with Elion and Hadwin to my sides. Then again, I wasn't sure of *their* preferences.

I opened the door again to speak to Elion and Hadwin, but the common room had emptied. Biting my lip, I considered. I could just wait, but I really wanted to know.

I strode through the common room and entered the men's corridor. I hadn't memorized which room was which yet, so I had to glance at each door as I passed. Finding Hadwin's, I knocked.

He opened the door, a toothbrush in hand. "Darling?"

My heart was such a plaything when he called me that, and I couldn't keep a smile from my face. "I wanted to ask… I'm assuming you'd still wish to lie next to me?"

He smiled warmly in return. "Absolutely."

"Okay. And … do you have preferences on the bed arrangement? Elion will be on my other side, and Haan in my pond, but I'm not sure of the others yet…"

Squinting, he considered. "Is it selfish to ask to take up the edge of the bed?"

I shrugged. "Not really." Assuming Gald wanted to be close, he could be by Elion. And I didn't even care what Findlech or Tyfen wanted.

Hadwin rubbed my arm with his free hand. "I'm sure I'll come to terms with this whole arrangement and sharing you, but if I'm honest…" He hesitated. "I'm sure this will become a cooperative brotherhood, but I'm not here for the rest of the Coterie. My relationship is with you. I like the idea of just being next to you, though I understand that won't always be an option."

I really couldn't expect less devotion, or hope for less of a request from a mate. "I understand. We can do that." I squeezed his hand. "I'll see you in a little while."

Haan was already in the common room when I returned.

"I pack rather light." He chuckled.

I was of half a mind to tell him he could take the underground tunnel to my pond already, but I thought better of it. "I'll let you know when I'm ready. I'll try not to keep you waiting long."

After returning to my chambers, I made a beeline for my dressing room. My aides spent a few minutes taking care of my jewelry and undoing my hair. They offered to wash and dress me, but I declined and sent them away. I had another plan.

I called for a guard in my outer corridor and asked him to discreetly fetch Elion for me.

And then I paced my room, hoping I'd made the right decision. I didn't want the others to get annoyed with Elion, so hopefully allowing him one more quick chance to get relief would help.

Taking the long way to my bedroom, he soon arrived, escorted by the guard. He was shirtless, and I wanted him so badly inside me, despite having been with him just a couple of short hours ago.

He shut the bedroom door behind him, and I leaned against a bedpost.

"You called for me?"

I couldn't take my eyes off his chest and abs. "Um, yes…"

He reached for his pants.

"Let's talk," I said.

Halting, he met my gaze. "I want you."

"I know. I just want to make sure the others don't get jealous."

"You're my mate," he said, mildly offended.

I didn't get upset at his possessiveness, not when he couldn't help it. "Yes, I'm your mate. But I'm not yours alone. I need you to remember that."

He put on a brave face and nodded.

"Once we're done, you need to go back and finish getting ready like the others."

Nodding again, he started undoing his pants.

I was tight, craving him, ready for him already. Thank Hoku I'd been created to have the mating bond so tamed, or I'd do nothing else but let him fuck me.

"One request," I said, ready to strip off my dress. "Can you be a little more gentle, and no clothes this time?" I was used to my pleasure instructors making love to me before bed, and so far, all but Tyfen had taken me in the bedding chamber with clothing on. My body begged for that skin-to-skin contact.

"Yes." He dropped his pants, his full erection on display.

I wanted to taste him, but I controlled myself while he removed his socks, and I shed my dress.

His fever still somewhat under control from earlier, he didn't pounce right away, but his eyes brightened as they lingered on my curves. His breathing picked up.

"Here." I pointed to the daybed. "Come join me." I crawled forward onto the bed and draped my arms over the back of it. "I'm sore from a long day, so be gentle."

"Okay," he breathed, his voice husky and labored. He knelt behind me, and I shuddered when he rested his hands on my hips to adjust me. The mirrored partition wall in front of me gave me a perfect view of his face as he penetrated me.

He glided his cock into me softly this time, and I almost whimpered at how agonizingly slow it seemed. His knot grew inside me, and fresh pleasure bloomed within me.

His hands slid up my bare sides to grip the back of the daybed. "How was that?"

I could barely answer with his naked chest pressed to me. "Perfect." Our eyes met in the mirror.

"Good," he purred into my ear, pulling himself partially out.

His thrusts were punctuated by possession and meaning, softened by intention and sweetness. I was grateful I'd chosen this position because I needed the support of the daybed to keep me from melting altogether.

He soon picked up speed, plunging deeper into me. I couldn't refrain from moaning and uttering a dozen goddess-damned curses.

"Harder," I begged, desperate.

He happily obliged, slamming into me as I gasped, as my core was on fire, as I careened into sweet relief, and he followed soon behind me.

"Fuck," I whispered, panting. I liked this mate thing.

He held me from behind as we both cooled. I loved being one with him in the soft fallout of furious lovemaking.

"I love you," he said.

I hesitated to respond. He barely knew me. That was the mating bond speaking. But love came on a spectrum, and he already had a corner of my heart that could never be replaced. "I love you too."

After another sweet moment, he unknotted and withdrew from me. Thank all the goddesses my rooms were equipped to take care of my sexual existence, so it was easy to clean up.

He dressed again, and I sent him on his way before quickly washing myself.

Twice now we'd had sex without the others knowing, and I felt guilty for that, but only mildly. He wasn't an ass like my fae and elf men, and I was happy to meet his needs when he fulfilled my own so well.

Still, we wouldn't be able to keep this up with the others now so ingrained in my life.

I chose a silky gold nightie that hit me midthigh. I usually slept naked, but I did enjoy pretty clothes, too.

Ready to end the night in cuddles and dreams, I took the door to the common room.

All my men were ready, most of them in shorts. My lust grinned at the sea of flesh. They were all mine. Even stupid Tyfen wore his shorts, and I hated how his tattoos drew my attention to his groin.

"Please, come in."

Haan dove under the water's surface while the others followed me in. They surveyed the giant room and bed for a moment.

I pointed to the washroom. "The toilet's there, if you want to use it instead of your own." Since Findlech was still fully dressed other than having taken off his circlet, and Hadwin wore a casual shirt with his shorts, I gestured to a large set of drawers. "There's a drawer for each of you, if you'd like."

Findlech took the offer, stripping down to his shorts. He was muscled but thin, his posture impeccable. Hadwin didn't take the offer, though.

"You're comfortable?" I asked.

He smiled at me. "I am."

I wanted to kiss him and that subtle smile, but I didn't.

"So… The bed situation." I hoped this wouldn't be too awkward since I'd only discussed it with half the men. "Haan will be in the pond."

"Happily," he said, the pond water gracefully rippling as he swam to the far corner with the most soft seaweed.

I pointed to the bed. "I'd like Hadwin on the left side, next to me. Elion will be on my right. And I'll leave it to the three of you to choose what you'd like from there." I guiltily acknowledged Findlech, Tyfen, and Gald.

This was uncomfortable… While I didn't like the idea of ranking or picking favorites, it was somewhat inevitable.

Hadwin politely claimed his spot on the left edge of the bed, and Elion eagerly took his place. Tyfen, still utterly disinterested in me or the rest of the group, plopped himself down on the far right, farthest away from me.

I had made my statement, and he was making his. So be it.

Findlech nonchalantly squeezed on the bed beside Tyfen, leaving space for Gald between himself and Elion.

Tyfen had the audacity to glare at Findlech, then turned around, resting his head at the foot of the bed.

I eyed him, perplexed at that tension. Surely the cousin races would be best friends, especially since they were both at odds with me right now, but apparently not. Findlech, as he often was, remained unfazed.

Gald waited to take his place, approaching me and holding me by the waist.

I frowned. "Sorry…"

His expression was hard to read, his emotions masked by a small grin. "It's fine. I trust I'll have lots of opportunities with you."

"Yes, you will." I stole a glance at him. He wasn't the most chiseled of the men in my Coterie, but he was still attractive.

He proceeded to feel me up, his flirtatious eyes noting I wore absolutely nothing under my nightie. "Can I have a consolation kiss?"

I gave him a toothy smile and leaned in, enjoying the kiss. He caressed my ass like it was a prized possession before pulling away. He made a brief comment about how he liked the mirrors in the room, then claimed his place on the bed.

"Right." I swung my arms, then hurried onto the bed, crawling under the covers between Elion and Hadwin. It felt right to be between my mates, honestly.

I lay on my back as Elion wrapped himself around me.

"Shoot." I pouted. "The candles."

Gald lifted a hand in the air, and they all snuffed out immediately. I almost laughed. I hadn't ever had strong mages in my family or circle of friends, and I still wasn't used to it despite my five years here.

"Thank you, Gald."

"At your service," he said brightly.

"Rather useful skills. I think I'll keep you around."

He hummed, silky and seductive. "My hands aren't even the most skilled part of my body…"

I giggled. "Go to sleep."

The room fell silent, and Hadwin scooched closer. He leaned in, brushing my ear with his cold lips. "Any preferences on how I hold you?"

"Not really." Elion had enveloped me already with his arms and legs, but Hadwin could sort out what he wanted.

And he did. He dared to move Elion's hand from my chest, pushing it down to my waist. Elion gave a low rumbling warning.

I softly shushed him. "Share."

He exhaled a sigh, then ground his cock against my leg a couple of times. "Sharing," he mumbled.

Hadwin cupped my breast, placing a kiss on my bare shoulder.

I smiled, happy as can be as I quickly found sleep.

24

Nightmare & Daymare

In the haze of a vision, I strolled along the bank of a murky pond. Foreboding settled in my stomach, but I couldn't get myself to move away from the waters. Moss squished under my bare feet, critters chirping all around me, and the twin moons illuminated the dark waters.

I had never been here, but like so many places in this realm, it carried familiarity. Hoku often sent me dreams and visions to show me this realm—the beauty and the cruelty. The realm she had preserved and blessed with gifts of mortals like me, to keep it well. It was common for her Blessed Daughters to have the visions.

The pond stirred, and my senses heightened. I swallowed, surveying the woods around me. The area was deserted, at least by land-walkers.

I kept walking, and the water stirred again. Thin strands of seaweed floated to the surface.

My eyes widened. That wasn't seaweed—it was hair.

Enormous beady eyes stared at me from just below the surface, but the creature did not reach for me. It was a mermaid with long, spindly arms, simply observing me.

It was grotesque, but my curiosity got the better of me. I crouched, getting a better look. "Hello."

The creature poked its head out of the water, its sunken eyes taking me in more fully.

I smiled at how calm it was, how it shared my curiosity. Perhaps they weren't as bad as people assumed. Perhaps they could still be helped and reintegrated into normal society.

"I won't hurt you," I said softly.

That was the worst thing I could have said.

Its long arms reaching, it grabbed my wrists and pulled me into the murky waters. I lost most of my air on the way down in a surprised scream. Much stronger than it looked, it yanked me deeper with it.

I kicked and fought, but my dress weighed me down. Despite my strength as a swimmer, the monster thrashed me, crushing my wrists without mercy.

It shoved me deep, letting go and hovering over me. With the tiniest pinprick of moonlight to guide me, I used the burning air in my lungs to aim for the surface.

I was too weak.

Faster than I thought possible, it lunged for me, baring its jagged teeth and ripping into my arm, tearing off a chunk of my flesh.

I *screamed*, letting the rest of my air go.

Water and blood filled my lungs.

I was choking and drowning. Gasping and bleeding. Fighting and crying for help, all the while sinking and being fed on.

It had brought friends.

"Sonta," a voice called.

I was past hope.

"Sonta!"

My eyes jolted open, and I gulped air.

"Darling, are you okay?" Hadwin's voice was full of concern.

I blinked in the dark. *Right, just a vision. Just a nightmare.*

"Did I … scream?" The room was quiet save the trickle of the pond's water and a bit of soft snoozing at my side.

"No," Hadwin confirmed. "Are you all right?"

I licked my lips. "Yes. Just a nightmare." I was still confused. I had never once woken any of my pleasure instructors in bed. The visions didn't work that way. I was a heavy sleeper by nature. Granted, the visions weren't often this vicious. It had probably been prompted by my claiming with Haan.

"How did you know I was having a nightmare?" I whispered.

"Your heart thundered. I worried."

I turned, nuzzling his cool neck and wrapping an arm around him. "Thank you." It only then dawned on me how intriguing it was that he could sense my heartbeat so well. Vampires were notoriously light sleepers, but it had woken him, and he had woken me with a whisper quiet enough to not stir the others.

Elion had turned to hold me again, and I found peace between him and Hadwin.

Hadwin was sweet—absolutely nothing like how much of society pictured the blood-sucking race.

Then again…

"Get the FUCK off her!" Hadwin belted.

My eyes shot open again, this time taking in morning rays. Elion must have grown too needy, because he was already inside me, already knotted.

"She's my mate," he growled, thrusting gently.

"I will rip your—"

"It's okay!" I yelled. Elion couldn't get out right now even if he wanted to. And I found pleasure as his cock worked its magic. I took care to put my face into my pillow to stifle my moans this time. I ought not to enjoy it when it had worked Hadwin up so badly, but I wasn't in full control.

Elion had taken me four times now, and had yet to disappoint me. This time was no different as he released inside me. It was dead quiet as we lay there waiting for him to shrink enough to pull out.

"My mate," he whispered.

"She's not yours alone," Hadwin snapped.

"You should have asked," Gald said.

"Stop," I muttered, covering my ears and further burying my face in my pillow.

After another moment, Elion pulled out.

I wanted to stay buried there, drowning out the six men who surrounded me and the tension the room had become thick with. This was not my ideal way to start the day, to start my time with my Coterie.

Forcing myself up, I sat in place. The four other men on the bed all wore obvious looks of disdain for Elion. Haan had stirred in the pond, and his look was more of wise curiosity. Consent was not much of a thing for his people, though he was educated enough to understand it played a large role for most land-walkers.

Elion's expression oozed defiance for those around him. "You liked it, right? The way I took you? No one can deny that. I know what my mate likes."

I pressed my lips together. "I enjoyed the sex, yes."

"Exactly." He aimed his retort specifically at Hadwin this time.

"But Gald is right, Elion." I gazed into his eyes. "You should have asked. You should have waited until I was awake." I couldn't baby him, not in front of the others.

He grappled for words, clearly confused. "You… I asked you in the bedding chamber, and you only said you didn't want shifting…"

I closed my eyes and blew out a breath. No, I hadn't told him not to fuck me while I slept, had I? I'd only told him I didn't want to fuck a full-on animal. And the truth of it was—I often *liked* being woken by my partner already starting things. It wasn't for everyone, but I'd enjoyed it when Schamoi and one of my other instructors had done it.

"Here's the thing." I met Elion's lycan gaze again. "When it's just you and me, we can do things differently. That goes for any of us—I don't expect us to all have the same rules or tastes within the Coterie. But when we're in a group like this, you have to respect the others' wishes for you to not do that. Okay?"

Mildly ashamed, he looked down at his hands. "If that's what you prefer."

"I do."

I glanced at the others in turn. "I could have been more clear with Elion. Please don't be upset with him. Because I'm not, and his act doesn't concern you."

"Does that mean we'll all get two chances today?" Findlech asked plainly.

"What?" I scrunched my eyebrows.

"That's three times he's taken you now. Let's not pretend you didn't satisfy him last night when that guard pulled him away. So, he's contributed seed three times to our one."

I was instantly uncomfortable… Four times. He'd taken me four times.

"He has different needs than everyone else."

"Does the divine mother promote favoritism because *he* struggles to control his urges? If I recall, her divine edict and your very creation are about unity and equality for the races."

I blinked. It was true, but I didn't particularly like having that thrown in my face. "She outlined the Great Ritual the way it is. You all got a chance, and then I get to continue how I wish."

"I propose we track," Findlech said. "A chart or something. Any true Blessed Vessel would agree in the spirit of equality."

Dangerous words. I wanted to rip off his stupid pointy ears. "Does anyone else agree with Findlech?" I tried to conceal my anger.

"I would agree to a chart," Tyfen said.

Of course the prick would.

I eyed the rest of the men, and no one else piped up. "*I* decide who shoves their cock inside me, starting now. You don't get any say in this. I will not keep reminding you two that I am a *person*."

Awkward silence.

After a moment, Gald shifted on the bed. "You know, many of the temple scholars believe our seed contributions are not even equal."

"Oh, shut it," Tyfen muttered.

"No," Gald said. "And I believe them. Chancellor Haan's ejaculations have more force and liquid, but yours might naturally carry more life. So, it's not necessarily a simple numbers game."

I wasn't sure of that conclusion, but I'd side with it simply out of principle. "Thank you, Gald."

Hadwin chuckled. "Sounds like you have no choice but to be with *me* nonstop, darling. We vampires apparently have no life-giving seed, so the statistics are not in my favor if we go by Findlech and Tyfen's way of thinking." He playfully brushed a finger across my arm. "What do you say to making love with me all day every day, just to even the odds?"

Gald laughed with him, and I had to bite the insides of my cheeks to not join them.

I held my tongue. Tensions were still high. Elion refrained from speaking, still embarrassed and annoyed. Naturally, hailing from the two proudest races, Findlech and Tyfen didn't take too kindly to being mocked.

"Let's reset our morning," I said, straightening the sheets around me. "Everyone can go get ready for the day, and we'll reconvene in the private dining hall for breakfast. The servants will show you the way."

Without complaint, the group filed out of the room. I pulled the covers over my face, wishing I could pick and choose my responsibilities. It wouldn't help, though.

Getting up, I strode to my dressing room, opting not to ring the servants' bell. I wanted to be alone.

I wiped myself clean and took my time picking out a magenta dress and matching jewelry. I gave myself a bit of a pep talk as I did so, reminding myself I was strong enough to handle these men and to navigate the social and political landscape that came with them.

Smiling in the mirror, I admired the simplicity of this dress and the matching underwear. Unlike with the last two days, I dressed to please me and me alone.

As I applied cosmetics and put my hair into a ponytail, I allowed my mind to wander to my other loved ones. What were Lilah and Schamoi up to? And my mother? Traditionally, a Blessed Vessel and her Coterie were given ample privacy when they first came together in the Great Ritual. Many more mornings like this one, and I might run to my comfort people more often than I'd planned.

By the time I entered the private dining hall, everyone else had already arrived, sharply dressed. Haan's waterway led to the end of the long table, and a spot reserved for me sat at the opposite end. The other five men had chosen seats as they'd desired.

"Sorry to keep you waiting."

A servant pulled my chair out for me, and I sat.

"You look great," Hadwin said.

I smiled. "No better than all of you."

Several servants entered the room with platters and trays, laying them on the table for my Coterie. The meals were an exciting mix, and I was interested to try some of them as I got to know my Coterie better.

"Here's yours, Your Holiness." My personal chef set a plate in front of me. "Please do let me know if you need anything different. I'm happy to see to your needs."

I nodded. "Thank you."

The plate was loaded with all my favorite things—heaps of them. I picked a strawberry first.

"So, we really have to plan ahead, don't we?" Gald asked. "If we want to do something fun with you that involves food?" He loaded some fried potatoes onto his plate.

I wrinkled my nose. "Yes. Unfortunately."

From the moment Tyfen had claimed me until the moment I bore a child, I had a highly trained, highly screened private chef, and only certain servants were allowed to even deliver my food and drink. They'd done a good job being discreet thus far, but I'd been aware of the precaution.

Just because the men of my Coterie seemed sweet—for the most part—didn't mean they wouldn't value their own people over me or my child. It made my stomach churn just thinking about it. A previous Blessed Vessel had been poisoned, jeopardizing the life of her growing child. In the end, they'd discovered it had been the aide of one of the Coterie members, having suspected the conceived life was not his. She'd hoped to restart the fertility process.

Luckily, the mother and child were both healthy in the end, and war was narrowly avoided, but the public execution had made its mark in the history books.

I drew a deep breath, taking a bite of my strawberry. I didn't want to live in fear. The danger was minimal and rare, the precautions just an added measure.

"It's *obviously* necessary, Gald." I made my sarcasm apparent to lighten the mood.

Elion shrugged, cutting into a rather bloody steak. "You'd think your Coterie was a den of wolves, but I only count one of us here." He smirked, and I couldn't hold back a laugh.

As we ate, we discussed our agenda for the rest of the day. There were no set plans. I'd show them around my tower and get settled more, taking time to get to know them each. And … bedding them. It was hard to know when a pregnancy took, so Coterie members were always eager to keep trying until a pregnancy was confirmed. Thank Hoku I had a great sex drive and a quick-healing body…

As we finished eating, a servant delivered a message to me. I opened the parchment, reading the shortest scribble. My nerves bundled into a tight knot in my throat.

Please see me in my office at your earliest convenience.

Signed by the emperor himself.

It was rare the emperor and I talked, or that he called on me. That made it even odder to happen on the first day of my Coterie's seclusion.

I handed the parchment back to the servant. "Please let him know I'll be there shortly."

"Everything all right?" Hadwin asked, setting down a goblet.

"Of course." Having lost my appetite, I pushed my plate forward. "I need to go attend to something, though. I trust you'll all be fine back in the common room or your personal rooms?"

Several nods answered me.

"No wandering the palace by ourselves?" Gald asked.

"I'd just like to see to the introductions the first time around. There are some areas that will remain private for myself and my other guests."

"Fair enough." He folded his napkin. "We'll fend for ourselves for entertainment without you for now."

I smiled, standing. "I'll try to be quick."

Elion caught up to me before I exited the room. "Can I…"

"I really should go." I frowned.

He took my hand. "I just wanted to apologize for earlier. For angering everyone in bed. When I woke and you were there, and…" He closed his eyes. "I just…"

"I told you—it's fine. That's behind us now."

His grey eyes searched mine.

"When it's only the two of us, I don't mind a surprise to wake me. Sometimes."

He wore a small smile. "Sometimes. And not when sharing."

"Yes."

His smile faded. "I don't like everyone hating me, but I don't know how to do this when I need you so much. All the time. No one understands how hard it is."

I kissed him. "We'll manage. Your fever will ease. I need you to try, though. I can't be with you all the time. You'll need to take care of yourself and control your urges more often than not."

His expression somber, he nodded.

"And … when it's too difficult, I don't mind helping you in ways the others can't object to. If it's only release you seek, and not winning the paternity race, there are other options."

A hint of relief crossed his face. "Thank you."

I squeezed his hand. "I really do need to go, though."

He released me without too much trouble.

I walked alone in the hallway, aiming for the emperor's tower.

Put out one fire, now to the next…

25

Spirit of the Law

"Please take a seat, Sonta." The emperor gestured to a chair opposite him.

My hands were clammy. "Thank you."

He surveyed me, his elf ears and greying hair adding to the solemnity of his expression. "How are things going?"

"Umm…" The emperor and I didn't casually chat, and he certainly wouldn't ask about the intricacies of my life. He didn't care to know I had a huge crush on Hadwin already, or that Gald's charm and intellect were winning me over. "Everything's fine. Was there something specific you wanted to know about?"

He gently tapped his desk. "I wanted to ensure there is no trouble with your Coterie, that everything is going well…"

Surely no one had sent word of the debacle this morning… I could handle things.

"And you're giving your Coterie fair and equal access in the Great Ritual?"

My jaw dropped. "Did someone say something?"

"No. No one needed to. It wasn't like you danced alone at the celebration last night. Your emotions were easy to read."

Ashamed, I looked down at my lap.

"You don't seem all that fond of Lord Findlech or Prince Tyfen…"

I met the emperor's gaze. "I'm not. They're arrogant and disrespectful. And as for 'fair access'… *I* choose who I spend my time with within my Coterie. I could choose to never give them another opportunity with me, and it would not break the law or divine edict."

He raised a hand. "I do not mean to stir you up, child. I merely wanted to remind you there is more nuance to your position."

"I—"

"It is not all about romance and love. You're a representative, a beacon to this realm, showing we can overcome our differences."

I bit my tongue, allowing him to get out what he wanted.

"Not all Coteries remain a full unit for the rest of their lives. I would know…"

It was exceptionally rare for him to speak of his own mother and her lovers, of his private upbringing. I was intrigued. It was true that after the birth of a ruler, the Blessed Vessel didn't always keep all six men close to her. There was more choice, and she often kept those she'd bonded with the most with her, to have an influence on her child. The emperor's mother had only kept three of her six Coterie members with her at the palace after his first year.

Speculations could be made, though the realm was generally respectful of Coterie happenings. It was understood they wouldn't all be compatible—the forming of it was primarily a political alliance.

Curious, nervous of the intimacy of the topic, I dared to probe. "Does your opinion of fair access stem from your mother's choices with her Coterie before your confirmed conception?" Had she drafted a chart and bedded them all equally to ensure peace?

He angled his head. "Like all Blessed Vessels, she was touched by the divine for a higher purpose. And she remembered that purpose."

"I haven't forgotten my calling," I muttered. "And I *have* obeyed every letter of the law, despite my feelings."

The emperor blew out a breath. "Within the constraints of the divine edict, your body is your own to choose what you will. I would not and could not issue orders about what happens behind closed doors. I simply want to kindly remind you of the *spirit* of the law, Sonta. That is all."

I waited a moment to respond, collecting my thoughts. Perhaps I'd been unfair or I hadn't been objective enough. The conversation was already uncomfortable, so I asked the question I had always wanted to. "Did… Did your mother and father love each other?"

His father was an immortal, centuries old and spending most of his time back in elven territory now. He had been one of the three to stay by the last Blessed Vessel's side—though that was a requirement for the paternal Coterie member.

Sire the next ruler, and you would be by her side to raise the child to maturity together. The other two had stayed with her by choice—presumably for love.

The emperor nodded in thought. "Love is a multifaceted word. Not all races agree on what exactly it means. Not all *people* even agree within a given race. There is passion. Fondness. Respect. Did my parents carry at least some of that for each other? Yes."

A politician's answer, but I'd have to accept it. My journey was my own, regardless of the experiences of the previous Blessed Vessels.

"I'll try to be fair," I said. "It's hard to have respect for them when their arrogance blinds me."

The tiniest smile graced his lips. "They all have their flaws. You are touched by the divine, and you possess your fair share of flaws as well, do you not?"

I hated being humbled. Did I have flaws? I had them in spades.

Averting my gaze, I focused on a bookshelf in the room. "Spirit of the law. I understand. Is there anything else I can help you with?"

"That was all. Enjoy your day."

I muddled through my thoughts on the long walk back to my tower. I wasn't a child. Yes, to the emperor and many in this realm, a twenty-five-year-old was only a child, but…

"Ugh."

I took the general entrance to the common room, where all the men had gathered, waiting for me. Gald chatted with Haan, but the others sat quietly, reading.

Everyone's attention snapped to me as I entered.

"I…" I surveyed them, considering the best course of action. I still needed to settle something.

"I'm not quite ready for a tour, but will be soon." My gaze landed on Findlech. "Could we please talk in my room?"

"Yes, Your Holiness." He stood and approached me.

I simply pointed to my door, and he went to it. I didn't want to make things worse, and I didn't want to spend time with him, but we needed to clear the air.

Elion focused on me, and I strained under the pull of the mating bond. He wanted me again already. His gaze was nothing short of a plea.

"No. Not for some time." I was firm, but tried to be kind. He nodded in understanding. He would have to take care of himself for a while.

I followed Findlech into my chambers, closing the door behind me. He stood there, his hands clasped in front of him.

"When was the last time you spoke to the emperor?" I asked.

He cocked his head. "At the celebration last night."

"Did you talk about me?"

He narrowed his eyes. "Perhaps generally."

I tapped my foot, annoyed. "I'm not doing you any favors just because the emperor is half elf."

"I wouldn't expect it."

"And I'm not doing a chart or guaranteeing perfectly equal access to me."

"So you have made clear."

I gritted my teeth.

"I'm sorry I'm not one of the Coterie members kneeling to flatter you. I'm simply here to represent my people for the next reign."

Spirit of the law.

I bit my lip, hesitating. I wanted a *proper* apology from him.

"I don't mean to cause you offense, Your Holiness, truly. I'm still getting accustomed to your human sensibilities."

That was probably the closest to an apology I'd get from someone who was more than thirty times my age.

"I'm assuming you'd like to … make a contribution today?"

"Yes, if you're willing."

Let's get this unpleasantness out of the way, then I can enjoy more of my day. "Okay. Here on the bed, now."

I stripped off my underwear and practically flopped on the bed. Spreading my legs was as much as he'd get from me. Seemingly unfazed, Findlech put his hair up, removed his vial of gel, and went to work.

It was dull, like some of the inexperienced young men I'd first fooled around with as a teenager. Granted, he lacked passion but had some semblance of skill, whereas it had been the other way around for the young men.

If I had to describe it to Lilah—which I probably would eventually because she'd be hot for gossip—I'd say it was a replay of the bedding chamber. He got the job done without a word, over me and inside me. My heart had no pleasure in it, but at least I was easy to orgasm, so there was the tiniest bit of relief.

After putting himself away, he thanked me, then let his long hair loose.

I grabbed my underwear. "You're welcome."

"I'll return to the common room?"

"Yes, please."

He reached for the door.

"Findlech?"

"Yes, Your Holiness?"

"I'm fine if we do things this way, but don't oppose me again in front of everyone like you did this morning. If you have a problem, you take it up with me in private."

His expression was contemplative for a moment. "It felt pertinent to the topic of the shifter lad taking you the way he did."

I straightened. I didn't care if it seemed pertinent, and I shouldn't have to repeat myself.

"But," he continued, "I will certainly do my best to wait until we have privacy to discuss what you might consider sensitive."

It took all I had to not roll my eyes at his wording. "Thank you. I'll be in the common room shortly."

I took a minute in the washroom to refresh myself and put on my underwear again, fixing my hair and makeup, then returned to greet the men.

Curious and happy eyes greeted me. I didn't care whether they were guessing if Findlech and I had only chatted or if he'd bedded me. A weight had lifted off my chest just by doing it—on my terms.

"Is everyone ready?"

A chorus of yeses responded as they stood. Even Elion held himself together well—he must have taken some personal time in his room.

"It will just be an overall tour. Nothing in the daylight and not that in-depth in some places for now."

I glanced at Haan. "Our first stop will be at the lounge three stories up."

He nodded and took off to meet us, diving out of sight.

Some of the halls would be narrow on this little tour, so I picked someone to be by my side. "Gald, would you walk with me?" I didn't want him to feel left out after the sleeping situation last night…

Grinning, he hopped up to meet me, his curly hair framing his bright face. "I'd love to."

He then proceeded to grab my ass and pull me against him. "Sounds like fun." His fingers roamed, exploring, catching on the thin line of my underwear. "Mmm… Fun to unwrap, like a package…"

I had to fight off a laugh. "You have no shame in flirting in front of the others, do you?"

He swooped in with a kiss. "Nope. They've seen what I did to you, and they're aware there's plenty more of that to come…"

My cheeks warmed at his playfulness, at his utter lack of propriety. I didn't mind it.

I glanced at the others. "Follow us. Let's go check out your new home."

Gald wrapped an arm around my waist, and we walked out of the room.

"How's this going to work with Haan?" he whispered.

"He was given a map of the waterways and the parts of the palace he has access to. Unfortunately, not all rooms are accessible, but you'd be surprised."

The waterways were so intricately woven into the structure, many of them between walls and floors. Some rooms only had small tanks sufficient to hold one merperson peeking in, while others, like the ballrooms, could accommodate quite a few.

We spent nearly three hours as a group strolling through the halls and checking out the rooms. Many rooms, we didn't even step into—they'd have free time to explore when they were bored or had an inclination to. I made sure they understood my personal guests' floor was strictly forbidden—Lilah and my mother deserved privacy. Just as the two women would not enter the Coterie's common room or the men's rooms, they wished to have their space respected. Most of the tower and wing, however, was common ground I was happy to share. They weren't my prisoners, and I didn't want them to feel cooped up.

"It's an impressive library," Hadwin remarked, glancing at the books in one of our last rooms.

"It really is." I stepped to a window, looking out.

He took the opening, joining me at the window, squinting. "A lovely day."

I nudged him. "Is it? Would a vampire honestly consider this sunshine and warmth a *lovely* day?"

He kissed my temple. "Nostalgia from my younger years. I don't actually dislike the warmth, either. I hope we're not refraining from going outside on account of me…"

"No. I figured that's a venture for tomorrow. There are well-shaded places, and the servants always have umbrellas at the ready for vampire guests. We'll take good care of you."

"I feel it should be illegal for me to even look in a room like this," Haan remarked from his small tank.

I laughed again, facing him. "The waterproof books are a meager selection, I'll give you that, but don't hesitate to come here whenever you'd like."

We'd spent so much time wandering around that we decided to go straight to the dining hall for lunch. Elion kept me back while the others entered.

He held me tight. "Please. I need you. Real quick."

I pressed my forehead to his. "You can push past it, Elion. I have a strong mate."

He shuddered at the word 'mate.' "I've been fighting it. I can only do so much…"

I craved him, too, but I had set a bad precedent already for letting us satisfy our urges when it came to fairness with the others.

"You're drinking your calming tea?"

"Yes." He pressed his bulge against me.

Damn it.

"And you took care of yourself earlier…"

"It's not the same."

"You still have my underwear?"

"Yes. In my pillowcase, but your scent is wearing off."

I met his gaze, forcing myself to stay strong. "You'll have to wait a few hours for my help."

I may as well have slapped him, given his look of despair.

"We'll have the chef see about a stronger tea. And until I can help you…" I hadn't had a full bath after Findlech had taken me, but I had washed up well. Unless we were in a group activity, it didn't seem right to have another man's scent so fresh on me, though they had to allow for *some* degree of it in our situation.

Reaching down, I took off my underwear and handed it to him. "Fresh scent. If you need time alone in the toilet or another room…"

He fisted the fabric, resignation in his eyes. "Fine. I'll hurry." Turning, he headed down the hallway.

"Do you want us to wait until you're back?"

"No."

Every ounce of me felt guilt as he bounded to the nearest washroom. And, honestly, I was jealous of his hands at the moment.

After composing myself, I entered the dining hall.

"Is the young one all right?" Haan asked.

Sitting, I flashed them all a confident smile. "He will be. He'll be back shortly."

Servants brought food, and we tore into it. Haan ate his raw fish and seafood, Hadwin blood and a few sweet berries, the others a mix of regional delicacies and comfort foods.

I made sure to discreetly ask my personal chef to see about a stronger tea for Elion's relief.

Elion joined us soon enough, much calmer and lucid. He sat in his place without a word.

We could all pretend it was normal for him to jerk himself off before meals, at least until the mating fever eased.

"I *have* to ask, Elion," Gald piped up, tearing a hunk of bread. "Do shifters suffer a lot of bruised and raw cocks from your insatiable mating fever?"

Tyfen rolled his eyes, and Haan abruptly seemed much more interested in his remaining shrimp.

"Gald!" I scolded.

He looked at me defiantly. "Sonta, it's just a question. I'm curious."

His tone *had* conveyed a smidgen of playfulness, though it mostly came across as curiosity.

Elion didn't seem too offended, grabbing his knife and fork. "Usually we mate with other shifters, right? And our saliva has healing properties; we generally take care of each other…"

Gald hummed his understanding while chewing. "I see. Sonta *did* enjoy tongue in her pussy, didn't she, while up in the bedding chamber?"

"Gald!"

This time, he grinned wickedly.

"I don't think we need to hear about her bedding habits or genitalia as we eat," Findlech said, his tone annoyed and words clipped.

Gald was seated across from him at the table. He grabbed a sausage from a platter and licked it rather suggestively, pointedly staring at Findlech. "Okay, Your Lordship. No more discussion of pussies or cocks over food."

They eyed each other a moment, then Gald winked at me. I just shook my head. Was Gald really that horny, or was he playing a game?

I took a sip of my tea as everyone went back to their meals. Hadwin caught my gaze and shyly smiled. He always kept an eye on me, and usually remained silent in the group, but gave me the warmest acknowledgement when I turned his way.

"Hadwin, would you like to peruse the library with me after lunch?"

"I'd love to."

26

Books & Blood Play

Hadwin and I strolled down the hallway in silence. I held out my hand, and he took it, intertwining our fingers.

"Do you like reading?" he asked.

I shrugged. "I was never much of a reader growing up. And I'll confess this private library doesn't get much use from me for pleasure reading." Maybe someday… "Studies, meetings, and lessons have taken up my time since moving here."

"Understandable." He lifted my hand and kissed it. Little butterflies flitted in my stomach.

"But *you* seemed rather fond of books on our tour," I said.

We approached a set of stairs.

"I am," he said. "I've done a great deal of reading. My type of immortality gives the gift of time but limits the enjoyment of many outdoor activities."

"True." I was dying to know more of his story—about his life as a human and since becoming a vampire. How and why he'd become one. But it was a touchy subject for many vampires…

"Do you have a grand library on your estate?" I asked.

"Decent… I've been rebuilding it since the original manor burned down."

Once Hadwin had been announced as my vampire Coterie member, the palace had looked into him, as they had with all my Coterie members. Hadwin's past was mostly unknown, though there had been a note about the fire.

"That had to be scary. I'm glad you're okay."

We rounded a corner, and he gave me his usual soft smile. "I'm glad to be okay."

"Will you miss it there? I suppose … we don't really know how things will go…" He might be here for a couple of months or the next year. Or the next twenty years, or the rest of my life…

He squeezed my hand. "I hope to see it now and then, and I'm excited to take you there, but I'd happily stay by your side as long as you want me."

I stopped and turned. "Because we're mates? You still really don't know me all that well…"

His hazel eyes were mesmerizing. "Yes, because we're mates. And because … I know enough about you." He pursed his lips. "You know where my estate is, right?"

"Yes. Not all that far from where I grew up." I smiled. "Maybe that's why we get along so well—we're both from that same area near the border."

He released my hand and slid his arms around my waist. "As a young lad, I grew up rather near where you lived. I … have friends still in the area."

My smile grew. "That's exciting."

Hadwin hesitated. "I saw you once."

"What?"

"We all knew another of Hoku's daughters was bound to be discovered soon… Then everyone had their eye on you after your identity was announced."

"Yes, they did." That had been awkward for the two and a half years between the formal announcement and moving into the palace. I hadn't been ready to leave my mother and hometown behind yet, but the attention did become daunting.

"I was told you were friendly to vampires." He averted his gaze. "I hope you don't hate that I came to see for myself once… I was in the area, you were nineteen, and…" He shrugged. "I wanted to see if Coterie life was something I would like, if mating with a Blessed Vessel was a path I may want to take. So, I visited the temple when you were there once."

My jaw dropped, the gesture somewhat playful, though I was genuinely surprised. "You stalked me?"

His voice was soft. "Not stalking, just stealing a peek."

I put my hands on his waist. "And your conclusion?"

Grinning, he met my eyes again. "You were young, but I was impressed with the stories and the way you carried yourself. And you're … pleasant to the eyes."

I pressed myself against him. "Just to the eyes?"

His expression was hungry. "No. Not *just* the eyes."

Biting my lip, I gestured with my head. "Come on, let's check out that library again."

Once we entered, I made sure to lock the door. While Lilah and my mother would probably steer clear for some time, I'd rather not have surprises…

"You'll have to recommend some of your favorite books to me," I said.

Hadwin happily obliged, and we took time perusing the shelves while we chatted. He occasionally gave me his opinions on books he'd read, and we pulled out a few, but mostly I loved our personal exchange.

As a human, he'd grown up staggeringly close to where I'd been raised, so we talked a lot about the local landscape, as well as how much had changed in the eighty plus years since his birth there.

We were so at ease in conversation, and I couldn't stop smiling.

After a long while, we set down a few books he'd picked to read. I sat on a long table, and he stood in front of me.

He rested his hands on my knees. "I'm glad you're feeling better after last night and this morning…"

I looked down. "You were rather angry at Elion, weren't you?"

He grumbled. "I still say he should have asked."

Resting my hands on his, I savored his cool touch. "He feels bad enough. Please don't hold it against him."

Hadwin sighed. "I'm learning to let it go. Learning to share you. I understand he's a young pup. And I understand there's a … unique pull that comes with mates."

We met eyes, and I smiled again.

"How is it you were identified as the Blessed Daughter so late in life? Aren't most discovered before they even hit puberty?"

"Ah, yes… My mother has never been a devout temple-goer, and given the circumstances of … our lifestyle, she couldn't fathom her own daughter was Hoku-touched." Half my mother's doubt had been the fact she had never considered a goddess would share her divinity with the offspring of a poor prostitute, but I didn't want to delve into that.

I continued. "Wealthy folks or those with status always screen their children, but it wasn't a consideration for my mother."

He arched an eyebrow. "But the visions…"

Tracing a spiral on his hand, I admired the contrast in our skin colors, his ivory to my warmer tone. "The visions… My mother thought I had too vivid of an imagination, that I liked telling stories. We hadn't realized I wasn't just daydreaming, that my dreams weren't just nightmares."

"Like last night?"

"Yes. I'm still amazed you could sense that, and that I woke so easily." I grasped his shirt. "I might keep you around just to save me from the scarier night visions."

He smiled wide, wider than he had since our meeting. He usually kept his mouth closed.

"You have a nice smile."

He immediately closed his mouth, softening his smile.

I cocked my head. "Now, why would you do that after I complimented it?"

Hadwin shyly pressed his lips together. "Vampire smiles can be intimidating. It reminds people what monsters we are."

"Monsters?" I frowned. "You're quite possibly the kindest and sweetest of my Coterie. You're not a monster."

"No?" His voice lowered to a whisper. "You were terrified of me in the bedding chamber… When I went to bite you, when you tasted my blood."

My heart dropped into my stomach. I wanted to lie, but I couldn't. "I'm sorry."

He gave me a look that conveyed he'd been hurt by it. "You didn't know me, darling. I can't blame you."

"Honestly, I think I was more scared of the blood than you. I've always been weird about it."

He let out a soft chuckle. "That doesn't bode well for me when I'm hoping you'll carry my child."

I would crave blood during a half-vampire pregnancy. The thought of it sent a shiver up my spine. "If I do conceive your child, I imagine I would be less fazed by it due to the cravings."

"I hope for your sake that's true." He sweetly rubbed my knee. "If I'm lucky enough to be the father."

My heart skipped a beat at the notion of him being the one. "Do you hope to be a father for the sake of politics alone, or do you wish for a child personally?" It just now occurred to me he'd been in his thirties when he'd given up his humanity. He'd been old enough to have children as a human before becoming immortal. "Do you already have children?"

He opened his mouth for a moment, then closed it. "I was not lucky enough to have children as a human. As for now, nothing would make me happier than sharing a child with you, Sonta. Personally or politically."

We shared a smile.

"Can I…" He hesitated again.

"You did that in the bedding chamber, too. You can ask me anything."

A tint of red shone in his eyes. "Can I kiss you?"

I chuckled. "Hadwin… You've had your cock inside me. I think it's safe to say you can kiss me!"

He chuckled as well. "That was … duty… This is more personal."

I scooted forward on the desk, my legs spread to get closer. "Kiss me."

Leaning in, he did just that, holding the nape of my neck. Like him, the kisses were sweet and soft. I pushed for more, and he reciprocated. He slowed as I carefully explored his mouth with my tongue, barely gliding across his fangs. With the slightest pressure, I would have cut myself.

We navigated it together, my heart beating wildly. I reached for his pants and scooted myself closer to the edge. With minimal work on my part, his pants fell to the floor, and I rubbed his large cock through his shorts.

He shuddered and pulled back. "We don't have to if you don't want to."

Panting, I narrowed my eyes. "Do you not want to?" Wasn't that the central purpose of the Coterie?

His eyes—now a deep red—spoke volumes of his desire. "Of course I want to. For pleasure and for my people, but … I don't want you to feel…" He rested his hands on my hips. "You're more than the Blessed Vessel. More than even my mate. You're a person, Sonta. And you deserve to be made love to for the sake of it, not just for politics."

I reached a hand up, brushing his lips with my thumb. "Do you regret your service to your people?"

"No."

I slid forward, to the very edge of the table. "Neither do I. And if I'm to spend the next couple of decades side by side with a member of my Coterie because his seed created the realm's next ruler, I would love nothing more than to have it be with someone I genuinely fancy." I would aim for fairness, but I'd prefer bearing Hadwin's child any day over Findlech's or Tyfen's.

After a quick pause to read my face, Hadwin pulled down his shorts. "Do you … want to warm me again?"

Grinning, I drew a finger down his bulging pale cock, and it twitched. "I want it cold this time."

He hiked my dress up more, one hand on my ass as he used the other to guide himself into me.

I took a few measured breaths at the shock of the cold inside me as he eased in, holding me with both hands now.

Once he was all the way in, he leaned in and kissed my neck—right over his love bite. I didn't flinch, but my heart did skip a beat.

I slid my arms around his neck, kissing where I'd reciprocated the bite, and wrapped my legs around him.

His body temperature and the friction were just right as he thrust, his hands keeping me in place on the table. I helped him, working in tandem, taking him deep each time. His shallow breathing mirrored my own pants of pleasure.

Hungry, desperate, I clawed at his back, trying to get closer, to take him farther into me. He thrust so hard, my ass kept lifting off the table and smacking down each time.

"I waited all this time for you," he moaned.

"I'm yours," I whispered between breaths.

He slammed into me so beautifully, so greedily yet so perfectly, as though we'd made love as a couple for centuries.

Near climax, he gazed into my eyes. His irises were fully bloodred; he looked as though he wanted to devour me altogether. Had he been a stranger, and not a Coterie member making love to me, I would have run for my life.

But Hadwin was not a monster, at least not to me. At least not a monster I didn't enjoy…

I tilted my head to the side, offering my neck. Hadwin snatched the opportunity. The pinch of pain was brief, quickly giving over to pleasure that intensified my tightness as he sucked.

He barely tasted me before we both came. Putting his hand over the bite, he leaned his forehead against mine as he finished.

"Thank you," he whispered. "You are just…"

I tightened around him, squeezing where he was most tender.

"Fuck, Sonta," he wheezed.

Leaning in, I nibbled his earlobe. "You just did."

He let out a low laugh.

I wasn't in a rush to move on, and neither was he. He stayed inside me, and we held each other.

"I'm glad your people sent you, Hadwin."

Rubbing my back, he gently hummed.

After another minute, he pulled out and offered a handkerchief from his pants pocket. I accepted but lay down lengthwise on the table. I hadn't lied about the fact I'd be happy if he were my child's father, and I was fine lying there a moment to keep more of him inside me.

"The table's large enough to cuddle if you want," I said.

Smiling, he cleaned himself and pulled his shorts and pants back up. "I enjoy cuddling."

Using our arms for pillows, we lay there, gazing into each other's eyes.

"The cold didn't bother you?"

I grinned wickedly, stroking him again through his pants. "I like your temperature."

He stole a kiss. "I'll confess—I enjoy your warmth around me."

"I'm sure you say that to all your warm-bodied lovers." I winked.

"I … haven't had any, since I became a vampire."

That genuinely surprised me. Many men intended for a Blessed Vessel's Coterie often bedded human women to practice.

"Five decades and only vampire lovers?"

"Well…" He cleared his throat. "I've only had two of those, actually, spanning six months and four years."

Four and a half years out of fifty… "That sounds lonely."

He shrugged.

"Then again, most of my lovers have either been horny young men, experts paid to pleasure me, or … well … politicians in my Coterie."

Hadwin cringed. "I'd rather not be considered a politician."

I ran my fingers through his blond hair, adjusting on the table. "Fair."

"I'd choose you even if I wasn't here for that." His voice and expression were so genuine, so sweet.

"As I would you…"

We chatted a minute more about the dynamic we worked with. When asked, I confessed I did miss some of my pleasure instructors. Not that I was starved for sex, but we'd grown so close. Hadwin confessed again he'd prefer to have me to himself, but that he was trying to cooperate with the others. I let him know he could duck out of uncomfortable situations when he needed to.

Before we got up, my curiosity wouldn't let one question go unasked, not now that I'd offered my neck to him twice.

"Are you familiar with blood play when making love?"

He smirked. "Have you been to a Suck and Fuck, Sonta?"

My cheeks warmed. "No. But my friend said they're pretty amazing. I was always too scared."

"But you're not too scared now?"

I would never grow tired of that face. "Not anymore. Not with you."

He slid a hand to my breast, under my dress, and rubbed my nipple with his thumb. "I've never actually practiced, but I studied. Just for you, in case you'd be interested."

My smile was a mile wide. "Let's try it together."

"Right now?"

I nodded, my nipple rigid. Hadwin slid one of my dress straps off, exposing my breast. "Shall we start with this one?"

He wrapped his lips around my nipple, and I prepared myself for the pinch. He didn't bite right away, instead circling with his tongue playfully. It was divine.

Then he raked his regular teeth against me, nipping.

The pinch of his fangs piercing me was brief, and I inhaled sharply. He released and began sucking.

Goddess save me—it was one of the most *exquisite* things I'd ever experienced. Blood rushed to my nipple, and Hadwin suckled me.

It tickled just right as he drank me in, stimulating me to the extent my whole body became rigid, and my toes curled.

His breath rattled as he voraciously took me in, his free hand groping my other breast.

I could orgasm again in another minute.

"Please," I begged.

He stopped. "Too much?"

I craved him, and he had to be large again already from the consumption of his mate's blood. "I want you inside me."

With a dark exhale, he yanked his pants open and brought himself back out. Not sparing a word, he shifted me to lie straight, hiked up my dress, and plunged himself into me.

Licking up the blood on my nipple, he stared me down as he alternated between quick sucks and thrusts.

This orgasm was so full, so complete and swift that I gasped loud and unrestrained, his name on my lips. He released inside me a second time, and stopped sucking.

The pleasure came in waves, and I couldn't find words. All I saw were stars; all I knew was ecstasy. Lilah *knew* what she was talking about, and she'd been right to save every coin she'd had in our hometown to visit the Suck and Fuck.

After we collected ourselves again, Hadwin lay beside me. "I'd say that went well…"

I laughed, and my muscles ached from having been wound so tight. "That's a mild understatement."

Sticky and bloody, we cuddled, and I didn't give a damn about cleanliness, time, or responsibility. I couldn't have even told you my name. I only knew pleasure and joy in my mate's arms.

27

GALD'S AGENDA

Hadwin and I spent much more time in the library than I'd planned, but every moment had been worth it. Once we gathered our strength to get up and clean the scene of our lovemaking, we also picked up the books Hadwin had wanted to take back to his room.

We were all smiles as we returned to the Coterie common room. I left him with a kiss before he entered, opting to go to my chambers' private entrance and freshen up.

The neck bite had been perfectly placed over his claiming love bite, and was barely sore. My nipple was the one that really ached, but I couldn't stop grinning about it. Luckily, his feeding on me should be relatively safe even during my pregnancy. He'd promised to be careful to not take too much. He had well-paid servants who came regularly to provide blood, and the palace kitchens could always supplement with pig's blood.

I wasn't a meal for Hadwin—I was a sex snack.

In a new dress, I went to the common room. It was nearly dinnertime already.

Gald and Findlech shared a sofa, discussing politics. Hadwin sat in an armchair, freshly dressed with his hair brushed, reading a book.

Hadwin gave me another toothy smile when he saw me, and I blushed.

"Enjoyed the books?" Gald asked knowingly.

I bit my lip, not giving a response. "What are the others up to?"

Gald pointed at the door to the Coterie corridor. "Tyfen has been hiding away in his room. Elion is in his, probably taking care of himself to survive without you. And Haan … he's swimming around somewhere. He got bored of us a while ago and said he was going to explore."

I nodded. I especially couldn't blame Haan. He was the odd man out. "I'm pretty hungry…"

"Worked up an appetite?" Gald smirked. He *really* enjoyed this, and all I could think of was his remark on how much he'd liked my bare ass smashed against Haan's tank glass.

I traded him smirk for smirk. Findlech ignored us both, standing and stretching.

Deciding to take an early dinner, I strode to the Coterie corridor. I knocked on Tyfen's door first.

It opened, and he surveyed me. "Yes?"

"We're going to dinner." I could have just left him in his room, and I probably should have. Why had I even given him any consideration?

"Okay. I'll be right out."

I turned and went to Elion's room, nervous to knock. He answered quickly, his fever apparent. "My mate," he gushed in relief.

"No." I stepped back. "Well, yes, but no—you can't have me right now."

His look was that of pure agony.

"We're going to dinner in five minutes. Do what you need to with a cold cloth and drink your tea, okay?"

He whimpered, and I died a little inside. I almost offered to let him have me, but he needed to push through this fever.

And, frankly, I'd so enjoyed getting to know Hadwin on our little date that I wanted to spend time with someone who had a clear head. I intended to take Gald up to my studio after dinner, getting to know him and giving him another chance with me.

"Before we retire for bed, Elion. I promise." I'd make time for him after Gald.

Nodding, Elion closed the door.

Reentering the common room, I went to the tank and pulled a string. An entire underwater system had been set up to help notify Haan when he was wanted.

Hadwin silently read his book, other than the second I caught him glancing over the pages at me. It may have been the new short dress and me bending slightly that drew his attention.

I sauntered up to him, taking the book from his hands, and sat on his lap. He wrapped his arms around me. "Hello, darling."

Never stop calling me that.

Tyfen walked into the room and waited next to the exit. Gald and Findlech had gone back to chatting about politics.

"So…" I leaned into Hadwin. "Are you joining us for dinner? Or are you already full?"

He let out a breathy chuckle, grazing my neck with his lips. "I may not be hungry." He licked my neck, and I enjoyed the tingle that shot through my body. "But I enjoy the company. And the sweet treats."

Vampires needed blood to survive, though many still enjoyed traditional food as more of a treat or delicacy.

"Good. I enjoy your company, too."

The tank water sloshed with Haan's arrival, and Elion made his appearance, somewhat calmer.

"I'm going to dinner if anyone wants to join me," I informed Haan. "No obligations."

Hadwin didn't give me a choice after I stood—he held my hand right away. Together, we left the common room, Haan diving away again, and the others following after us.

As we sat to eat, I asked Gald if he was interested in touring my studio. He accepted with a smirk.

After leaving dinner, he wrapped an arm around my waist, pulling me closer. "I like the dress change."

I smiled. "I thought you might like it…"

As we strode for my art studio, I asked him about his political conversations with Findlech. Gald's blue eyes lit up as he passionately discussed policies and law.

While I understood law more now, after five years of intensive tutoring in the palace, it still wasn't exactly a passion of mine, not the way it was for Gald.

"You really are here for policy and representation, aren't you?"

He glanced at me. "I told you that upfront, Sonta. But I was also honest about what I think of our union. I *do* think we'll be great friends and lovers." Sliding his hand down, he cupped my ass, then returned it to my waist.

I slung my arm around his waist. "And how could you possibly have known that before meeting me?"

Gald bobbed his head. "I looked into you before making my bid with the high mage council. You seem to have a good head on your shoulders, having spent your youth away from the elite… And I thought you were adorable during your Blessed Daughter acceptance speech when you came to live here."

I shook my head. At this point, I really shouldn't have been surprised anymore that the men of my Coterie had looked into me and even snuck a peek at me. I was one of a kind, unique and necessary to the realm. Gald had come to the palace with thousands at my official speech. I had dripped sweat and stumbled over my words that day, despite the practice.

We approached my studio.

"You wanted to be with me even after you saw me stammer and stutter?"

He stopped at the door, leaning back against it and pulling me in. "I wanted to be with you *especially* because you stammered and stuttered."

I stood tall. "Because you like to have the upper hand?"

Sighing, Gald gave me a look. "That's what you think of me?"

"Well…" I pursed my lips. "Just checking. You're obviously clever to have been chosen as my Coterie member at your age. And … your views are a bit aggressive."

He looked down, thoughtful. "Aggressive? Perhaps. I think of it more as progressive and passionate."

"I hear you want to do away with the unicorn hunting ban." I'd been shocked to hear it.

He met my gaze. "I do. And humans like yourself—all mortals, really—could benefit from the potions and spells we mages can do with their blood and horns. Surely you know how much power they hold."

"They're nearly extinct!"

"Yes, they are. And they're all 'safe' in fae forests." He rolled his eyes. "Don't pretend the fae don't slaughter them for their own pleasure without the emperor knowing. The king himself has been seen wearing unicorn horn adornments, purely for show. At least we mages want to do something with the animals that benefits others."

"They're nearly extinct," I repeated in a whisper.

"Then shouldn't we be doing something about that? My people are willing to cooperate with the fae to bring them out of those forests safely and to start breeding programs. Wise animal husbandry can multiply their numbers, and their byproducts can benefit us greatly."

I took a deep breath, setting a hand on his chest. "I…" It was over my head. It all sounded lovely, but I'd been warned about Gald's agenda… "I like the way it sounds. But implementation is probably trickier than you imagine."

"Not if we work together, Sonta. Isn't that our purpose here? Cooperation? We mages have been trying to head *multiple* projects like this, but we're constantly ignored." He softened his tone. "We have a lot of hope in you. In the Blessed Vessel, raising our voices."

The pronouncement made me a little uneasy. "And if my child isn't yours?"

He frowned, then kissed my forehead. "Sonta… I'm not making threats or demands. I'm frustrated with the issues, and wouldn't take it out on you, no matter the outcome. Okay?"

I gazed into his eyes. He exuded sincerity as far as I could tell.

"It's not like you and I make the final call anyway, right?" I smiled. "But it's good to consider the issues, and I'm always learning."

He smiled as well.

"Is this how you won your bid to become a member of my Coterie at such a young age? You talked your people's ears off? Or did you flirt with them all until they advanced you?"

Gald chuckled, tucking my hair behind my ears. "First of all, I'm eight years your senior. Who's the young one?"

"You're not a grand master… I expected someone much older."

He clutched a hand to his chest in feigned shock. "Ouch. Now you insult my position within my own order…"

I giggled. "Come on. They usually send someone at least a decade older for Coteries…"

His tone was friendly, his expression mirroring it. "Yes, I was given the privilege of coming here because of my research and passion about many topics. And … perhaps I flirted my way up, too." He winked. "Now, are we going to talk politics in this hallway all night, or are you going to show me this studio of yours?"

"Come inside."

As soon as we entered, he waved his hand and lit the candles in the room. He *was* rather handy to have around.

Gald studied the room, wide-eyed. "I'll be honest—part of me wondered if 'studio' was code for something a little more…"

I grinned. "I have a playroom. But when I say studio, I mean studio."

My drawings and paintings covered half the walls.

"I didn't realize you were an artist."

I almost laughed. My work was *not* that astounding. I had never even been properly trained. "If these ever make it into a museum, it will be because of their significance, not my skill."

"You're not half-bad. What's the significance?"

I glanced at the fullest wall, admiring the collection of scenes, the splashes of color. "These are my visions from Hoku. I draw or paint each time I have one." I pointed in the far corner at the shabbiest-looking ones on scraps of paper from my childhood. "My mother kept them all."

Gald stood with his mouth open, dumbfounded. "Wow."

Him being speechless warmed my heart. I may not be as smart as him, but he was genuinely taken aback by this. "Surely you knew the Blessed Daughter has the gift of visions."

He blinked. "Yes, yes, of course… I just… Wow." He turned to me. "Can you train your visions? Divine from them?"

"No. They happen as they will, leaving me with impressions and reflections, but they're not predictive. They teach me the past and the present, if anything." There actually *was* one exception to the rule—a Blessed Vessel secret I safeguarded.

Gald approached the wall, zeroing in on one painting splashed with autumnal colors. "This looks like the high alpha's private garden." He glanced at me, confused. "I thought you hadn't traveled the realm. Not even to shifter lands."

I raised an eyebrow. "Visions."

He shook his head, focusing on the painting again. "I haven't been there myself, but I've seen these decorative structures in a shifter cultural center in the heart of their lands."

I looked forward to traveling more once I was pregnant, but the visions gave me a head start on getting to know my own realm.

"If you want to take a look around, feel free to. I did actually want to paint one real quick about a night vision I had, if you don't mind." I had hoped this would be a multipurpose visit.

"Sure thing."

I sat at my desk and pulled out my paints, dripping some water into each of the colors I expected to use. Gald studied my paintings intently.

Blowing out a breath, I closed my eyes and returned to the night vision—the horrible mercreature in murky waters drowning me and feasting upon me. It made me want to lose my dinner.

Shaking the unease away, I opened my eyes and set to work, dipping a brush into the blue and black. I lost myself with each stroke, having picked a scene from under the water—after being pulled in but before the beast bit me.

Like a scholar in a museum, Gald giddily assessed each of my paintings, commenting now and then. He recognized several scenes, either from their historical significance or from having been to the location.

When I was halfway through my painting, he walked behind me. "Dark." He gently rested his hands on my shoulders, massaging.

"You don't know the half of it…" It was mostly dark blue at the moment, with a pinprick of moonlight near the center; I hadn't even added the creature yet.

He watched and massaged. I tried not to get distracted. As I painted in a faint image, I explained to him my vision.

"That's rather bleak and ghastly," he said, his tone matching his words.

I shrugged. "My divine mother sends me many more pleasant than painful visions. But there must be balance. There exists both good and bad, right?"

"True."

"And I think…" I focused on painting the sharp, spindly fingers it had held me with. "I think it's a reminder to not let your guard down, to not disregard the warnings of others, and to accept that some things truly are past our help." My acceptance of it saddened me, but the wisdom was sound, and it rang true with each stroke of my brush.

"Let us hope the unicorns don't fall to such a fate as these monsters."

I frowned. "Not if we can help it. It's not too late."

Gald crouched, kissing my neck. "I like the way you think." He kissed again, and again.

I shrugged him off. "I want to finish, then I can show you some more attention?"

"Of course." He backed up and looked around the room. A few minutes later, he said, "Now *that's* a painting…"

I glanced behind me. "Oh, please don't touch those." He'd taken the covering off a large easel. "Those aren't mine. I share the studio with my friend."

He had the covering still lifted. "One of your friends in the bedding chamber and at the celebration?"

"Yes." I smiled. "Her name's Lilah. I'll introduce you all soon."

Gald studied the painting again. "This is you. And not a speck of clothing on you."

I grinned wider as he made eye contact.

"Did you pose for it?"

My cheeks warmed. "Yes." She'd painted it less than two weeks ago, and we'd made love after she'd finished it.

His eyes twinkled. "Do you think she would paint me fucking you?"

I swallowed. "I'm not sure. I'll have to ask."

He stole another glance at the painting before lowering the covering. "I hope she says yes. She certainly seemed to enjoy watching you get taken in the bedding chamber. Perhaps as much as I did."

My heart skipped a beat, and I let out an awkward chuckle. "I guess she's as much of a voyeur as you are."

Gald angled his head, his gaze piercing. "Is she a lover?"

And now my heart raced… I wouldn't deny Lilah. She wasn't exactly a secret; I just hadn't been ready to broach that topic with my Coterie.

He smiled knowingly. "I could tell."

"How would you know that?"

"I'm good at reading people." He shrugged.

"I do plan on telling everyone, truly. And we're not breaking the divine edict. I swear it!"

Gald scrunched his eyebrows. "I wasn't questioning your integrity to the Great Ritual, Sonta. I was just curious. And that secret's yours to keep for as long as you wish. You can trust me."

I shrank in embarrassment for panicking about his motives. "There's just a lot going on right now…"

He nodded. "Will it be hard for you two to be separated?" Glancing at the covered canvas, he added, "Perhaps she would not like to paint me taking you."

"We'll be fine. We're casual about that part of our lives. She's my friend, first and foremost. And I honestly don't think she'd mind painting us…" Given her enjoyment in the bedding chamber and allowing me to watch Schamoi take her in my bed… "Though…"

I faced Gald more directly, crossing my legs. "Maybe I don't want to be painted having you take me." I grinned. "Maybe I should be the one taking *you*."

He matched my grin. "I'd enjoy that. Are you ready to practice? Or do you want to finish your painting?"

I gestured behind me with a thumb. "Just a little more work on painting the creature. I don't always have animals or people in my visions, and when I do, they're more of blobs when I paint them." Lilah was much more skilled than me at portraits and body form. "But since this one looked so ghoulish, I'm not afraid it will turn out poorly if I add a little more detail."

"If you'd like to practice painting the human form, I volunteer to be your subject." He gestured at his well-dressed body.

"I really wouldn't do you justice. Maybe another time… I just wanted to do this one before the vision faded."

Gald looked hurt. "I see… It's not often I offer to strip down for a partner and they so easily refuse a look."

I liked him. "Fine. Let's see what we're working with." I folded my arms, leaning back.

He wore a look of satisfaction, unbuttoning his vest, shrugging it off and draping it over the back of a chair. Next came his shirt, and I didn't at all hate his muscles. He wasn't as well built as the immortals, but he still took care of his body.

Gald removed his shoes and socks, then started on his belt.

"Thank you," I said softly. "For using your ceremonial robe to cover me in the bedding chamber. I really appreciated that."

Meeting my gaze, he gave me a gentle smile. "You deserved the privacy and respect, no matter how limited."

I glanced at my wrist inking for a moment, running a thumb over it. Allies, friends, and lovers. Intentions and promises Gald and I had made to each other.

He removed his pants and shorts, standing bare before me without a hint of shyness. Then he started to flex his muscles.

I laughed.

"I'll try not to take that personally."

His mop of curly red hair did him no favors in the 'strong, dark, and broody' category, but he was nonetheless handsome. I lifted a finger, spinning it.

Following my instructions, he slowly turned, flexing more. He did have a nice ass. Why was I such an ass person?

After he made a full circle, he stopped, holding his arms out. "So…? Do you want to paint me?"

My eyes wandered from his locks to his feet, drawing a line down his chest, to the hairs near his groin, to his cock… "An admirable subject, but I fear you would still look like a deplorable blob."

"If you're not ready to paint me, how about you *paint* me?"

I furrowed my brow. "You just said the same thing twice…"

He winked. "I'll be your canvas."

Accepting the challenge, I picked up my brush and approached him. "And what should I paint? The night sky on your chest?"

Grabbing my waist, he pulled me to his bare body. "This is the first time you've seen every inch of me. I'm curious what you like. You could show me what you like on my body…"

He toed a fine line between confident and arrogant, but he wasn't wrong. I'd barely seen any of him in our claiming, and he'd worn shorts to my bed last night.

"I can do that." I stole a kiss, and he released me. "I won't paint your lips, because I don't think paint tastes good. But you're not a bad kisser."

He raised his eyebrows in acknowledgement.

I started with his face, dotting my brush onto his cheeks. "I like your dimples."

His instant smile displayed them.

"And I'd rather not blind you, so this will have to do for your eyes…" I swiped a line next to each, then I dabbed a dot on his nose. "For the piercing."

"I've been considering getting more…"

"Where?" I asked. He already had one each in his nose, lip, and tongue.

A smirk preceded his suggestive answer. "There are a few imaginative places I can think of…"

Clearing my throat, I ignored the obvious flirtation. One of my pleasure instructors had a pierced cock, and I had never complained about the sensation it brought me.

"Well… I won't hold you back."

I moved on, fighting my grin. I felt guilty for not marking his ears, but there was nothing really noteworthy about them, and as for his hair… Red wasn't my favorite, and his ego could handle the blow.

I took another step back, glancing at his chest. Swiping an *X* over his heart, I smiled. "Allies, friends, and lovers."

He looked at his matching magical bond mark. "We already have something for that."

"Then let it be for having a good heart."

"I would like to think I do have one."

Looking him up and down, I contemplated what to do next. "Legs are legs, right?"

"Are they?"

Just for fun, I swiped on each of his knees. "Gotta have those for a lot of different positions I like."

He hummed his approval.

I spared a glance at his feet. "No offense, but I'm not a foot person. Nothing against them, just not a fetish of mine."

"I can accept that."

Whirling, I went back to my desk.

"That's all?" he asked.

"I was low on paint." It wasn't true, but it gave me a moment to do what I wanted.

With my back to him, concealing my actions, I painted the palms of my hands, then dipped my brush in paint again. Once I returned to him, I gingerly set the brush on Lilah's table, then held up my hands.

Smirking, I pressed against him, reaching around and grabbing each of his cheeks. "I really like your ass, Gald."

He chuckled, kissing me a few times, sliding his hands up my dress to caress me. I'd worn undergarments just for him, and he seemed to approve.

I stopped kissing as he hardened against me. "Not quite done."

As he released me, I grabbed my paintbrush, stroking a line from his chest X down to his navel and just a little beyond. Without another word, I returned my brush to my desk. Luckily, I had a large washbasin next to my desk, so I cleaned my hands off.

"You're kidding me," he said, half-playful, half-wounded. "You would injure me so deeply?"

Fighting another smile, I turned, grabbing a towel and wiping my hands clean. "What do you mean?"

He angled his head. "You insult me for not being a grand master, and now this? I am a *healthy*, *virile* man, sent here to impregnate you, and you don't even do me the decency of painting my cock?"

I belted out a laugh, gripping my painting chair. "Don't be so fragile, Gald. I didn't paint your lips because I don't want the paint in my mouth. And I didn't paint your cock because I don't want paint inside me when I'm ready to fuck."

I sat in my chair and picked up my detail brush again. I dipped it in the watercolor, but the pan dried up instantly. Pursing my lips, I held back a sigh.

Gald had been one of the most forthcoming about himself when the mages had submitted him for my Coterie candidate. His control of the candle flames in my chambers had already confirmed his born-magic—he was an elemental mage.

Facing him again, I crossed my arms. "I'm not ready yet. You're going to have to sit tight—cold, naked, and drying—until I'm done painting this vision. Stealing my water won't speed me."

Challenge glistened in his eyes as he swished a hand through the air. Water pattered on the paints behind me.

"Well done." Far too satisfied with myself, I returned to painting. I wanted him to work for this.

Gald dragged a free chair opposite me, watching me work. "Don't mind me."

I stole a glance to confirm he'd covered the chair with a dropcloth—it would have nice handprints on it now. Gald stretched himself out like he owned the place, grabbed his cock, and ever so slowly pumped himself.

My mouth went dry as he hardened, as he peeked out of his foreskin with each deliberate stroke.

"I'm sorry. I'm not distracting you, am I?"

My eyes snapped up to his. "No. Not at all." I coldly focused on my painting, *fully* distracted, and now wet.

He softly moaned. "I guess I'll just keep myself company over here."

"I guess so." I painted a skull on the mercreature.

"You're killing me, Sonta."

"I doubt that. I've never known a man to actually expire from lack of arriving in a woman. Though, there's a first for everything."

"You're wicked."

I hummed my satisfaction. After a minute, he stood and walked back to Lilah's painting station. No sooner had he returned to my side than he'd set his wooden wand on my desk.

That intrigued me… I met his gaze. "I don't know how to use a wand, especially not with paints."

Wearing a crooked grin, he narrowed his eyes. "I can wait all night for you to finish your painting. You won't make me beg for sex." His eyes flickered to the wand. "You'll be the one begging."

My core heated at the threat, at the fierceness of his promise. I failed to sound properly disinterested as I returned to my painting. "Good to know."

28
ART IN MULTIPLE FORMS

It didn't take me long to finish my painting. Gald waited in his chair, naked and hungry for me.

Lifting the paper, I showed it to him. "There we have it."

"I'd say it was beautiful, but…" It *had* been a rather ghastly vision.

Shrugging, I stood. After selecting a spot on the wall, I tacked up the new contribution.

I returned to my chair, crossing my legs elegantly. "I'm trying to remember… Were we going to do something else tonight?" I didn't allow my eyes to leave his, didn't allow them to trace his every bare feature.

"I want you naked," he said, almost in command.

"Hmm…" I playfully bobbed my head as though I considered. Without much delay, I got up. "You said you like to unwrap things. Surely you don't expect me to do it myself when I dressed for your preferences."

Gald gave me a satisfied smile. "Come here." He stood, and I did as ordered. With a swift motion, he grabbed my dress and lifted it over my head, tossing it to the side. Licking his lips, he surveyed me, then hooked his fingers through the waistband of my underwear and dragged it to the ground.

He didn't lose eye contact.

My breasts peeked out of a corset, and he took a moment to enjoy the view before ordering me to turn around. He undid my corset with skill, though not gently as he tugged it loose.

"Arms up, love."

I enjoyed being undressed, and readily obeyed. After Gald set the corset aside, he took his time with his hands, caressing me. His gentle touch made it hard to breathe properly.

"Do you want the paintbrush?" I asked as his hands drifted from my hips to my front.

"I'm a tactile person. I didn't get a proper chance to study and assess my favorite parts of you in the bedding chamber, now did I?"

I sharply inhaled as he slipped a finger to my clit, pressing himself against me.

He let out a satisfied groan, then nibbled on my ear as he gently circled my clit.

If this was a game of wills, I was royally screwed. My breathing was absolutely ragged.

"So tense already…"

"I, uh…" I whispered.

"You what?" He pressed his cock harder against me.

"Nothing." I wouldn't beg. Instead, I let his hands roam.

After a moment, he spun me around, taking me in from head to toe. "Lovely." He smiled.

I reached to my desk and picked up the paintbrush, offering it to him.

Gald plucked it from my hand and set it back down.

My jaw dropped, and I angled my head. "I don't paint more of you, so you won't paint me *at all?*"

He reached a hand forward and held my chin. "I wouldn't taint your perfect form." He softly kissed me, his free hand taking mine and placing it on his erection. "Plus, I'd need a whole vat of paint to dunk you in if I wanted to point out the best parts of you."

No wonder he'd been given the chance to represent his people in my Coterie. He knew how to speak, how to wrap me around his finger. As I held him, I *almost* asked him to end my torture.

After one more kiss, Gald let my chin go. "Take a seat."

Not having a clever response, I obeyed again.

"Might as well make use of my knees since you've marked them." He grinned, and I spread my legs for him as he knelt before me.

"If you're uncomfortable, tell me to stop," he said. "If you need me inside you, I'm sure you'll find the right words to convey that."

I simply shrugged, as if he wasn't about to find out how absolutely wet I was…

Gald held up his hands, and all the candles in the room snuffed out, save the closest one to us. Small flames lit at the end of Gald's fingertips. I blinked, mesmerized by the way the light danced and formed shadows around us.

He lowered those hands to my skin and caressed my arms. The flames didn't burn my flesh, didn't singe my hair, but they were hot. As he gently swiped his fingertips down my arms, the heat left temporary trails of red skin.

He had promised me magic with our sex, after all.

Neither of us said a word as he worked his magic on my chest, stomach, and legs. It was like a hot rock massage—far above body temperature, and just leaning toward a hint of pain.

Tracing his hands back up my legs, he tickled my thighs just right. Then he extinguished his finger flames.

Opening his mouth, Gald lit a flame at the end of his tongue. His eyes looked menacing as he leaned down, keeping my gaze, and dragged his tongue from my clit to my opening.

Goddess save me…

If my insides weren't on fire before, they were now, especially with the extra sensation of his tongue piercing. I gripped my chair like my life depended on it, forcing myself to not moan, to not move. Sweat beaded on my forehead.

Snatching his wand from the table, Gald extinguished his flame and pulled back. "Is there anything you wanted to ask me, Sonta?"

"No," I panted.

His grin told me he enjoyed watching me suffer. "We'll soon see about that…"

He slid his wand into me. I sat carefully as he went deep. Rotating it, he scraped me, applying gentle pressure.

And then I lost all hope as he tapped the end and it began to vibrate like one of Lilah's charmed tools.

"Shit," I muttered, clenching my teeth as he angled and rubbed it inside me with precision.

Gald hummed with delight at my torture.

I could barely breathe as I wriggled, as my desire built, as I tightened.

"What do you want?" he asked.

"I…" *Oh, goddess…* "I'm fine. Your wand can give me all I need." He could leave it there, and I'd complete without his cock just fine.

The wand stopped vibrating. "We wouldn't want that…"

"No!" I pleaded as he withdrew it from me.

His blue eyes gleamed in the candlelight. "What do you want?" He stood and sat back on his own chair, massaging his erection, running his tongue piercing against his teeth.

Maybe on another day I would be stronger, but I wanted him like a drowning person wanted air.

"I want you inside me," I blurted, aching for release.

He released his cock, opening his arms. "Come take what you want."

In the blink of an eye, I leapt from my chair and mounted him. Every inch of him slid into me like it belonged there.

His fingers dug into my hips as I rode him, as we moaned and panted and kissed. I would definitely not complain if he chose to get more piercings, or if he expanded his magic use during sex, but he was perfect as he was.

Unrestrained, I called his name into his ear as I came. He kept thrusting underneath me until he found his release, calling my name as well.

With my arms wrapped around his neck, I crumpled, my breasts to his chest, his hands on my ass.

"Thank you," I whispered, kissing his neck.

He kissed mine in return. "Thank *you*."

We stayed there for a while, both spent, holding each other.

Gald caressed me. "I can't promise we'll always see eye to eye," he whispered, his voice sweet. "I'm too practical for that. But I'll always listen."

It was as good of a promise as anyone could make in a union. I appreciated his honesty amidst all the flattery and lovemaking.

I nuzzled his neck. "Me too."

After seemingly forever, I leaned back, holding tight with my legs. I pulled my wrist to me, rubbing the magical bond mark. He brought his next to mine.

"You really mean it?" I asked. "Friends, allies, lovers?"

He nodded. "I'm not perfect, but I am honest. And a hard worker, and that extends to the relationships I'm in." He lifted my wrist and kissed the mark. I returned the favor with his matching mark. We shared a smile and another kiss on the lips.

I glanced at his chest, and my smile grew to a smirk. We were a mess. Sweat and rubbing had smeared some of his paint onto me. "We should clean up."

He nodded.

I stood, and his cum dripped down my leg. Hopefully enough had stayed inside to do its job. So far, from what I knew of the man, I would be happy to bear his child and work alongside him.

Gald was a perfect gentleman as we cleaned ourselves and the studio. I asked him why he never called me or the other Coterie members by our titles. He had addressed me formally a couple of times, but he'd almost immediately become casual with me.

"Would you rather I be formal with you?" he asked.

"No…"

"I'd like to think we're not so different, I guess. We each have gifts—yours from deity and mine from my parents. Neither of us grew up amongst the elite."

I smiled. "But what about the others, like Findlech? You don't address them formally either."

He shrugged, grabbing his shorts. "Yes, they're more experienced and titled than I am, but we were all chosen for this Coterie. I call it an even playing field. Others can stroke their egos; they don't need me to."

Yes, I definitely liked Gald.

After redressing, he held me from behind, the candles relit, admiring my paintings again. He said he'd be happy to join me here again—with or without sex. I loved the idea of it. I already looked forward to seeing if Lilah would paint us making love, or more fully painting each other again, or simply having his companionship while I painted.

"Life is art," he said. "And so is love."

After he extinguished the candles, we walked hand in hand through the quiet palace hallways. Night had long since fallen, and we took our time.

He gave me another kiss at the common room door.

I rested a hand on his chest. "I think I'm going to sleep alone tonight, so you don't have to stay up wondering." I didn't want to ruin the nice day with any more drama like I'd woken up to, with my bed full of Coterie members.

"Sounds good. I'll give my own bed a try."

We entered together, and I couldn't be too shocked to find most of the men occupying the room. Findlech was gone, and I wasn't surprised at that. He'd made his 'contribution' of the day, and it wasn't like either of us had a mind to cuddle each other.

Tyfen sat alone, brooding and sparing me a glance.

Elion sat alone, obviously suffering from mating fever, a pillow covering his lap.

Hadwin leaned against the wall, chatting with Haan in his tank.

Giving my hand a squeeze and kissing me on the cheek, Gald bid me good night and left through the Coterie corridor door.

I assessed the others as they looked to me. After making up my mind, I strode for the tank.

"I'm planning to sleep alone tonight," I told Haan and Hadwin. "Haan, if you'd *prefer* to sleep in my pond, I wouldn't mind, but I don't plan to share my bed tonight."

He nodded. "I'll take that offer."

I smiled. "Great. I'll let you know when I'm ready." I turned to Hadwin. "As for you…"

Haan interjected, excusing himself for the time being, swimming to his room.

Hadwin embraced me. "How has your evening been?"

I pursed my lips, taking in his eyes—now mostly hazel. "I thought you didn't want to know about me and the others…"

He smiled awkwardly. "True. I don't need details. I just want you to be safe and happy."

My heart warmed, and I lifted a hand to his face scruff. "I enjoyed myself. I painted my vision from last night."

His smile grew. "Glad to hear your evening was a good one. I rather enjoyed the book I read."

I pulled myself closer, wrapping my arms around him. "If we read through them too quickly, we'll have to visit the library again soon."

A red gleam in his eye told me that was exactly the kind of challenge he enjoyed.

I kissed him, and he gave back more than I'd expected him to. I didn't mind.

"Will you … often … sleep alone?" he asked.

Why was he so sweet and cute?

"Probably not. I'd just like to tonight."

He nodded.

Since he'd prefer to not constantly know about or see me being intimate with the others, I decided to pay him fair warning. "You should probably go to bed." With Elion and Tyfen remaining in the room, I'd already formed a plan. While Gald clearly enjoyed watching, Hadwin wouldn't.

Hadwin nodded, kissing me one last time. "Good night, darling."

My smile followed him as he left the room.

The room fell silent and awkward. Tyfen looked like he had been stewing alone all day. Elion looked like he'd been suffering all day.

I walked to Elion, kneeling before him, resting my hands on his knees. "How are you doing?"

He panted out a breath. "I'm fine." His voice shook with the lie.

Frowning, I rubbed his knee. He was showing remarkable restraint for not having been able to take me since this morning.

"I'd like to help you," I said. For show, I ought to have made the offer in front of the others, but at least Tyfen would know I was trying to be fair.

"You've already had me more than the others," I said. "But I wouldn't mind sucking you off."

He groaned with anticipation, shifting in his seat. "I'll take it."

We could have gone to either of our rooms and had privacy, but I was still bitter toward Tyfen, and he would pay for his humiliation in kind.

I removed the pillow from Elion's lap. His pants were already bulging. As I went to undo them, he joined me, making quick work of freeing himself.

His lycan eyes were sharply fixed on me, his strong hands firmly planted on my shoulders as he scooted closer.

I first circled his cock with my tongue. He twitched and shuddered. I wouldn't torture him. He'd already endured enough.

Opening my mouth, I took him in deep, and sucked.

Lilah and I had joked for years about her having the larger capacity for alcohol and me having the larger capacity for a man's dick and cum.

Shamelessly, Elion moaned as I sucked. It didn't take long before his fingers dug into me as he thrust and fucked my mouth with fervor. I had long since learned how to do it well, and how to not choke on a man or his cum. Granted, his knot definitely made it trickier…

Elion ravaged me, and I kept sucking until he arrived and his salty seed filled my mouth and drained down my throat. I sucked even after he released, drinking him in, savoring the sweet look of pleasure on his face.

He leaned back after a moment, running his hands through my hair. "My mate," he whispered.

I looked up at him with a smile, removing my mouth. "My mate." Thinking back to Gald's question about Elion getting a sore cock, I said, "Sorry my saliva doesn't heal as a shifter mate's would."

Nonetheless, I licked him clean. A knotted cock was a curious thing to behold, though it quickly shrank to appear normal.

He groaned through half-closed eyes. "You're more than enough as you are."

After I'd cleaned him up, he put himself back in his pants. I smiled up at him again.

"You're sleeping alone?" He frowned.

"Yes. This time. You can be the first to claim me tomorrow."

He calmly blew out a breath. "Okay."

I didn't even spare Tyfen a look as I rose to my feet. Despite the emperor's reminder about the spirit of fairness surrounding the Great Ritual, I was still angry with Tyfen.

Yes, Findlech was rude, but that was mostly his elf nature and age. I could endure bland sex with him for the sake of political equality.

But Tyfen… He had intentionally made a spectacle, had insulted me and demanded to bed me at least once a day. I didn't need to trade barbs with him to make my sentiments clear.

"Good night, Elion." I gave him one last smile, and strode to my private chambers. I closed the door behind me with great satisfaction.

On His Knees

I took my time washing up, cleaning my mouth of Elion's cum and soaking away any remaining paint and cum from my time with Gald in my studio. I'd really enjoyed getting to know Hadwin and Gald better, and I was more at ease with both of them. As for Elion, I looked forward to the morning already, and was proud of him for pushing past his mating fever.

I savored the warmth of my lavender bath, getting out before it turned cold. Dressed in a slinky nightie, I looked at my wardrobe, deciding what I'd wear first tomorrow.

"You would slight me so publicly?" Tyfen said behind me.

I whirled. "I didn't invite you into my chambers."

"Exactly." His stupid green eyes stared me down.

"Get out."

"No."

My nostrils flared. He wouldn't *dare* hurt me. At least I hoped not… "Get out, or I'll call the guards. And if you force yourself on me…" I gritted my teeth. "You'll wish you'd never been born. Get the hell out of my room!"

He rolled his eyes. "I wouldn't hurt you or force myself on you, *Your Holiness*. But it's *your* responsibility to see to it that all races get an equal chance at rulership representation. Or have you forgotten that?"

I took a step forward. "It's *your* responsibility to not be an asshole so I *want* to give you more chances after the claimings. Or have you forgotten that? You brought it on yourself. I told you in that bedding chamber to not make demands, and then you sided with Findlech this morning.”

“And yet you let *him* fuck you, didn’t you?”

Unintimidated, I stood tall. “Yes, and that speaks volumes, doesn’t it? About how detestable I find you…”

“It’s not fair for only the fae to be unrepresented.”

I shrugged. “Haan hasn’t gotten a second chance with me. Perhaps after I let him take me again…”

Tyfen’s expression darkened. “You haven’t been with him again because he’s a fucking fish who would drown you, and we all know it. Stop acting like a child.”

My ears heated. “You have no right to talk about him that way, or to have *any* time with me. Get out of my chambers. *Now.*”

He stood there, blocking my dressing room exit.

After a moment of staring each other down, I stepped closer. He was much more intimidating so close.

“Get out of my way.”

His expression softened a degree, but he didn’t move. “This is about my people and your calling, not you and me.”

“Like hell it is. Get out of my way, or I’ll scream for the guards. If you want to be spared utter shame and possible war, I’d suggest going to your own room.”

Tyfen pursed his lips. “Please,” he practically whispered.

It caught me by surprise as he met my eyes, his anger now melted away. “Please,” he repeated.

I said nothing.

“I… I’m sorry. I shouldn’t have agreed with Findlech.”

“You shouldn’t have said and done *several* things, Tyfen,” I said coldly.

Closing his eyes, he tilted his head back. “You’re right. And I can’t undo that, but I also can’t…” He sighed. “I can’t go back to my people and look them in the eye knowing I ruined the likelihood they’d get fair representation.” He met my gaze, searching.

His change in demeanor cracked a thin layer off the ice around my heart, but a small show of penitence would not induce me to take him to bed. “Your conscience is your own to suffer with. It’s not my fault you’ve treated me the way you have. I never provoked it.”

Tyfen’s throat bobbed. Slowly, he got to his knees. “Please,” he firmly pleaded with more emotion than I’d thought possible from a prick like him.

“My people don’t deserve to be ignored. *I’m sorry*, Your Holiness. It’s not their fault I was an idiot. Please don’t punish them.” He lowered his head to the ground at my feet. “I *beg* of you. I *don’t* ask for myself.”

I honestly didn't know how to feel or act. He was groveling, something I hadn't expected at all. And he sounded genuine.

Considering his plea, I thought of his people. But my pride was still wounded. "Your parents should have chosen their own people over their son, then. They were fools to send a prince who would so easily destroy their chances of producing the next ruler."

Silence hung in the air for a long moment.

"You're right," he said softly. Looking up, he met my gaze again. Tears coated his eyes. "I'll never argue that point. They should have sent *anyone* but me. But we can't change that now. I'm here, and I'm asking you to overlook my faults, for my people."

Actual tears… Something akin to true regret laced his words, and I was faced with a decision I truly didn't want to make.

I let out a heavy sigh. "If you behave, then you can have a chance sometime tomorrow."

"But the sooner, the bet—"

"Tomorrow or not at all," I rebutted. "Speak another word, and you've chosen the latter."

Tyfen pressed his lips together, slowly nodding.

"Now get out of my room, and if you *ever* come in here again without my permission, I'll more than deny you chances to sire a child."

Swallowing, he stood, turned, and walked back through my chamber to the common room.

I drew a calming breath, then let it out. He drove me mad; he didn't have a right to me or my pity. Why had something in me ached at seeing his eyes tear-coated?

Flopping on my bed, I closed my eyes, cooling and meditating. All I could see were Tyfen's eyes.

Frustrated, I got up and went to my pond. I pulled Haan's call string, and he swam to me in no time.

"How are you doing?"

I forced a smile. "Fine." I almost asked if he wanted my company—I could lie on the floor next to the pond… But it was a silly question, since he always slept underwater.

Sitting on the ledge of the raised pond, I gently swished my legs through the water. "How was your day? I'm sorry I've neglected you."

His smile didn't waver. "I don't expect you to dote on me. I came here with an understanding of how rare our representation is, and how hard it can be to fully coexist with land-walkers."

I frowned, and he chuckled.

"I do like swimming," I said. "I'd like to swim with you sometime."

His turquoise scales flashed in the candlelight as he adjusted his grip on the edge of the pond. "I'd love that."

"Great. We'll plan on it soon."

We chatted for a while about his exploration of the palace waterways and his taste in food, as well as his discussions with the others. It was cute when he explained how much he'd already learned from talking to Hadwin since he could provide both a human and vampire perspective.

My eyelids grew heavy, and Haan called me out on my exhaustion. "Tomorrow's another day, and I'd be happy to talk more then."

I gave him a tired smile.

"Would you like a kiss?" he offered, his voice laced with that usual husky airiness.

It was sweet he wanted to try again. "Sure."

He puckered his lips, and I lowered mine to his. He was still stiff and untrained, but I'd be up to the challenge of teaching him. I gave him a few passes to demonstrate, and left it at that.

"Thank you, Haan."

"You're welcome. Have a good night, Sonta."

"Good night."

He dove to a comfortable corner of the pond, curling up, and I returned to my bed.

After blowing out my candle and slipping under the covers, I lay for a while, simply breathing and soaking up the calm quiet. A picture fluttered through my mind.

No, not just a picture… Another vision.

I let it take me where it wanted.

Barefoot, I strolled through a field, morning dew on vibrant green grass, surrounded by enormous mountains. Early autumn leaves from tall trees drifted to the ground in every color as I walked toward an ancient stone wall. Moss and bright lichen clung to the rocks, and in the center of the wall, giant ornate iron doors had been locked shut.

Glancing over my shoulder, I verified I was alone. A bird cawed in a distant tree, and a light breeze rustled the leaves. I carefully tried to open the door, but to no avail. Instead, I peeked beyond it as much as I could.

Other than some flowering bushes on the periphery, the only thing in view was a massive intricately carved statue. I didn't recognize the design, but it sure was grand and ancient. It blocked whatever hid behind it.

Before I was of a mind to walk around the wall for another way in, the vision dissolved.

I blinked, reconnecting my senses to my chamber, the soft trickle of the pond grounding me.

The vision hadn't been so much eerie as it was a mixture of peace and sorrow… While my visions were sometimes influenced by events or emotions I'd recently experienced, I didn't usually have them so close to each other.

This one had to be a coincidence, a random vision from Hoku for me about somewhere in the realm. My heart was still hesitant, though, and then I realized why that emotion had been attached to such a beautiful place—Tyfen.

Perhaps our encounter tonight had evoked more pity in me than I'd realized. His tears had really affected me, and the way he'd said his parents should have sent *anyone* but him.

He didn't deserve my pity, or visions cropping up that mirrored the emotion his words had evoked in me.

Forcing myself to close my eyes, I hiked up my sheets and turned on my side. It took me a while to fall asleep, but I slept soundly.

30

MATING FEVER

I dared to take a dip in the pond shortly after waking. Haan quickly stirred and swam up to me. We exchanged morning greetings.

We practiced kissing. I made sure to not wrap myself around him, to not bump or rub him wrong and incite a sexual frenzy. He took instruction well when I gave him tips on kissing. It was sweet that, despite him being twenty years my senior, he was perfectly teachable. And, unlike with Findlech, I rather enjoyed the fact Haan was an older man. His maturity was attractive in its own way. I genuinely regretted not being able to be with him right now, even if it were only for cuddling.

Before getting out of the water, I swam a couple of laps, and he accompanied me at his leisure. I soaked an extra minute before getting out, and at my request he showed me his aquatic earrings more closely.

"Haan, would you … be up for more sex? If we could make it safe?"

He smiled wide. "I absolutely would. I found it pleasurable." Shrugging, he added, "And of course another chance to sire a ruler would be important for my people."

I nodded, returning his smile. If I was going to take a risk, it should be soon. Several months pregnant would not be the time to allow him to constantly beat me against the edge of a tank or pond, or deprive me of oxygen. And his companions in my Coterie were gaining the advantage with my womb already.

"We'll sort something out." I gave him a peck on the cheek. "I'm going to get out and ready for the day…" It was mostly true.

He took the hint, offering a bow. "I'll see you soon, then."

As I climbed the stairs out of the pond, his tail splashed the water in a dive, and he disappeared through a tunnel that connected my chambers to his, with a stop at the common room in the middle.

I wrung my hair out over the pond and stripped off my soaked nightie.

Knowing good and well that Elion would already be chomping at the bit to have me, I remained naked as I popped the door open just enough to peek.

"My mate!" He jumped up from his seat and rushed to me.

I let him in, smiling. Our relationship so far, because of his mating fever, was a simple thing. It was lust and pleasure, and fast fucking. But it was also untainted devotion and care. I'd happily endure his constant need if it meant I was able to enjoy everything else.

"You're already naked," he panted, practically tearing his clothes off.

I was wet for him, and quickly backed up onto the bed before his shorts were off.

The ferocity in his grey eyes grew as I backed away from him. "I want you."

Grinning, I scooted further back. "Is that so?"

A low growl rumbled in his throat, and it brought me great delight.

"Maybe you should show me how much you want me…" I challenged with a raised eyebrow.

In no time flat, he'd sprinted onto the bed and grabbed me, flipping me over like he had in the bedding chamber.

I was all smiles as he lifted my hips, spread my legs, and plunged into me.

Lost in pure ecstasy from his unrestrained pounding into me, I didn't even have it in me to pretend I wanted to try to get away. Not with that knotted cock rubbing me just right.

Elion came forcefully, and it tipped me over the edge. No one made me moan and gasp the way he did.

Recovering, he rested on my back, still inside me. He kissed my shoulder. "Good morning."

I squeezed my pelvic muscles around him, making him shudder. "Good morning."

He kissed me more. "How many times can I have you today?"

Sighing, I considered my day. I hadn't worked it all out yet. "I'm not sure."

"Yesterday was too hard. Only the once, and then before bed…"

"I'm proud of how well you did…"

He softly moaned. After a couple of minutes, he pulled himself out and licked me clean. I was so stimulated I relished every second of it.

While I enjoyed sucking off a partner now and then, licking them clean wasn't always my thing, and he didn't seem offended when I turned down his offer to return the favor. But I did wipe him off.

Kneeling beside me, he kept an adoring smile on his face.

"Cuddle and chat for a little while before we go to breakfast?" I asked.

Without a word, he lay next to me, wrapping himself around me. I cherished every inch of skin that touched. He gently fondled my breasts, and I bolstered my courage to ask him a question that had been drifting in my mind for some time.

"Would you be against helping heal any injuries I have?" I wouldn't ask him to take care of Hadwin's love bite, as that was healing fine, and it felt too intimate and disrespectful for one mate to override the claiming mark of the other. But the nipple he now rubbed was still rather sore from yesterday's blood play.

"I'd do *anything* to heal you," he said emphatically. "You're my *mate*."

I pursed my lips. It was more complicated than that. He was possessive with the mating bond, more so than any of the others who held claim on me. "Even if it's an injury from another lover? From another member of the Coterie?"

His expression flashed dark. "Who hurt you?"

Shrinking a little, I broached the topic carefully. "You can't be angry, because I asked them to do it." I cupped his cheek. "Okay? I like things … rough, sometimes, and that occasionally means injury."

He didn't seem much at ease. "Would you tell me if they hurt you when you didn't want it?"

Accidents obviously happened from time to time, and I wouldn't fault them for that. I rubbed Elion's cheek. "If they hurt me against my will, I…" I *almost* promised I'd let him know, but I had to ask myself if I truly would… "What would you do?"

"I'd kill them," he said as plainly as though he'd just told the servants he wanted his venison more rare.

My stomach clenched, and I locked eyes with him. "Not unless I say so."

"I should be allowed as your—"

"No," I asserted. "I don't care if this is the fever talking or the regular mating bond. You need to remember your place in this palace and Coterie. You have to share, and you have to follow my orders. Especially when it comes to something like that."

His fever had mostly subsided for the moment, so fresh after sex, and it worried me he was so fervent in his declaration despite that.

Elion searched my face for quite a while. "I won't kill anyone unless you say to."

I rested a hand on his chest. "Good. No hurting them either."

He rolled his eyes.

"Elion…"

He huffed. "Isn't it enough I always kind of want to wring their necks to have you to myself, but I don't do anything about it?"

"Well…" I swallowed hard. That hurt to hear. "You're already miserable? You don't like your companions?"

"I can't say I'm miserable when I have my mate close to me. And I don't have any personal problems with those men. I'm sure I'll grow to like them. It doesn't mean I don't daydream of slaughtering them all and fucking you for hours."

I fought a smile at his candor. "I think we'll keep those desires just between us, okay? And I don't see a need to dwell on whether they'll harm me against my will." I blinked away the image of the common room bathed in the blood and carcasses of my other lovers…

"I only brought it up to ask a simple favor. I asked Hadwin to feed off me, and I'm tender. I was only offering to let you help it heal faster if you'd like."

His face was contemplative for the briefest moment. "If you ask me for help, I'll always offer it. If I can make you feel better, I'll always say yes."

Smiling, I pointed to my nipple. "That's sore. Want to help?"

He slid down a couple of inches and wrapped his mouth around me, running his tongue around my nipple. It was divine, and he apparently enjoyed himself, as he started to hump my thigh.

It didn't take long for the pain to subside, though I ran my fingers through his hair. "Thank you, Elion."

Removing his lips, he gave me one last lick. "Always happy to help my mate."

He cuddled me again, slowly grinding his already hard cock against me.

I kept running my fingers through his hair. Since we were clearing the air and setting boundaries, I had two more questions that had been nagging at me. "You've never called me by my name. Would you mind calling me Sonta sometimes?"

He stopped grinding, confused.

Surely he remembers my name…

"You just call me your mate all the time, never by my given name… And I'm more than a mate. I'm a person…"

Narrowing his eyes, he said, "You're more than just a person. You're my mate."

He'd said it so simply, so genuinely, and I couldn't fault him or restrain a smile. He was a shifter, and in his culture, 'mate' wasn't a cold title. It was revered above one's self-identity in many ways. I had to respect that.

"You're right." I gave him a kiss.

"I… I can call you Sonta sometimes, if you'd like it."

My smile grew. "I would like that."

"Okay… Sonta."

I could make a more concerted effort to meet in the middle, too. "Thank you, mate."

A growl of pleasure left his lips as he dipped and claimed my own, as he began grinding again. I wanted him again already, too.

But there was one last question. I freed my lips. "One more thing… Do you ever enjoy different sexual positions? Or just taking me from behind?"

His face showed confusion again as he considered his own preferences. "I guess it's just the most natural for both the wolf and human in me. You don't like it?"

With a feral smirk, I ran a finger down his cock. "I didn't say that. I absolutely love the way you take me."

Another growl of pride.

"But … I would like to see your face sometimes. I'd love to see my lover's eyes now and then when we're intimate."

He nodded. "I've practiced. We can do that. Would you like to right now?"

I hesitated. To keep things as 'fair' as possible, I shouldn't let him already make another 'contribution,' but the position I craved didn't work so well for back entries or oral. I'd let Hadwin complete inside me twice yesterday, though, and neither Haan nor Tyfen had been given another chance.

The battle was short in my heart. I was trying to be fair, but I also got to choose, and deserved to be happy.

"Lie on your back," I said.

A smoldering look told me he didn't mind being ordered around now and then, likely since he'd just been the dominant one.

Elion did as told, and I happily mounted him.

My mate.

After a glorious but quick ride with Elion, I made sure not to dawdle. The others all had to be waiting to go to breakfast. We dressed for the day, and he especially enjoyed watching me.

We entered the common room together, and I *was* a bit embarrassed to have everyone all dressed, waiting for me. The seated men stood, giving me their full attention.

I wrung my hands. "You don't *have* to wait to eat meals with me, but you're welcome to. Sorry to keep you waiting."

Hadwin walked up to me, taking the hand Elion wasn't holding. "Maybe we enjoy spending time with you…" He kissed me, his lips cold.

It was crazy how much I already looked forward to seeing some of these faces each day.

"Plus," Gald said, dressed sharp as ever, "if we're going to eat, might as well enjoy a view of your perfect breasts while we do so." He smirked in his usual fashion, his eyes darting to my low-cut dress.

"I almost feel like that's a downgrade. Not exactly a vat of paints."

He busted out laughing at our private joke, and I gestured for us all to head out.

Haan beat us to the room, and we all soon sat around the table. We traded general chatter as the servants brought food. Hadwin, Elion, and Gald gave me most of their attention, though Gald struck up politics with Findlech too. Tyfen sat at the far end again, next to Haan's tank, and rudely ignored Haan's attempts to converse.

A wicked part of me enjoyed how humbled he'd been last night, how it felt to have him kneel and beg. I had warned him to play nice if he wanted more chances to sire a ruler. Whether rude to me or to other members of the Coterie— it was unacceptable. Especially after he'd degraded Haan the night before by simply calling him a fish.

"Tyfen?"

Annoyance on his face, he looked up at me. I offered him a sickeningly sweet smile. "Is it true what Hadwin said?"

The others quieted, having no doubt picked up on our tension.

"Is it true that even *you* waited for me to have breakfast because you enjoy spending time with me?" I dared him to disrespect me, especially in front of the others.

He pursed his lips, and then forced a smile. "Of course. Why else would I be here?"

I cut into my pastry. "That's so *sweet* of you." I popped a bite into my mouth, keeping eye contact.

Tyfen lowered his gaze to his plate once more, cutting his ham. "I do what I can, Your Holiness."

Subtly uncomfortable looks passed between the others as I ate another bite.

"And what of you, Findlech?" Gald asked, smoothing out the awkwardness. My contention with Findlech was just as apparent, given the others didn't know about Tyfen's rude visit to my chambers last night.

Findlech finished a bite of food, dabbing a napkin to his lips. "Most people address me as *Lord* Findlech."

Gald wore a satisfied expression, and I could only imagine how he'd tackle that reply. "Even in the elven parliament? And your family? Your community?" His grin widened. "Even your *lovers*?"

I couldn't say I was upset to watch Gald play with him, to break down his stiff titled exterior. Granted, perhaps *break* wasn't the right word, since I couldn't imagine Findlech being anything but set in his cold and rigid ways.

Before Findlech answered, Gald continued, spearing a sausage and putting it on his plate. "Surely some of them call you Findlech. Or something shorter? Fin? Findie? I could see you being a Findie…" He narrowed his eyes.

Findlech's mouth hung open a moment as he processed Gald's lack of propriety. "No, not everyone calls me by my title." He glanced about the table. "If you're so insistent on it, the Coterie may call me by my given name."

Gald frowned. "No Findie?"

"Findlech." He made sure to enunciate well.

Leaning forward on his elbows, Gald pressed his luck once more. "*Lord* Findie?"

I almost spat out my juice as Findlech's mouth hung open again. I loved nothing more than Gald using his charming and playful manners to undo the stiff elf.

Gald held up a hand. "I don't want an answer if it will be no. You think about it." He sat up straight and took a bite of his sausage, sending a wink my way.

31

LOVE & THE LIBRARY

For the sake of convenience, I could have asked Findlech if he wanted his chance to bed me in a nearby storage closet or something, but that actually sounded like it would be too much fun for him.

We all returned to the common room, and I asked Hadwin if he'd stick around, assuming he wanted to spend some time with me. He happily took a seat.

I asked Findlech to join me in my room, and he readily obliged for his turn to 'contribute' for his people. Luckily, the sex itself wasn't horrible. I still enjoyed his long and large cock inside me with the tingling gel he used, for the sensation itself, but other than that…

After a minor orgasm and cleanup, we left my room. All but Hadwin and Haan had cleared out. Hadwin stood, giving Findlech a polite bow as he passed.

"I'll be out and about," Haan said.

"I look forward to seeing you later," I said.

Findlech had made a beeline for the Coterie corridor, so only Hadwin and I remained. He took my hands, smiling. "Hello, darling."

I stood tall and kissed him. "Hi, handsome."

He enjoyed that. "What would you like?"

"I was hoping you'd want to accompany me to the library again. I had another vision, and it's driving me crazy that I can't identify a giant sculpture."

"I'd accompany you to the edge of the realm and back." He held out his arm. "And this sounds like a fun mystery."

I hooked my arm through his, and we walked together, talking about the vision and other things. An embarrassed servant apologized for crossing our path and sped past. I shook my head at the absurdity of it. They didn't normally do that. What had she expected? Yes, I enjoyed a great many things with sex, but I hadn't planned to scar any servants who may not wish to see it.

As soon as the door closed behind him in the library, Hadwin took me in his arms, digging his fingers through my hair, and backing me up against the wall. "Maybe she had the right idea. Then I wouldn't have waited an entire hallway to do this…"

He leaned in, first kissing my love bite, then trailed kisses up my neck. I giggled at his sudden playfulness.

Someone cleared their throat. "Sorry."

Hadwin straightened, pursing his lips.

Gald stood in front of the shelves, holding a book. "I figured I'd grab something real quick." He shrugged. "Hadwin's not the only one who enjoys reading."

"Yes, of course. You have full use of the library." We should have checked that it was empty, though I hadn't exactly planned to skip straight to sex.

Gald held the book up. "Great. I'll see myself out, then…"

I'd wanted to do some research before today's intimacy with Hadwin, and Gald was so well traveled he might have a clue about my vision's setting. "Actually, would you like to join us?"

Glancing between the two of us, Gald cocked his head. "I enjoy group activities."

"Great!" It took me a second too many to realize we weren't on the same page. Gald knew nothing of the vision.

I held up a finger. "I… I meant joining us for some research, not sex…" Honestly, the image now danced in my mind of them both taking me at once, and I would have been more than okay with it, but I wouldn't press Hadwin into a situation he was uncomfortable with.

Gald chuckled. "I'm fine with that too."

I snuck a peck on the lips with Hadwin, and he placed a hand on my back as we approached Gald.

After a brief description, I sat at the table Hadwin and I had made love on. Gald asked me questions, and the suggestions volleyed back and forth.

The vision had taken place in autumn—that often had no meaning I could decipher, unless the visions were from specific important instances like a battlefield right after an ancient war had ended.

We focused on the types of trees and the enormous mountains that had surrounded me. The trees had been generic. The mountains were likely taller than most, which narrowed down the possible locations, but it gave us nothing definitive. I hadn't even grown up around mountains, so I wasn't great at comparing, beyond those surrounding the palace and those from previous dreams.

Gald shrugged. "Maybe once it's painted, I'll get a spark that tells me where it is, assuming I've come across the place in my travels." He glanced at my chest. "I *am* a rather visual creature."

Hadwin so far had been fairly calm around all the extra demands and flirting. That didn't mean his hand under the table didn't ride a little higher up my thigh with Gald's flirtation just now.

"So, it's down to the sculpture?" he suggested.

"Yes. It looked important." I grabbed a notepad and sketched out a rough drawing.

Both of the men peered at the paper, thinking.

"Hmmm…" Gald angled his head.

Hadwin scratched his beard. "Sorry, I don't recognize it. But I'm more than willing to help you search through the books."

Gald snapped his fingers repeatedly. "I think…" Lifting a finger, he walked away, soon returning with a red book. He set it on the table and flipped through the pages.

"You think…?"

He waved off my question as he turned another page.

"It's good to know you're capable of thinking, Gald," Hadwin said with a touch of humor to his voice.

Gald glared at him, and I couldn't help but laugh and lean my head against Hadwin's shoulder. Gald rolled his eyes and returned to the book.

"It's…" He flipped one last page. "Yes!" He rotated the book, pushing it in front of us. "Could that be it?"

I closed my eyes and compared the inked image. "Similar. Not exactly." Biting my lip, I opened my eyes. "It's got the same swirls here and those hash marks, so the symbols that are likely there for meaning and not decoration are all represented in the central figure of the statue."

I dragged my finger along the sides and base. "But what about these?"

"I'm guessing ancient Elvish," Gald said. He tapped the book page. "That's the high lord's family insignia."

Hadwin and I both raised an eyebrow. "No, it's not…" Hadwin said.

I wasn't as old or well traveled as either of them, but I at least recognized the royal symbols of the fae kingdom and elven nation…

Gald sighed, flipping the page forward a couple of times. "Thus why I said it's probably *ancient* Elvish… Their insignia has changed over a few millennia…"

I turned the pages myself and compared. He was right. The modern symbols were similar, yet different enough that we hadn't recognized it.

"You've seen this in your travels?" I asked Gald. "The ancient version?"

He shook his head. "I've barely been permitted access to elven lands, nowhere near the palace or cities. They're so closed off." He pointed to the book again. "But like I said: I like reading and learning."

None of us knew Elvish—ancient or modern—well enough to decipher the rest. Maybe I'd ask Findlech down the road to translate the rest for me.

Gald closed the book and shelved it. "I'd still love to see your painting of it when you're done with it." He returned to the table, glancing at us. "So…"

"So…"

He looked between the two of us. "I suppose this group activity is done… Unless you've reconsidered *other* group activities."

"We're fine on our own, thank you," Hadwin said confidently.

I had to smile at Gald's repeated offer, and while I'd previously enjoyed the thought of being sandwiched between them, blood play didn't sound as delightful when shared. I wanted all of Hadwin's attention as my vampire mate fed and thrust us both to ecstasy.

"Thank you for your help, Gald." I stood.

He picked up the book he'd originally come for, then gave me a kiss on the cheek. "Enjoy yourselves."

After the door clicked closed, Hadwin rose and held me by the waist. "You're not disappointed, are you?"

I smiled. "I don't think I could ever be disappointed in what you offer me."

His eyes reddened a shade, a sign of his desire. "So, is the library to be our love nest, then?"

I leaned my forehead against his chest and chuckled. "Love nest?"

"Sure? I'm assuming you wanted to again…"

My mind was caught on the 'love' part. Only Elion and I had exchanged that. Love came faster with some people in my life than others. I couldn't imagine it would take long for me to utter that word to Hadwin and truly mean it.

I gazed into his warm eyes. "Beds are generally more comfortable, and there are other options, but this can also be our special little place."

He tenderly kissed my love bite. "I consider anywhere with you a special place, darling."

Hadwin made fantastic love to me, this time only once before we wrapped things up. Since I didn't want to rush things with Gald, and lunch was fast approaching, I asked Hadwin to return to the common room and ask Gald to come to my art studio in a while. I wanted him to get one good look at my painting just to confirm the visual didn't stir any memories to help identify the place. Other than not wanting to carry around a wet painting, I also didn't like the idea of my paintings leaving the studio.

My studio wasn't exactly a sacred place like a temple built to one of the goddesses, but it was my own place of reverence. Well … reverence and fun and sex, but it felt wrong to take one of my vision paintings from the room, to separate it from the others. Lilah called me superstitious, but I'd always been that way about my divine mother's visions and the art attached to them.

Gald joined me and confirmed he still didn't recognize the location of the vision. It had been a long shot. Despite his vast travels, he hadn't recognized even half my many paintings.

We joined the others for lunch. As we stood to leave the table, I asked Gald to please stay. He smiled and nodded. Tyfen looked to be struggling with the fact that I was again leaving him for last, but we still had hours before nighttime… While I liked getting Findlech out of the way in the mornings, I was genuinely intimidated to be with Tyfen in bed again. Gald could help take my mind off that.

He scooped me up after the others left, grabbing my ass. "Does this mean what I think it means?"

I hummed. "How about we try something a little different this time?"

Into the Playroom

With all of Gald's suggestive flirtations and his quick offer for a threesome, I had a strong feeling he found pleasure in any number of kinks like I did.

He would be the first of my Coterie I'd introduce to what my pleasure instructors and I had coined the 'playroom.' It was a room up one level that I hadn't shown my Coterie on our initial tour.

The moment we entered, Gald's eyes lit up. "Damn, Sonta. I knew it… You can't enjoy yourself so much with six different men without … knowing proper fun."

I stood by the door, locking it as he explored. He recognized quite a bit of the equipment in here—all sorts of swings, benches, and chairs for sex, as well as mats on the floor. There were a few things he wasn't familiar with, though.

He particularly liked perusing the wardrobe for restraints and costumes, and a set of drawers for all sorts of smaller plugs and tools.

After looking it all over, he returned to me. His blue eyes shimmered. "So, am I to make you wet and wanting until you beg again? Pleasure you until dinnertime?"

My cheeks warmed. "Would you be upset if we actually didn't take too long in here this time?"

"I can manage a quickie. You're a busy woman." He kissed me.

"Thanks. I just want to spend some time with my mother and friend before dinner. Since the celebration was the last time I saw them…"

Gald leaned in, kissing me again. "You don't have to explain yourself, Sonta." He slipped off my dress straps and reached behind to loosen the bodice. "I'm just happy to get time with you."

In no time flat, I was undressed and undressing him. I let him pick what he wanted. We went with a chair that made things easy and fun, opening my legs and tilting my pelvis just right.

He still worked me up a little with his flame magic, and we were both satisfied by the end of it.

Both naked, we held each other as we cooled down. "You have a great pussy, you know that?" he whispered into my ear.

I chuckled. "Thanks. Your cock's not too shabby, either."

He also laughed, pulling himself back, still pressed against me. "I think we would make a beautiful child, honestly." He smiled. "It would be exciting to see."

I rubbed his thighs. "Have you always wanted children?"

Wincing, he shrugged. "Not really. I've been busy with my career and travel, and children would weigh me down."

"So, you wouldn't want any unless it's my firstborn?"

"I…" He searched my face. "Do you want a bunch of bonus children with your Coterie? I know it's done sometimes, but I honestly don't see myself being one of those men…"

It was my turn to shrug. "I don't know what I want after my firstborn. It wouldn't be horrible for him or her to have siblings—other mixlings to be raised around, but I don't have expectations and plans." I gave him a calming smile. "I'm just getting to know your heart and goals as much as your cock, Gald."

He snickered, swooping in for a kiss. "Good to know. No matter the outcome, I will be loyal to you, and my people, and this Coterie. I'll help however I can with your firstborn, and if you choose to have more children with the others, I'll happily be a supportive uncle. I don't dislike children; I just don't have a great desire for more beyond the one."

I nodded, and he rose. We set to work cleaning and dressing. "What did you think of the chair?" I asked.

"Not bad. I like variety." He withdrew his wand, stroking it on my thigh. "But I don't mind a longer timeframe to work you up. Pleasure is just as important as duty, if you ask me."

We left the playroom with smiles, he to the library and me to the floor where my mother and Lilah lived. I'd asked Gald to inform the others in the Coterie that I would be taking dinner away, so they could choose for themselves when they ate.

I first knocked on Lilah's door. Her eyes grew wide the moment she opened it. She snatched me up. "Sonta!"

I held her tight. "It's good to see you. It feels like forever already." I sniffed her subtle perfume, soaking in the memory. "Do you have plans? I was hoping to spend the afternoon and dinner with you and Mother."

Lilah pulled back, giddy. "I can rearrange my plans. I'm excited to see you so soon. I thought you'd be flat under those men all day every day for a month."

Rolling my eyes, I stuck out my tongue. "It *is* possible for them to perform their duty rather swiftly and for me to go about my day if I want…"

She frowned. "Please tell me it's not so dull. You deserve better than bland sex just for politics."

"No." I bit my lip. "I mean, there are a couple I'm still not all that fond of, and Haan and I haven't had another chance, but I rather like three of them."

Her smile returned. "Want to come in? And give me all the dirt?"

I held her hand. "Maybe after I quickly go say hello to Mother?"

"Oh! Yes, you should!" Lilah wiggled her eyebrows. "She has a dinner date."

Hmmm… "With Kernov? A proper date?"

"Yes!"

My heart was full from the confirmation. "I have to hear about this."

Lilah joined me as I ran to my mother's chambers and knocked. My mother was just as surprised to see me as Lilah had been. She hugged me.

"Is everything all right?" she asked.

I smirked as I pulled back. I wouldn't worry her about anything, and she certainly didn't want intimate details of my sex life. "I'm great. I'm here to make sure you pick out the cutest outfit possible for your date."

My mother gave Lilah the stink eye. "You did *not* pull her from her Coterie by telling her about this, did you?"

"Yes," I lied. "And I'm glad she did."

Lilah elbowed me. "Liar. I told her not two minutes ago."

Mother shook her head. "Come on in, it'll still be a while. You two can obsess over my hair and wardrobe."

We entered her chambers and did just that. Madam Gaffey had designed her a few special dresses to choose from for the Great Ritual events, and Mother was going to wear one she had left over.

Lilah and I scoured through her jewelry and played with her hair to make her look sharp.

"I *do* know how to dress myself," she reminded us.

"Mammi," I scolded. "You would deprive us of this? We want things to be just right for your romantic night."

Once we'd done up her hair and picked everything out, we sat to chat awhile; there was still time before Kernov picked her up.

I told my mother and Lilah how sweet, shy, and devoted Hadwin was. And how playful and clever Gald was. And how Elion was working through his fever, but things were going well, all things considered.

I explained how thoughtful and understanding Haan was. As for Findlech and Tyfen, I swept most of their details under the rug. "Sometimes it's simply about siring the next ruler, and I can accept that."

Mother and Lilah caught me up on what they'd been up to the last two days. While the thousands of spectators had dispersed from the palace grounds after the celebration, the palace was still buzzing and packed with servants and dignitaries. The numbers would slim over time, but there continued to be a large presence from all six territories of the realm. Mother and Lilah had been invited to some of the more casual banquets and activities.

My mother gave me a small smile. "It's exciting to be around such important people, and such variety, but it's also tiring to be in such a crowded place."

I crossed my legs, playing with the tassels of a throw pillow on her sofa. "It's not *usually* this crowded, though, just as a reminder… In case you ever take me up on my offer to move in." I cleared my throat. "Even if you move in and it's not in *my* tower of the palace."

She knew what I was alluding to with my grin. "Please don't tease. And tonight is just a date…"

I hugged the pillow. "Fine. No teasing. But I'm happy for you. And I wish you were closer. I'll never be too busy with my Coterie or responsibilities as Hoku's daughter and the next ruler's mother to be *your* daughter."

She nodded. "Time will tell." She shyly pursed her lips. "I'm sure Kernov and I will have lots to discuss when he escorts me back home next week."

My jaw dropped, and she jabbed a finger in warning. "No teasing or making a big deal of it."

Despite closing my mouth, I was positively giddy. It *was* a big deal if Kernov—the magistrate's workaholic advisor—was taking a decent chunk of time from work to personally escort my mother all the way out to her quiet little cottage. I hoped he'd planned a couple of extra days into that trip…

Not wanting Kernov to be greeted by all three of us when he picked her up for their date, Lilah and I took off, leaving Mother to dress.

Lilah and I decided to take dinner in her chambers. It was a little awkward entering her room again since we'd made love the last time we'd been in here together. Part of me struggled with our friendship, that years of platonic fun mingled with sexuality, and the boundaries muddied sometimes.

Lilah's dark brown eyes studied my face as I looked at the bed, a lump in my throat. "Dinner. No dessert." She winked and took my hand.

I frowned. "I'm sorry for kissing you in that hallway during the celebration. I shouldn't have. I should have left our romantic farewell as it was."

Her expression was soft. "We're allowed to live without regrets. It was a fun moment—that was all."

Nodding, I guided her to a massive sort of pillow sofa she kept in her sitting area. It would be a while before our food was ready. "How have you been? And how was Schamoi when he left?"

We sat together, and she sighed. "It's been a busy couple of days, but it's still only been two days… Schamoi was fine." She played with the hem of her dress. "I made sure he had a decent sendoff."

I smiled. "Do you think you'll share a bed when he comes to visit?"

She shrugged. "We'll see. I could go either way with him. For now, I'm having fun getting to know more people at these gatherings." She shifted. "I've been too busy to sort out anything else."

That was hard to hear, and I didn't need her to explain. She was still trying to sort out her life. We had talked for years, since we were little girls, about how we would someday learn an important skill and set up a shop together.

But my life had taken a sharp turn, and instead of losing each other, she had come with me. My destiny had been laid out for me; she had halted her plans and had yet to find her true passion and new dream. I'd support her in anything she chose. Her latest interest was in art and architecture, though she hadn't committed to serious studies.

"You know… Gald thinks you're a great painter…"

She furrowed her brow. "He's the … mage, right?"

"Yes. I hope you don't mind. I had him up in the studio, and he snuck a peek at your last painting."

Smiling, she played with her earring. "The subject was pretty sexy, so it was easy to paint her."

I hesitated to pass along Gald's question. "He… He asked if you'd consider painting him and me someday. While he … takes me."

Lilah purred playfully. "That doesn't surprise me. He seemed to enjoy watching each of your claimings in the bedding chamber." She drew a breath.

"As for the painting… To me, he's just another man, but it could be a fun adventure to try to capture that kind of moment."

I took her hand. "No pressure."

"I have to know, though. When you say you had him up in the studio, does that mean you…" She clicked her tongue, making a gesture for an erection. "Had him *up* in the studio?"

Unable to control myself, I giggled my confirmation.

A servant knocked with dinner, and we got up to take the trays. We reconvened on the pillow sofa to eat and cuddle.

"I want *all* the dirty details about those men, though," she insisted.

I caught her up in more detail than I would have dared to in my mother's presence. I explained my predicament with Tyfen in particular.

"I know I shouldn't hide from him, but I don't want to have sex with him. I'm still … annoyed. And I feel bad for him after the way he begged me." It had been the *way* he'd begged, the words and tone, the tears.

Lilah chewed on a grape, contemplative. "I can't make your choices for you. I wasn't there, and I don't have your skills, gifts, or calling."

I frowned.

"But I trust you to make the right choice. Everyone does."

Wrinkling my nose, I chomped down on a grape of my own. "No pressure…"

She chuckled. "Follow your heart. You didn't tell him he would *absolutely* get to bed you, just that he would *probably* get to. And he was a complete ass, so I don't blame you for wanting to avoid him. But you have your duty and your heart to balance." She wrapped her arms around me, holding me on that soft sofa. "You'll make the right choice."

"Yeah…"

"Treat him like that Lord Findlech if you have to. All business—just get it done with. And Prince Tyfen *does* have the most impressive cock out of them all, doesn't he?"

My mouth went dry at the memory of seeing him for the first time. "Well, that's not all that matters…"

"No, but it certainly doesn't hurt his case when it comes to duty." She added resolutely, "Just make sure he remembers who's the boss."

33

Good Girl

I returned to the common room after some great cuddles and conversation with Lilah, hoping my mother's date with Kernov was going well.

Surprisingly, everyone but Haan was in the common room. I'd assumed the men, other than Elion, who had already had a chance with me would have found somewhere else to be. Their rooms were large and customized to their needs and liking… And the grounds were expansive.

Elion looked at me hungrily—no surprise there. Gald waved, then went back to chatting with Findlech. He even laughed at something Findlech said, which took me by surprise. I couldn't imagine Findlech capable of joking. Then again, I listened for a moment… They were talking about tax allocation. I refrained from rolling my eyes—I should have known these two would be chatting it up about politics again despite their complete opposite personalities. They had both made it abundantly clear it was their main focus.

Gald's laugh was cute, though.

Hadwin gave me a smile from his corner chair, closing his book.

Tyfen sat alone on the other side of the room, his arms folded, barely making eye contact with me before averting his gaze.

I walked up to Elion first, crouching to his level. "How is my mate doing?"

A growl rumbled in his throat. "Fine, Sonta." He struggled with saying my name, or speaking at all. I suddenly imagined the common room walls splattered with the blood of others and him taking me in the middle of it.

I held Elion's hand. "I'll help you in a few minutes, okay?"

"Okay," he breathed.

I kissed his cheek and strode to Hadwin.

He stood and wrapped his arms around me. "Hello, darling."

"Hi. You didn't have to spend your time in here if you didn't want to…"

With a shy smile, he admitted, "I know. But you'll always come back here, even if it's not to see me…"

For having such icy skin, he sure knew how to warm my heart. "Would you like to share my bed tonight?"

"That will always be a yes." He kissed me.

I beamed. "Great. I'll probably have Elion join us. I've got to … sort out a few things first. You can obviously stay in here if you want, but if you'd prefer to read in your room, I'll collect you when I'm ready."

He nodded and stole another kiss. "I think I'll read in my room until then." After picking up his book, he strolled to the Coterie corridor.

Turning, I sucked in a breath. Gald was next. I walked up to Gald and Findlech and stood behind the sofa.

"Hello, gorgeous," Gald said.

Findlech nodded politely. "Your Holiness."

I sighed. "If you're allowing the Coterie to call you by your given name, I feel it's right for you to call me mine."

"My apologies, Sonta."

"Thank you. Anyway…" I pointed to Gald. "My bed tomorrow night?" I wanted to limit it to two men a night—I had two cuddleable sides, after all.

Gald smiled. "I'll be there." He glanced around the room. "Do you want us to leave?"

"No. No, you're fine. This is your space more than mine. I just wanted to let you know."

"Sounds good. Because I'm still here trying to make sense of Findlech's nonsense about why he thinks humans should be taxed more heavily just because we have more representation in the capital, given his own people won't volunteer their population statistics." Gald smirked at Findlech in challenge.

Findlech sighed. "Like I said—"

I rested a hand on Gald's shoulder. "I'll let you get back to your discussion…" *Absolutely riveting…*

I walked to Elion and took his hand. "I haven't seen your room yet. How about you show me?"

He eagerly jumped up.

Tyfen cast me a glance from his seat—somewhere between pleading and angry, but not rude enough to upset me. I'd throw him a bone. "I'll be out in a little while."

He gave me a single nod.

Elion led me to his room and immediately began stripping down.

"Hold on."

He grunted. "What?"

"I need to be fair to the others—you know that."

"I know. And I don't complain," he half whined.

I swallowed a lump in my throat. "I don't mind backdoor sex sometimes, or oral like last night."

He frowned. "I don't like it as much, but I'll do it."

"But sometimes I just like normal sex, and we have to consider some sort of equality with how often your seed gets a chance…"

His grey eyes studied my face.

"Surely you've used barriers on your cock before?" He'd mentioned having other shifter lovers before and hadn't impregnated them…

Elion's frown deepened. "Yes."

"You don't like them…" Honestly, *I* didn't even like them that much, though they were handy for easy cleanup and preventing diseases and pregnancies. I'd used them loads in my teenage years with young human men.

He wrung his hands. "I just hate the idea of having anything separate me from my mate," he whispered, defeated.

If it were any other man making excuses, I would have been annoyed, but I couldn't fault him for struggling to compromise with such a fierce biological craving, especially with fresh mating fever.

I tried to reason with him. "After I bear a child for this realm, do you expect me to constantly be pregnant with your cubs?" There were teas I could use to prevent pregnancy, but the point remained.

He looked confused. "No… But I…" His eyes were so vulnerable. "I hope we have some cubs together … even if the ruling child isn't mine."

Cubs. Plural. My heart raced.

"You don't want to?" he asked.

I shouldn't have brought it up, not when he didn't have a clear head. "I don't know. We don't have to make that decision for a while, right?"

"Right…" he said cautiously.

I walked up to him, taking his handsome face between my hands. "I'm not saying 'no' to my mate. I simply wanted to ask if you had a barrier for this time."

He averted his gaze. "Yes. We…" Sighing, he turned and practically leapt to his washroom. His delegation would have understood the delicate balance we had to maintain, and the primary purpose of the Coterie. I had some in my room, but we were already in here…

Elion quickly returned with one. "Put it on me?"

I smiled. "Absolutely."

We enjoyed each other like we always did, like I imagined we always would. He still wanted to lick me clean of myself afterward, and I loved it. I took some time cuddling with him on his small bed. Granted, it wasn't actually small, but compared to my huge thing, it was.

While I loved several orgasms a day, I wanted a *little* breather between him and Tyfen.

Elion and I talked while he had more clarity, though I avoided the topic of children so as not to ruin the mood. Elion's room was simple and filled with reminders of nature. Haan's room was the only one out of the Coterie to have a real window, but each of the men had an enchanted window, showing an identical view in real time. Even bigger than that, a large painting of the central plains in shifter lands took up a significant portion of one wall.

I rested a hand on his bare chest. "You won't miss it? Living with your family and people?"

He breathed peacefully, tucking a strand of hair behind my ear. "When will my mate stop questioning my devotion?"

I gave him a half smile. "I believe in your devotion. It doesn't mean you won't miss it."

His fever temporarily subsided, his grey eyes had dulled. "I will. I don't think I'm really built for a place of formality like this. But I'll get used to it. And as the future ruler's mother, you'll travel a great deal to enrich the child's life and understanding of the realm, so I'll get to visit with you." He smiled sweetly.

I hooked a leg around him. "I mean no disrespect, but why were you chosen for my Coterie? Especially when you were next in line for regional alpha, and when it's so hard to control your fever at this age?"

He gazed lovingly into my eyes. "You're worth more than being alpha."

That was the fever talking… Or at least the mating bond in general.

"I'd take you and this position any day, Sonta. My younger brother will do well as the next regional alpha. My place is here." He chuckled. "Want to know the other reason they chose me?"

I furrowed my brow. "Yes…"

"It's simple, really. I'm only two years older than you. My parents thought you might prefer youth over crusty geriatric men for a partner, so it might improve our chances."

I had to laugh. It wasn't kind to most of the others, but the shifter alpha and his wife had been wise in that regard.

Before getting up, I asked Elion if he wanted to share my bed tonight, with Hadwin on the other side. He, unsurprisingly, gave the quickest possible yes. I dressed and let him know I'd come for him when ready. Since I wasn't going to let him take me again until sometime tomorrow, I reminded him to top up on his calming tea.

He nodded. "I'll bring some barriers for tonight. Because if that's the only concern… I'd rather wear that than not have you at all…"

I fought a smile. "No need for that. I have some in my room, but please do remember that, even though I'm the Blessed Vessel, even *my* pussy needs a break sometimes." I amended my statement. "*All* of me needs a break sometimes."

"Okay," he breathed.

I left him with a kiss, and he did a good job letting me go.

Candlelight flickered in the common room. Tyfen stood, now all alone. We stared at each other a moment. I hoped he was too afraid to ask again in case I turned him down for good.

"Come on. Let's get this over with." I made a beeline for my chambers.

Tyfen entered my room behind me, closing the door. "Thank you," he said plainly.

I blew out a breath, glancing at the bed. I didn't want to share my bed with him again, not now, not ever. "The daybed." I walked over to it.

Tyfen followed, reaching for his belt. "Did you, um… I'm not really a fan of another man's seed on me like that."

I rolled my eyes. "I am clean. Elion and I used a barrier, not that it's any of your business." I glared at his stupid dark brown hair and bright green eyes, at those slightly pointy ears and his muscled, tattooed form. "You and Findlech would be proud to know I've done a pretty good job of being fair, and without an idiotic chart."

His nostrils flared. "It was a simple question."

"And you have your answer."

"Fine. Like you said: Let's get this over with."

I folded my arms and sat on the daybed.

Instead of reaching for his belt again, he pulled off his shirt, then went to his shoes, socks, pants, and shorts.

It wasn't fair in the slightest he was so attractive, or that his tattoos swirled suggestively to his massive cock. He wasn't even erect yet.

"So…" he said.

My eyes snapped up to his. Was my brain faulty? It had to be… I hated the carnal attraction I had toward him.

Tyfen wore the tiniest hint of a smile, as though he remembered all too well how I'd gawked in the bedding chamber, and how I'd accidentally let slip on the dance floor that I thought he had a great ass and cock.

"You *are* capable of fucking a woman with your clothes on, right? The others seem competent enough to do it."

He rolled his shoulders, flexing. "I suppose I am, but it's not as comfortable. They limit my range of motion."

My stupid traitorous thoughts suddenly melted into scenes of him pinning me against a wall and a few other things.

I huffed. "We're not doing gymnastics."

Annoyed, he tilted his head. "Can we just do this instead of arguing?"

I rolled my eyes. "Fine. I'm not getting out of my dress." He didn't deserve to see me naked after unnecessarily stripping me down in the bedding chamber.

"Fine." He gestured to the daybed.

Much like I did for Findlech, I lay down and spread my legs.

Tyfen took his place above me, and zoned out a moment, staring at my dress. He blinked and focused. "Right…"

I couldn't make heads or tails of him. His mannerisms were like a torn and tossed map—confusing and inconsistent.

He shook his head and drew a deep breath, then pumped himself until he was erect. Without looking at me, he lifted my dress and pressed himself to my entrance.

This time, he didn't slip in as easily. I had already cooled from Elion, and my momentary lust for Tyfen hadn't done enough.

His massive size genuinely hurt me as he tried to push in, and it made me clam up more. I'd never had that happen… Then again, I wasn't used to his impressive fae size…

Tyfen kept trying, and I got annoyed.

"Could you stop trying to *cram* yourself into me like that? It hurts."

He glared at me. "It's not my fault. You were ready for me last time."

Not his fault? My jaw dropped. "How the hell were you chosen to represent your people? It sure wasn't for your personality or wit, and apparently not even for your bedding skills. I pity your former lovers if you have not learned in two *fucking* centuries how to make a woman wet for you."

His eyes darkened at the insult. "I know how to bed women I *want* to bed just fine, thank you." He swiftly slid my dress straps off and yanked down the top to reveal my breasts. Staring at me, he bent down and sucked my right nipple.

It would have felt divine if that hadn't been the one Hadwin had pierced and fed from earlier. I winced at the soreness. It was my own fault for not having asked Elion to help heal it up.

Tyfen stopped sucking and jerked back. He looked startled. "You're … bleeding…" His eyes met mine again.

If I didn't know better, I would have mistaken his reaction for concern.

I gently pinched my nipple to stop the bleeding. "What I ask my mate to do to me is none of your business."

He nodded, averting his gaze. "Right… Your mate…"

I swallowed. "The other one won't have any problems."

"All right." His tone and expression had softened, and I had to wonder if he disliked blood as much as I usually did. Not that I should care one iota.

Tyfen leaned down again, more gently sucking and licking my other nipple, slowly pressing into me.

Goddess damn me. My core heated at the pressure on both fronts.

With a beautiful rhythm, he kept pushing in. I *loved* the way I stretched around him, and I hated that I loved it so much.

He glanced at me cautiously when he'd made it halfway in. "That's a good girl."

That shouldn't sound good. Not in his voice. But it did.

Averting his gaze again, he returned his attention to my breast. "You can take me," he coached with another thrust. "A little at a time." He licked and sucked me.

I was putty in his hands. My brain had left the building entirely as his pressure inside me increased. Once he was finally fully inside, he stopped and looked up at me. "That's a good girl," he repeated.

Had I still possessed any semblance of pride, I would have argued that I was not a girl anymore, but a woman. And I certainly didn't need praise from an astoundingly handsome prince just because I'd successfully taken his cock.

But my pride and sense and even words were gone.

He pulled himself most of the way out, and thrust. It took *everything* I had not to moan with just the first one. I was hopeless.

Smoothly and steadily, Tyfen worked his magic, building up speed, plunging into me repeatedly. I didn't know what to do with my hands on that daybed, but I needed *something* to hold on to. I reached for his bare sides, gripping him.

Just like in the bedding chamber, he didn't make eye contact as he took me, and a part of me hated that. I didn't miss that intimacy with Findlech, but I did with Tyfen. I somehow craved Tyfen's approval more than I did 'crusty' old Findlech's.

Strong and fierce with his work, Tyfen soon came, though he pushed through it to keep pounding into me until I came moments later, gasping against my will.

Neither of us hid our pleasure well. And why should we? Even some animals seemed to enjoy sex. And that was all this was…

Tyfen stayed on his knees, breathing heavily, his eyes closed. I had the urge to run my fingers through his hair, but I wouldn't.

Surprisingly soon, he yanked himself out, grabbed cloths for us both, and snatched up his clothes. "Thank you."

Still completely naked, he carried his clothes and marched right out of my chamber.

Had I not been so stunned by his flight, I would have admired his ass a little more on his exit.

He was so utterly perplexing.

I blinked and forced myself to clean up since his cum spilled right out of me. The daybed wasn't as easy for the servants to clean as my regular bedding was…

While splashing my face with water in the washroom and then changing into a nightie, I kept mulling over his odd behavior. I reminded myself it wasn't my job to fix or understand a rude man. This was politics. No more, no less.

Instead of collecting Hadwin and Elion personally, I pulled the strings that rang to their rooms so they'd know they could join me.

I propped myself against the wall, still dwelling on Tyfen.

Why did it have to feel like being with him was more than politics?

34

In the Bathtub

I thoroughly enjoyed sleeping between Hadwin and Elion. I was safe in their arms. As silly as it was, part of me felt like the armies of the six territories could all take on the palace but I would still be okay with my two mates looking after me.

Elion was chomping at the bit to have me by morning. At least he waited this time and asked. Hadwin kissed me and excused himself so he didn't have to be there for it.

This time, Elion took me from the front, and he called me Sonta again. For less than a week after becoming mates, he was actually rather restrained and conscientious for his age. I was proud of him, and as always—satisfied.

It was still early in the morning, and Haan and Tyfen hadn't made their way to the common room, so I invited Findlech to fulfill his primary Coterie duty.

I'd started to run through my daily to-do list while he was inside me, my mind wandering and preparing. This time I kept fixating on the sketch of my vision I'd brought to my chambers. The painting still remained in my studio, but I'd brought the sketch in case I got the courage to ask Findlech if he could translate the ancient Elvish for me.

He thanked me as he always did while putting himself back in his pants. I almost didn't ask, but Findlech had been less terse with me since we'd come to our agreement, and I shouldn't have to worry about confronting him or asking anything of him.

"Can I ask you a favor, Findlech?"

"Of course, Your Holin—" He corrected himself. "Of course, Sonta."

"Do you read ancient Elvish?"

He raised an eyebrow. "It depends on how ancient and which dialect."

I grabbed the sketch from my bedside table drawer. "What about this? I know the central stuff is ancient Elvish representing the high lord's family, but I can't make out the rest of it."

Findlech took it, studying. He gave me a quick side eye, then looked at it again. "Who wrote this for you?"

"No one." That was an odd question to ask. Why would anyone have written it for me? We had so few elves working at the palace, and I would never trouble one of them for something like this, especially because they were centuries younger than Findlech.

"It's from one of my visions," I added for clarification.

He angled his head. "Hoku sent you to this place?"

I nodded.

"This is a place not for public eyes. Very few have seen it, and you should not have. I would ask that you not share it with others." He handed it back to me.

My jaw dropped, but I took the sketch back. "I think a goddess can decide better than you what I'm allowed to see of this realm. Have you forgotten who you're speaking to?"

He considered. "Hoku's visions do not tell you of the future, correct? Only of the past or present, and not all of them are of times or places of significance?"

"Yes…"

"Then it does not matter. It doesn't shape the future ruler's decisions for this realm."

I was genuinely dumbfounded he would stonewall me. If he hadn't known because it was too ancient, that would have been another issue. "You won't even tell me what the writing says?"

"You'll have to forgive me, Your Holiness. No. That is a sacred site few elves have even laid eyes on, and I do not wish to taint it. And, given the circumstances, it would be indelicate to discuss the place anyway."

I narrowed my eyes. "Given what circumstances?"

Expressionless, he kept eye contact. "I have nothing else to say about that drawing. I beg of you to keep it private. It may make sense to you someday, but today is not that day."

I had no choice but to accept his plea. I also had no reason to chase the location down other than for curiosity itself. He was right that many of my visions had seemingly minor or insignificant meaning to the history of our realm and peoples in general.

He bowed. "Thank you again, and I'm sorry I can't be of more assistance."

I shook off the odd interaction and joined the others for breakfast. Later, Hadwin welcomed me into his room for coitus. I enjoyed cuddling and chatting as much as I did the sex. He didn't feed off me this time; we instead focused on more gentle foreplay with my sensitivity to his cool touch. It was odd he still wore a plain, casual shirt, that he almost seemed to redirect me whenever I tried to get him fully naked. I wanted to take in all of him, but decided to be patient. He was shy, and we had years together ahead of us.

His room surprised me. It was a false stereotype to assume he'd find comfort in some dark dungeon-like room, or that the décor would be bloodred and gothic.

Including a map of the realm and several books, he'd decorated the place rather neatly. The color scheme was blue—represented in various shades. A large painting portrayed a meadow of sunflowers with a bright sun high in the sky. When asked about it, he said he found peace in seeing the sun in a painting, since it hurt him so much in his daily life. It made me adore him even more.

I often had to remind myself that vampires never started out as such; that they had all begun as humans. So far, Hadwin had only told me of hobbies and fun adventures as a small child, and that he'd had a fairly happy childhood. That was all. I trusted he would open up in his own time.

The rest of the day went swimmingly, honestly. Gald and I enjoyed time in his room. I was pretty sure he'd noticed Hadwin had taken me back to his and decided to make the offer. Gald's room was as quirky as I'd imagined it would be, also loaded with books. My favorite part was him letting me wear his ceremonial mage robe while he made love to me.

When it came time to bed Tyfen again, I struggled with my heart and mind… Where to do it?

I didn't want him in my bed, but part of me didn't even want him in my chambers. The intimacy of it had probably been what had made it awkward last time.

I introduced him to the playroom. Shyly standing by the door, I locked it and allowed him to take in the room.

He surveyed the pleasure furniture out in the open, but didn't look in the wardrobe and drawers like Gald had. Unreadable, he glanced my way. "Interesting choice."

My cheeks warmed. I hadn't brought him here for anything kinky like I had Gald. "It's … neutral. Then we don't have to use either of our beds."

Tyfen nodded. "Where would you like?"

I pointed to a padded and formed bench and then to some mats on the floor. "They're soft enough. You choose."

He chose the bench and dropped his pants and shorts, this time keeping his shirt on. I had to stop myself from admiring his giant cock again as he took his place over me.

"If you'd prefer we use some type of gel like Findlech did in the bedding chamber, I could get some. Or I could…" He glanced at my breasts as they peeked out of my dress, as if he cared that I might be injured again.

My heart skipped a beat, but my mind put it in its place. He didn't care. He simply didn't like the taste of blood.

"I have no injuries today. My tits and clit are pretty much always a safe bet."

He nodded and set to work, using both his hand and mouth this time until I was wet for him and took him in. I couldn't muffle my moans as he made me orgasm, but I hopefully hid how much I loved how he praised me, and his coaching me as he penetrated.

As quickly as the time before, if not quicker, he pulled out after coming. This time he hastily dressed, thanked me, and departed.

I should have been happy to have him go, but I was cold and lonely after he left…

The rest of the week went well. I visited my mother and Lilah once more, and had a brief meeting with the magistrate and emperor.

I met with the palace's appointed mage midwife for a reading. Fertility was a guaranteed gift from Hoku to her Blessed Vessels. With how much my Coterie and I bedded each other, we were certain to conceive in the first month. Some mages with special gifts could sense the formation of new life, and even confirm the type of life, but it took time for the reading to be accurate.

At only one week in, she couldn't confirm a pregnancy, and my body hadn't given me any hints yet.

As for sex—things continued as they had. Elion took every opening he could with me. Hadwin's fanged smile always warmed my heart. Gald was always down for something kinky and made me laugh at least once a day. Findlech and I did our duty and nothing more. Tyfen and I had mind-blowing sex despite hating each other. He never once looked at me as he climaxed or after he pulled out. It angered me. We bickered sometimes like we had on my daybed, but it ironically made the sex even more enjoyable, more intense.

I made a concerted effort to spend more time with Haan. We spent a whole evening and night in his room once. It was so bare compared to that of the other Coterie rooms I'd been in. A pond a third the size of mine was built into it, leaving room for a narrow bed for me. It had a large window overlooking the grounds, and a small sitting area for me.

We stayed up late, only dim fairy lights to cast our shadows in the room. He entertained me with wonderful stories of his people and life before joining my Coterie. I wanted nothing more than to swim to the depths of the sea and witness it myself.

Merfolk culture was rich and as ancient as the oldest of the races.

"I miss it, to be honest," he confessed, laying his chin on his hands at the edge of the pond. "It's nice having access to the far palace lake, but it's not like back home. It's … unnatural to be on the surface so much."

I frowned. "Sorry you're homesick."

He gave me a smile. "I shouldn't be complaining. I understood the sacrifice. And I trust down the stream you wouldn't keep me captive when I wish to leave for visits."

"Of course not!" I adjusted on the small bed, lying on my side.

"You're sweet, Sonta. And I trust you do want to help my people, no matter the father of your child."

I felt guilty he'd been given only one opportunity so far. "No matter what, I've taken an oath to do my best to balance the needs of the realm, and to help my child do so. Your people are just as important as any of the land-walkers."

A smile twinkled in his purple eyes as much as it did on his lips.

I asked him what some of the most important issues were for him as his people's choice for their Coterie representative.

"The usual, honestly…"

There was always the concern of the murky-water merfolk and the harm they inflicted on the local ecosystems and on unsuspecting land-walkers. My heart went icy as we discussed them. I hadn't told Haan about my horrible vision and didn't plan to. Some people thought they should be hunted down and eradicated, simply because of the threat they posed, and many merfolk didn't appreciate the beastly reputation the creatures gave them. Other folks were adamant they should be allowed to exist as they were, and that the areas they were found in should be better marked to warn land-walkers of the dangers.

When asked what his opinion was, Haan told me he wasn't sure. Even the merfolk population was split or undecided. I reminded him his people needed to form their own opinion before the empire could override their rights since the murky creatures were little more than an inconvenience for anyone wise enough to understand the threat they posed.

We also talked about a more disturbing and dark past, which apparently was more present than I'd realized. In ancient days, merfolk were sometimes hunted for sport. Trophy tails had hung in galleries of the wealthy, and savage kings had feasted upon merfolk flesh as a rare delicacy. The image made me sick to my stomach.

"Some of the territories still keep those trophies when they should be given a proper water burial," he said. "I'm sure you can imagine which territories."

I pressed my lips together. "Yes." The fae and elves, as they often were, had been the perpetrators of that bloodthirsty violence. I'd heard of humans sometimes eating merfolk flesh after 'accidentally' spearing one, or because they found a particularly old and weak one washed up, though it was usually extreme poverty that drove humans to such a low place. Merfolk scales, however, were sometimes worn in jewelry by the ultrawealthy in human society, though the rich always swore they'd been ethically sourced.

It was still less of a problem with humans, given geopolitical borders in relation to merfolk seas, and I'd never heard of my people keeping trophy tails.

"I agree," I said. "I hope we can take care of that problem."

Haan's expression was woeful. "It's not like that's the most pressing issue though, right? A trophy tail represents a soul needing rest, but the living are more important. The youngling trade always haunts me."

My heart broke in half at the mention of it. Mermaid pregnancies were short, the children birthed relatively small. Just like the hunting of merfolk had been outlawed centuries ago, so had the capture and private possession of merfolk. Merfolk admittedly weren't always the most protective parents. They had their distractions, and sometimes priorities put their offspring at risk. A male may take an unwilling female in a mating frenzy while her recently born children were nearby. A fisherman may seize the opportunity to net the little ones and sell them on the black market for private collectors' tanks.

Life in a display tank was not a life at all.

"That's been outlawed for so long!" I said. "And the penalty is so harsh." To be found with a captive merperson meant to be stripped of every last possession. The terms of your sentencing to empire-operated workhouses depended on factors like how well the merperson had been kept, how long they'd been in captivity, and if you had more than one. Even with my humble education, I'd learned in my youth of a gruesome execution that had happened in an eastern human town a century ago where an entire family of nobles had been dragged to the town square and publicly beheaded. They had been found with a dozen merfolk on their private estate, inbreeding them.

That story had always haunted me. "I can't believe anyone would be foolish enough to capture your children anymore."

His voice was airier and huskier than usual, his slitted purple eyes haunting. "They do. It may be rare, but it happens. Just last year a fisherman in the Southern Dalia Sea netted some without releasing them. And you don't net younglings and *accidentally* bring them to shore."

No, it wouldn't have been an accident. They may have been netted somehow by accident, but should have been released immediately.

I was horrified. "Does the emperor know? The local governor?"

Haan nodded. "The captain was slaughtered on sight and the younglings released once others caught him trying to unload his cargo at night. His crew is still serving in workhouses."

He let out a gurgled sigh. "My people may someday consider disregarding Hoku's wishes about sending a representative for the Coterie. We could live in peace without land-walkers. Many of my people have never even seen one because they're too scared to surface within miles of any waters that may be fished." He held up a hand. "And while the resort merfolk life would not be my choosing, I don't fault them for finding a way to coexist with the local land-walkers. But … harmful old practices must die. The law is not enough if there are not more raids or investigations. Surely this fisherman had intended buyers… His property had only small tanks that would not have allowed the younglings to grow much; they weren't for a personal collection."

Frowning, I nodded. "I'll do everything in my power to work on that."

Glancing at my stomach for a moment, Haan opened his mouth. "Strictly speaking, you are not the lawmaker or enforcer in this palace, Sonta." He didn't say it disrespectfully, and I caught his meaning.

"I'll make sure my child is raised to respect your people, and I can still raise concerns in meetings with the current emperor and magistrate."

He gave me a polite smile. "Let's hope the child is not too distracted with the priorities of its father. It often swings that way, and we can't deny that."

I swallowed. He was right. Another reign with a half-merfolk emperor or empress may finally stamp out this unacceptable behavior. Merfolk were underrepresented in the Great Ritual results, and it was no secret as to why.

"I did rather enjoy our time in the tank," I reassured him. "Your cock and everything." Goddess, I could still feel his unique cock snaking into me. And how much had I loved him pounding into me?

Haan grinned wide. "Don't flirt with me too much, Sonta. I might get tempted to drag you into this pond." His joyful expression faded. "And no one would like the Blessed Vessel or her unborn child harmed."

"I'm not confirmed pregnant yet, and I'm sturdy."

"But without gills…"

I shifted on the bed. "I've considered a different option than a tank… Something safer we could try…" Another Blessed Vessel had written about it in one of the journals that had been passed down.

"I'm listening…"

The next night, Haan and I carried out our plans. No giant tank with ropes, nor guards with spears at the ready.

We used my smaller clawfoot tub. I lined it with pillows and blankets to soften his blows as he slammed into me, and filled it halfway with my pond's semisalty water. He couldn't drown me easily here with so little water.

I stripped down naked, and Haan dragged himself out of my pond, all the way to my bathing room. It was the first time I'd seen him fully out of the water. His scales didn't shimmer as much as they dried.

"You're sure?" he asked at the edge of the tub.

I lowered myself in, spreading my legs. "I'm willing to experiment if you are." It would be lovely for me to ride him; it would honestly solve most of our problems, but it wasn't that easy.

His cock simply didn't get as rigid as the others'. It was long and pleasurable, but it snaked and bunched inside me. We needed water, and hopefully just gravity to make this work in this environment.

I was extra impressed with his sheer strength and the definition of his muscles as he pulled himself up the tub and gently lowered himself onto me. I enjoyed the pressure, and ran my hands along his shimmering scales.

"You really are handsome, Haan."

He smiled and kissed me. He was getting better at it. "You have a beautiful form, Sonta, and a beautiful soul."

I beamed at the compliment.

Raising his arms, he gripped the head of the tub to aid his thrusting. He situated his groin scale near my opening.

I tightened in anticipation. "Ready?"

"Yes."

Lifting my hips, I coaxed him. His head did a little bob, his eyes sharpening. His cock snaked into me, latching in with a barb once he was as deep as he could go.

I couldn't remember the last time I was so excited. Everything had gone well so far.

Haan shoved and dipped, grinding and thrusting into me. I tried to open my legs wider to help.

It did not feel great.

Water sloshed about, much of it right out of the tub. Any lift Haan got meant the whole force of his body pounded into mine. This environment was *not* conducive to proper merfolk sex. Instead of his cock penetrating and bunching well, his whole body crashed down onto my flesh and bones.

It didn't take long before I started to silently cry in pain. I told myself I could endure it, hoping he could somehow climax soon. But to no avail. His frustration at flailing about made him more unforgiving in his attempt.

"Please stop," I begged.

He looked at me, pausing, his gaze still frenzied. I was terrified he wouldn't be *able* to stop himself. He grunted, his gills rapidly flashing. Holding himself up, his arms extremely rigid, he stared at me for a solid minute, perhaps more.

"Please, Haan," I whispered, a tear rolling down my cheek. "It's not working." I was devastated for the both of us.

It took another minute before he blinked away the frenzied look and wore a frown.

"I'm sorry." I frowned in return. "I never should have suggested this. It's my fault."

He shook his head. "I…" He closed his eyes. "I… I should have known. And I can't retract my barb easily…"

I nodded. It had been a risk we'd agreed to. Without him completing, the barb stuck inside me wouldn't naturally release. We'd be connected for *several* minutes now, sharing in the shame of this flopped attempt. I wrapped my arms around his back. "We can cuddle and even practice kissing if you want, until your barb releases…"

"Okay." He gently lowered himself fully onto me, and I tried not to wince at the pain in my ribs.

We held each other and kissed a little. I would *definitely* be writing in my own journal to pass on this failure to warn other Blessed Vessels that I wouldn't recommend it…

35

Tonic & Terror

After nearly a half hour inside me, Haan's barb had finally released and he'd withdrawn himself. He'd dragged himself back to my pond and swum to his own room.

I ached from head to toe, carefully ensuring I didn't slip on the water around the tub. It hurt to even breathe. Still wet and naked, I curled up under my covers and cried myself to sleep.

First thing in the morning, I opened my door for Elion. I asked him to be gentle, and he was as gentle as he knew how to be. My rib still seared, stealing from the pleasure of him taking me.

I let Findlech take me, and fought the pain again.

"Could you … let the others know I won't be joining everyone for breakfast?" I asked after he'd finished.

He said he would, and I took a few more minutes to lie in bed, miserable.

I forced myself to stand and called for a servant. My aide quickly arrived, and I asked her to send for my midwife.

I lay back down and waited. The visit was quick, my midwife giving me a gentle scolding for hurting myself. I wouldn't disclose how it had happened.

She used some healing magic and prescribed me a tonic for the remaining pain. Ironically, it was easier to heal a broken rib than a bruised one. I would be sore for a couple of days at least. As the midwife left, I asked my aide to order food to be brought to me for a late breakfast.

I didn't particularly like the kind of tonic my midwife had prescribed. It smelled like horse piss and was supposed to make me drowsy. I'd be fine without it.

As I finished my meal, the pond's string rang a bell—Haan's way of knocking on my door. I frowned but responded by pulling my coordinating string.

He rushed into my chamber pond, the water splashing as he crested. "You were hurt?" Guilt covered his every feature.

"No. I'm fine."

His skepticism was clear.

"Don't baby me, Haan. I'm *fine*. I'm tougher than most humans and heal faster. I just wanted to eat alone this morning…"

"I never should have agreed to that." He frowned.

I gave him a sad smile. "I asked for it. You're not at fault. You did a marvelous job stopping when it wasn't working."

I insisted again that I was fine and asked for some privacy for myself and another Coterie member. If I checked them all off my list, then maybe I'd go to bed early and down some of the nasty tonic.

Peeking into the common room, I asked Hadwin to join me. He, like the others, had been curious about me not joining them for breakfast, and I told him the same lie, that everything was fine.

I asked him for blood play, and he did a good job of both bringing me pleasure and distracting me. I guided him to rest his hand on my rib afterward, though he didn't understand why. The cold helped a bit.

As much as I wanted him to hold me all day when I felt cruddy, I also wanted to complete my duties quickly. I took my leave and asked Tyfen to join me in the playroom again.

Tyfen seemed a bit confused when I asked if he would take me from behind. I couldn't bear to have him see any weakness in my face, not him.

He obliged, warming me up by rubbing my clit. My rib was screaming by the time he'd finally eased all the way into me.

"What are your powers?" I asked.

Tyfen halted. "Does … that matter right now?"

My annoyance flared. I wasn't asking him to bring magic into this like I'd been enjoying with Gald, and I certainly wasn't going to hope he had fae healing powers beyond that of the palace's own mage to beg for help. If he wasn't going to volunteer his powers, I wasn't going to continue this conversation.

"Never mind," I muttered brilliantly. "Just get this done with."

He pulled back and thrust into me. "Aren't you a ray of sunshine today?"

"Shut the hell up."

"Whatever you say, Your Holiness." He didn't take me gently. Granted he never was all that gentle, and I had come to crave his ferocity, but my eyes were fully coated in tears by the time he was done with me.

As usual, he went on his way without checking on me, and I was happy for it. I curled into a ball and cried again.

At times, I hated being weak and mortal. I was so frail compared to these men, and I'd been so quickly humbled in that bathtub.

Not allowing myself to wallow too long, I forced myself up. Gald… I just needed to let Gald fuck me, and then I could feel better. I'd have given them each a fair chance.

I walked back to my room and downed the tonic the midwife had left me. "Horse piss," I muttered. After brushing my teeth, I opened the common room door. "Gald? Can I see you?"

He jumped up from his chair and joined me. "Hey, beautiful. What's going on?"

My head swam already. "Fuck me." I sat back on the bed and spread my legs.

He raised an eyebrow. "I thought you came to the common room to announce you were ready for a late lunch."

I blinked. Time had blurred already. "No. Yur hungry?"

"Aren't you?"

Now that I thought about it, I was starving, but I was also in no shape to walk and eat. That tonic wasn't a light one, apparently. "No. I jus' want youuu in meeee."

Concern painting his face, he crouched. "What's wrong with you, Sonta?"

The tonic was taking me a lot faster than I'd expected. "You heal?"

Gald narrowed his eyes. "No more than the palace healers… Do you need a healer?"

I shook my head, and the room spun. "No… I…"

A rushed knock pounded on my door to the common room, and I was out.

A bird chirped, and I sighed, smiling.

"Darling," Hadwin exhaled, sliding a hand to caress my cheek.

"Mmm."

"You're feeling better?"

My eyes fluttered open, then the confusion struck. "When did you get here?"

Someone yawned behind me, sliding his hand off my hip. "That was *not* fun, Sonta…" Gald lay behind me.

I turned to sit up, only wincing a little. The pain in my rib had subsided quite a bit. "That tonic sure worked."

Gald's curly red locks were a mess. He glared at me. "It would if you were daft enough to down an entire day's worth of doses in one go…"

"What?" I glanced between them, panicked.

Hadwin's soft hazel eyes confirmed the truth. "Why would you do that?"

I searched my memories. "I…" I'd been an idiot. I had wanted to speed through the midwife checkup to ensure I could eat breakfast soon and return to normal daily responsibilities without my injury being noticed. I'd brushed off the instructions because I'd hoped to be strong enough to not have to take the tonic.

"I was only supposed to take a little at a time, wasn't I?"

Both of them nodded, and I dropped my face into my palms. "Please tell me this wouldn't do a child harm…"

Hadwin rubbed my back. "No, not even at that dose."

I blew out a breath of gratitude. How had I gone from perfectly balancing the needs and demands of my Coterie and my calling to failing so miserably?

A bird chirped again at the window, which was odd for this time of day. Then again… "How long was I asleep?"

"It's early morning the next day," Gald answered.

I glanced about the room. It was only the three of us. "Where's Elion?"

Neither answered right away.

"Why wouldn't he want to be by my side?" Not that I wasn't fine with these two, but that was rather unnatural.

"He's … sleeping … in his own bed right now," Gald answered.

I stared him down. "Why? And why do you say it like that?"

"His mating fever was out of control, and…" Hadwin started.

"And he's on a rather strong sleeping potion right now."

That made me frown. "I guess that was easier for him with his urges."

"Well … darling…" Hadwin cleared his throat. "It wasn't really his choice."

My eyes grew wide. "What?"

Gald took my hand. "We were a bit panicked. Things … devolved rather quickly. *This* ass practically knocked down the door when you passed out because he sensed your heart had slowed. He thought I slit your throat or something."

"I did not," Hadwin mumbled.

"Liar," Gald retorted. "And things just got ugly from there…"

If I could have shrunk into a hole in the ground, I would have. "What happened?"

After Hadwin had been assured I wasn't being murdered, he'd yelled for a servant to fetch the midwife. The next hour had been a nightmare of chaos. Elion had heard the commotion, and things went to hell rapidly in his concern for his mate. Tyfen first got the blame since he'd been the last with me. Upon her arrival the midwife had swiftly spotted my empty tonic cup and confirmed I had drunk too much, but then they'd all turned on Haan when he confessed I'd hurt myself the night before 'tripping while getting out of the pond in my room.'

I closed my eyes in chagrin. Gald got up and called for a servant. They ordered for food and my midwife to be brought right away.

I smoothed out the bedding around me. "Great to know the one person divinely appointed to keep peace in this realm almost started the next great war…" I was winning at this.

Hadwin chuckled and gave me a kiss on my cheek. "We managed."

Gald returned to the bed. "Do you want to see your mother? We hesitated to mention this to her since we don't know her and didn't want to worry her. It's honestly felt a bit treasonous keeping this within the Coterie and a few servants…"

"No. Don't worry her. No one needs to know. I was stupid and then doubled down on my stupidity."

My midwife showed up to check on me, stern and frankly a smidge insulting about my hearing and intelligence because I'd drunk so much of the tonic in one go. She confirmed I was fine and should take it easy, then reiterated the tonic's instructions slowly as if I were a small child.

As she finished, my personal chef arrived with food. "I've been so bored the last couple of meals…"

Gald reminded him it was none of his business, and shooed him away.

I scarfed down eggs and toast.

"Will you tell us what really happened?" Hadwin asked cautiously.

I chewed slower. "The midwife already confirmed that. Like Gald said: I was daft."

"I think you know what we mean, Sonta," Gald added.

I took another bite, avoiding eye contact with them both. They wanted to know how I'd come by the injury. "Haan told you. I tripped."

"I don't think either of you are particularly good liars," Hadwin said.

I swallowed. "You could really sense my heart slowing from the common room?"

"Yes."

I hadn't realized the vampire mating bond was quite that strong. Now I was a bit mortified. "So, if I'm … in here with another member of the Coterie, and we're…" *Hot and heavy…*

He looked properly embarrassed. "I try to stay on the far end of the common room and distract myself…"

This day was just getting better… "You should have told me. I feel bad."

Hadwin sighed. "It's fine. I have to get used to it." He rubbed my knee. "But do you know what *you* should tell *us*?"

They wouldn't let me deflect the injury question. And I wouldn't start more problems or so fully shame Haan by telling the truth. "Haan had no reason to lie. I slipped. My answer won't change, no matter how many times you ask."

I gave them both a look to let them know not to press the issue.

"Fine," they both uttered.

I happily took another bite of my breakfast.

Gald reached under the covers, sliding his hand up and down my thigh. "You know, Hadwin, I don't think she would lie to us…"

"Really?" Hadwin asked skeptically.

"No," Gald practically purred. "Sonta is like a *baby foal*, so young and inexperienced. She's *clumsy* like that. She barely knows how to control her own body." His soft brush against my inner thigh made me rigid.

"Riiiight…" Hadwin answered dully.

Gald was turning me on just to make a point. I was not clumsy. I knew how to move and manage my body well.

"You can have me after breakfast settles."

Chuckling, Gald pulled his hand out. "You should take a day or two off."

"I'm fine, really. And you were the only one other than Haan who didn't get a chance yesterday."

He lightly kissed my cheek. "I know you're trying to do your duty, but part of that duty means taking care of yourself."

36

Fun in the Sun

The men of my Coterie had agreed they would give me a full two-day break. I insisted I was fine, but they wouldn't have it. None of them would bed me. Granted, Elion hadn't been awake to make that promise, but they'd ensure he did when he woke.

Embarrassed by all the fuss, I quickly finished my breakfast and washed up while Gald and Hadwin assured the others I was fine. They all anxiously eyed me when I entered the common room. The central coffee table had been replaced, and I couldn't help but wonder who had tackled Elion and kept him down while a sleeping potion had been fetched. It had likely been more than one of them.

Haan eyed me nervously, but I gave them all a bright smile.

"Well, I can't remember when I've been so well rested."

No one laughed.

I wrung my hands. "It's no one's fault but my own. I tripped and hurt myself, and then I was silly to take the wrong dosage of the midwife's tonic. That's all."

"And let us hurt you further by keeping it a secret," Hadwin added, censure in his low voice.

I pursed my lips. "I thought I could handle it. And I'm fine now. So let's move on from this. There will be no more blaming or arguments. I don't want to hear about this anymore. And if you need to take out your frustration, then you can do it on me. Not Gald, Tyfen, Haan or even Elion."

Everyone nodded their agreement.

"And I think we should do something fun tomorrow. I'd like to introduce you to my mother and friend, if we're going to take some time off…"

Gald and Hadwin seemed most excited about that.

For the first time since the Great Ritual celebration, I didn't have to worry about who I wanted to take me next, and I genuinely enjoyed just sitting with the men in the common room and chatting. Granted, Haan kept pretty quiet, and Tyfen was silent with his arms crossed in the corner like he always was, but I sat on Hadwin's lap and talked with Gald and even Findlech for a good two hours.

During lunch together, I struggled. It was sweet that they'd all taken a pact to give me time off, but they seemed to forget I was a sexual creature. I'd been this way since my teenage years because Hoku had touched me in my mother's womb.

I could be convincing…

Eventually, I lured Hadwin away and asked for relief. He refused to bed me, but he worked wonders with his fingers. Later, I asked Gald to accompany me on a walk, and ended up gasping to his wand inside me.

By bedtime, Elion still had not woken, but he was expected to soon. I had to be there to help calm him, so I told the others I'd be fine. He was really sweet lying in his bed, and softly woke up. Once he really came to, though, it took a lot of assurances to make him not storm out of the room to confront the others.

He did calm, though, and was elated his mate was fine. Understandably, he wanted to claim me anew. I told him of the pact, and he thought it wasn't fair since he hadn't done anything wrong, and he hadn't agreed to it.

I was wet for him, but I didn't want to break the trust of the others, even if they never found out. With surprising clarity of mind, Elion suggested an alternative. Never had I had a man reach his tongue so far inside me, eating me out so fully, as he did when I rode his face, gripping his headboard. He used his hands on himself, then cleaned me so thoroughly, I came twice.

'Taking time off' wasn't so bad, after all.

I stayed the night with Elion, and he was the most adorable with pillow talk in the dark. He'd already started calming down with his mating fever after the first week, but this night was exceptional.

Still, the next morning, I didn't turn down the offered repeat of the feast…

After breakfast, I changed into a swimming outfit, and the men all wore swimming shorts, Haan obviously excluded. I had to force myself not to laugh at how stiff Findlech looked with some kind of shawl or scarf draped around him. I'd never swum with anyone other than humans and Haan before, so it may hold some sort of significance I hadn't learned about. As always, Findlech didn't have a single long hair out of place.

Hadwin still wore a casual shirt instead of going bare chested. It had been just over a week with my Coterie together, but in such close proximity, I'd hoped he'd feel more comfortable by now.

Surprisingly, Tyfen wore a shirt, too.

"Look at you, Sonta," Gald said, wearing the skimpiest and tightest shorts of the men. "You rarely wear undergarments under your dresses, but this is like the reverse…"

I laughed far too hard. "Thanks, Gald."

For some reason it felt absolutely scandalous to lead my men through the corridors and out into the sun together. A pair of servants offered Hadwin some dark glasses and shaded him with large umbrellas. Haan had taken the tunnels and had likely beaten us to the pool.

We were quite the parade onto the grounds, but I loved it. I not only had my own tower of the palace, but my own private gardens and a large pool. Lilah looked stunning in her suit, which rivaled my own. Squealing, she ran to me and hugged me. "Sonta!" She squeezed so tight she actually hurt my mostly healed rib bruise.

"Lilah." I sniffed her hair, happy to see her again.

She glanced at the land-walkers of my Coterie. "I look forward to getting to know you gentlemen." She wrapped an arm around me. "Come on, your mother is already talking it up with the chancellor."

She led me and my party to the pool.

My mother had indeed been speaking with Haan, crouched low to get closer to his level. Only then did I realize how truly odd being around my Coterie might feel for her. Haan would be more her dating age than mine, had we all been humans and I not Hoku's daughter.

I strode to my mother, and she rose. Wrapping my arms around her, I kissed her on the cheek. "Mammi!"

She hugged me back. "Sonta."

Pulling back, I took a good look at her. She'd worn plenty of layers to be poolside. "You don't even intend to tan?"

"Well… I didn't think the first time you'd formally introduce us, we'd all be in our underthings, Sonta. I…"

I frowned. "You're leaving me tomorrow, and I wanted a fun day with fresh air…"

She kissed my forehead. "I'm still happy to be here." She spared a quick glance at my barely there suit. "I suppose everyone in attendance has seen every inch of you already." She grinned.

My eyes went wide. She wasn't wrong, but Lilah… Gald was the only Coterie member to know she and I were intimate, and I never openly spoke of it with my mother.

My mother winked. "You look well. I'm happy."

Lilah interrupted, throwing an arm around each of our shoulders. "I think we should meet the men who *ravage* her day and night."

My nostrils flared, and my mother scolded her. Gald, having apparently heard, belted out a laugh. Pride gleamed in Lilah's eyes—without question, they were going to be good friends.

I spun. "Well, everyone … this is Vesta Gwynriel—the best mother a human girl could hope for."

She gave me one of our thick-as-thieves 'I love you' glances before stepping forward to shake hands with the men. Lilah stayed back with me, holding my arm, assessing.

Elion was a wonderful gentleman, thanking my mother for raising me.

Hadwin stepped forward and took her hand. "It's an absolute pleasure."

She smiled. "Thank you. I knew some lovely vampires in the town I raised Sonta in."

"That's great to hear." He smiled back, though it was his closed-mouth smile he'd originally used with me to hide his fangs. That twisted my heart a little.

One by one, they each introduced themselves. Gald layered on the charm, Findlech acted regal as always, and Tyfen greeted her as cordially as he had me the first time we'd met before the bedding chamber.

I then introduced Lilah. They'd all seen her in the bedding chamber, though that wasn't mentioned by anyone. Tyfen was visibly colder with her, and she with him.

Elion walked behind me and held my hips. "I'll save you a seat?"

"Sounds great."

The men dispersed to different lounging chairs, and servants came to collect orders for food and drinks.

I first sat with Mother, squeezing tight on the same lounge chair. Lilah sat on one next to us.

"So…" Lilah started in. "Do you think you could be, you know…?"

I rolled my eyes. "It's too early to tell, but I've already started seeing the midwife."

My mother gave the men a scrutinizing glance; most of them sat a few yards away under sunshades. "And they're treating you well?"

They'd all been thoughtful since my stupidity with Haan and the tonic, even if we weren't usually on the same page. "Yes." I threw a glance at the pool, where

Haan cautiously swam laps. We hadn't talked since the incident, and he had to be uncomfortable. "Lilah, would you mind paying Chancellor Haan extra attention? Talking him up and swimming with him?"

She raised her eyebrows. "Do the others not like merfolk? Have you had issues in the Coterie?"

"No. I mean, there was a small thing, but really, I mostly feel bad that I sometimes neglect him. It's hard to pay everyone attention, especially him… I want to make sure everyone enjoys today."

Lilah smiled and gave me a firm nod. "At your service, Your Holiness."

I lightly smacked her arm.

She laughed, and leaned in. "But in all seriousness … he's not going to accidentally try to take me and drown me, right? Not unless I feel up his man-scale?"

"Yes, Lilah." I rubbed my face. "You'll be fine. Don't feel up his scales…"

Without another word, she jumped up and stepped toward the pool. "Hey, Chancellor!" She ran and did a cannonball.

After she popped back up, Haan swam to her. "Miss Lilah."

"Has Sonta told you we swam together all the time growing up?"

He smiled. "She did."

"Did she tell you I was faster than her?"

"Hey!" I yelled.

She laughed again. "I've never raced a merman…"

He chuckled in return. "I'd be delighted." He would easily win, but it was a good diversion.

I leaned into my mother. "I wish you would stay, at least until I'm confirmed pregnant or we know who the father is…"

She frowned. "You know how I feel about the palace and all the commotion. It's hard for me to be here."

I batted my eyelashes at her. "But Kernov…"

She blushed. "I think going away will be good for us. Just me and him, to see if there's anything actually there."

My heart was full. "Then may you two stay away all you need."

A servant asked my mother and me if we'd like anything to drink, and we placed orders.

"Do you want me to stay with you?" I asked. "Or do you want to join us on the other side of the pool?"

My mother removed her shirt, revealing something much more 'tasteful' than I wore. "I'm fine here. You don't have to dote on me. We have all day…"

I glanced at the men of my Coterie. Tyfen, consistent with his disagreeable nature, had chosen a lounging chair at the far end of the giant pool.

Under a large shade, the others sat in a row—Hadwin on the far right, then Elion, Gald, and Findlech. The group always fell in line this way, with my two mates next to each other.

"All right. I'll be back to chat later," I told my mother, standing. Sauntering up to Elion, I rested my hands on my hips. "I thought you were going to save me a seat…"

He smirked and held out his arms. "I did. Right here."

I couldn't hold back a smile as I sat on his lap and his arms wrapped around me. It didn't take long for him to go hard. Leaning back, I whispered to remind him he had to be careful, that I did not want my mother to be uncomfortable.

He kissed my cheek, whispering back. "I guess that means you'll have to stay right here to cover it up."

I intentionally shifted on him, and he growled in my ear.

"Or," I said, "you can use a towel."

He snarled in fun.

"Your mother's delightful," Hadwin said.

I turned. "She is. And so is Lilah, so you can cut it with the shy smiles."

He gave me a full smile, fangs and all. "You'll have to get used to that. I always do that when I'm first meeting a nonvampire. You never know what reaction you'll get."

I held out a hand, and he took it. A servant delivered a copper tumbler with a straw for Hadwin.

"Would you like a sip, darling?"

"You know I can't do that if my personal chef didn't make it…"

He frowned after taking a drink. "It really is delightful. Give it a smell at least." He tipped it so I could see inside.

My stomach churned at the bright red blood. He chuckled.

"No thanks."

"It's not just blood this time. It's a drunk man's blood…"

I furrowed my brow. "What?"

He grinned. "It's equal parts human blood, pig blood, and spirits."

"Huh…" A vampire cocktail. "I'd be interested to see you drunk, Hadwin."

His expression sobered. "I'm afraid I'm not that lively. I don't drink much."

I read his face to understand his meaning. It was harder with his shades on, but, then again, it wasn't really all that hard to understand his implications. He was not the jovial sort when drunk…

"What about you, Elion?" Gald asked. "What kind of drunk are you?"

Elion grinned. "The kind who thinks he can hunt anything in the woods for hours until he wakes naked and lost in the morning."

We all had a good laugh.

Gald stretched out on his lounger. "I'm pretty fun. Then again, when am I not?"

We all stared at Findlech, expectant.

"Come on, Findlech…" Gald prodded.

He gave us a judgmental glance. "Very few living beings have ever seen me intoxicated, and I plan to keep it that way."

"We don't have to see you drunk to hear the stories," Gald teased.

Findlech wore a look that told us all his history was hidden in a deep vault. It made me want to know even more, and I kept imagining all sorts of wild behavior from the most regal and proud of us.

Elion kissed my neck. "What about you, Sonta?"

I leaned into him. "We were talking about Coterie members…"

Hadwin's cold fingers brushed my arm. "Oh, now that's not fair… You're the head of the Coterie, and we won't get a chance to find out for ourselves until after you've borne a child…"

Smiling, I acknowledged his point. "And isn't that a shame?"

He replied with a sinister glance at the pool. "I bet your friend has a treasure trove of stories."

"You wouldn't! *She* wouldn't!"

Lowering his shades, he met my gaze. "Wouldn't I? She seems the type to enjoy sharing stories."

I stuck out my tongue, and he snickered.

"Fine," I said. An approved servant handed me a frigid smoothie I'd ordered, and I thanked him. "Alcohol amplifies whatever I'm feeling at the time. If I start drinking when I'm happy and excited, then I'm fun. If I drink when I'm sad, I'm pathetic and weepy."

Gald slurped up his drink and set his glass to the side. "Well, I can't stand to waste an opportunity to sun and swim. It looks like Lilah is already worn down from her race with Haan." He stood and dove into the pool.

After finishing my drink, I looked at Elion and Hadwin. "I think I want to go for a dip. Want to join?"

"Sure!" Elion said.

Hadwin shrugged. "I think I'm going to work on my tan."

Yes, the vampire who couldn't tolerate the sun…

"We can have the shades shifted to cover part of the pool, Hadwin."

"I'm fine here, but thanks, darling."

Elion lifted me, ran to the pool, and jumped. The two of us together made quite a splash.

The next little while was fun. Elion, Gald, and I raced a few laps, and then Lilah chatted them up. I didn't hate the occasional physical touch I got from Lilah in the pool, either.

"So, Gald… I understand you want me to paint a portrait?" she asked.

He slid his hands to my hips. "Don't you think a beauty with the touch of the divine should be … properly worshiped? And have that immortalized?"

Lilah grinned. "Sounds like a fun project."

Findlech got up from his seat after a while and sat next to my mother, starting a conversation. That was rather kind of him.

Not much later, I challenged Haan to a solo race, just to allow us some privacy. On the return, we stopped halfway across the pool.

"How are you truly?" he asked, his eyes full of guilt.

"I'm fine. I've been swimming all this time, haven't I?"

"I never should have let you do that."

I sighed. "I practically talked you into it. And it wasn't your fault I was stupid about the tonic."

"Still…"

"Did anyone try to hurt you?"

He gave me a half smile. "Not really. But it's funny how slurs and threats come right out—not just aimed at me—when the Blessed Vessel gets hurt."

I frowned. I hadn't asked for details because I honestly hadn't wanted to hear them. I wanted to forget it had all happened and move on…

"Well, I'm glad you're all right as well. And I'm still sorry it didn't work out." I kissed him. "And I don't kid myself… Most people don't even know me, don't even love me for me." Perhaps it was my need to let him know he wasn't the only vulnerable one here… I wasn't blind to the facts, and didn't usually dwell on them, but they existed. "My pleasure instructors and I had great relationships, but how deep is love when it's paid for? My Coterie is faithful and pay me more than enough attention, but I don't pretend it's not mostly politics and hormones in mating bonds."

He frowned in return. "Don't think of it that way. All relationships are transactional in one way or another." He tucked a strand of hair behind my ear. "And I often stay quiet in our group, observing all you land-walkers. They like you."

Findlech and Tyfen obviously excluded. "Maybe I should use you as a spy. You can lurk in your tank while I'm gone and report to me what they all say."

He chuckled. "I'd rather not make enemies of the others."

"Fair. I've already done that for myself with Findlech and Tyfen. You don't need to as well." I rocked my head side to side. "Well, Findlech's made it clear he's just not fond of me. Tyfen, on the other hand…"

Haan narrowed his eyes. "Is that why he's always staring at you?"

I glanced in Tyfen's direction. He *was* indeed staring, though he quickly glared and looked away.

"A real charmer, that one."

37

SCARS

I'd had enough of Tyfen's behavior. Yes, he was being reasonably civil with me, but the point of the Coterie wasn't solely to create the realm's next ruler. He needed to get over himself and try to socialize with the others instead of constantly pouting in the corner.

I got out of the swimming pool, walked up to him, and sat on the chiseled stone flooring. "How long are you going to keep this up?"

He barely glanced at me before crossing his arms and closing his eyes. "I don't burn in the sun, so I suppose I'll stay here enjoying it until we're done with this frivolity."

"I meant being an ass and avoiding everyone."

Opening his eyes, he glared at me. "I'm here. I'm civil. I'm fucking you for my people. How much more do you want from me?"

"I don't think it's unreasonable to ask for a *little* more than that…"

He pulled his shirt off. "Is that enough for you, Your Holiness?"

Deep into his flesh, right through the large tattoos on his chest, a slash of claws remained, raw and red. I gulped. "Was that…"

"Your damn dog? Yes. *Someone* had to hold him down."

"Don't call him that."

"That's what he was at the time…"

I *did* feel bad, though the fact that severe of a wound wasn't bleeding was a credit to the palace healers.

254

"I guess this means you don't have healing powers of your own, then?" I asked.

"No. And I'm guessing that's why you asked me about my powers again when I was already inside you… You hoped I'd heal your rib more…"

I rolled my eyes. "I wouldn't lower myself to ask you to do more than the bare minimum, Tyfen."

His expression darkened. "What's the purpose of a Coterie if the Blessed Vessel is going to put her own life and the life of her child at risk?"

"I'm fine! And any child inside me would have been fine! I'm not as fragile as you think just because I'm not an immortal prick."

He shrugged. "You're right. Fragility and idiocy *are* different issues."

Balling my fists, I wanted to throttle him. "You know, at least Findlech knows how to fuck me without annoying me with talk." The words tumbled out, and I instantly regretted saying too much—he didn't know how much I secretly enjoyed his subtle praise.

I expected him to look confused.

Instead, he surprised me. His words were clipped and feral. "Don't ever compare me to Lord Findlech. I am *nothing* like his kind."

My shot hadn't been all that coherent, but neither was Tyfen's. I hadn't said they were similar… "What do you mean?"

Tyfen shook his head, looking away. "Don't you have other people to attend to? People who will happily fawn over you?"

Standing, I glanced once more at his handsomely muscled chest and the poor exposed injury. "Yes. I do."

I marched past him, spying Hadwin in the shaded hot tub.

Perhaps it was petty or childish, but I wanted affection and approval. If Tyfen saw it, all the better.

Hadwin sat alone on a ledge, his lap and half his chest in the hot spring water. I straddled him, kneeling, facing him on his lap.

He took off his shades, his hazel eyes squinting slightly in the daylight. His cool arms caressed my back. "Hello, darling."

I wrapped my arms around his neck and kissed him, hard and fast. By the time I stopped, his eyes were red, and his erection was hard to ignore.

"I should be insulted to receive affection simply because you're mad at another Coterie member, but I'm happy to have it nonetheless."

I looked down. "Sorry," I whispered. Of course he'd felt my heart race with my anger at Tyfen, and had likely overheard some of our conversation.

"Didn't I just say I was happy about it?"

I gave him a smile. "I was going to come see you anyway…"

He stole another kiss. "Are you having fun?"

I glanced over my shoulder. Findlech still chatted with my mother, and other than Tyfen, the others were all enjoying themselves in the pool. "I think it's going all right. I'd love to see you joining the others, though."

He wrinkled his nose. "I like the warmth in here." Grinding his hips suggestively, he added, "Just like the warmth inside you."

I laughed. "That's it? Warmth for your cold cock?"

"That, and I'm not a great swimmer."

I ran my hands through his blond hair. "You told me you enjoyed swimming as a little boy."

"Yes, but vampire buoyancy is different…"

"You've had fifty years to relearn."

"So I have. I just haven't made the time for it yet."

Imagine not finding the time to enjoy swimming… He never really talked like the others did. He sweetly always made it seem like our relationship was personal and not political. Perhaps he'd done a lot more campaigning to get here than he'd let on, and that had claimed all his time over the last few decades.

"Well, if you're not going to swim with me, you should at least be nearly as naked as me…" I slipped my hands under the hem of his shirt and slid them up.

He slapped a hand over his shirt to block me. "No."

I stared at him, confused. I still hadn't seen him without a shirt. Ever. He'd seen every inch of me. And I hadn't complained…

"Everyone knows you're pale. And no one will judge you for not being as muscular as some of the others…"

His throat bobbed. "I… It's not that."

I eyed him, looking for an explanation.

He softly blew out a breath. "Fine. You can feel it, but please don't lift my shirt."

Feel what?

He dropped his hand from his shirt, and I glided mine up onto his pecs.

My left hand ran into a bumpy scar of some kind, and my jaw dropped. "Is this from the other day? Did Elion get you?"

"No. I've had it for some time now." His voice was low, and it twisted my stomach.

"Does it hurt?"

"No. Not anymore."

I gazed into his eyes as I ran my fingers across the scar. It was deep and gnarled, and my horror grew.

Vampires simply didn't scar like this.

A major benefit of envenomation was the healing process. Once humans turned, their old injuries and scars disappeared. It was one of the reasons people willingly chose the vampire life—they'd been on the brink of death and opted to trade their humanity for healing.

This wasn't from his human days. But vampires were also far more sturdy than they generally looked. As long as they had a healthy and regular blood supply, they could live almost indefinitely. Just like with the prick I'd given him for the mating ritual in the bedding chamber, he healed almost instantly.

But there were some vampires, always associated with dark cults, who would intentionally scar themselves. To do so, the ritual cuts had to be made deep and repeatedly. Days, months, and years in a row until their bodies kept the wounds.

I swallowed, removing my hands. My heart raced. "Why?"

He wouldn't look at me. "It's not what you think, Sonta."

"Then what's the meaning of—"

"Now is not the time or place."

I stared at him in disbelief. "Hadwin…"

He took his hands off me and put his shades back on. "Please go enjoy the others. Your mother isn't here for much longer, right?"

I frowned. "Why can't you just tell me?"

Pursing his lips, he still refused to look at me or touch me. "We'll talk tonight. Please leave me and join the others… If you can't agree to that, then I think I'll go back inside for the rest of the day."

Bewildered and without much choice, I stood and left him alone in the hot tub.

"Sonta!" Elion called out. "Come swim again."

Hugging myself, I returned to the edge of the pool and dangled my feet in.

Elion held my legs, leaving a kiss on each knee. "What's wrong?"

I forced a smile. "Nothing."

His eyes were so clear lately, along with his head. "I know my mate better than that."

Part of me wanted to run my hands through his hair and kiss him just like I had Hadwin, simply to get over my unease about Hadwin, but I was stopped by the greater part of me that knew I wouldn't feel better by doing so.

I glanced around at the pool. Gald had gotten out and sat under the shade again next to Findlech. Lilah had joined my mother poolside. And Haan floated in the corner, munching on some raw shrimp.

How much did I still not know about these men? I'd always assumed Hadwin was shy, but not keeping something so… Not keeping something like that scar from me.

I returned my attention to Elion. He was cut-and-dry, happy and sweet, prone to act on his emotions. "One thing I don't know about you is how you look in wolf form…"

His smile was bright. "You've never asked."

"Just because I don't want you bedding me as a wolf doesn't mean you have to hide that part of yourself."

"You want to see?"

I nodded, and he climbed out of the pool. He backed up a bit and transformed before me.

To say he was massive and impressive would be a gross understatement.

He had menacing claws and paws the size of my face, a magnificent tail and a grey coat that matched his eyes.

"You're beautiful," I whispered, pulling myself out of the pool to examine him closer.

His fur was so soft that it brought a genuine smile to my face. "I have an impressive mate, don't I?"

Even as a wolf, his eyes were piercing. He growled his approval.

I stroked his fur near his ears. "I wouldn't mind cuddling with you this way sometimes."

He gently licked my cheek, and I giggled.

"And … while I'd prefer to ride you in other ways while in human form, you do look strong enough to ride on this way for other fun."

He softly growled again, wagging his enormous tail.

Then I noticed his torn swimming shorts on the ground.

Shit…

"Do me a favor and stay in your shifter form…"

He cocked his head, which was twice as adorable in wolf form.

"My *mother*, Elion…"

His lycan eyes widened, and he glanced past me.

"Yeah…"

It was already enough for her to know these men all railed me regularly. She had not signed up to see one of my mates' cock or bare ass.

Elion lowered his head and licked my leg.

"Would you mind running inside to change?" I asked.

He nodded, and turned, picking up his torn shorts by his teeth as he darted away.

I sat poolside with my head on my knees. Today was supposed to be fun… Instead, things were mildly awkward with Haan, I'd fought with Tyfen, Hadwin had puzzled me and pushed me away, and Elion had almost flashed my mother. Lilah, too, though I thought she'd get a good laugh out of it.

Warm hands rested on my shoulders, and I jumped.

"Just me," Gald said. He knelt behind me and massaged. "That was about to be a good show."

I scoffed.

"You're not having fun?"

Sighing, I popped my neck. "It's fine. It could just be better…"

"I bet you're tense…" We both knew I hadn't orgasmed in hours and was wanting. "I could help."

"Are you offering to take me behind a bush with your wand?"

He leaned in, his lips brushing against my ear. "If you're referring to my magical cock, that would break the Coterie pact to not take you today. But if you're referring to my *actual* wand, I'm curious where you think I stashed it in these swimming shorts…"

Unable to stop myself, I laughed. They *were* rather revealing… "Good point."

Gald continued massaging my shoulders. "Why don't you swim a couple of laps to calm you."

"I don't think it will help much." Especially not with sexual urges…

"Trust me," he whispered.

I sighed. "Sure. Why not? Want to join me?"

"No. I'll let you enjoy your time alone."

He stood and strode back to his lounger, then gave me an urging nod.

Whatever… Servants would be taking orders for lunch soon, and I might as well swim a couple of laps.

I got back into the water and swam alone. It was fairly calming. After two laps, I stood in the pool, propping myself up by my arms on the edge, and made out shapes in the clouds. A light breeze blew them past the tall hedges.

A small whirlpool brushed against my leg. I bunched my eyebrows, glancing at it. It wasn't like the pool was draining below me…

The whirlpool tickled me as it drifted up my leg to my thigh. Damn if it didn't tickle me in the right way for being sex-deprived.

Invisible from the surface, it grew in speed and force, and shifted right for my groin. I gasped and blinked as it found its way to my center.

I held my ground, searching around me. No one else noticed what was going on, except for one grinning son of a bitch.

Gald winked, subtly swirling his finger through the air at his hip. He lifted his other hand and kissed the identical magical bond inked onto his skin.

An elemental mage. He didn't need a wand or spell to control this water.

I accepted the favor and challenge, concealing how amazing it felt as the vortex of water entered me, spinning and rubbing and tightening me perfectly.

Despite my best attempts to conceal what was going on, my breath was heavy. It took every last bit of my resolve to not shake or gasp as the water brought me to completion.

"Would you like to make a special request for lunch, Your Holiness?" a servant asked behind me.

The vortex dissipated, and I stood there panting. "Um, no. Whatever the chef wants to prepare."

"Right away."

Wearing a self-satisfied look, Gald turned and started talking to Findlech.

I allowed myself to cool and my muscles to relax before I exited the pool. Walking back to the loungers, I claimed Elion's seat next to Gald.

Gald rested a hand on my thigh. "So nice of you to join us."

I gave him a look to let him know I'd pay him back the favor tomorrow.

Hadwin strode over carrying a shading umbrella, reclaiming his seat next to me. "I trust you're fine."

It took me a moment to understand his meaning. My heart rate… This vampire mate thing kind of sucked if he could always sense my heart rate. "I'm all right. How far away can you sense my heart?"

"Depends on the walls. Usually two or three rooms away."

I nodded.

He lowered his shades. "Are you upset with me?"

"For sensing my heart?"

His glance indicated otherwise. "The hot tub."

Was I? I was scared about why he would have disfigured himself, what kind of cult he may have aligned himself with. I was hurt he'd shooed me away and had hidden it from me in the first place. "I don't know what I am with you, Hadwin," I muttered.

"I promise, we'll talk about it tonight," he said softly.

"I just want to enjoy the rest of the day with my mother here."

He gently rested a hand on my other thigh. "And I want that for you."

I blew out a breath and took his hand.

Elion returned shortly after, dressed in new swimming shorts. Instead of getting up to sit on his lap, I let the men know I would be eating lunch with my mother and Lilah, and they were all welcome to move their loungers to join us.

Once lunch arrived and everyone except Tyfen gathered around my party at the poolside, Haan included, things got better. My Coterie didn't hesitate to ask Mother and Lilah questions, and they in turn didn't hesitate to embarrass me with stories.

My stomach and cheeks hurt from laughter after a while.

We chatted, and played games in the water for hours, past dark. Servants brought elegant meals and decadent desserts onto the patio, lighting torches.

Shortly after dinner, Tyfen gave up on his solo pouting and went inside without a goodbye. It grew cold the later it got, and Elion warmed me on his lap again.

I could have stayed up all night, but my mother was leaving with Kernov early in the morning. I wished the men good night, letting them know I'd likely sleep alone and may be up for a while in my mother's room.

They all bid or kissed me good night. Hadwin lingered a little longer. "I'll be up, in my room, whenever you're ready to talk."

I squeezed his hand. "Thank you."

38

Hadwin's Suffering & Sins

Lilah wished me and Mother a good night, and Mother safe travels. I visited with Mother a while longer in her chambers before giving her the biggest hug. Distracted, I didn't even tease her about Kernov escorting her back to her cottage.

I walked the corridors a bit slower than usual, my heart and mind uneasy about going to speak with Hadwin. Those scars—what kind of vampire cult had he signed up for, and what did that mean for the empire if he'd weaseled his way into my Coterie?

What did that mean for my heart when he'd already claimed it?

As expected, the common room had emptied for the night, and I quietly tiptoed down the Coterie corridor to Hadwin's room. I sucked in a deep breath and knocked.

He opened the door with a cautious smile. "Sonta, come in."

I hesitated, but did so.

"Would you like to sit?" He gestured to his sitting area.

I wrung my hands. "Sure…" I claimed a solo chair, and he sat on a sofa.

"I'm sorry I spoiled things this afternoon the way I did," he started.

"Shouldn't you be apologizing for keeping something so big from me? Did you really think I'd never find out? You planned to *never* take your shirt off? *Ever?*"

He sighed. "Obviously I didn't expect to keep it a secret from you forever. I just hoped you'd get to know me better before it came up."

I shrugged.

"So… When I was a human, I only ever had two lovers. The first barely even counted, honestly."

Arching an eyebrow, I held up a hand. "I know how injuries heal when you become a vampire. And I don't really care about your former lovers as a human." I pointed to his shirt. "I want to know why you did that."

"I'm trying to tell you, Sonta."

I crossed my legs and leaned back. "Fine. Cut to the chase."

"It's not an explanation I'm used to giving. I'm … trying to help you understand." He surveyed my face. "Like I said, I had two lovers. The latter wasn't until I was in my early thirties." He pursed his lips. "I've never been all that bold."

My patience was thin, my anxiety high. None of this mattered unless he was leading up to say his choice to become a vampire and join a cult had to do with revenge on women who'd jilted him or something like that…

"So, the second one… Well, I told you I grew up poor, right?"

I nodded. "You've mentioned it."

"I had an older brother. He passed from the powder plague, along with my parents, when I was fourteen."

My heart went out to him. I wouldn't have known what to do without my mother at that age. "I'm sorry," I whispered.

He gave me a half smile. "Me too. And it wasn't easy financially, either. I became an apprentice and fought to make ends meet, and kept my head above water for years, but just barely. So, the woman in my early thirties… I loved her dearly. Or so I thought. And I thought she loved me." He rubbed the knee of the slacks he'd changed into. "I saw myself building a life with her, having children with her. And I finally found the courage to bring it up one day."

Hadwin paused, swallowing. "She broke it off. I could never afford to provide her with the kind of lifestyle she wanted, and she knew it. I begged her to reconsider, swearing to make something of myself. I was a fool to believe her when she told me she'd reconsider once my situation had significantly changed."

I almost commented that it obviously had, though not in the have-children-together kind of way. But he *was* wealthy as a duke.

"I did what many humans in poverty do—I started selling my blood to local vampires on the side for extra income. Payment back then wasn't what it is even now… It barely made a dent, but I kept doing it. A wealthy vampire gentleman started coming into town regularly for business. He said my blood was worth a premium, that it was like a delicacy."

All I could think of was Hadwin's disgusting blood coating my mouth in the bedding chamber. Granted, it wouldn't have been so thick when he'd been human…

"He was charming, too, and chatted me up. Under the guise of generosity, he made a proposal. He understood how desperately I needed the money to please the woman I loved, and he craved my blood. His one main criticism was that my blood would taste even richer if I had a healthier diet. He proposed I come live on his estate. That way, I'd have access to the finest foods I could imagine, and he'd have regular access to feed upon me."

I was queasy just thinking about that, as if he'd walked into an animal pen to be fattened for slaughter, or—in this case—regularly drained of blood.

Hadwin scoffed at himself. "But I was *smart*. I wouldn't leave town. I didn't care for money other than to please my former lover, and I wanted to make sure no other suitors swooped in while I was trying to improve my situation. But everyone has a price. The man offered me jaw-dropping sums to move to his estate, outlining how he would not only pay me for my blood, but also as a servant for extra work.

"I agreed. Things went well for a while, though I was a little uncomfortable when it came to the rare visits he allowed me back in my hometown. He made me swear to not disclose where I'd gone to work. I dismissed my discomfort by rationalizing that he was a wealthy man who simply didn't want people getting into his business. Swearing her to secrecy, I still told my lover, hoping she'd keep her heart open with the news."

Clearing his throat, Hadwin adjusted his seat. "One winter day, I stood outside chopping wood when a bloodied and beaten vampire ran through the grounds past me. I'd never seen a man take an arrow through the head until that day." His gaze was distant. "My employer did the shooting. I was a witness."

My blood ran chill. "A trespasser?"

Hadwin shook his head. "A fellow servant—one I hadn't yet met because he'd been locked up in the cellar."

I gulped.

"I promised to keep my employer's secret, but I wasn't a great liar… He didn't even wait a week before taking me down to that cellar, draining half my blood in a feeding frenzy, and giving me an eternal bite."

An eternal bite—the kind with venom to turn a human into a vampire.

"You didn't choose this life?" I said.

"No. I never would have."

I was appalled at the injustice. "Did you seek out someone from the emperor's enforcement offices?"

Hadwin let out a wry chuckle. "It wasn't that simple, and it's not really done that way, darling. That servant had been in the cellar for eight months as punishment for accidentally spilling hot water on our employer's lap."

"For such a small offense?"

"Yes. I took his place down there. I remained in the dark for nearly a year until I agreed to stop trying to kill my sire for turning me. Somehow, I didn't break. I made him think I had, but I didn't. I'd mourned my lost love because I knew without a shred of a doubt that she would not have me this way, but I still had a lot of fight left in me."

I still didn't understand Hadwin's choice to be scarred, but I loved his strong will.

"Once I stopped fighting and uttering threats, he allowed me to leave the cellar. He *praised* his brand-new lifelong servant, and I played along, utterly grateful."

"Sounds like he was delusional."

Hadwin gave me a sad smile. "To some extent. I eventually hatched a plan to run for help, to find someone from the emperor's enforcement office. The issue was, I was watched like a hawk, and I hadn't realized how devoted some of his servants were to him, despite him having done this to several of them. I was betrayed."

For a moment, Hadwin eyed me. He reached for the hem of his shirt and pulled it up and off. The scar was much more gruesome than I'd imagined when feeling it in the hot tub.

"Did you think I'd joined one of those outlandish cults?"

I averted my gaze. "I didn't know what to think." It was clear now that this wasn't a ceremonial scarring, at least not from the way I'd had them described to me.

"Take a closer look."

I studied the gruesome thing. The thick red scars contrasted with his pale skin, centered on a concave spot in the middle and spidering out, the size of his fist. Hadwin turned, showing me his back. I nearly gasped. The scars on his back were almost identical.

"What happened?"

Hadwin glanced at his own scar before answering. "Twenty years of hell is what happened... Lashings when I was disobedient. Throwing me out in the sun naked until my skin blistered anytime I talked back. And the multiple times I attempted to run away? That's when I earned these scars."

It was hard to look away.

"For the most obstinate servants, he had a pole cemented into the cellar wall, where he impaled them. Nowhere close to their heart so they couldn't end their suffering. In just the right place so their bodies could heal enough to still cycle oxygen. I spent the better part of five years straight on that pole, locked there with chains and deprived of proper feedings for strength."

"Please tell me he's dead."

Hadwin nodded. "He won't hurt anyone else."

"Good. How did you escape?"

"I never fully did... I tried, time after time. That's why the scars are so bad, because I wouldn't sit tight. I got lucky one day, though. A drunk servant came to bring me a meager blood ration, and I tripped him. I..." A dark look crossed his face. "I did what I had to and got free. At that point, I was half-feral, barely capable of coming up with a well-planned strategy. But I didn't really need one. I slaughtered most of the other servants, any who sympathized with my sire."

They'd all deserved a proper trial, but I honestly couldn't blame Hadwin...

"My sire had been away on business, and I ambushed him upon his return, impaling him on the same pole he'd kept me on for years."

"He deserved it."

"Yes, he did."

"And then you killed him."

"Eventually..."

The word hung thick in the air.

"Why wouldn't you have just done away with him and run away?"

Hadwin hesitated, his mouth open a bit. "I didn't tell you my story earlier because I didn't want pity. Yours or anyone else's."

He still had it...

"And I also didn't want to be feared..."

My heart skipped a beat. "Why? Why would you be feared? Your actions were justified."

Averting his gaze, he continued. "Did the palace's background researchers tell you how I inherited my title of duke?"

"No..."

He met my eyes again. "It's the vampire way... If a man is clever and strong enough to take a titled vampire's life and establish their place there, they earn that vampire's title, estate, and wealth."

My eyes grew wide. "Your employer, your sire—he was a *duke*?"

Hadwin bit his lip with a fang. "Yes. I had to work with the remaining decent servants to put on a farce for quite some time to establish my claim on the land. That duke had actually been somewhat antisocial, so he didn't have many people calling on him other than business partners. We deflected any visitors and conducted his business through forged letters.

"I… I may have been more brutal than necessary in some of my retaliations in the meantime."

I glanced again at his scars. "I find it hard to believe any punishment could be considered too brutal after everything he did to you."

The look on Hadwin's face as he stroked his beard told me I hadn't been imaginative enough. My mind returned to the poolside, when he'd insinuated he wasn't all that fun when drunk.

"Either way, by the end of his twenty-first year straight in that cellar—one more than he'd kept me as a slave—I finished building a brand-new manor on the opposite end of the estate. And then the old one burned down."

"*You* burned it down."

He nodded. "I couldn't go back to my old life. My old life didn't even want me—no one ever came looking, not even the woman I'd gone out there for."

My heart broke at that revelation.

"And I didn't want to live in that filthy place, so I moved into the new one, burning the old manor down with him still alive inside."

We sat and stared at each other for a while.

"I don't blame you for what you did, but shouldn't you have turned him over to the emperor for justice? Vampires like him need a reminder that none of that behavior will be tolerated!"

Hadwin cocked his head. "That's not the vampire way, darling. We deal with our own problems, in our own way."

I furrowed my brow. "The vampire way? You had never set foot in proper vampire society when you did that, had you? He deserved a *public* execution!"

In his wisdom, Hadwin eyed me again. "What good would have come from that? Realistically? Humans would fear us more than they already do. We rely on them to survive. I didn't choose the life of a vampire, but now that I am one, I won't jeopardize the lives of those like me—victim or not—by getting personal vindication that way. I won't further demonize my people for justice the empire's way."

My heart volleyed between his logic and the law. Crimes against nonmage humans tended to be severe since we were viewed as the weakest race. "A lot of people in my hometown were friendly to vampires. And the Coterie is all nice to you."

Hadwin winced. "The Coterie often ignores me, and I'm not complaining, but they wouldn't openly come after me, just like I wouldn't go after them for their races' faults. It's politics…"

Fair point.

"And I killed the man and took his place ten years ago. Things have improved a bit since then, but there's still strife and prejudice… Even *you* were terrified of me in that bedding chamber."

I frowned. "I'm not anymore."

He smiled. "Not even after learning the truth?"

I stole one more glance at his chest, then at his lips. Standing, I bridged the gap between us, then sat on his lap. His cool hands slid to my back and knee.

Angling my head away from him, I presented my neck. "*Especially* not after learning all that."

Red bloomed in his hazel eyes, and he glanced at my neck. "Thank you," he murmured. Instead of taking the offer to bite me, he sweetly placed a kiss on my two tiny scars.

I leaned into him. "I'm proud to have you in my Coterie, Hadwin."

He kissed the top of my head. "And I'm proud to be here."

We sat together for a moment, and the temptation got the better of me. "This doesn't hurt at all?"

"No. It's all numb."

"Can I … touch it?"

"Sure."

I traced the stiff scar on his chest, my eyes glazing over as I imagined years of torture and the strength it had to have taken to make it as far as he had. I wanted to cry when I considered how lonely he'd been, and how his former lover had callously turned him away. "What ever happened to the woman?" I asked.

"She married well, had children, and ended up dying a few years ago."

I held his hand, meeting his gaze. "She never deserved you. And I…" I shouldn't say what I wanted to—it was wholly inappropriate, given my position, and rather unlike me to make promises I was unsure of. "I still have to give the others equal chances with me."

"I understand that."

"But I kind of hope I end up having your child. And if the heir isn't yours, I'd be willing to have one for you down the road…" I was the only being in existence who could bear a vampire a child, and I'd happily give him what he'd missed out on.

He wore an adoring smile. "I've waited a *few* years for someone to care enough to offer me that chance. I wouldn't rush you or expect you to make a promise."

I caressed his cheek, running my thumb over his soft beard. "As long as you want me, I'm yours."

Hadwin panted a breath. "And as long as you want me, I'm yours, darling."

39

BACK TO BUSINESS

I leaned in, kissing Hadwin. His hands slid around me as he returned the kiss. Time after time, our lips met, our tongues tangled.

Straight from his lap, he picked me up, carrying me to his bed. He gently set me down, then laid me down. I grappled for his belt, and he came up for air.

"I guess it's a good thing it's after midnight," he said.

"Like I would've let your stupid pact stop me right now."

His irises were fully red with want as he helped me remove his pants and shorts. I took a second to appreciate his entire naked body for the first time—massive scar and all.

"You're beautiful."

He smiled softly. "Allow me to return the favor." It didn't take him long to strip me down and take me in.

We kissed more, taking our time. 'As long as you want me, I'm yours,' we'd both said.

It was nice to have riches, to live a comfortable life and make sure those I loved were taken care of. It was beneficial to be worshiped. But my Coterie was still a precarious environment, and I felt my heart was safer with Hadwin than I did with most. He wanted *me*.

Hadwin adjusted my hips, but I didn't open my legs for him. I pulled back, studying his lethal eyes.

"What's wrong?"

My heart was full, and I only hesitated a moment. "I love you, Hadwin."

He stared at me, his throat bobbing. He said nothing.

It would be disingenuous to say my pride wasn't a little wounded. Though, we'd known each other barely over a week, and not everyone was so quick to throw that statement around. "You don't have to say—"

"I love you too, Sonta," he answered just above a whisper. "With everything I have." He swooped in for another kiss, and I spread my legs for him.

We were both so ready that he slid in smoothly. I loved his frigid body within me.

Taking our time with each thrust, we made love. Not fucking, sex, or a 'contribution.' Proper lovemaking as I squeezed him, as he plunged in as deep as he could go.

I needed Hadwin like I needed water or air, my body craving him, my heart and soul mingling with his as my vampire mate.

The orgasm was nothing short of a masterpiece as we panted and kissed, as we held each other skin to skin for the first time.

He stayed inside me a while, cuddling. "I really do love you, darling."

I nuzzled him. "I love you too."

We stayed up for hours talking, wrapped up in each other. I fell asleep in his arms.

And we made love again early in the morning; this time he fed on me.

I'd told the others I would be sleeping alone in my own chambers, so I didn't want to stay too late in Hadwin's.

Somewhat unsurprisingly, Elion already sat in the common room, bouncing his knee and staring at my door. I frowned.

"Good morning, Elion."

He whipped his head around. "Sonta! You… You said you were sleeping in your…" He glanced behind me at the Coterie corridor. "Who were you with?" Hurt shone on his face.

I clasped my hands before me and gently reminded him he needed to share. "I know I'm *your* only mate, but you're not *my* only mate or partner."

He averted his gaze. "I know… I'm trying…"

I walked up to him and caressed his cheek. "You're doing great, mate."

His eyes flared silvery grey. My heart was still back in Hadwin's room with him, and I wanted to savor the moments we'd shared the night before and this morning. My hormones, however, were tugged by the stronger shifter mating bond.

I blew out a breath. "Can you wait until I bathe? You'll be the first one in my room today."

Elion rubbed himself, nodding. "I can."

"Thank you."

Hadwin had cleaned me up after sex, but I'd still not properly bathed after the long day at the pool. Choosing myself, I took my time in the bathtub, inhaling the jasmine scent of one of the salts from my collection.

I forced myself to not allow guilt to rush me as I made a quick entry in my personal journal, too. I kept my Blessed Vessel journal locked up with the others in the library.

Only after finishing did I allow the warmth in my center to motivate me to open the common room door for Elion.

Hadwin sat in his usual corner, a book in hand. He'd cleaned up nicely.

"Sonta," Elion said, standing.

Hadwin glanced up at me, the sweetest look of adoration gracing his face. "I love you," he mouthed.

My heart fully skipped a beat, and I smiled.

Elion came up to me and kissed me. "You smell wonderful."

With a grin on his face, Hadwin focused on his book again. I let Elion into my room. No sooner had the door closed than he set to work stripping down. I'd only thrown on a bathrobe.

"Can we … be gentle again this time?" I asked, still lingering in the sweetness of the morning.

Elion slowed as he freed his cock from his shorts. "Yes. Are you still hurt? Because if you are…"

His clearer mind and concerted effort to care for me was endearing. "I'm fine. *Sometimes*, I just like it softer, remember?"

He nodded. "Of course. I'd do anything for my mate. For the woman I love."

I kissed him. "I love my mate, too."

As promised, he was gentle, and it was a nice change of pace from the ravaging I generally craved from him.

By the time we emerged from my chambers, most of the Coterie had appeared in the common room. Only Tyfen remained in his room.

I was hungry, and frankly would have been happy to leave without him after our argument yesterday. I was so happy from having bonded with Hadwin last night.

Taking my time, I greeted the men in the room. Gald stood and gave me a hug and kiss. Findlech acknowledged me in the formal way he always did. Haan and I exchanged pleasantries.

I lingered in the corner with Hadwin, getting lost in his hazel eyes. I couldn't stop smiling as he wrapped his arms around me and kissed me on the forehead. "Hello, darling."

"Hello." I already ached to be with him in private again. To hell with obligation and equality in the Great Ritual.

Hadwin sat, pulling me onto his lap. We chatted for a while about the book he'd been reading, while the other men conversed amongst themselves. My stomach growled, and Tyfen still hadn't shown his face.

"Hungry?" Hadwin asked.

"Yeah. Not all of us have already had breakfast."

He smirked, glancing at the fresh bite mark on my neck. "It's a shame."

"Do you want one of us to knock on his door?" Elion asked.

I shook my head, standing. "No. No one's obligated to share meals with me or each other. Tyfen can do as he wishes. But I'm starving, so I'm heading to the dining hall."

The others followed me. Tyfen never showed.

After breakfast, I gave Findlech his chance with me in bed. The rest of the morning consisted of group chatter in the common room. I sat between Hadwin and Elion, each resting a hand on my thigh. It was genuinely enriching to swap stories about our childhoods and to even dispel some racial misunderstandings within the group.

This. *This* was what the Coterie was about. This was the type of environment I would raise my child in as he or she prepared to rule this realm someday.

After lunch, Gald and I went for a stroll on the palace grounds. While I'd originally planned to take him back to my room for sex, we ended up sneaking it in behind some bushes. Not exactly romantic, but certainly fun, with an element of risk that a gardener would spot us.

We kept laughing as we picked twigs out of each other's hair on the stroll back to the palace.

"Perhaps we could have planned that location a little better," Gald said.

I snickered. "Perhaps." At least I was having fun while completing my duties. And now that my first week in seclusion had passed, I'd have more meetings. "As long as I don't have a twig sticking out of my ear for my meeting, though, I'm fine."

Gald grinned, checking me over again. "You're good."

I had to attend a short meeting with the emperor's and magistrate's advisors—nothing out of the ordinary for my position. I'd rather not look a complete mess.

As we walked on the paved path back to my tower of the palace, Gald held my hand. "So, will you ever tell us the truth of how you hurt yourself?"

I swallowed. "There's nothing to know."

"No?" He raised an eyebrow.

"No."

"Then what did Haan mean when he told you 'I never should have let you do that'?"

I stopped dead in my tracks, dropping Gald's hand. Gald had eavesdropped on Haan and me during our *private* conversation in the pool. "What magic did you use to overhear that?"

"I didn't use magic."

My ears heated at the lie and the invasion of privacy. I smacked Gald on the arm. Having forgotten our magic bond, I flinched at the swift sting in my own arm. "Don't. Don't play political tricks on me. I deserve privacy, honesty, and respect."

His jaw dropped. "I didn't lie, Sonta. I happen to be great at lipreading. And you can't fault me for not buying your and Haan's lie. Not when the others in the Coterie wanted to rip my head off because you fell unconscious with me alone in your bedroom."

I averted my gaze. "Even if that's true…"

"It is true, *Your Holiness*," he bit back.

Him calling me by my title somehow hurt worse than if he'd smacked me in return. I hugged myself, meeting his gaze. "Fine. It's still an invasion of privacy. I'm sorry the others were angry with you. I don't want *any* trouble in the Coterie." Not for him or Haan, or even Tyfen. I also didn't want the others to realize how stupid I had been for trying to have sex with Haan in a bathtub; they were all already older than me, some considering me childish simply because of my youth. And then I'd proven my stupidity by downing several doses of the medicinal tonic in one go.

Gald crossed his arms, but it was hard at times to take him seriously. Not with such a youthful face, that curly red hair and those dazzling blue eyes. "And what about accusing me of political tricks? I may aspire and work hard for a place in this realm, but that does not make me a snake." He held up his wrist where his twin bond tattoo lay. "I am loyal to you. I care about your well-being. I made this as a personal promise, not just as a politician."

I sighed. "I know you care. I'm sorry. I just wanted things to be fair…"

His firm expression softened a bit. "I accept your apology." He rubbed his arm. "But next time you strike me, it better be your palm on my ass in foreplay."

Unable to stop myself, I smiled.

He cracked a small smile too. "What do you mean by wanting things to be fair?"

I drew a deep breath. So far, Gald *had* kept my secret about Lilah and me being lovers… "Can you promise me you won't tell anyone? Even Haan?"

Gald shook his head. "I don't make blind bargains."

I furrowed my brow. "Then I won't tell you."

He rolled his eyes. "If you told me you and Haan were making plans to assassinate the emperor, you'd expect me to keep a secret?"

I scowled. "You get upset at me for claiming you're thick into politics, but you jump to treason for me?"

"My word is my bond. I simply don't like making promises I can't keep."

I walked away from Gald, continuing on the path.

"Sonta!"

Huffing, I kept my pace.

He ran up to me. "Fine. I'll keep your secret."

"Even if I'm planning treason?"

"You're too sweet for treason."

I stood tall, puffing my chest. "Maybe you don't know me as well as you think you do."

He had the audacity to laugh. At first it annoyed me, but it did soften me. He wasn't wrong, after all.

Taking my hands, he gave me a pleading look. "Allies. Friends. Lovers. I'll try not to invade your privacy like that again. And you're allowed your secrets. It just worries me when it has to do with your safety. Even if you're fine now, you *could* have hurt yourself if you'd passed out in a different place…"

I frowned. "I feel like an idiot. And Haan's not at fault. And he would feel so … emasculated … if the others knew…"

"The others don't have to know," Gald said softly.

I bolstered my courage and told Gald how foolish I'd been by going through with the bathtub attempt.

Gald nodded, listening intently. "I can see why Haan would be embarrassed if he wasn't able to finish… And scared of the others because he hurt you—accident or not."

"Exactly…"

"Won't the palace provide you with similar conditions to the bedding chamber to ensure you can copulate with him again safely?"

"Yes, but neither of us want that. It's dangerous, and I can't imagine having guards standing over me with spears again."

He pursed his lips. "True. Surely there are other alternatives…"

We brainstormed a while, and I kept shooting his ideas down. There was a split there between merfolk pride and simple logistics. Merfolk were a bit more limited on how they could do the deed… Unlike land-walkers, who were able to contort themselves as long as they could fit their dick in my pussy, Haan was at a physical disadvantage. And I was sturdier than most humans, but not *that* sturdy. If I held on to a rope the entire time Haan took me, I'd have burned hands and dislocated shoulders at best.

"It's not like we have to be so primitive about it…" Gald said. "We *did* use magic in the bedding chamber, with the protective enchantments."

"Yes, but we both know why that was the only magic allowed in that setting…"

Merfolk possessed no magic, and many were fairly superstitious. Beyond that minimal protective spell they'd allowed palace mages to put on the consummation tank, the merfolk wouldn't accept further intervention by the magical races.

"Haan seems reasonable, though," Gald remarked.

I wore a faint smile. "Yeah, he's a sweetheart."

"I was given the opportunity to be in your Coterie because, despite my youth, I'm damn good at what I do."

My smile grew into a grin. "Yes, you are."

He chuckled. "What I'm saying is I would be willing to help you."

I wrinkled my nose. "Haan would be humiliated to have a bunch of people in on this, especially after the bathtub incident."

"I didn't say a bunch of people. Just me. I'm powerful enough to charm your personal pond like they did for the bedding chamber. And I *am* an elemental mage…"

I narrowed my eyes, considering his proposal. "You could make sure I don't drown… Controlling the air and water…" Just like he had in my studio and when he'd made me orgasm in the pool.

"Yes. I was ready to do it in the bedding chamber if needed." He shrugged. "I'm glad it *wasn't* needed."

Looking at Gald with newfound admiration, I stood there with my jaw open. "But why? Why would you offer to help?"

He slid his hands onto my back. "Why wouldn't I?"

"Because you've been honest about wanting to sire the next ruler. What happens if you help Haan have another chance with me and he becomes the father instead of you?"

Gald held my chin. "Then I'd hope to earn favorite uncle points with the next ruler for being a good example, for offering a better chance at equality for all races."

I glided my hands down to Gald's ass, grabbing it as he often did mine. "I like you, Gald."

His smirk was feral. "Mutual. We can iron out details later on, but you have a meeting you don't want to be late for."

I'd nearly lost track of the time. I gave him a quick smooch. "Thank you."

40

Two on Top

My meeting was rather dull but thankfully not long. By dinnertime, Tyfen had still not left his room. He wasn't my problem, and I certainly wasn't going to beg him for sex, no matter how mouthwateringly large he was.

After dinner, I spent time with Haan, swimming in my personal pond. I did my best to bring up the idea of Gald helping us to have sex again so he'd have another chance at siring the next ruler. It wasn't like we hadn't enjoyed our time in the tank together anyway…

Haan flat-out refused to entertain the idea. As much as he wanted to represent his people, he wouldn't risk hurting me again or facing the wrath of the other Coterie members or worse.

In the end, I sought out Hadwin. If Tyfen wasn't going to ask for sex, and if Haan wouldn't accept it, I was going to enjoy some time under the sheets with someone I'd stepped it up with in the relationship department.

I savored my time in Hadwin's bed, teasing him. I worshiped every inch of his body, kissing and biting him, eventually sucking him off. Not much later I let him feed on me, then we practiced a few rather gymnastic moves.

Should we have used a barrier? Yes, in the spirit of fairness. I didn't want to.

At the end of the night, I chose Gald and Elion to share my bed, letting Elion take me a second time as well before inviting Gald into the room. Gald may have enjoyed watching, but I wasn't sure Elion would want it.

I slept easily and peacefully with the two of them wrapped around me.

In the wee hours of the morning, I woke to only Gald holding me. Elion had to be in the washroom.

"You really do sleep soundly, don't you?" Gald said, his voice froggy.

I smiled. "I have you all to thank for wearing me down during the day."

He softly chuckled, kissing my cheek and slipping a hand to caress my breast. "Speaking of…" He pressed his erect cock against my side. "How would you feel about starting the day off this way?"

Still tired, I quietly moaned. "Sure."

Gald shuffled under the sheets to take off his shorts, and soon straddled me. Still sleepy, I'd let him do the work.

He slid in without resistance. "Damn, I like mornings with you. Much better than a man's own hand."

I laughed. "So flattering, Gald."

Smiling wide, he made his first thrust. "Seriously though, you're so perfectly tight, always ready for more, despite how much cock you take each day."

Grinning, I flexed myself around him. He shuddered.

Sweet morning sex was never something I complained about, and I would milk Gald for all he wanted to give me as he steadily built up speed.

A whimper came from behind Gald.

Shit… Elion hadn't seen another man take me since the bedding chamber.

"You'll have to wait," Gald said firmly. "Sonta and I are going to enjoy each other before I let you have her."

I glanced at Elion. Luckily, he didn't look murderous. His breathing was heavy, though, and his shorts tight. He distracted me from the building tension in my core as Gald slowly did his work.

"Can I…" Elion looked me in the eye, desperate. "Can I at least watch?" He pulled himself out of his shorts and pumped himself.

Any release in my presence was better than no release, right? "I'm fine with that."

Gald thrust again, massaging me deep inside. "That's fine." He paused. "Unless you'd like to join us, Elion."

'Group fun' as Gald had called it before…

To my surprise, Gald shifted, throwing off the blanket and exposing his bare ass. "I'm staying in Sonta, but there's an opening you can take if you'd like…"

Gald was offering himself as the middleman, and I couldn't say I was all that shocked. He was easily the most adventurous of my Coterie partners.

Elion still gripped his cock, staring between Gald's ass and me as Gald started up again.

"Sonta?" Elion panted out.

Gald leaned down and sucked my nipple. I bucked my hips with pleasure. "It's up to you, Elion. You can take his offer if you want."

Gald sucked my other nipple, and I let out a small moan.

Elion whimpered again, indecision dancing across his face. His pumping slowed, then stopped. Then he dropped his shorts and crossed the room.

Bracing himself, Gald stopped thrusting as Elion mounted him. Hungry, Elion slid into Gald from behind. A measured amount of relief showed on his face at his cock being caressed. Gald's own expression was one of ecstasy.

Fevered, Elion greedily thrust into Gald, and Gald moved in time with him while inside me. Twice the weight behind each thrust, twice the panting and fucking, meant twice the pleasure as Gald slammed into me time and time again.

Every inch of him inside me hit right. Every slap of skin and balls and each whisper carried lust and love and pure pleasure to me.

Then the cascade of relief hit us, crashing like waves one at a time. Elion went first, then Gald, and with a couple more thrusts, I found my orgasm.

I was all smiles, and frankly very proud of Elion. Gald adjusted himself a bit, still inside me.

"What did you think, Elion?" Gald asked.

"I… Um…" He caught his breath. "Sorry, it takes a while for the knot…"

"And what about you, Sonta?" Gald purred.

"Mmm. I'm not complaining." I flexed around him again.

He claimed my mouth, his tongue playing with mine. I always enjoyed the skillful rub of his piercing.

I moaned again. "I like this," I whispered.

Elion pulled himself from Gald's entrance. "I'll be in the washroom."

Gald stayed on top of me.

"Group activities?" I said. "Adventurous."

He smirked. "You barely know me. Perhaps someday we'll find out which of us is more wicked and perverted than the other."

I wanted to prolong the moment. "Kiss me."

He fondled both my breasts, passionately claiming my mouth. We panted, grinding. If he'd been a vampire or shifter, he'd have been hard again already.

Elion shuffled back into the room, and Gald stopped kissing me. "Well, perhaps I'll use the washroom now. But, for the record, I adore waking up next to you."

I gave him a smile as he got off me.

"What did you think?" Gald asked Elion as he grabbed me a cloth for wiping.

Elion had just finished putting on his shorts. "It felt nice, thanks." He glanced at me. "I'm going to use my own washroom to get ready for the day."

"Okay."

It was a nice lazy morning. I let Findlech have me, as well as Elion again before lunch, then Hadwin and I spent time together before dinner.

Tyfen hadn't shown his face all day.

The rest of us enjoyed a fantastic dinner together. My roast was perfectly juicy.

"Should someone check on Prince Tyfen?" Findlech asked.

The others looked to me. No one had seen him leave his room in nearly two days. I was mildly concerned, given the nasty gash Elion had left him with, but I wasn't going to baby Tyfen, and I certainly wasn't going to beg him for sex.

"I'm sure he's fine." I drank from my goblet. "If flies aren't collecting at his door, he's probably alive."

Gald shot me a surprised look, and I felt guilty for being so openly harsh.

"I'll check on him," I said.

"Do you want me to?" Elion shyly offered. He likely blamed himself for Tyfen's injury, but it wouldn't go well to throw those two together like that.

"I'll be fine on my own, but thank you."

Since we were already on a bit of an uncomfortable subject, I decided to loosely address what had happened this morning in my bed. Elion had been uncharacteristically shy around Gald all day, and I was ready to let the men of my Coterie know where I stood on the issue. It also wouldn't hurt to ease them into the mindset for when I was ready to disclose more details of my own sexuality…

"Unrelated, but I got to thinking…" I cleared my throat. "I would just like it to be known that I'm okay with … more adventurous pairings in this Coterie. I'm not a stranger to group activities, and it's not like I haven't seen two men … involved before. I'd never expect you to do something you don't feel comfortable with sexually, but you also don't have to worry about me shaming you for something you like. You can be open with me…"

All I got in return was a slew of nods.

After dinner, I let the men know I'd be spending the evening with Lilah, and I'd eventually fetch who I wanted to share my bed with.

Before going to see Lilah, I discreetly checked with the servants to ensure Tyfen was fine. They confirmed he'd been having meals delivered straight to his rooms. I'd done my duty and hadn't needed to see him—even better.

Lilah and I had a great evening. We played cards and gossiped forever, especially about Hadwin's blood play. Lilah went into great detail about the sucking points the ladies at the Suck and Fuck had used on her. Hadwin had mentioned a couple more, but we'd been hesitant to try because they required such precision that Hadwin wasn't experienced with.

I wanted to share with Lilah so much that I couldn't. I didn't tell her about the flop with Haan out of respect for him. And I didn't tell her about Hadwin's devastating past for the same reason.

We shared the regular sofa in her sitting area, splitting a dessert at the end of the night.

"I got to thinking about your request with your mage partner…"

"Yes?"

"Full paintings … good ones at least, take me a while."

I licked caramel sauce off my finger. "Right…"

"I'd be willing to do multiple sketches if you'd like? Showcasing different positions?"

I smiled. "If it's too much work, you don't have to do it at all."

"I *do* think it would be fun, but I was considering focusing on a slightly different painting project."

"I'm all ears."

"What if I painted you alone during your pregnancy? It would be a beautiful way to document your growth, and it would also be something all your lovers could enjoy, not just Gald."

Smiling, I almost cried. "I love that idea!"

She shrugged. "What are friends for? Plus, I'm still a lover, right? Just dormant?"

"Yes!"

"And if you wanted something a bit more tasteful for when that little one joins us, maybe I could paint a *little* something to cover your more private bits…"

I blinked. "Not a bad idea." Sometimes, it still seemed unreal that I would be a mother in a year's time. Sometimes, I also forgot I wasn't just Sonta—Vesta's daughter—but also a major figure, and things like a gallery of me naked might be odd to keep in the public eye for centuries.

Lilah and I stayed up late, catching up. I eventually gave her a massive hug and went on my way.

I took my time strolling the silent hallways. The still of the night was peaceful and healing. Once I arrived at my chambers, I undressed myself and bathed.

After crawling into bed, I blew out my candle. Oddly enough, a knock sounded at my door to the common room. I bunched my eyebrows. Who would be up so late? Elion, despite his mating fever, never interrupted my sleep like this.

They knocked again. Grunting, I stood. Since servants would have knocked at a different door, I approached naked. It wasn't like my Coterie hadn't seen it all anyway.

I opened the door, and only a dim sconce flickered in the common room. Tyfen, of all people, stood before me. He was shirtless, leaning against the doorframe, reeking of strong wine.

His gaze dragged across my naked body. "I want my turn."

41

THE DRUNKEN DEED

I gaped, reading Tyfen's face. "Excuse me?" Naked, I concealed myself a bit behind my door.

"I want my turn with you," he said.

"You're drunk, Tyfen. Go back to your room."

"No I'm not."

His slight drawl and the strong wine that wafted to my nose with each breath suggested otherwise.

"Yes, you are. And I was already in bed."

"I'll join you. I haven't had you in days."

No, he hadn't. He hadn't touched me in four days.

"That sounds like a demand."

"Not demands. Statements." There was a softness to his tone that surprisingly kept me calm. Were he a drunk *human* man, I might actually be afraid, or I might laugh in his face about even being able to get it up to bed me. But Prince Tyfen of the fae was not the sort of man to become impotent just because of a bit too much wine.

As I surveyed him—his muscled body leaning against my door, his face mostly hidden in the shadows—I had to accept one thing about myself. I was a weak excuse for a goddess's daughter, because I obviously had a soft spot for handsome damaged men.

Two weeks as partners and I still knew next to nothing about Tyfen, but I would never forget the way he'd teared up as he'd begged me to let him bed me for the sake of his people. His green eyes had matched the dewy grass in the somber vision I'd had later that night. Something in my heart had pinched at the way he'd admitted his parents should have sent *anyone* but him.

"For my people?" he whispered.

I drew a deep breath. "It's not my fault you hid in your room the last two days."

He didn't respond.

"If you want me, then I want something in return." I crossed my arms. "I want to know about your powers."

He narrowed his eyes, considering. Those who possessed magic often kept their abilities a secret. To expose your talents would be to let your enemies know how to handle you. While there had been peace in the realm for a long while, the logic was still sound.

But he was a member of my Coterie, pledged to me, and I deserved something out of this exchange beyond an impressive cock inside me.

"I can winnow," he said.

I blinked. Winnowing—instant transportation—wasn't the most rare gift, but one I'd always been impressed with. Some mages could perform travel spells, but winnowing belonged to the fae and elves.

"Oh." I didn't have anything particularly clever to say. I waited a moment to see if he'd divulge more, but he didn't. "Fine. You can have me, but not here." I didn't want him in my room, and I didn't want him to bed me in the common room or his room, either.

Tyfen reached out a hand, caressing my bare hip. His touch was soft, coming from a drunk brute. It sent shivers down my spine. "Your other room?"

The palace had wards to prevent winnowing, so we'd have to walk together. "Sure. Let me get a robe on."

I turned and grabbed one from my dressing room, the twin moons' light helping me see well enough. I returned to the door, wearing a silk robe. "Okay, let's go."

He stepped back to allow me past him, then followed me through the common room and into the hallway.

Torches lit our way, the soft patter of our footsteps the only sound punctuating the quiet night.

"Your chest wound looks better," I said. There was barely anything there now from where Elion had clawed him a few days ago.

"It's fine," he muttered. "Good healers."

We didn't talk for the remainder of the walk. My playroom was dark upon our arrival, and it took a moment to light a couple of sconces. Tyfen watched as I did so.

I faced him. "Where would you like me?"

He stepped up to me, wordlessly untying the knot in my robe and slipping it off me.

I hadn't been fully naked in front of him since he'd claimed me in the bedding chamber. And I didn't really know what to think of him at the moment.

Tyfen's gaze raked over me again, his face unreadable. He swallowed. "Wherever you want."

I chose the same formed sex bench he'd taken me on before, scooting myself back.

He dropped trou, now also completely naked.

There was something different in the air between us, something soft and sensual. It was probably the alcohol. What all would he say and do with his guard down?

Tyfen approached me on the bench, laying his hands on my thighs and gently spreading them. Instead of straddling me right away, he bent. He took in my scent and licked me, setting my core on fire.

He didn't stop at one lick. He lazily drew his tongue through me, dipping inside me and also pressing against my clit.

I had definitely been hasty in my previous insult about him not knowing how to make a woman wet. He was skilled when he wanted to be.

Why did he want to be now?

I remained silent save for the occasional instance I couldn't stop my breath from catching. In mere minutes, I was drenched and ready for him.

Tyfen straddled me but didn't enter. He was already erect. He met my gaze with his handsome green eyes; it was unlike him. "You like my cock."

I looked away. I'd already accidentally admitted as much once. He didn't need another confirmation for his pride. Then again, he'd stated it matter-of-factly, not with an arrogant grin.

"But you've never held it." He took my hands and placed them on his cock.

My mouth watered, and I couldn't resist looking. I grasped him tighter, truly admiring his girth, visually tracing his ab tattoos, which swirled down to his impressive manhood. I had to remind myself he was a complete asshole, and that size didn't matter all that much.

His cock twitched in my hands, and I gave Tyfen a gentle squeeze. He let out a moan. I dared to glance at his curved, pointy ears. It was common knowledge the fae and elves had sensitive ears. A well-placed stroke could arouse him further.

I stopped myself from doing it. We weren't truly lovers in that way. This was *just* obligatory sex.

Tyfen removed my hands from his cock, setting them to my sides. Dipping, he put his tip to my entrance and slowly slid in.

If I lived to be a thousand, I would never *not* be impressed with how it felt to have him stretch and rub me so effortlessly.

I panted out a breath.

He kept his eyes squarely on mine. This uninhibited Tyfen finally gave me the sense of intimacy I'd been irrationally craving from him.

A small smile graced his lips as he reached halfway inside me. "That's a good girl."

I was putty in his hands again, and I unintentionally flexed around him.

A spark in his eye shone; he'd recognized how much I enjoyed him saying that. I swallowed, praying he'd forget it by the morning when he sobered up…

"Why were you hiding in your room?" I dared to ask, distracting him.

He rolled his bloodshot eyes. "Just sex, Sonta."

My heart twisted at that. It had no right to. It had no right to betray me like that. This *was* just sex. Just duty. I didn't need to care for him personally.

Keeping his gaze on me, studying me, he finished sliding into me, all the way to the hilt. My body begged for him to continue, and it was cruel for him to pause.

With a short glance at my breasts, Tyfen licked his lips, and pulled himself most of the way out. He looked back up, then thrust.

I gasped, and his expression also faltered, betraying his own pleasure.

Happy to surrender in the moment, I joined him in the next thrust. He grasped my sides, and I his, and we lost ourselves in each and every instance he plunged into me as I took his cock deep.

It was the closest to lovemaking Tyfen and I had ever done, as he kept his eyes on me.

I savored the pain of his fevered thrusts as we built, and when the time finally came for me to find my release, I didn't try to hide it. I gasped just like I always did for Elion.

The sweetest moans shivered through Tyfen as he shook with pleasure. I enjoyed his unrestrained honesty.

His mouth open, he blinked a few times, then met my gaze again.

My heart warmed at the unity of the moment, at him giving me something he never had before—eye contact, a moment of tenderness together as we cooled instead of immediately pulling himself out and leaving me alone.

I had no words. Neither did he.

I slid my hands to his groin, at the base of his shaft, daring to gently massage him. His chest heaved as he let out a low and feral groan.

Then his gaze left mine, studying my breasts. Were he not absolutely drunk, I would have thought he'd never seen tits before, given the way he looked at them.

He glided his hands to them, palming them.

Fuck.

His curious expression didn't match the skill with which he groped me, nor the way his thumbs circled my nipples perfectly, making them hard.

My heart and lungs raced at the attention.

Fully taking me by surprise, Tyfen leaned down, still buried deep inside me. Was he going to kiss me?

What would his lips taste like? I was hungry to find out.

He didn't kiss me, at least not on the lips. He angled his head and aimed for my neck.

A tingle ran down my spine the moment his lips pressed to my neck. He breathed me in, whispering in my ear, "You smell good."

Smoky cologne mingled with the wine on his breath. I didn't return the compliment.

Had he kissed me on the mouth, it probably would have been sloppy anyway, given his current state, but I couldn't pretend I didn't enjoy the way he worshiped my neck with several kisses.

Whatever his motivations, this wasn't *just* sex.

Tyfen sucked on my earlobe, and my entire body went rigid. I dug my fingers into his thighs as he gave a small thrust.

Fuck.

His lips touching my ear, he whispered again. "I hate that I love being inside you."

I swallowed hard at the confession. It hadn't been said with malice, but more as a tragic resignation. I shared that same feeling, and while I couldn't pretend I hadn't enjoyed him taking me—not with the gasps and moans—I wouldn't give him the satisfaction of me openly admitting it.

He kept kissing my neck, reaching a hand down to grope my breast again.

His lips rested on the base of my neck, and he sucked. The sharp pinch of his sucking meant only one thing—he was giving me a hickey.

I stayed still, analyzing him. But how much could one truly analyze a drunk man for his actions? He'd wanted to fuck. He'd wanted a release, and to do his duty—that was all… His muddled brain had made this something more than it was.

He finally released his suction and sat up, resting his hands on my sides. He stared at the mark he'd left, his expression hazy. "There. The others left their marks, and so have I."

My brain stuttered. It hadn't just been a sloppy hickey? He'd left it on the opposite side of my neck from Hadwin's love bite.

Did he *want* to claim me like Hadwin, Elion, and Gald all had? Leaving a mark on my body that way?

And did *I* want him to?

Tyfen and I weren't mates. Fae and elves hadn't had human mates for ages. And if the bond were there, wouldn't I have known? Fate itself would have likely snapped that bond into place by now, and we'd have matching tattoos like the ones covering his perfectly chiseled body.

I wasn't his one and only. And I shouldn't care about that.

He looked at me again, and I couldn't bring myself to ask him why he'd done it.

"I'm still hard," he uttered.

"Yes you are." Hadwin could arrive twice in a row with me because of his vampire nature, given he'd had fresh blood. Elion could as well, mostly because of his mating fever.

But Tyfen? He was a strong fae male, and something of a sex god by my estimation. As I was the daughter of a goddess, my admiration would have been a massive ego boost had I dared to admit as much.

He didn't ask if he could take me again, could add to his chances of siring the next ruler. And I wouldn't ask either, at least not with my words.

I flexed my muscles tight around him. He panted out a breath, taking the cue, and pulled himself halfway out again.

This time, he bent lower as he thrust greedily, every moan, groan and grunt of pleasure making its way to my ears. He sounded like Elion whenever he was desperate for me.

That, or like a drunk fae losing himself while seeking satisfaction.

Turning off my brain, I stopped trying to analyze, giving in to animal instincts. I dug my fingers into his back, helping him with each thrust. Every muscle would ache from the work and the buildup and the extra release, but I chased the feeling I craved.

His fevered thrusting nearly pushed me off the bench. He held my head and neck for support, yanking me back before continuing. I was his to do with as he pleased, and I didn't care for the why or how or even the who.

We were flesh and sweat, a chorus of breathy moans.

My legs shook, my abs on fire as I met my second orgasm. He kept slamming into me, and it hurt from how big he was and how wound up I'd become.

I was just trying to catch my breath when he came the second time. He was much more vocal than me this time around.

I lay there stunned, not a coherent thought in my brain.

Clearly worn out, he tucked his arms in, lying on me. He was as sweaty as I was, as spent and breathless.

After a minute, I relaxed more under his weight, savoring our lungs working in tandem. His head nestled between my breasts, he kept his eyes closed.

After a while, he slid his hands between us, to my abdomen.

It was kind of sweet. Maybe if he'd let his guard down, and if this was the real him, he wouldn't be so bad to raise a child with.

"I hate this," he whispered.

My heart cracked. How could he be so sweet, so passionate, and yet so hurtful? Maybe… Maybe he hadn't meant it in that way…

My emotions raw, I dared to ask for clarification. "Hate what?"

It took him a moment to respond. "Everything."

I swallowed, devastated. 'Just sex,' he'd said. And I needed to remember that. I needed to take him at his word. He owned no part of my heart. He didn't even want it.

But I was a stupid young girl, especially in his eyes. And I *wanted* him to like me, to love me. I wanted great sex to mean something. I almost cried.

"I want to go back to bed," I said.

He pressed his forehead to my chest. "Right. Bed."

Like he always did, he peeled himself off me without meeting my gaze. He withdrew slowly, his seed spilling out.

He grabbed some cloths from a nearby table and handed me one, cleaning himself off. I scooted back, wiping him off me, and he moved to take care of the mess on the bench.

"I can handle this. Go to bed." I wanted him gone.

"Fine." He grabbed his shorts and pants, dressed again, then left the room without so much as a thank you or goodbye.

I sopped up the rest of our mess and threw the dirty cloths in a hamper. After putting my robe back on, I curled into a ball on the floor mats.

I let myself wallow, tears dripping onto the mat. I hated Tyfen for the way he made me feel.

Worse than that, I hated myself for being so fragile, for *allowing* him to make me feel this way.

Since when did I need everyone's approval? I didn't. I didn't much care that Findlech barely respected me.

Tyfen should be no different.

I stayed there so long, huddled and miserable, that I nearly cried myself to sleep. As soon as I jerked awake, I forced myself up and back to my chambers. I could barely walk from how intense the sex had been, how much my muscles barked. I didn't come by my toned figure from boring exercise… At least there was that.

Not caring to even remove my robe, I slipped under my covers and crashed.

PRIMAL PLAY

I blinked, the early morning rays hitting my face. No one held me.

Right… I never invited anyone to bed with me.

My stomach muscles were sore as I turned in bed.

I sighed. Tyfen…

How much of our crazy night would he remember? The good and the bad? At least no one had seen me fall apart over it. That was a secret I'd take to the grave.

I lay in bed for a while, closing my eyes and conjuring up one of my favorite visions from my childhood. In that vision, I'd climbed a snow-covered mountain, viewing the palace itself being constructed several centuries ago. I'd been chilled in the dream, but not too badly. Part of me wished for a snowpack right now. My eyes were puffy from crying and my pussy still tender from taking Tyfen twice.

Eventually, I found the will to drag myself out of bed. I had a servant draw me a warm bath while I put cold compresses to my eyes. She glanced at my neck a couple of times.

Only after I'd dismissed her did I look in the mirror.

"Shit." No wonder she'd glanced at my neck. Tyfen had left quite the mark on me…

I took my time in the tub, then eventually called the servant back to braid my hair after I'd dressed.

"Would you like help concealing that mark, Your Holiness?" She bound my braid.

Did I? I could apply makeup myself, but I wasn't sure I even wanted to… I wanted to see Tyfen's reaction, wanted to see how much he even recalled from last night.

"No thank you."

After dismissing her, I selected the most ornate necklace I had that drew the eye right to it.

I took more time to ready myself than I had most mornings lately. I was starving by the time I entered the common room.

All eyes immediately turned to me.

Elion leapt up, closing the gap. He noticed the hickey right away, pausing. "Do you want help with that?"

I gave him a soft smile. "No thank you. I'll heal fine on my own." I kissed him.

"Okay. Can we…"

"After breakfast?" Not only was I hungry, but I was still healing.

"All right," he breathed.

I glanced in Tyfen's direction for the briefest moment. He was actually dressed rather sharp, with his hair combed to the side, not a single hint of a hangover. His eyes were wide, though, his expression pure shock as he stared at what he'd left on me. I hid a smirk, capturing a mental picture.

Hadwin took his turn greeting me, pulling me in for a hug and kiss. "Good morning, darling."

"Good morning." I gazed into his hazel eyes.

He looked at the hickey. "I trust you didn't … fall … again?"

My smile brightened. "No. I didn't. Thank you for caring."

I nodded my hello to Haan and faced the others. "I'm ready for breakfast. Why don't we eat, and we'll take it from there today."

Haan splashed away, and the others stood. Hadwin kept a hand on my back, escorting me as the others went into the hallway.

Tyfen hung back, lingering by the door.

I paused at the door. "Hadwin, go ahead without me. I'll be there in a minute."

He glanced at Tyfen, then kissed me on the cheek. "Okay, darling."

I made sure he'd followed the others down the hallway quite a bit before facing Tyfen.

"Can I help you?" I clasped my hands in front of me.

"I, uh…" Tyfen swallowed. "I don't really remember anything from last night."

Didn't that bring me a mix of emotions…

He continued. "So … I hope I didn't say or do anything too stupid…" He kept looking at the hickey.

"No more than usual." I smiled wryly. "Everything was … *sufficient.*"

"Right…"

We stood in silence. It was nice to see him unnerved.

"Is there anything else you wanted?" I asked.

He sucked in a breath. "Why didn't you hide that?"

The elephant in the room, the mark of his drunken stupor…

I batted my lashes, lifting my chin. "Was I supposed to?"

He blinked, and I would have paid good money to know what ran through his head, to know what exactly he remembered.

Without another word, he walked around me and followed after the other men.

I blew out a breath and braced myself against the door, and swore to myself in that moment that I would *never* cry over him again. I was made of tougher stuff than that. And I deserved better.

The rest of my day was rather average, aside from asking the men in private to be a bit gentler with me.

Tyfen didn't ask me for sex again that day, but he did the next. I made a new rule. Not only did he have to be civil with me and the others to earn a chance to bed me daily, but he had to divulge something about himself. He wasn't pleased with that ultimatum, but eventually gave in, making me swear to keep the secrets between us. I agreed.

He had masking powers—they made it hard for enemies to trace him, a great tool for battle.

Our sex took place again in the playroom—neutral ground—and he went back to his sour mood, not looking at me or staying long inside me.

By the end of the second week of my Coterie being together, I was healed of every injury and had another meeting with my mage midwife. It was still too early to tell if I'd conceived, but she gave me a clean bill of health.

The next few days were interesting.

Hadwin was as sweet as ever, and we even said our first public 'I love you' in front of the others.

Gald was still sexy and playful.

Findlech was Findlech.

Haan continued to refuse to let me try taking a spin in the tank with him again, but we enjoyed lots of great chats.

Tyfen was his usual reclusive self, but he came to most meals, begrudgingly divulged small details about himself before bedding me, and was perhaps a *tiny* bit kinder.

I tried not to let it hurt my pride that he now usually had alcohol on his breath when he approached me for sex. He wasn't drunk, but he apparently needed something to take off the edge when it came to intimacy with me…

And then there was Elion… His fever continued to slowly calm, but he was still skittish around Gald, and I had my suspicions.

After a nice hangout with Lilah, I decided to finally tackle the issue. There was something special I'd wanted to do with Elion anyway, even before I'd ever met him.

I carved out an evening just for him. We had a picnic out in my personal gardens. The sunset was brilliant, and we chatted over policy. Now that he was capable of seeing beyond fucking me every moment of every day, it was a good time to discuss what he wanted.

Elion wasn't the most eloquent speaker, but he also wasn't an idiot. He presented his biggest political concerns, most of which were understandable. Shifters always fought for more and better land. They used to have free rein over the realm, but they'd been granted space specifically for them where they could be safe from hunters mistaking them for wild game. The land was tight, and not as fertile as they often wished. He begrudgingly added that the fae often overstepped the bounds of their kingdom anyway.

I admired Elion for the wisdom his parents had imparted to him in his youth, and he had sound logic of his own.

He fed me strawberries as part of our dessert, and we lay, cuddling and kissing. He was ready for more, but patient.

I stroked his cheek, gazing into his silver eyes. "Will you be honest with me if I ask you something?"

He smiled. "I'm always honest with you, Sonta. I have nothing to hide."

"What did you think of the time you shared me with Gald?"

He looked away. "I… It wasn't my favorite."

That had become apparent by the way he'd avoided Gald after that; I just wasn't completely certain why.

"You said it was nice," I reminded him. "Have you been with a man before?"

Elion cleared his throat. "No."

"Oh… Did you feel pressured into it?" I was all for people experimenting, but on their own terms. I hadn't thought Gald and I were particularly coercive that morning…

"Not really." He met my gaze again. "It was just hard to see him inside you when I wanted to be, and he offered… I wanted to be close, so I thought I'd give it a try."

"But you didn't like it…"

He drew a breath. "It felt better than my hand, but not as good as being inside you."

I nodded. "You don't have to be with any of the others if you don't want to be. Or even in the same room when I'm with others in that way. Just let me know what you prefer." It wasn't like I didn't thoroughly enjoy Hadwin despite him not wanting to share.

Elion considered. "I … think I just don't want to be inside anyone or to have them inside me unless it's my mate."

"Even another woman?"

"Even another woman. I love *you*."

"I can be okay with that. If anything changes, let me know."

"Thank you." He paused. "I honestly think I might not hate sharing you, but separately, if that's something you want."

I grinned. "Like you're each taking a different entrance?"

He mirrored my grin. "Yes. Especially with this constant sharing business. The others don't want me to be with you so often, but I still want to be inside you *constantly*. Even if they're just making a daily political contribution, I could enjoy you an extra time…"

All sorts of wicked positions danced in my mind. "You'd be fine with that even if it's Gald taking me?"

"Sure."

Something told me Gald would be happy, too.

As darkness overtook the sky, I leaned in and kissed Elion again. I slid a hand across his chest, undoing the top button of his shirt. He growled in anticipation, reaching for his belt buckle.

"You have to wait," I said, moving to the next button.

He grunted in protest.

"Wait," I repeated.

His eyes shone brighter, his hand instead finding its way inside my dress to fondle me. My heart beat faster as I finished the last buttons, then felt his bare chest.

"My mate." He claimed my mouth, reaching for his pants again.

I wanted to prolong this a little longer, and wanted to position myself better.

Pulling back, I grabbed his hands. "No." I was firm as I removed his shirt completely, rolling him onto his back and straddling him.

His breathing was guttural and forced. He didn't want to be dominated this time. "Yes," he muttered through clenched teeth. The bulge in his pants was telling, not that I needed it to tell me how he felt. Not like I wasn't already wet for him, too.

"I'm going to undo your pants, but you're going to stay put, Elion."

He growled, and I hid a smile.

With his trousers undone, I slowly stood and backed up.

His breathing only grew heavier with his barely there restraint.

"Do you want me?" I asked.

"Obviously," he choked out.

I prepared myself, stealing a glance out of the corner of my eye. "You only get to have me if you can catch me."

I bolted to the side, ducking behind a row of bushes, running like my life depended on it. I'd waited until nighttime to avoid any gardeners, but it wouldn't give me an advantage with Elion's better night vision.

But I had studied every possible path in my private gardens. My home advantage evened things out.

Or so I'd thought. The rapid crunch of gravel behind me begged to differ.

Wrapping my arm around a tree, I swung myself around a turn, glancing behind me under the moonlight.

Elion had shifted, running me down on all fours.

A nervous squeak escaped me as I darted faster down the next lane of bushes. In no time flat, I reached a clearing at the end.

I didn't take time to congratulate myself, nor did I deserve to. Elion tackled me, and we went rolling together.

"Ouch!" I yelped.

He paused on all fours, then shifted into a man, naked and staring at me from a couple of feet away. He searched me for an injury, and I took the opening to jump up and run further.

My hair was a mess, and my dress likely torn, but I enjoyed the chase too much to give up now.

"Sonta!" he barked, sprinting after me, this time on two feet. Even as a man, he had impressive speed and stamina.

He caught me by the waist, yanking me back. My sides were already hurting from running so fast, and I couldn't hold back a laugh.

"Mine," he said as he pinned me against a tree from behind.

I panted, trying to jerk away.

He pressed me more fiercely against the tree, reaching a hand up to grab my hair. "Struggle again, and I'll take you harder."

My grin was positively feral. "I'd like to see you try."

He tugged my hair, lifting my dress to take me. I'd worn underwear this time, though it barely delayed him as he shifted his hand into a paw, dragged one sharp claw down, and sliced my underwear clean off me.

"Mine," he repeated in a low rumble.

There was no easing into it as he plunged into me. I held tight to the tree as he slammed into me repeatedly. Observers couldn't have easily viewed us where we were, but they may have been able to hear us with the goddess-damned noises we both made as he fucked me relentlessly.

I was too lost in pure ecstasy to care even the smallest amount.

The pressure built quickly as his knot rubbed me, as the friction hit just right.

He went first, something of a strangled howl escaping his lips. He filled me, still thrusting as though he could get further inside me. That was all I needed to complete.

"Elion," I gasped. "My mate."

We held on to that tree together, gulping air.

He kissed my shoulder. "I liked that."

I moaned my agreement. "I think we could make plans to do this more often."

"I love you," he whispered, kissing my shoulder again.

Wearing a lazy grin, I adjusted my grip on the tree. "I love you too."

After he unknotted, he released me. "Thank you." His smile was so wide and tired he may as well have been drunk.

I picked up my torn underwear, dangling it in front of him. "Would you like these? Freshly scented just for you…"

He snatched them out of my hand. "Yes."

I almost giggled at the fact he didn't have pockets to tuck them into. My dress hung off me, with one of the straps having been broken in our tumble, but he didn't have a single stitch of clothing on.

Teasing him, I stroked his slick cock, then licked his cum off my finger. "What do you think? Share a bath with me? Then share a bed with me?" I'd planned to spend the whole night with just him this time.

Elion pressed his forehead to mine. "Why do you always ask me questions I would never answer no to?"

I giggled this time. "Come on. Let's go find your clothes and our picnic stuff."

43

An Unexpected Partnership

Three weeks had passed since my Coterie had come together. Nothing all that much had changed in the last week. Findlech and I had actually started to chat a little, though. It was our job to discuss elf concerns and equality, after all.

Tyfen still tugged my heart and body in different directions. He fit me so well at times, but was still cold and disinterested. I continued to make him tell me something about himself before bedding me each time. Once, I'd asked him to tell me about his tattoos. He'd refused, instead glamouring them away. Then he'd started volunteering stupid things about himself like 'I think it's usually wrong to kill people.'

How enlightening…

I'd asked if he spoke Elvish, hoping he might be able to translate that ancient writing from the vision I'd had over two weeks prior. He'd rudely reminded me that fae and elves had separated over a millennium ago, and that their tongues now had significant differences. He was not fluent in Elvish, nor was he fluent in ancient Fae. He'd commented that his brothers and sisters were more scholarly than he, and I'd made a harsh comment on his brain capacity. He'd fucked me pretty hard after that, and I'd enjoyed his insults just as much as his praise as he drove into me.

No one knew I'd started imagining him inside me instead of Findlech when Findlech made his daily contributions…

I wasn't *absolutely* certain I was pregnant, but it was more than likely I was. Hadwin had informed me, with a hungry smirk no less, that he would gladly help me with anything I wanted if and when I had cycles in the future. He wasn't shy of anything that involved blood.

While I appreciated the offer, it wasn't likely he'd get that chance anytime soon. At my three-week appointment, the midwife's reading was still uncertain. I, however, had an inkling I was pregnant. Lack of a cycle in my first month wasn't proof—the change in hormones given the two mating bonds alone could throw that off.

But it was something I felt in my heart, a freshness and glow. I kept it to myself for now. At the one-month mark, the midwife should be able to confirm. So, for now, it was business as usual with the demands and pleasures of my Coterie.

One day, I was preparing for an evening stroll in the gardens with Hadwin when I realized my favorite hair clip was missing. I searched high and low in my chambers, unable to find it. Then I remembered taking it off in Gald's bedroom earlier in the afternoon.

He wasn't to be found in the common room. The men had started venturing out more, so he was probably in the library or somewhere else. I trusted he wouldn't mind me ducking into his room to take it back.

I quietly walked into his entryway. The familiar squeak of his bed made me stop—I'd told him to speak to the servants about having that fixed.

Panted breaths came from the bedroom, and the smart part of my brain told me I ought to leave. Then again … by law, the Coterie was a closed unit until I'd given birth to my firstborn. Who the hell was squeaking that bed?

I peered around the corner and glanced in. My jaw dropped immediately. Gald was here, all right. His partner, however, was unexpected.

Neither of them had a stitch of clothing on them, and both seemed to be enjoying themselves *immensely*.

Findlech was on all fours on the bed, his long hair dangling over his shoulders, Gald fucking him from behind.

My eyes were wide and unblinking. Perhaps it was the fact I had never once seen Findlech naked like this, and never could have imagined his face so relaxed, so lost in pleasure. Or perhaps it was simply because these two were such an odd pair.

Gald thrust greedily, and Findlech moaned.

"Harder," Findlech breathed.

I should have left immediately, but I was still too stunned.

Gald adjusted his grip on Findlech, plunging himself in. The moment I moved a muscle to back away, Gald looked in my direction.

Shock overtook his expression, and my heart rate doubled.

"Sonta!"

In the blink of an eye, Findlech looked up, horror covering his face. I slapped a hand over my eyes. "I…"

I turned and left without an apology or explanation.

Hadwin had just left his room when I got to the corridor. "Hello, darling."

In my retreat to my chambers, I simply put up a hand. "I'll be late. I'll let you know when I'm ready."

He tried to make sure I was okay as I ran through the common room, and I yelled a quick 'yes' before opening my door and slamming it shut.

I dove onto my bed, my brain mush. What had I just walked into? And how were the chips going to fall with me being caught spying on them?

I might choose to stay in my chambers the rest of the night. Or for the rest of my natural life…

After a few minutes, I got up and sat on my daybed, biting my nails. The knock on my door from the common room was a playful one—one Gald usually used.

I didn't know what to say, but I could at least apologize. My stomach in knots, I opened the door.

Now dressed, Gald stood looking down. "Can we talk?"

"Of course." I let him in, stiffly walking back to my daybed.

He took a seat next to me. "So…"

"I swear, I didn't mean to invade your privacy," I blurted. "I realized I left my hair clip, so I went to grab it…"

His beautiful blue eyes met mine. "Understandable. And we should have locked the door."

I sighed. "No, your room is your sanctuary. I shouldn't have gone in without permission."

He surveyed me silently, his eyes narrow. "You're not upset?"

My mouth opened, but words initially failed me. "I'm not sure. I'm certainly surprised…"

Gald rubbed his thigh. "I'm a bit unsure of what to say, too."

"Do you like women, Gald?"

He scoffed. "Seriously? How many times do I have to say I like you? It's a little harder for a man to fake pleasure, and I never have with you."

That made me feel better; it hadn't all been a lie. "But you obviously like men, too…"

"I've traveled a lot, and along the way, I've enjoyed shes, hes, and theys from every territory." He wrinkled his nose. "Merfolk excluded for obvious reasons, though watching Haan take you has given me the hankering to try it out." He flashed a crooked grin.

"I think that's great. And I'm really not all that surprised. Not with how adventurous you are with me, or with your invitation to Elion that one time… But Findlech?" I raised an eyebrow.

Gald leaned back, crossing his legs. "What about him?"

"He seemed to enjoy what you were doing…"

Gald blushed.

"So, he likes men… Does he like women too?"

Hesitating, Gald paused. "He does not."

I blew out a breath. "So the sex is bland, and he doesn't really like me, because he's never been attracted to me."

Gald winced. "I won't comment on the sex, because we obviously have different experiences and opinions on that, but it's not just that… No, he doesn't exactly look forward to fulfilling that part of his duties with you, but let's not pretend you're not just very different people. And you two had a rough start."

I folded my arms. "And he's arrogant."

Not picking sides, Gald gave me a look. "Surely, the Blessed Vessel, arguably the most worshiped mortal alive, is not that wounded because she's not one man's cup of tea."

I bit my cheeks at the absurdity. Yes, I'd been offended. Why did I even care? "You promise you still like me? I'd be hurt to learn you were faking it all along."

He leaned in and kissed my cheek. "I promise. And frankly, I'm flattered. Imagine such an important woman being hurt because a lowly mage, who, as she has reminded me, *isn't even a grand master in his order…*" He cleared his throat, and I couldn't help but smile. "Well, it's nice to know I'm cared about."

I looked at my hands. "Why didn't you tell me you liked each other? Finding out this way *is* pretty cruddy…"

"I'm sorry," he whispered. "We wouldn't have dared to start something if you hadn't announced over dinner that one time that you were okay with mixing within the Coterie. Still, I'm pretty sure you meant that about your men bedding each other in group activities involving you, not in private."

He bit his lip. "Findlech is … a private person. I don't know how comfortable he'd be with me sharing much beyond that."

I nodded, trying to sort through my feelings.

"He would like to speak to you, though, if you're okay with it."

Gulping, I nodded again. How could I ever look Findlech in the eye again after this? This wouldn't be a pleasant talk.

"Is there anything else you want to know from me?" Gald offered.

I considered. My mind retraced the last three weeks. Gald had enjoyed watching other men taking me—it wasn't just voyeurism. He and Findlech *constantly* chatted politics, and who knew how much more they did in private when I was out in meetings or with the others? And Gald's teasing—it was flirting, not just fun to unnerve Findlech.

"I think half my shock, honestly…" I pursed my lips. "It's finding out Findlech is a bottom."

Gald laughed. "Goddess damn you, Sonta." He shook his head. "You really don't know the man. And we *do* take turns…"

I didn't need that image of Findlech in my mind. "Right…"

Gald's smile melted into a calm expression again. "We'd like your permission to continue seeing each other. We would obviously have to stop if you wished it."

I selfishly wanted Gald to myself. Once my pregnancy was officially confirmed, Findlech and I would stop having sex anyway. Still, Gald deserved to be happy, and Findlech had never offended me so badly that I could imagine blocking his happiness either.

"You really like him?" I asked. "How long has this been going on between you two?"

"I do like him," he answered calmly. "And I've told you I'm good at reading people, just like I was right about Lilah, so I had a feeling about Findlech pretty early on. But the intimacy and all that is really new…"

I nodded. "I'm sure I won't mind. I think I'm just still in shock."

"Understandable. We didn't come here to find male companionship. We came for duty and for you, and neither of us would neglect our duties or you." He took my hand. "Why don't you spend a few minutes with him?"

I agreed, and Gald squeezed my hand. Not wanting to have others see Findlech enter my room right after Gald had, he asked me to meet him elsewhere. Gald let Hadwin know I'd be a while longer, relaying my apologies. I went to my library and waited for Findlech to arrive.

I was all nerves as I sat at a table facing the door. Findlech arrived soon after, closing and locking the door behind him. If only they'd locked Gald's door earlier, we wouldn't be having this awkward moment. Then again, how long would they have kept their relationship from me if I hadn't walked in?

Findlech approached. I couldn't meet his eyes.

"Your Holiness." He sat across from me at the table.

I shyly glanced up. He wore clothes, but all I could see was his flesh and cock, his long hair swaying with the force of Gald's thrusts. I blinked. "Are we going back to titles, Your Lordship?"

He gave me a polite smile. "I suppose not."

I looked at my hands as I fiddled with a ring. "I'm not sure if Gald told you why I was in there. Either way, I'm sorry for invading your privacy."

"I appreciate that." His voice was low and formal, though softer than usual.

I didn't know what to ask Findlech since Gald had said he was so private. He was so duty-bound, I didn't doubt he'd come here sincerely for his people. Intentionally entering a Coterie just to find a male partner wouldn't have been the wisest strategy.

Still, if we were going to get through this, I needed to understand Findlech better. "You're okay with being here? Are you upset your people chose you to come bed a woman?"

He shrugged. "I'm perfectly fine with it. And my people don't know my preference. I'd like to keep it that way."

I blinked again. "Oh." Sexuality was treated differently in each race, and elves were the most secretive, so I genuinely didn't know what their norms were.

"I…" He tapped the table. "My attraction to men is a fairly recent discovery for me. I've only had one male lover before Gald, and that was only for twenty years. Practically no one knows."

Only for twenty years? I was only twenty-five!

Findlech continued. "I'm just not ready to share that knowledge. I hope you don't find it disingenuous, and I sincerely apologize we kept this from you."

I picked at my nails. What did I want? It wasn't like I wanted Findlech to love me—I'd given up on that long ago. "I guess I'm just wrapping my head around possibly having a child with a gay man… I have nothing against you being gay. I just … imagined I'd be a bit closer to the father, given the dedication it will take to raise a good ruler." I'd envisioned myself continuing to share a bed with the father…

He nodded. "This is a challenge I signed up for but has already been much different than I'd anticipated. I'm not used to being around mortals. And I know we haven't seen eye to eye, but I think we could work on that, Sonta. And whether or not the child is mine, I will only ever treat you with the respect you deserve as its mother. I wouldn't let my feelings for Gald get in the way."

"Thank you for that." It warmed my heart a bit for him to admit his feelings for Gald out loud.

"Of course," he said. "I respect all my children's mothers. You'd be no exception."

My jaw dropped. "You have other children?"

"Yes. Several, with several women."

I was flabbergasted. "And you thought coming here and being bound to me for the next twenty years would be the best idea? How often do you plan to leave my side to take care of your other children?"

He gave me his signature 'you're a stupid young girl' look. "My youngest is eighty-seven. I trust all my children are capable of taking care of themselves at this point."

Immortals… Findlech was over eight hundred years old. How had I forgotten that?

My face warmed with embarrassment. "Right."

"Your child won't live as long as my full elf children, but I'll be dedicated to it each and every day."

It was impossible for me to fathom how someone as old as him perceived time and relationships. In the grand scheme of things, Findlech's dedication to me and my Coterie and even my child—his future ruler—would all be over in the blink of an eye.

"Thank you."

"Thank you for the honor."

I looked him in the eye; I so rarely did that. His dark brown eyes held wisdom and perhaps a kindness I hadn't allowed myself to see. Some of that was my new perception of him as a man who had already fathered several children.

"Do … we have your permission to explore a relationship?" Findlech asked.

I smiled gently. "Don't break his heart, because I share it." I already loved Gald in my own way. We were friends and lovers in a more jovial, less deep way than I was with Hadwin or Elion, but he still had a place in my heart.

Findlech looked down. "I'll do my best."

We sat there a moment, silence filling the space between us. What more needed to be said? He'd already been more open about himself and his sexuality than I'd expected him to be.

"I think I'm already pregnant, but I can't be sure until my midwife officially confirms it in a few days. I don't expect you to bed me when it's not your preference, but I can respect you've chosen to do so for your people. I … will still allow you to do so if it's your wish."

Findlech furrowed his brow, taking a long moment to consider. "I *should* continue to for the sake of duty until it's confirmed, but given the circumstances, I think I'll pass."

Pressing my lips together, I nodded. I'd honestly expected him to take the opportunity in the name of duty, but I wasn't disappointed. He and I had never done it for each other, and I would have been happy on a personal level to never have given him another go with me after the bedding chamber in the first place. His denial did make me feel guilty, though. For a man so focused on duty, it wasn't a small thing for him to turn down the offer. For a man as proud as him, having me catch him naked in his secret had to make him feel vulnerable.

"Your secret's safe with me. I generally prefer men, but I do enjoy sharing my bed with women as well." I smiled again. "And no matter what, I'd very much like to be your friend, Findlech."

He would never be the toothy-smile sort, but his smile *was* the most genuine I'd seen from him. "I would like that as well, Sonta."

44

In the Hate of the Moment

There were two things about Tyfen that continued to be true. One: He was an ass. Two: He had a great ass.

In his attempt to be civil to earn my favor in bed, he joined me and the rest of the Coterie on a picnic on the greater palace grounds.

The six of us strolled along a pathway to the picnic site, Haan swimming in a canal to our right.

Gald and Findlech walked in front of Hadwin and me. As usual, they talked politics. It had only been four days since I'd walked in on them. I smiled as I watched them now. Everyone would just think they were doing their usual boring chatter about policies, but I knew there was flirtation hidden in the arguments.

Just as Findlech had requested, no one else knew his preference. He still came into my room for a few minutes daily, though. Instead of him bedding me, we took the opportunity to discuss elven representation in the empire's capital.

"What are you thinking?" Hadwin asked.

"What?" I glanced at him.

"Your beautiful smile. I'm curious what's on your mind."

While I was not at liberty to tell the truth, I could give Hadwin a different truth. "It's a lovely day for a picnic, don't you think?"

He held his own shade umbrella this time. "As a vampire, my feelings are conflicted."

I chuckled and squeezed his free hand.

Lilah met us at the picnic spot, eager for a chance to see me and get to know my men better. Unsurprisingly, Tyfen was barely tolerable. His annoyance with Lilah was apparent when she and I laughed too much. He also snapped at Findlech to leave him alone when Findlech asked him how he was doing.

I shot him a glare to tell him to mind his manners. He rolled his eyes and went on a stroll alone.

After an otherwise great picnic, I dropped Lilah off at her room, then met the men in the common room.

Everyone was jovial, save Tyfen in the corner. He was the last Coterie member I needed to bed today.

I approached him. "I'd like to talk."

"Then talk."

"In private."

He huffed, standing. I pointed to the door leading to the main hallway.

As soon as I closed the door behind us, I laid into him. "What the hell is wrong with you!? Why can't you *ever* get along with others?"

"I get along with who I want to!"

"Which is no one. I'm tired of your shit. If you roll your eyes one more time at Lilah or Findlech…" What was I going to threaten aside from withholding sex? I was now absolutely positive I'd already conceived, and my midwife would confirm it in a couple of days.

Tyfen's voice was low and threatening. "Maybe they deserve it. Maybe *you* deserve it."

"Why? What have any of us ever done to you? We didn't force you to join my Coterie!"

"But I'm here, and I'm doing my *fucking* duty, Sonta. What do I have against your little friend? I find it interesting you haven't told us she's your lover."

My heart skipped a beat. "What?"

"Don't deny it," he muttered through clenched teeth. "Fae have strong senses, and her scent was all over you when I took my turn in that bedding chamber."

I stood there, flabbergasted. I hadn't fully bathed after Lilah and I had made love before the Great Ritual started, but that shouldn't matter…

He didn't like that Lilah and I were a couple? My heart froze as I connected the dots. Findlech… Tyfen also didn't like him, and had made it clear on more than one occasion.

"You hate Lilah, Findlech, and me because we're gay?!" A prick I could stand, but this…

Tyfen bunched his eyebrows. "What? I don't have a problem with gays, you moron! But it's rather insulting for you to show up with another lover's scent on you at the Great Ritual. You bathed after me, but I didn't get that same courtesy?"

This time I rolled my eyes. "I'm so sorry your giant ego couldn't take the hit."

He jabbed a finger at me. "You criticize me constantly, acting high and mighty, but maybe you should look in the mirror. I'm doing my duty. Are you doing yours? Or are you busy fucking her, *against the law*, when we're not looking?"

The accusation stung. "I haven't been with her in that way since the afternoon of the Great Ritual. Don't you dare accuse me of breaking the law. And do you want a round of applause for doing a better job than me in the Great Ritual? Because *I'm* trying to get along with everyone, and all you seem to be capable of is inserting your cock where it needs to go on occasion."

He took a step toward me, looking down at me. "Don't pretend you don't like it." It sounded more like a threat than anything.

That familiar feeling flared up in me like it always did when we bickered. I was either going to punch his nose or reach for his pants.

I stepped back against the wall. "What about Findlech, then?"

Tyfen's eyes darkened. "I'm certain he knows why I dislike him. It's a personal matter that doesn't concern you or this Coterie. I don't know what kind of lies he's making up for you to think otherwise, but you're absolutely wrong on that account."

So … it was all just Tyfen judging me for not taking my oath more seriously for the Great Ritual, and some stupid personal feud with Findlech?

"Well, you're still a complete jerk. You constantly shoot me down when I'm trying to get to know you."

He towered over me. "Trying to get to know me? More like manipulating me to get information you want."

"Do you even know how relationships work? Friendships?"

Tyfen shook his head, a vein on his neck bulging. "I'm not here to make friends. I'm here to *fuck* you."

We stared at each other a moment, his face red, his stare intense. My breathing was heavy, my heart racing. My core heated, my body aching for him.

I shouldn't want him so badly right now, but I did. I did the math. Aside from Haan, Tyfen had the worst chance of being my father's child. That meant he was free to leave me once the paternity reading was conclusive. He'd likely stop bedding me long before that. In two days' time, my pregnancy would be confirmed, and I'd lose access to him. Just like Findlech and Haan, there would be no more sex with Tyfen.

The self-respecting woman, Hoku's own mortal daughter, did not agree with what my heart and the rest of my body craved.

I didn't care.

I lifted my chin. "Then fuck me."

Tyfen's breathing sped up, and he stole a glance at my chest. His hands drifted to his pants.

He was going to take me against this wall, and I was going to love it.

His pants and shorts dropped, and he picked me up like I weighed no more than a feather, pinning me against the wall and spreading my legs. He was already large, and I was already wet.

"I can't stand you," he uttered. Pinning my arms above me, he plunged into me.

I gasped, wrapping my legs around him more tightly as I took him in, as I tried to catch my breath. "I can't stand you either."

Those brilliant green eyes bored into me as he pulled out and slammed into me.

"Shit!" I wheezed.

He didn't stop as he withdrew again and plunged. "I can't stand *anything* about you. Not your face or your voice, or *anything.*"

I could barely speak with the way he pinned me against the wall, with how beautifully forceful his thrusts were, but I could say *something* in my defense. "Not anything? Don't you hate how much you love being inside me?"

He paused, locking eyes with me. He remembered saying that when he'd made love to me drunk...

"Shut the hell up." He thrust again.

"Make me, Tyfen," I whispered.

Leaning in, he claimed my mouth, thrusting at the hip, assaulting my lips and tongue with his own.

Goddess damn me... I lost myself completely in it.

He'd never kissed me on the mouth. Like with sex, he was exceptionally good at it.

When we both came, our moans were muffled by our passionate kissing. I kept kissing him, unable to stop myself. I wanted every part of him.

Tyfen was the first to pull away, and he stared into my eyes. Before I knew it, he'd averted his gaze, dropped my hands and set me on the floor. I barely maintained my balance by leaning against the wall, his cum dripping down my leg.

He put himself in his pants and left for the common room without a single word.

I stood there a moment, dazed. I'd never had hate sex before, and I couldn't say I was disappointed. Except for his abrupt departure, because I could still feel his lips on mine…

Calming my racing heart, I straightened and made my way back to my chambers through my private door. After cleaning myself up, I sat on the daybed.

Words… Thoughts… The two of us intertwined…

A few minutes ticked by, and Gald knocked playfully from the common room. I got up and opened the door.

His face was somewhat somber. "Hey, Sonta. Can we chat?"

"Of course, come in."

We sat together.

"What's wrong?"

He drew a deep breath. "Are you okay?"

I straightened my dress, suddenly shy. "Yes…"

"I, uh, snuck a peek in the hallway when you and Tyfen were…"

My face warmed.

"I normally wouldn't, but with the yelling and, you know, picture frames on walls getting knocked about."

Gulping, I looked away. "Wow. That's not embarrassing at all…"

Gald rubbed the knee of his trousers. "It's not like we don't all know you two don't get along, or that you're having sex with us all." He paused. "The thing is…" He met my gaze, pursing his lips. "I guess we learned today that your personal chambers are a lot more soundproof than the common room wall to the hallway."

"I'm sure it didn't help we were yelling."

"No. It didn't. And now the entire Coterie knows about you and Lilah, and about Findlech's preferences."

My eyes widened. "Shit!" It wasn't a huge deal about Lilah and me, but Findlech… "Shit, shit, shit!"

Gald didn't console me, nor did I expect him to. "Yeah, Sonta."

I had sworn to keep Findlech's secret, and then blurted it in an argument. "I didn't mean to. I didn't realize…"

He rubbed his forehead. "I can't imagine why you would think Tyfen would have known Findlech prefers men... Me, perhaps, but Findlech's not exactly openly flirtatious..."

I blinked. Why *had* I thought that? Tyfen had been rude to him on numerous occasions, starting with the very first night when we'd all shared a bed. And there was that time he'd snapped about not wanting to be compared to Findlech's 'kind'... And there had been other instances, but... "I guess, just because he was being an ass about both Lilah and Findlech today, so I..." Tears pricked at my eyes. "Is Findlech okay?"

"I'm sure he will be..." Gald answered softly. "I don't know what quarrel there is between Findlech and Tyfen, but it has nothing to do with sexuality."

I stood. "I need to go apologize to Findlech."

Gald took my hand. "No, you don't. At least not yet. Give him some space and time."

Easing myself back down, I wiped away a tear. "I *really* didn't mean to say that... I'm usually great with secrets."

"I know. What's done is done, but you're going to have to clean up this mess, Sonta."

I nodded, sniffling. "It won't be a big deal with Lilah, but what can I do about Findlech?"

"Things got awkward, and everyone went to their rooms. It would be a good start to ask them to keep that information to themselves for the time being. Give Findlech the night, and we'll sort more out then..."

"Absolutely. Right away."

Gald stood, forcing a smile. "It'll be fine. I'll be spending the night with Findlech, and we'll talk."

I frowned. "Thank you."

After giving me a reassuring squeeze on the shoulder, he left me alone in my room.

It took me a few minutes to gather myself. How could I have done that to Findlech? How had I managed to mess something else up?

I couldn't wallow for too long; I needed to do some damage control.

My heart heavy, I strode through the empty common room and entered the Coterie corridor. I stared at Tyfen's door for far too long.

Eventually, I found the courage to knock. Tyfen opened the door in his shorts, holding a wine bottle.

Lovely... It was admittedly hard to look him in the eye after what we'd just done, and hurtful to find him already drinking away the memory of it.

"Yes?" He narrowed his eyes.

"I … need to ask a favor."

He scanned me. "I'm not in the mood for favors, Your Holiness."

I sighed. "I shouldn't have said some of the things I did in our argument."

He leaned against the doorway, curious.

"What we discussed about Lilah and Findlech. Please don't speak of it. Especially about Findlech."

Tyfen stared at me, then took a drink from his bottle. "Honestly, I don't give a shit what people do with their bodies as long as they're not hurting others. And I have better things to do than gossip about the bedroom habits of others."

I glanced at the wine bottle. "Better things to do like drinking?"

He gave me a wry smile.

I held out my hand for the bottle. "Let me have it."

"Mmm… But the Blessed Vessel can't drink during the Great Ritual. Especially not something that hasn't been handed to her by an approved chef or servant…" He raised the bottle. "I'm not selfish. I'm drinking for the both of us." He took another swig.

My heart ached at seeing him this way. While I'd loved the way he'd been raw and vulnerable when he'd made love to me drunk, I couldn't bear the sadness that blurred behind the alcohol.

I kept my hand outstretched. "Please."

He pressed his lips together. "Don't pretend you care about me."

I swallowed, and I hated that I did care about him. I never would have imagined I'd be giving him a chance after the constant insults, but I liked him despite myself. I couldn't say when someone was past hope. He certainly wasn't one of the murky-water merpeople.

We stared at each other without a word. There was kindness and goodness *somewhere* behind those stunning green eyes—I knew it as well as I knew my own name.

Tyfen averted his gaze, handing me the bottle. My heart fluttered as his fingers brushed mine in the exchange.

"Thank you," I said, pulling it to me.

"Whatever." His voice was soft and resigned.

"And thank you for not discussing Lilah or Findlech further."

He simply shrugged.

"Good night."

"Good night, Sonta." He closed his door.

I liked my name on his lips; I just wished he'd use it in a different way. Sighing, I swirled the bottle—it was about half-empty. Were I not likely pregnant already, I may have considered taking a healthy swig from it to numb myself for the task I needed to finish carrying out.

Since I wouldn't risk it, I carried on with this unpleasant necessity. I skipped a couple of doors, knocking on Hadwin's. He opened it with a warm smile. "Darling."

I handed him the bottle. "Will you please dispose of this?"

He gave me a questioning glance as he took it from me. "I trust you didn't…"

"Of course not." I tried not to be humiliated about everyone having heard Tyfen and me fucking against the wall. Hadwin in particular would have disliked it. "And I'm sorry about what you had to hear earlier."

He frowned. "I just want to know you're okay. That's all."

I hugged him. "Yes. I just hate myself for being stupid." With my words and with my heart.

Leaning, he set the wine bottle down, then wrapped both arms around me, threading a hand through my hair. "You're young, not stupid."

I could be both.

"Did you want to share a bed tonight?" Hadwin asked.

Despite what he'd assumed, I hadn't come for comfort or companionship. I didn't deserve either.

"No." I pulled back, wringing my hands. "I came to ask a favor."

"Anything, darling."

I had to smile, though it faded. "I didn't realize I could be overheard from the hallway, and I said some things I shouldn't have. I'm not ready for the realm to know about my relationship with Lilah, and I had no right to talk about Findlech's preferences. Can you please keep that information to yourself?"

"Of course."

"Thank you."

His expression soft and loving, he took my hand. "So, it's true your friend is also your lover?"

"Yes, though we're obviously practicing abstinence with each other during the Great Ritual." I searched his hazel eyes, a smidge nervous. He wanted me for himself, and Lilah meant one more lover to share me with.

"She's a lovely young woman." His smile was genuine. He'd gotten to know her well enough during our pool day and picnic. "I'm sure she misses you, as I would." He tucked a strand of hair behind my ear, then trailed his finger down the strand, along my breast, to rest against my stomach.

Hadwin exhaled. "I'm assuming you're with child…"

I slid a hand to cover his. "I'm certain I am."

He nodded. "Good. I'm sure it will be nice to not have to deal with so many demands, especially with … Tyfen." He looked down. "I've never liked the way he treats you."

I frowned. I should also be rejoicing that I could reject Tyfen's requests to bed me without an iota of guilt soon. Why wasn't I rejoicing?

"Thank you for your support," was all I could say to that.

I gave him another hug and kiss and wished him good night.

I went room by room, asking the others to not mention Lilah or Findlech's sexuality to others.

Elion agreed, but was worked up about Tyfen. He'd been ready to rip him apart for yelling at me and being so rough with me in the hallway. I calmed him, eventually leaving him with a kiss.

Haan easily agreed to not speak of it. He confessed he'd already suspected Findlech and Gald of liking each other. He'd swum into the common room tank once when the two had sat next to each other alone, their politics laced with land-walker flirtation as he'd observed.

It gutted me to have to skip those two last doors again. I didn't even know which of their rooms Findlech and Gald had chosen to stay the night in. I desperately wanted to apologize to Findlech, but honored Gald's wishes to let them sort things out first.

I didn't want to go to bed alone, or at all right now. I'd never be able to fall asleep. At bare minimum, I needed to talk to Lilah.

45

CLEARING THE AIR

ragging my feet as I went, I headed for Lilah's door. I knocked, and she quickly answered. "Hey, love!"

I frowned, and she mirrored my frown. "What's wrong?"

"I suck."

She scooped me up into a hug, pulling me into her room. "No you don't. And when you do, I happen to *like* it."

Had I been in a better mood, I would have laughed.

"What's wrong, Sonta?" She held me at arm's length, searching my face.

"I screwed up."

Closing the door, she nodded to her sitting area. We claimed the sofa, and she held my hand. She was already in a short nightie, ready for bed.

"The Coterie knows about you and me."

She gently rubbed my hand. "I didn't know that would be such a personal tragedy…"

I cocked my head. "Of course it's not. It's complicated…" I squeezed her hand. "I'm not ashamed of you. I'd just hoped to wait until after one more activity together so they'd get to know you better."

Lilah nodded. "Are they upset? They don't like me?" There was a tinge of hurt in her voice. She normally didn't care what people thought of her, but it reminded me how she'd been afraid my Coterie would force her out of the palace.

"They love you!" I gave her a smile. "After finding out, Hadwin even called you *charming*." I shrugged. "He clearly has questionable taste, but I can't help that…"

She laughed. "You know you're insulting yourself right now, right?"

I chuckled. "True."

She asked me how they'd come to find out if I hadn't been ready. I shared with her my idiocy and the unfortunate revelation thanks to the thin common room wall. She winced. I explained how Tyfen had been offended I'd shown up to the bedding chamber with her scent on me. She winced again. As humans, we often forgot some of the other races had different sensitivities with senses.

"And then of course he accused me of breaking the law by being with you."

She rubbed my thigh. "Which is exactly why you were keeping it under wraps in the first place…"

I nodded, my shoulders slumping.

"Honestly…" Her dark brown eyes focused on mine. "I'm happy. I've never liked having to hide who I am. And now none of your men will think I'm flirting with them just because I'm being friendly. Men can be stupid that way sometimes."

Lilah adjusted her seat, crossing her legs. "And they have to trust you… Schamoi will be here to visit any day, and are you not allowed to have a single moment in private? Just because you physically *can* fuck someone doesn't mean you will." She rolled her eyes. "And while I understand the required devotion and building political allies and relationships bit, it's a little ridiculous to prohibit you from spending your time with anyone you love. It's not like sharing a bed with *me* will somehow produce an illegitimate ruler."

I pursed my lips. As much as I agreed with her, I would not blaspheme as she did. Hoku was not the softest, kindest goddess, but she also wasn't the cruelest. She wouldn't strike anyone down for merely questioning her edicts, but I did not wish to walk that path when I'd accepted my role as her daughter.

"Sorry," Lilah said. "I just mean to say those men are idiots if they feel threatened by me or anyone else."

"True." Lilah was okay with the men knowing, and we got to be our true selves. I still felt awful.

"What else?" she asked, tucking a hair behind my ear.

"I can't really talk about it, but I said something else that was insanely stupid. And I can't take it back." Tears pricked at my eyes again. Lilah had always freely been herself, but it had taken a while for me to recognize I had an attraction to women. And then to accept it. I'd have hated if someone had outed me before

I'd been secure in that. And I still wasn't in some ways. Asking my Coterie to believe in my devotion to my calling was one thing. Asking the realm to accept my relationship with Lilah would be a bigger issue we both understood.

I'd been born to bear a ruler. My focus should be with my Coterie and my child. In my heart, I knew Hoku would not deny me happiness in the long run. She'd given me many gifts—sexual pleasure, strength, fast healing, a place of power, and even mild pregnancies compared to other humans. But some people thought my entire existence should center solely on the one task I'd been created for.

"We all make mistakes, Sonta," Lilah said softly.

She shifted closer, holding me in her arms. I nestled into her embrace. She was warmth and safety itself.

She kissed my head. "You'll be fine."

I soaked up her kindness, trying to believe that. If I could wish away these troubled feelings, I would. I secretly prayed to Hoku for a vision of the future to ensure things would work out.

It was a prayer she would not answer. There was only one exception to the visions Hoku gave her daughters, and I could not force her hand.

Lilah and I cuddled for a while, nothing more.

"I should probably go back to my room for the night," I whispered as it grew late.

"Probably," she whispered back. "Would you like company?"

I frowned. I would take her cuddles in bed in a heartbeat. "No. Not until everything has calmed down."

"Okay."

She walked me to her door, offering one last hug and a kiss. "You have my vote of confidence."

"Thank you. Love you."

"Love you too, Sonta."

On my way back to my chambers, I ran across a servant doing her nighttime duties.

I stopped her. "Can I ask a favor?"

She bowed. "Of course, Your Holiness."

"I'd like to restrict alcohol from being delivered to Prince Tyfen's room."

She blinked. "Okay…"

"I understand it's an abnormal request, but please see to it the others who service his room are aware of the restriction. If he complains, you can let him know to see me."

"Yes, Your Holiness. I did just deliver a bottle to his room a few minutes ago, though…"

I gritted my teeth. "Thank you for letting me know."

I should just let him drink himself into a stupor again, but I was annoyed he'd already replaced the bottle I'd confiscated.

After striding to his room, I knocked on the door. He answered, again in his shorts, holding his fresh bottle.

"Sonta." He slurred a bit, wine on his breath.

I grabbed the bottle, yanking it to me.

He kept his hand on it. "That's mine. You don't need it."

"You don't either. Go to bed."

He raked his gaze over me like he'd done the first time I'd seen him drunk. "What do I get if I give it to you?"

"I guess we'll find out when you do." I wore a disingenuous smile.

It took him a moment, but he surrendered it, his hand sliding from the bottle to my hip.

My heart sped up. I knew that look and touch, and as much as I wanted him in the moment, I didn't deserve the pleasure or even the pain of it.

"Thank you." I stepped back and turned.

"I get nothing?"

"You get a good night's sleep."

"Bitch," he mumbled.

I threw him a vulgar gesture as I walked away. "Sweet dreams, Tyfen."

After returning to my rooms, I drained the bottle and trashed it, then readied for bed.

It was so cold and lonely, but I eventually found sleep.

I woke to a knock on my door early in the morning, coming from the common room.

Stumbling out of bed, I straightened my nightie. My mouth went dry as I opened the door. "Findlech…"

His face was somber. "May I come in?"

"Of course." I opened the door wider, giving him space.

He was fully dressed, as proper as ever.

I shut the door. "I'm *so* sorry, Findlech."

"As you ought to be."

"I didn't mean to share your secret. I swear it."

His face was still terse. "I'm sure you didn't. But I would expect more of the Blessed Vessel, of the woman who would shape this realm through her womb and influence."

Chewing on my lip, I nodded.

"I suppose I shouldn't expect so much of one so young, but I hadn't planned to be dragged through the mud in a scandal in a single month after centuries of respect from my people."

My stomach twisted. "Is that what will happen with your people if they find out you like men?"

He pinched the bridge of his nose, then gestured to the daybed. "Shall we sit?"

I nodded, and we took a seat.

"I don't really know how your people view sexuality, Findlech." I wasn't sure if I should go back to calling him by his title, or if that would just make things worse. "But even if they accepted you as you are, I still broke a promise, and I'm sorry."

His posture was rigid. "We elves pride ourselves on the wisdom of our years. Mortals such as humans are constantly changing, and traditions shift with each generation. It's frivolous. Were it not for Hoku and the empire's rule, we would happily keep to ourselves and our own ways."

It was always refreshing to be reminded I was so little in his eyes…

He continued. "As for our views on sexuality… It's like how we handle the mating bonds in our culture. We are the masters of ourselves."

Vampire mates were always made by choice. While shifters often had a biological pull to a particular person, their mating bonds were also by choice. The fae and their cousins, the elves, had fated mates. Whereas the fae accepted the unions fate gave them, the elves actively denied those bonds. Part of their pride was in making wise pairings, not in giving in to the demands of the flesh and fates. I'd understood that, and that was part of why I'd never questioned if Findlech would be my mate or if he'd be sad to give up one to be in my Coterie.

Findlech cleared his throat. "Were I your age or even a hundred, my people would not judge me harshly for loving a man. That's not the issue. I may not be the high lord, but I *am* a lord. For a man of more than eight hundred, I would be looked down upon for suddenly changing my romantic interests in the public eye. My people would not easily accept that type of change after centuries of me being with women. To them, I would look soft and frivolous. I may be accused of senility because I should have understood that part of myself long ago."

"People's interests do change, though. Do elves not pick up a new hobby after they're a century old?"

He gave me a tiny smile. "A hobby is one thing, something that perhaps may define us but is not so wholly a piece of how we view ourselves and our place in the world. I don't expect you to understand my people's mindset, Sonta, but I ask that you try to respect my wishes. I'm not ready for my people to know. I'm not at a place where I can shake their faith in my leadership, in the stability I offer those under my rule."

I nodded. "I never intended to harm you. And I already spoke to the other Coterie members. They've agreed to keep your secret."

"I hope they do."

A moment of silence punctuated the discussion. I almost assured him I trusted the others, but what did that really mean coming from someone who had just betrayed his trust?

Findlech adjusted a clip holding back his elegant long locks. "Not that all is well, but I suppose there's one good thing to come of this…" His voice was softer, his expression less confident.

I met his gaze, but he looked away.

"I hadn't planned to form any romantic relationships while in your Coterie, and I've never been in a relationship with a mortal… I would have been happy waiting a few decades before sharing any sort of knowledge of a relationship, but I don't think that would have made Gald happy."

Gald had felt so guilty hiding their relationship from me. Findlech was right about him. Gald loved open flirtation, and wasn't one to hide his sexuality.

Still, it was barely a consolation. I was genuinely surprised Findlech wasn't ripping me apart.

"There's one more thing I'd like to add to this," he said. "About the issue with Prince Tyfen… I suppose I can understand where you were coming from with your assumption about his dislike toward me if you thought he disliked you for your attraction to your friend, but I can't imagine he would have known about my change in preferences."

My face warmed with embarrassment. "I know. I don't know why I thought that. I wasn't thinking straight."

"Tyfen's dislike of me is … of a political and personal nature. I can't say much and indeed should not say anything at all on the matter, but I'd like us to be understood on this."

I nodded.

"About a year before you moved into the palace, the fae and elves almost went to war. I trust the emperor and magistrate have informed you of that?"

"Yes. The emperor's men reported increased battle training at the edges of both territories, but things settled…"

"Correct."

Most of the empire was not even aware of this almost-war. The fae and elves had stated it was simply a coincidence of training exercises.

"What happened with that?" I asked. "And what does it have to do with Tyfen and you?"

Findlech quietly sized me up as he planned his words. "The war was not for domination. It was about a grievance between my nation and the fae kingdom. But we know how these things work. The shifters and merfolk would have been affected at minimum, as collateral damage."

He crossed his arms. "As for Tyfen and me… I'd never met him before coming here. I can't imagine he tolerates *any* elves right now…"

I rolled my eyes. "Great. So he's just a racist?"

"I would not be so harsh on the lad," Findlech replied softly. "It's likely about my place in the elven parliament. And while he harbors hatred toward me, I do not return that to him. Despite having no fault in his pain, I would not deny him the right to his feelings."

Now it was just a riddle… "What feelings? What pain and fault and… And what does this have to do with almost going to war?"

Findlech hesitated again. "It's not for me to say. I've already said too much. I'm only telling you any of this to help clear the air. While I consider him young and foolish, I hold no personal grudge against him. I'm sure he was opposed to the war plans, as was I, and I'd like to see him move on in peace."

I stared at Findlech, confused and a bit frustrated at the half answers. It was generous of him, though, to try to help me see Tyfen in a different light, given Tyfen was a jerk to him despite his innocence in whatever 'pain' he held.

Gald's signature knock sounded at the door before I could formulate another question. I rose and answered. He looked handsome, and I had to hold myself back from hugging him.

He closed the door behind him, stealing a glance at Findlech. "How are things going?"

Findlech stood, approaching us. "We've sorted things. The only direction now is forward."

Several minutes later, we emerged from my chambers, and everyone but Tyfen was already in the common room. Elion was hungry for me, but I told him he'd have to wait until after breakfast. We needed to have a sit-down with everyone.

I strode for Tyfen's room and knocked. He didn't answer until I knocked a second time.

He glared at me when I opened the door. "I don't have any more wine for you to steal."

"Coterie meeting in the common room. Now."

He grumbled. "Let me get some pants on."

I returned to the common room and stood in the middle. After a minute he arrived, plopping into a chair.

"Thank you, everyone." My hands were clammy. We hadn't really had a formal meeting since coming together. "By the nature of this group, there are some things that stay within the Coterie, and we need to talk about that today. I said some things yesterday that were … not planned. What we discuss now needs to stay here."

Everyone nodded.

"First of all, I love Lilah. She prefers women. She's my childhood best friend, but we *are* also lovers. I haven't made that public because I don't want people questioning my devotion to Hoku and this empire. I can love her and still fulfill my calling. We're abstaining from sex as required, but that doesn't change my feelings for her. I will still spend time with her. After I've given birth, she'll have an even greater role in my life. I'm not asking for your approval, nor do I need it. I love many people, men and women. If you're not comfortable with that, then that is *your* problem."

More nods.

"But I let something slip last night that I shouldn't have, and I have to apologize to Findlech." I glanced at him, as did everyone else.

He stood and faced everyone. "As Sonta stated last night, I do have a preference for men. I've been honest with her from the start about my role here being purely to represent my people, however I wasn't fully honest until recently about my … sexuality. I'm not looking for a new partner as I have one already, but I would ask that this stays within the Coterie. It's not public knowledge, and I have my reasons."

Elion nodded. "Of course."

"Yep," Tyfen muttered from his chair as he picked at his fingers.

The others agreed to keep his secret.

Findlech sat, and Gald rose, turning toward the group.

"I feel it's not as big of a surprise that I love a wide variety of people. I'm open to adventurous things within the group if Sonta and others want, but I'm not looking for a new partner either. I'm already fucking both of these two."

I bit my cheeks, fighting to hold back laughter as Findlech raised an exasperated hand to his face. Findlech had agreed to allow Gald to share their status, but he obviously hadn't imagined him doing it so unceremoniously.

Gald gave him a playful smirk. I washed my hands of that—Findlech had understood what he was getting into with a wild spirit like Gald, and he probably secretly loved it.

"Well…" I said.

Gald sat again on the sofa next to Findlech, grinning at him. Findlech stared at him with a disapproving look. Their relationship was fresh, but now that I understood more of their dynamic, I could read the foreplay in their exchange. They still didn't hold hands or show physical affection, and I imagined Gald wouldn't tease or flirt with him as openly as he did with me, simply because of Findlech's desire for decorum.

I continued. "I appreciate the chance to put all that out there, and I again welcome anyone to let me know anything of the sort, even if you don't feel comfortable doing so in this group yet." Guilt twisted my heart. I'd keep my promise next time.

I looked over the group. "Does anyone have anything else they want to add before going to breakfast?"

The men glanced around the room. After a moment of silence, Hadwin raised his hand. "Mind if I say something?"

I blinked, fully in shock. Hadn't I pegged him well, with all our conversation and … pegging? "Anyone in the Coterie can be open."

He gave me a toothy smile, his fangs showing as he stood. He walked up to me and slid a hand onto my back. "I think it's great we can all be so open in this setting." Removing his hand, he unbuttoned the cuff on one of his sleeves. "We're all gentlemen capable of keeping secrets, after all."

Hadwin glanced at me, unbuttoning the cuff on his other sleeve. "And a gentlewoman, of course." He focused on the others again, his hands moving to the top button of his shirt. "We're not war generals, right? Just men and a beautiful woman, doing our duties for this honorable empire."

Another button undone. He was stripping in front of everyone? That was a bit much for even Gald to do, but Hadwin…

"I love this newfound sense of community and honesty," Hadwin continued. "It's refreshing that we can be ourselves and not be judged. That we don't have to worry about inconsequential things like a person's individual bedroom preferences, or their past."

He undid his last button, and my heart skipped a beat. He was going to expose his scars.

"We may not fully understand each other's cultures, but we trust that our leaders would not have chosen us solely because we best represent our people, but because we're the best to bring peace and understanding to this realm." He slipped off his shirt and draped it over his shoulder.

Everyone's eyes widened as they stared at his scar. I doubted Haan even understood the implications of vampire scars, but it was still a gruesome thing to behold. Questioning gazes bounced between Hadwin's scar and face, and also to me.

I smiled. Hadwin had just dared them to accept his scars without question. I wrapped my arms around him. "I agree. Having spent a month in the company of all you men, I'm happy with your leaders' picks. You're all doing this empire proud." Tyfen was an obvious exception, but I hoped he'd rise to the occasion eventually.

Hadwin kissed my forehead.

"Unless anyone has something else to add, I think it's time for breakfast," I said.

No one else spoke.

"Lovely," Hadwin said. "Let's go eat."

Tyfen stood and instead returned to his room. I held back my disappointment. The others filed out of the room, but Hadwin stayed to put his shirt back on. "Just because I showed the Coterie doesn't mean I want to scare the servants…"

As soon as he'd finished buttoning it, I undid the top two, kissing his cool, strong chest. "You can't see it with this much exposed."

He grinned. "I suppose not."

I loved those hazel eyes, those lips. "How did that feel?"

"Good. It felt like the right time. Diffuse some of the tension, give them something else fun to quietly speculate on, and get it off my chest."

I held him close, kissing his chest again. "I love this chest. The muscles, the scars, the heart within."

His eyes reddened. "I love you too."

Putting on a sober face, I stepped back. "But I learned something new about you just now."

"What's that?"

"You've been depriving me of a good strip show, and I'm a little offended."

He chuckled, drawing me close again. "Is that what you'd like this afternoon, darling?"

"Mhmm." I kissed him as he palmed my ass. Damned if I didn't want him to be first today.

After a minute, he let me go. "I did want to add one thing to the conversation today. About you and Lilah…"

I pressed my lips together. "Yes?"

"What makes you happy makes me happy. We all know what you two can't share until you've given birth, but if it would make you happy to invite her when you and I share a bed, then I'm fine with that."

I smiled, then narrowed my eyes. "When you say 'when we share a bed'…"

"Well… I'd still rather make love to you in private. I mean for the softer things. Cuddling at night. Intimacy has many levels beyond penetration and orgasms."

"I fucking love you so much, Hadwin." I kissed him without restraint, our tongues wrestling. I wanted him right now, every part of him. "We should go to the dining hall," I panted out. "And I promised Elion he could have me first, but you and I … we're going to have a *great* afternoon."

He grinned again. "I'm already looking forward to it."

Elion stood outside the dining hall when we got there, waiting for us. The three of us entered together. Everyone had taken their usual seats, including Gald across from Findlech.

Elion stood behind his regular seat, glancing at Gald. "Would you like to sit here?"

My heart melted. Why was Elion so cute? He'd always sat next to Findlech. Gald gave him a smile. "I'm fine here, thanks."

It was an incomparably lovely meal.

46

THE MAGE MIDWIFE

The day went so well after our Coterie meeting. Tyfen didn't show up all day, but I let him stew in his room. I was too happy with how things had smoothed over with Gald and Findlech, also with Hadwin and his courage to show his scar.

I was excited for the following day, too. I'd have my next meeting with my mage midwife for my one-month mark, and that was usually when Blessed Vessel pregnancies were confirmed.

My mother hadn't come to visit, but Kernov had given me a letter from her when he'd returned to the palace. Schamoi was coming to visit, though.

Things had gone so well that I took Hadwin up on his offer, inviting Lilah to share my bed along with him. She arrived before him through my private door. I gave her a huge hug and a kiss, welcoming her in.

She straightened her nightie; it was her longest, stretching to midcalf. "Is this okay? I've never shared a bed with a man when sober, and when I'm not sleeping with him… Again, usually because I'm not sober…"

I chuckled. "You're fine. He saw you in less at the pool, and he's sleeping next to me, not you."

"Okay." She bit her lip. "And you're sure your Coterie is fine with this?"

Smiling, I nodded. I'd confirmed with them at dinner for complete transparency.

Hadwin knocked at my other door, and I let him in. He wore shorts and a casual shirt.

"Hello, Lilah."

"Hi, Hadwin. I knew I liked you."

He grinned. "Glad to hear it. I've been learning to share our Sonta."

I wrapped my arms around him, facing him. "Are you going to wear that shirt all night?"

He pursed his lips.

I called to Lilah over my shoulder. "How do you feel about vampires who get scars from wrestling swamp beasts but don't like others to know about said scars?"

"Um…" Her confusion was apparent. "I'd say I know how to keep my mouth closed if they don't want anyone to know about it?"

I gazed into Hadwin's eyes. She could be trusted, and wouldn't judge him. "No pressure," I whispered.

He took a moment to consider, then grabbed his shirt.

I stepped back. "Ooh, another strip show." I winked.

Rolling his eyes, Hadwin removed his shirt.

I turned my back to him, and he slid his arms around my waist. I begged Lilah with my eyes to not make a big deal of it.

She swallowed, then smiled again. "I'm not that familiar with swamp beasts, but I'm glad you made it out alive."

"Me too!" I said.

Hadwin kissed my head. "Me three." He tightened his grip around me, and I angled my head. He rested his fangs on my love bite, and I grinned.

He only kissed me, then released me. "We have an early morning, right?" His hands rested over my womb, and my heart might burst. It killed me that I wouldn't know the father right away, but it would still be so great just to have the pregnancy confirmed.

Lilah claimed her spot on the bed first, climbing under the covers. I slid in next to her, and then Hadwin cuddled up to me after snuffing the last candle.

"So … do we both get to grope her as we sleep? How does this sharing thing work?" Lilah asked in the dark.

I busted out laughing, then stole another kiss.

"I just don't want to accidentally hold Hadwin's hand or something."

He quietly chuckled. "I'm sure we can sort it out, and you'll recognize the difference between our temperatures."

And they did sort it out. While I sometimes slept alone or with just one of the men, I usually still slept with two in my Coterie at a time. Hadwin had long ago learned how to share.

"He's not going to suck my blood during the night, right?" Lilah whispered intentionally loud. "Vamps are so sketchy."

I elbowed her. "Play nice, or he won't invite you back."

She gasped. "You wouldn't dare hurt me like that, would you, Hadwin?"

He hummed. "No, but I *would* intentionally withhold information about skilled lesbians I know who have worked in the Suck and Fuck business…"

"Hadwin!" she exclaimed.

I slapped a hand over both their mouths. "Sleeeeeeep."

Lilah licked my hand, and Hadwin opened his mouth, scraping his fang across my skin.

"You'll both be the death of me."

Hadwin removed my hand, kissing me. "Good night, darling."

I savored another kiss. "Good night, both of you."

In the morning, I was all smiles. Hadwin had a little fun while stretching, complaining about Lilah snoring. I was such a heavy sleeper I could neither confirm nor deny it. She of course denied it.

Lilah left for her room for breakfast and to ready for the day, leaving me with a satisfying hug and kiss. Hadwin pulled me back to bed and made love to me. It gave me less time to dress for my appointment with my midwife, but it was well worth it. Servants happily helped primp me anyway, making it all faster.

I ate in my room as I readied; Hadwin had returned to his own room to dress.

While this pregnancy reading would be more private and informal than the paternity reading, it was still a big deal. I had no doubt I was pregnant. My appetite had grown a bit, as well as my energy, and it was simply something I could sense within myself.

I took an extra moment of meditation to Hoku, thanking her for this opportunity. Despite any of the recent drama, I was safe and cared for, and loved.

Uncharacteristically, I wore full makeup, undergarments, and a long flowing dress made specifically for this event. I again wore the special necklace I'd worn to the celebration after the claimings. It rested on a long chain near my breasts.

I was ecstatic, near bursting when I walked into the common room. All the men had dressed well, and I took a moment to greet each of them personally, even Tyfen. He wasn't rude, but the interaction was short.

Guards led us through the long corridors to a central meeting room. The emperor and magistrate were there, as well as a few advisors—Kernov gave me a bright smile, carrying the warmth and presence of my absent mother. She'd be here in a month's time for the paternity reading.

Not only Schamoi, but three of my five pleasure instructors had come. I wanted to hug them as soon as I saw them, but I kept my distance for now. I so appreciated the visit.

Lilah was there, and so were some of the aides for the men in my Coterie.

I approached the mage midwife at the front of the meeting room, and she bowed. "Your Holiness."

My cheeks were already hurting from all the smiling.

"Let's check again, shall we?" she said, dabbing a special oil on her hands.

I pulled my dress open at a slit designed for this, and she said a quick blessing, sliding her hands onto my still-flat stomach. Her hands were warm as she closed her eyes and focused.

My heart raced. What if I somehow wasn't pregnant despite all the sex? Or if it was too early to tell? What if I'd read my own body wrong?

She smiled, then looked at me. "I can sense the life," she whispered.

I instantly teared up.

Standing tall, she removed her hands from my stomach. "The Blessed Vessel *is* with child."

A collective sigh of joy echoed in the room as I turned around. I wiped away my tears, wanting to hug everyone in sight, but I stayed in place.

Everyone wore smiles. It was a bit hard to tell with the elves, to be fair, but there was a hint there, and Tyfen's smile was barely there.

The emperor and magistrate bowed. "May Hoku's blessings continue with you."

Everyone else in the room followed suit, and I had to simply accept I was a ball of tears.

"Thank you," I whispered. Today would be a big day, a huge day, but it was also a little bittersweet.

I first approached the emperor and magistrate, and we shook hands. They offered me congratulations. Then I went to the men. Hadwin, Elion, and Gald gave me perfectly tight hugs, a twinkle in each of their eyes. My interaction with the others was naturally a bit different. I didn't see myself having sex with the last three anymore, and my heart was conflicted.

So as to not get me too wet, Haan shook my hands from his tank, and I kissed him on the cheek. I mourned the lost opportunity, since he had only gotten the one chance. I wouldn't risk the life within me by having sex with him again now that I was confirmed pregnant, nor would anyone else allow me to.

Findlech offered me congratulations and a handshake. I was so excited that I wanted to hug even him, though I wasn't sure he wanted it, given all the chaos of the last few days.

"Can I hug you?" I shyly asked.

He offered a small smile. "Of course, congratulations."

It was quite possibly the stiffest hug I'd ever had, but sweet of him to give it.

I stood in front of Tyfen, the last person I wanted to talk to at the moment. I … would miss him in bed, but I wouldn't miss his constant reminders that he only fucked me out of duty. If only we had made progress on our relationship over the last month…

I offered my hand to shake, and he stared at it a moment. It was almost like I could feel the emperor's eyes on me, assessing me for the awkwardness with the two men I'd struggled to get along with from the beginning.

Tyfen met my gaze and opened his arms. "A mother deserves a proper hug."

My heart skipped a beat, and I accepted.

His hug was tight, his muscles strong. "Congratulations, Sonta." His tone was oddly soothing.

I savored the unexpected hug. "Thank you."

As I pulled back, his smile was hesitant. It numbed my joy a bit.

I turned and accepted congratulatory handshakes from the aides and advisors in the room, a massive hug from Lilah, and handshakes from my pleasure instructors. They would have given me hugs, but it wasn't really appropriate with all the onlookers. Lastly, I shook hands with my midwife and thanked her.

She reminded the room we'd have a paternity reading in a month's time. That was usually the earliest mages could sense the race of the child.

The emperor dismissed the meeting, and everyone bowed as he and the magistrate took their leave.

The midwife left me with a reminder that she was available anytime I needed, and that I was to be the judge of what I could handle in my pregnancy.

I turned after she left; the men of my Coterie had already started speaking to their aides. Word would be sent to the leaders of each territory, confirming the pregnancy, but the public wouldn't be told until the paternity had also been confirmed.

While I waited, I hugged Lilah again. She kissed me on the cheek. "It took everything I had to not make a snarky remark, by the way—something about being *shocked* you'd possibly conceived since you never bang anyone."

I snickered. "You're wicked."

As the aides and the advisors filtered out of the room, I addressed my men again. We'd already discussed how the day would go, but it wouldn't hurt to recap. "I'll meet you all for lunch, then individually?"

I got nods of agreement, and they took their leave.

With the room nearly empty, I finally hugged Schamoi and the other two pleasure instructors. "Goddess knows I've missed you all!"

"Lies," one said.

"They're a handsome lot," another admitted.

I bit my lip. "It's not so bad."

Lilah joined us, wrapping an arm around me and Schamoi. "Look at this cute reunion. The Coterie really shouldn't be awkward around you fellows. Without you three, how would Sonta have been prepared to be railed so often?"

Schamoi chuckled; I'd missed that sound, and his icy blue eyes.

I rolled my eyes at Lilah. "I'd still be capable of being screwed simply by opening my legs…"

We both cringed, and I felt a bit bad about the imagery dancing through my mind of Findlech over me. It was what it was, and we were both happily moving forward.

"Anyway…" I stood tall. "The servants have prepared a lounge with sweet treats and drinks so we can all get caught up!"

47

Moving Forward

It was a lovely gathering with just the five of us. Lilah hadn't gotten to know my pleasure instructors well, so she and the other two chatted, and she and Schamoi did a little flirting, though they didn't openly discuss having shared a bed.

"I'm really grateful to see your faces," I said. "It already feels like it's been so long." How much had changed in a month's time…

The men talked about what they'd been doing since having been released from my service, as well as the other two who couldn't make it today. One of them enjoyed a new home, still living off their residual income from serving me. Two of them had set off traveling the realm together. One had saved away his money, moving back home with family and starting a new job.

"And what about you, Schamoi?" I asked.

He blushed. "I'm working. I, uh, hope I can make it to your tour after the paternity is announced."

It was a lovely gesture, given he hailed from a far region of human lands. "I really appreciate that. That's a long way to travel. I'll be busy, though…" The imperial tour wasn't about social calls. The empire had come to me for the Great Ritual's beginning, but my Coterie and I would go to the empire, its leaders and people, once the paternity of my child had been confirmed.

Schamoi looked down. "I'm not working in human lands."

I angled my head. "Really?"

He nodded. "I've taken a position with a vampire mistress."

I blinked. He'd … basically signed up to be a lover for hire again. It was above the rank of a simple prostitute or a Suck and Fuck worker, but along the same lines. Really, not all that different from being my pleasure instructor.

"Exclusive?" I asked.

He nodded again.

My heart hurt, and I had to remind myself he was not mine anymore, and I'd never had a guarantee he and I would reunite the same way.

"We're doing a trial for a year," he said softly. "Then we'll go from there."

One of the other men sucked in a breath, cringing. "How does it feel to have her drink from you?" He rubbed his neck.

Schamoi bit his lip. "Don't knock it until you've had fangs in your cock."

The other two men went pale. Lilah and I exchanged a playful look. We both knew the pleasure of vampire blood play.

Still, I couldn't help thinking about his new mistress. She would be wealthy, and the parallel to Hadwin's story made me sick. "I'd love to see if my Duke Hadwin knows her. You'll have to give me her name."

He said he would. After a couple of hours, I had to leave the group to rejoin my Coterie. They would all be waiting on me, and I couldn't be rude. At least Schamoi called me his dove again as he hugged me goodbye; it soothed my soul.

Lilah walked me out, and we chatted a moment. This was one of those bittersweet moments in my life, a reminder that time was a cruel mistress that constantly turned the page to the next chapter, even if I wasn't ready for it.

"I guess *I'm* not getting laid tonight." Lilah frowned. "I can't believe the stupid man decided to bind himself to a woman so quickly like that."

I poked her arm. "Was he so good you're now yearning for his cock?"

She shrugged. "I'm just in a dry spell."

I took her hand. "You haven't talked about Cataray for a while. She's not back from her vacation?"

Lilah looked down. "She extended it. I don't really want to talk about it."

Pursing my lips, I nodded. "Sorry."

"I'll be fine." Her beautiful eyes looked into mine. "Can I ask you a possibly inappropriate question?"

"There's no such thing between you and me."

She smiled. "After the baby is born, can I … try some of your milk … straight from the source?" She glanced at my chest, and my core heated.

"I'm sure I could spare some."

As expected, all of my Coterie waited for me in the common room. I got more congratulations as I returned. I thanked them for letting me spend time with the others first. We ate a nice lunch together, then reconvened in the common room.

I swung my arms, nervous about this next part. "Elion, do you want to talk first?"

He rose from his chair, smiling. "Yes."

I assumed he'd tear my dress off me as soon as we entered my room, but he didn't. His mating fever had essentially all dissipated, but that didn't mean he wasn't still a horny mate… And we had something to celebrate today.

I eased myself down on the edge of the bed. "What are your thoughts?"

Elion paced the room. "I'm … nervous."

"About what?"

"Everything. Nothing."

It was so unlike him to be antsy. "Won't you come sit with me?"

He quickly sat down, tucking his hands between his legs.

"What changed, Elion?"

His soft grey eyes were so vulnerable. "I'm worried I won't be the father."

I hugged my stomach. "What about that worries you?" We were public servants, not just lovers, and I understood a failure to father the next ruler would be seen as a failure of the man by his own people in some cases.

He surprised me. "I won't be as important to you."

I frowned. "You're my mate. You'll always be important to me."

"But I'll fall lower in the order," he whispered.

We all knew how the imperial tour would go. In many ways, it celebrated the child's father, and could be a bit emasculating to the other men—not intentionally so, but the display itself did highlight the dynamic.

I took his hand. "Between now and the paternal reading, I won't have as many men demanding my pussy, or equality in bed…"

He grinned, happy about that part.

"And I'll gladly bring you along for the entire tour if you'd like." He'd have to take a backseat, since his only official appearance would be in shifter lands if he ended up not being the father. The entire Coterie didn't always travel the full tour with the Blessed Vessel, but we could use as many carriages and resources as we desired.

"I'd like that." He hesitated. "I worry, too, that I might not be a good enough father, or that the father—if it's not me—won't want me so involved in the child's life or in yours."

My heart truly went out to him, because his concerns were valid. "We'll work it out. And you'll be fantastic, whether it's as a father to my child or as an uncle."

He searched my face. "Do you love me, Sonta?"

My jaw dropped. "Of course I do. You're my mate. You're great in bed and an absolute sweetheart. And I know I'm safe with you."

Elion smiled shyly. "Have you given any thought to whether you'd like to have cubs with me, especially if this child isn't mine?"

I swallowed hard. We hadn't talked about it since that one time in his room in the thick of mating fever. "I can't commit to that with any of the Coterie right now. Not when my priority is raising the next emperor or empress." I squeezed his hand. "That doesn't mean no. But I won't be able to commit for at least a year or two."

He slowly nodded. "I know. I just want to share more with you."

We had admittedly been more of a sexual pair than anything else. Now that his mind was clear and things were changing, I looked forward to sharing more time in conversation. "We're one month in. And I plan to spend the rest of my life with my mate…"

Grinning, he stole a kiss.

I kissed him back, our lips sharing a soft and sweet caress. I straddled him, prodding with my tongue to his lips. He opened for me, a satisfied growl in his throat as he lay down, grabbing my ass and sliding us further onto the bed.

I whispered against his lips. "I love my mate."

"I love you too," he panted.

Smiling, I added, "Is there anything else you want to talk about before I claim your cock?"

His hands had already started to explore my body. "No."

I didn't really have a planned order for the men, but after sending Elion on his way, I picked Haan to meet with next. It gave my body a break and allowed him to swim about afterward since our conversation would likely be short.

I entered my pond with Haan, wading in the water. He warmly congratulated me on my pregnancy.

"Thank you. I regret we didn't get another chance…"

He nodded. Not a lot needed to be said. The likelihood of him being the father was small, and we wouldn't have sex again, at least not for a long time.

"You're a lovely woman," he said in his airily husky voice. "And I very much enjoyed having you the once. Perhaps again after your divine duties are complete."

I smiled. "You'll always be welcome in my Coterie and life, even if you only wish it to be as a political ally and a friend."

We discussed contingency plans. By law, all of the Coterie had to remain at the palace until the paternity was revealed. After that, there was more flexibility. Assuming Haan was not the father, he wouldn't be present for any of the imperial tour beyond the merfolk stop. There were so many safety and logistical hurdles to have him travel about the realm, and he wouldn't want to unless it was necessary.

He'd likely go back to his people in the sea for a visit after the paternity reading, then would pop back to the palace now and then. I'd miss his sweetness, but things *would* be easier working with only land-walkers. If he ended up being the father, we'd have an unexpected adventure on our hands.

Before leaving my pond, he gave me a pretty impressive kiss. After he left me, I toweled off and put on a simple dress, calling Gald into my room.

He hugged and kissed me first thing when the door closed. "Congratulations, Sonta!"

I held him longer. "Thank you." I wouldn't forget his kindness in offering to let Haan and me have sex again with the safety of his magic, nor his generosity in even speaking with me after walking in on him and Findlech and accidentally outing Findlech.

"Let's sit down." I gestured to the daybed.

We had a good talk about where we were and where we planned to go. He of course hoped the child was his, and still wasn't interested in having children beyond that. He planned to be attentive, while taking a little more time now to work toward becoming a grand master in his order.

"I know the imperial tour order changes depending on paternity, but I'm hoping to be paired with the elven portion…" he said cautiously.

Since elven lands bordered human lands, there was a decent chance Gald would accompany Findlech and me naturally on the tour. "You're welcome to join, even if it's not traditional."

He smiled. "I shouldn't say anything. He'd kill me if he knew I told anyone…"

I raised my eyebrows high.

"He lets me call him Lord Findie in private. And he calls me his pet." Gald was positively giddy.

Personally, I kind of wanted to vomit at the notion of such a formal man using and accepting those pet names, but it wasn't my relationship. "You really like him…"

Gald looked down, playing with his hands. "I think I could love him. I know that's silly since we barely know each other, but…"

I nodded, admitting to myself I was jealous. Haan, Findlech, and Tyfen all pulling away was one thing… I hadn't planned on losing Gald.

Reading my face, Gald calmed. "That doesn't mean I love you any less, Sonta."

"*Do* you love me?" We'd never exchanged those words.

"Of course I do. I'm not the type to make a big exclamation about it, but I thought you'd understand that. There are many kinds of loves. I still think you're sexy as hell and great in bed. A kind soul with a fun sense of humor. I plan to make you laugh every day and warm your bed often, for as long as you want me, Sonta."

I hugged him. "I love you too. And I want you around. I know it's silly to be jealous of sharing you…"

He pulled back, holding my chin, and kissed me. "It's an adjustment for all of us." With his free hand, he traced my matching bond tattoo. "We'll navigate it."

I was safe in that reminder. "We will."

We discussed that more. I again apologized for the messy discovery with Findlech, and he forgave me. We would have to sort out intimacy, though. Findlech, much like Hadwin with me, didn't want to be with anyone beyond Gald. And, along the lines of Findlech's rigidity, he proposed we come up with a Gald-sharing calendar. I had to fight to not roll my eyes. I was more of a free spirit, and frankly, so was Gald. We'd find something that worked for us all— that was the point of the Blessed Vessel and her Coterie.

Satisfied, a calmness in my heart, I rested a hand on Gald's knee. "Is there anything else you wanted to discuss?"

He smiled. "I think that's about it."

I was nervous to ask, because we'd only been together twice since I'd walked in on him and Findlech, and not at all since I'd accidentally outed Findlech. "Do you … want to share a little more time together? The naked kind?"

He looked at my chest. "Did your breasts stop being perfect? Have you stopped being good in bed?"

I smirked. "I guess you'll have to find out."

Leaning in, he kissed me and slipped a hand inside my dress, fondling me. "Yep, this one still seems okay."

Stroking his cock, I played too. "Meh… Decent."

He stood, straightening his vest. "Well, if that's how it's going to be…"

I grabbed his wrist, pulling him back onto the daybed. He laughed.

I pressed my forehead to his. "Take your fucking clothes off, and go lie on the bed."

His grin was feral. "As you wish, Your Holiness."

After an exhilarating tussle in the sheets, we kissed. I'd needed to reconnect with Gald that way. We said our farewells at my door, and I peeked into the common room after he passed through to the Coterie corridor. I wanted to save Hadwin for my last. Glancing at Tyfen, I considered. He met my eyes, then looked away.

No, I didn't have the courage to put up with him yet. "Findlech?"

He stood and nodded, heading my way.

I made sure the robe I'd slipped on was closed well.

My stomach growled—it was dinnertime already. "Have you eaten?"

"Not yet," he replied.

We'd never broken bread alone together. "I'm starving. Are there any elven foods you'd recommend? My chef could whip us up something."

Findlech suggested a few items, and I had a servant order them.

We sat on the daybed and had a conversation, continuing while eating after the food arrived. It would take me a while to get used to sharing Gald in such close quarters, but we were all on the same page that it was more comfortable to let Gald be the main communicator between the three of us when it came to sexual things. Findlech and I were just too uncomfortable to talk about that with each other.

I profusely apologized again for accidentally prying into Findlech's life and betraying his trust. He was gracious, and I couldn't have been more grateful.

We'd obviously understood where things were going between us, but we confirmed. His sexual duty was complete, and he would remain in the palace until the paternity reading. After that, he planned to stay with me to help raise my child as I allowed, sometimes tending to matters as needed in his own lands.

Our meeting ended with a handshake again, and I was grateful to continue building our friendship with a new hope that it hadn't been completely derailed.

Taking a deep breath, I surveyed the common room again, ready to get my interview with Tyfen over. There was one problem—he was gone. I rolled my eyes and strolled out to Hadwin. "Where did Tyfen go?"

Hadwin pointed to the door that led to the main hallway. "That way. Not sure where exactly."

I sighed, straddling Hadwin on the sofa. His smile grew as he slid his hands up my thigh to my ass; I wore nothing under my short robe. "Do we have to use words in this interview? Or will moans and gasps suffice?"

I giggled, stealing a kiss. "I love you."

"I love you too. I'm so proud of you."

Running my hands through his blond hair, I admired his pale and eternal beauty, his cool touch. His hazel eyes as they slowly tinted red. "I also love that your eyes betray emotion, the way they perfectly turn bloodred…"

"Hmmm…"

Reaching a hand down, I rubbed his cock through his pants. "They just don't tell me which emotion. Are you angry right now?"

His eyes rapidly grew red, at the same rate his cock in my hand grew harder and thicker. "Not that emotion."

I grinned. "Which one could it be, then?" I was wet.

"I guess I'll have to show you." He lifted me effortlessly, carrying me to my room as I wrapped my legs around him.

And then he worshiped me, congratulating me through moans, pants, and passionate thrusting. Eventually, we cooled and cuddled. I didn't want it to end. We kissed plenty.

"So…" I rested a hand on his bare chest. "Talking…"

"Overrated." He stole another smooch.

"Come on…"

He cleared his throat, wearing a forced serious face. "Sorry. Yes, Your Holiness?"

I gave him the stink eye.

Softening, he adjusted his grip on me. "Yes, darling?"

"Moving forward…"

His smile was so soft, so genuine. "I'm yours. My estate is self-sufficient. My vampire court requires little from me. I plan to please you for the rest of your life, and parent with you no matter the father."

My heart might actually burst if he kept talking that way. "I accept it all."

He caressed my ass. "I hope this means I'll get even more time with you, now that the first duty has been completed…" Now that Haan, Findlech, and Tyfen were out of the picture, or at least out of my bedroom.

"I don't know… How many times could you even handle me a day?"

He narrowed his eyes. "You forget how much strength I possess as a vampire. As for the blood supply I need… I hope the emperor has a healthy herd of pigs, and that the palace's residents enjoy pork regularly, because I'll down gallons of that blood a day if that's what it takes to satiate you."

I placed the softest of kisses on his lips, already warm for him again, plotting a fun night. "You'll have to ask the emperor himself about his herds."

Hadwin silently chuckled. He wouldn't dare to ask the emperor about something so trivial or personal.

We cuddled a while longer, savoring each other's temperature and curves.

"Have you made plans for sleeping arrangements tonight?" he asked.

I hid a smirk. "Not yet. You don't have to wait up. I may just sleep alone tonight." I fully planned to surprise him with another good time in his room tonight—he'd told me I could do so anytime I wanted.

"Okay."

After we'd cleaned up and dressed, we said goodbye at my door. I watched his glorious ass walk away from me until he turned at the Coterie corridor, giving me one last smile before he went to his room.

My gaze turned to Tyfen. He'd returned, lounging in his usual seat. I walked up to him, my stomach and heart twisting. His would be the hardest conversation for me to have. We all assumed he and I would stop having sex because he was a complete asshole and because his primary duty was done.

Then why did I still yearn to be with him? His cock was undeniably fantastic, but it was more than that. I wasn't ready to give up on him, nor should I. The child in my womb *might* be his, and we needed to learn to get along for the sake of the empire if nothing else.

"So…" I said shyly. *How eloquent…*

Tyfen's gaze raked down my body, his face unreadable. Without a word, he stood.

He crouched, picking me up and throwing me over his shoulder.

I gaped, my bare ass in the air. "Put me down!"

He didn't answer, instead stalking toward the Coterie corridor. His grip tightened around me as I tried to free myself.

I punched his back. "What the *hell* are you doing?"

Tyfen stopped at his bedroom door, his voice gruff. "What I *want* to now that I don't *have* to."

My breath hitched as he reached for the door handle.

Finally.

The Blessed Coterie

Sonta's anticipation of the paternity results brings her enough stress. Amidst her growing feelings for the men in her Coterie, she also has to calm fights between them, uncover their secrets, and dodge unexpected political nightmares.

While experiencing the varied rich cultures of the realm during the imperial tour, Sonta endures her share of heartache and worry on the road. But with the fates seemingly doing everything they can to break her Coterie apart, she must find a way to keep all those she loves and make her Coterie a real family.

The thrilling conclusion to the Blessed Vessel duology, perfect for lovers of diverse steamy why-choose/reverse harem stories!

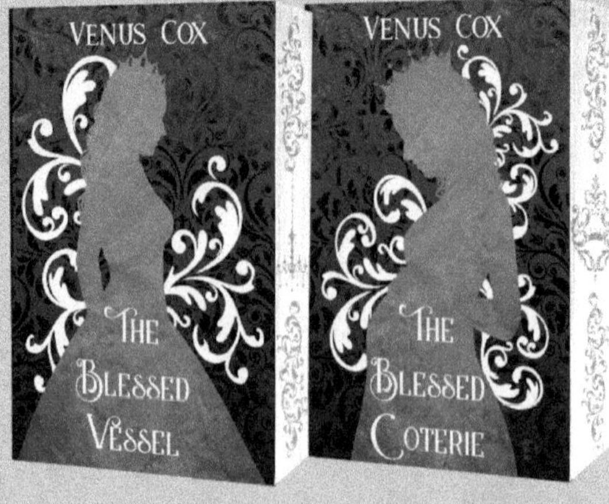

Remember to leave a review for
The Blessed Vessel!

Sign up for Venus's newsletter
for more book updates!
VenusCoxBooks.com

Follow her online @

https://www.facebook.com/groups/venuscoxbooks

https://www.instagram.com/venuscoxauthor

https://www.tiktok.com/@venuscoxbooks

Steamy Character Art & More!

Looking for steamy *Blessed Vessel* art?

Sign up for the author's newsletter for more information and access to exclusive offers!